ACCLAIM FOR BLACKBOARD BESTSELLING AUTHOR SANDRA KITT AND HER ROMANTIC NOVELS . . .

Significant Others

"Realistic, compelling, and peopled with thoroughly engaging characters. Don't miss it!"
—Brenda Joyce, author of *Finer Things*

"Her finest work to date; I loved it, I highly recommend it!"
—Heather Graham

"Once again, Sandra Kitt has tackled a sensitive subject with depth and compassion. . . . Wonderful!"
—Anita Richmond Bunkley, author of *Balancing Act*

"Excellent . . . I couldn't put it down . . . strong characters you find yourself caring about long after the story ends."
—Julia Boyd, author of *Embracing the Fire*

"Poignant and heartwarming."
—*Romantic Times* (4 stars)

PRAISE FOR

The Color of Love

"A moving novel."
—*USA Today*

"Tender, sincere, and provocative . . . A wonderful contemporary urban story of life and love . . . A winner!"
—Laura Parker, author of *Tempest*

"Read this book! . . . One of the most tender and rewarding love stories I've ever read! I loved it!"
—Susan Wiggs, author of *Dancing on Air*

"Sometimes gritty, always compelling . . . A powerful story handled with realism and deep emotion. If you're looking for something different, look no more."
—Christina Skye, author of *Key to Forever*

PRAISE FOR

The Color of Love

"With insight, sensitivity, honesty, and a generous dose of storytelling magic, Sandra Kitt storms stubborn barriers by drawing the reader under the skins of her characters. . . . A triumphant celebration of the true nature of love."
—Kathleen Eagle, author of *The Night Remembers*

"A tender, romantic, yet realistic look at the problems that still face an interracial couple in the 1990s. Talented author Sandra Kitt demonstrates her tremendous storytelling ability with this compelling, insightful and emotional novel. A truly marvelous read."
—*Romantic Times* (4 stars)

BETWEEN FRIENDS

Sandra Kitt

With praise, thanks, and love to *Him*,
from whom all blessings flow.

SIGNET
Published by the Penguin Group
Penguin Putnam Inc., 375 Hudson Street,
New York, New York 10014, U.S.A.
Penguin Books Ltd, 27 Wrights Lane,
London W8 5TZ, England
Penguin Books Australia Ltd, Ringwood,
Victoria, Australia
Penguin Books Canada Ltd, 10 Alcorn Avenue,
Toronto, Ontario, Canada M4V 3B2
Penguin Books (N.Z.) Ltd, 182–190 Wairau Road,
Auckland 10, New Zealand

Penguin Books Ltd, Registered Offices:
Harmondsworth, Middlesex, England

First published by Signet, an imprint of Dutton NAL,
a member of Penguin Putnam Inc.

First Printing, June, 1998
10 9 8 7 6 5 4 3 2 1

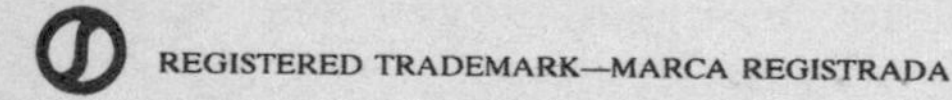

Printed in the United States of America

ACKNOWLEDGMENTS

Between Friends presented a number of research challenges. A great deal of information was needed for what turned out to be a very few pages, but these sections are visual and action-filled. I read lots of materials on scuba diving, Navy SEALS, New York Police Rescue and Aviation units, but extensive interviewing of the men and women who perform these tasks added immeasurably to a sense of the importance and excitement of their jobs. I am deeply indebted to all of them for their generosity of time, spirit, information, and sense of humor.

I am grateful to Brian Walker of the Naval Institute Press, who put me in touch with ex-Navy SEAL Dick Couch, USNR, who, with a few personal anecdotes, set me on the path to learn more.

Many thanks to Diane O'Connor (whose husband I interviewed when researching an earlier novel), Stephen M. Giaco, Community Affairs Officers, Officer Kevin Burns and Sergeant Edward Mountford of the Midtown North precinct of NYPD in Manhattan.

Sergeant Dennis M. Schoeller, a former five-year member of the NYPD Scuba Unit, gave me a thorough background in the history of the unit, as well as details on the kind of search-and-discovery assignments typically dealt with.

Doug Sherrad of Grumman Aerospace on Long Island, and a recreational diver, sent me articles to read on equipment and the physiological concerns of diving.

Pete Oliver, co-owner of Adventures in Diving on Staten Island, New York, was added to my list of experts when I spotted him on a local TV report about this company and dive shop. I also appreciate the female diver's point of view of Debra Williamson, a student of Mr. Oliver's.

David R. Getty, Marketing and Communications Manager of National Drager, provided crucial information on the LAR 5 rebreather, a respiratory unit used by Navy divers.

I was thrilled to have been invited to visit the NYPD Aviation Unit at Floyd Bennet Field in Brooklyn, New York. There, Captain Bill Wilkins, Commanding Officer, introduced me to his team of officers. I was given a personal tour of the hangar facility, equipment, and the helicopters frequently used in rescue or recovery missions. Police Officer Tom Kelley of the scuba unit and Officer John Galligan, aviation mechanic, spent a few hours answering my endless questions. I will always remember the enthusiasm and patience with which I and my research was treated.

Finally, I came away with a tremendous sense of awe, admiration, and respect for the work of all of the professionals mentioned above. I am inspired to complete my own diving certification, delayed almost *ten years*, by performing my required open-water dive!

Prologue

The door was unlocked.

She knocked anyway, as was her habit. It didn't seem the right thing to do, to walk into someone's house just because they knew you were coming. When there was no immediate answer after the second knock, she called out quietly: "Lillian? It's me, Dallas."

Sometimes Lillian just didn't hear her. Often the TV was on, or Lillian was in another part of the house. Several times she hadn't been home at all, but she'd never leave the door unlocked if she went out.

"Lillian?" Dallas called out again softly.

In the depths of the house she could hear music. Feeling more confident, Dallas opened the door and stepped inside the mud room just off the kitchen. She never came in through the front door if she could help it, although Lillian frequently showed her out that way.

There was no pot of hot water gently bubbling in a glass kettle on the stove as usual. Lillian always made her hot chocolate, and she'd have tea. But on the kitchen counter was a little plate of biscotti. The kind that was chocolate and crunchy with sliced almonds. Dallas smiled with pleasure because Lillian had introduced her to the hard cookies when she was seven or eight. She had shown Dallas how to dip them in coffee or cocoa to soften them so that they would be easier to eat. But Dallas didn't mind the hard texture of the baked biscotti. She picked one up and stuck it in her mouth.

She shrugged out of her jacket and draped it over the back of a kitchen chair and dropped her heavy schoolbag on the seat. She bit hard into the cookie, breaking off a piece to chew as she followed the music that was coming from the basement. The laundry room and Lillian's sewing room were down there, too.

There was a light on, illuminating half of the stairwell. She started carefully down the steps, expecting to find Lillian standing at an ironing board, or cutting out a pattern at the sewing table, or measuring out detergent for a wash. But the room was empty. Dallas finally realized that the music was not the kind Lillian would listen to anyway. It was rock music from a CD.

Dallas bit off another piece of biscotti, her chewing distorting her words.

"Lillian . . . are you down here?"

She heard a sound. Something moved in the room. Instinctively she sensed she'd wandered into a trap. Warily, her gaze swept around the paneled room. A large, husky body slowly rose up from the sofa in the family room. The motion made her jump. It was Lillian and Vincent's son.

Nicholas Marco was almost six years older and no longer a teenager. But Dallas didn't trust him any more now than on her first encounter with him when she was seven years old and he was a strapping thirteen. She was afraid of him. She'd always been afraid of him. It was the way he had of disregarding her, of looking not at her but right through her as if she weren't human.

Staring at him now, Dallas was speechless. It seemed like she'd spent all of her adolescence avoiding any contact with Nicholas so that there wouldn't be a moment like this. She was a friend of his mother's, but that wasn't going to help her at that moment.

There was a new and different look in his eyes.

Dallas could see it come over him as he stared at her. He was wearing a pair of black jeans and a long-sleeved shirt, unbuttoned to reveal his hairy chest and soft fleshy belly. He had a cigarette in his hand. No, not a cigarette. A joint. Dallas could smell the acrid tang in the air even though one of the basement windows was open. Dallas was too afraid even to chew the rest of the cookie she'd bitten off, and she tried to swallow the dry crumbs down her parched throat.

"What the fuck are you doing here?" Nicholas asked.

"I . . . I was just looking for . . . Mrs. Marco," she said, trying to keep her voice quiet and flat. Like an animal, she was sure Nicholas could smell her fear. She tried to take one tiny unnoticed step backward toward the staircase.

He stared at her thoughtfully, his narrowed gray eyes looking slowly over her as he took a deep drag, sucked, and held the smoke in his lungs.

"She ain't here. What do you want with my mother? How come you just walk into my house? Don't you know no better?" he asked.

Dallas took two more steps toward the stairs. Nicholas took two steps toward her. She stopped. "I . . . I just had something to give her . . ."

"More mail?"

Dallas nodded even though it wasn't true. It was an easier answer than anything else she might have said.

Nicholas dragged on the joint again. "I bet you come to steal stuff. I bet you go through things and my mother don't even know. I keep tellin' her she can't trust any of you niggers. Just 'cause you live in the neighborhood doesn't make you my neighbor."

Dallas froze at his ugly words. She'd learned to just stay still when anyone started in on her, hoping they'd run out of insults and stop. To fight back made it worse, as she'd found out. She was beginning to feel hot in the low-ceilinged room, sweat making her jeans and blouse damp and sticky against her skin.

She became even more frightened because she understood the drowsy consideration in Nicholas's eyes. She was not a little kid he could push around or ignore anymore, but a nubile fifteen-year-old. She presented a whole new range of possibilities and an opportunity.

"I'll go home . . ."

Quicker than Dallas would have thought him capable, Nicholas reached out and grabbed her wrist and held tightly.

"Not so fast. As long as you're here . . ." He tossed the marijuana roach into the cold fireplace and took hold of her other arm when Dallas tried to twist away.

"No. Let me go . . . I'll go . . ." she said in a rush.

His chuckle was soundless, his voice dropping to a thick burr. "You shoulda thought of that before. You're not suppose to be here, right?"

Dallas could see the interest perking up in his eyes. Boys in school sometimes looked at her this way.

"I have to go . . ." she uttered sharply, pulling herself free and running up the stairs.

She hoped that Nicholas would let her get her things and leave. She could hear his laughter behind her. In the kitchen she grabbed her jacket and canvas schoolbag. Dallas struggled with the strap of her bag and accidently toppled over a chair to the floor. She bent to pick it up but Nicholas had followed her and grabbed her from behind.

"Noooo . . ." she gasped in panic.

"Come on . . . don't fight me," he hissed, his strong arms locking around her. "You want it. You know you want it . . ."

"Let me go. Please let me go . . ." Dallas pleaded, twisting in his clasp. She felt his hot breath against her ear. He smelled of smoke and beer and sweat. He pressed his body against her back, and she felt something hard and stiff at her buttocks. Her recognition of his male sexual part churned her panic up even more. In the middle of her chest her heart was now beating too fast.

His hand was crudely trying to explore her body. He grabbed a breast and squeezed. "You got big tits."

When his other hand tried to push between her legs Dallas began to fight in earnest.

"Don't . . . *don't.*" Dallas began to cry, her voice quickly rising to form a scream. He covered her mouth and her words were cut off.

"Shut *up*! I know you've done this before. All you black chicks are really hot for it," he breathed heavily into her ear.

Nicholas was slowly forcing her back to the stairwell and down to the basement. Dallas dropped her jacket, using her hands to grab a hold of the table edge, the counter, the door, as Nicholas dragged her ruthlessly, his hold across her mouth restricting her breathing. She tried beating his arms, kicking wildly with her feet, swinging her bag to hit him. Nicholas cursed through his teeth, becoming angry at her resistance. He ripped the bag from her grasp and tossed it aside, the contents sliding across the kitchen floor.

"Cut it out, you bitch!"

Together they stumbled back down the stairs to the basement. Dallas felt the fight going out of her. She couldn't get a breath. She clawed his hand, scratching and digging, her screams shut off behind her covered mouth. The joint had made him impervious to the pain.

Suddenly Nicholas spun Dallas around and pushed her hard. She fell heavily and landed on her back on the sofa. Nicholas came down hard on top of her, momentarily knocking the rest of the air out of her lungs and causing tears of shocked surprise to stream from her eyes.

"Please," Dallas gasped. "I . . . I'll go. I . . . won't come back anymore."

Nicholas heaved and bucked his pelvis against her and Dallas again felt the presence of his hard penis between his legs. He was oblivious to everything but his own need. He tried kissing her, his tongue wet and aggressive like some sort of reptile. His hand yanked her hair, pulling it loose from the ponytail, to hold her head still. His other hand pulled up her blouse, freeing it from her jeans and causing the fabric to rip against the button closing. Then Nicholas began rubbing her groin area, squeezing her private parts as he tried to force his hand between her legs.

"I . . . I won't tell." Dallas began again pushing his chest, twisting her body to roll away. She heard her own voice trail into a whimper of helplessness. "Please don't . . ."

Nicholas bucked his body upward, pulling the zipper on his jeans. "You're fuckin' straight you're not going to tell anyone. My mother ain't coming home until late tonight." He laughed, trying to get his jeans down and hold her still at the same time. "I bet no one even knows where you are."

Nicholas dug beneath her blouse, grabbed her bra, and yanked it up, spilling her breasts out. Dallas tried to cover her bare chest, tried to keep her legs clamped together. She tossed her head wildly to prevent him from kissing her. The pressure of Nicholas's knee was painful and bruising as he forced her legs apart. He held her jaw and clamped his mouth over hers. Dallas tried to bite his tongue. Nicholas cried out and retaliated by backhanding her across her cheek. She lay momentarily stunned.

A door closed loudly somewhere above them.

"Anybody here? Lillian?"

Whoever had arrived started down the stairs to the basement.

"Lillian . . ."

Dallas whimpered and moaned.

"Who's down here? Nick? *What the hell are you doing?*"

Dallas heard the surprise in the new voice. A man. Someone standing behind Nicholas whom she couldn't see.

"Get the fuck outta here and mind your business. I'm busy . . ."

"Help me, help me!" Dallas twisted her head and cried hysterically. "Make him stop, *please*!"

"For Christ's sake, Nick. Let her go, man."

"Stay out of this. We just had a little fight, that's all. *Get outta here, will you!*"

Dallas got a hand free and grabbed a handful of Nicholas's hair, pulling sharply. Nicholas bellowed.

"Let her go, Nick. Can't you see she doesn't want to? You're hurting her." The man clamped his hand on Nicholas's shoulder. "Come on, knock it off."

Nicholas ignored him.

"I said, *knock it off!*"

Suddenly Dallas felt the weight of Nicholas Marco being pulled off her, and she could breathe freely again. She heard him grunt as he landed with a loud thump on the floor. He cursed violently. Dallas was too dazed to move. She drew in gulps of air. A scuffle was going on between Nicholas and the other man right next to her.

"Get outta here, you bastard!"

"Leave her alone."

Slowly Dallas tried to sit up, the relief of being able to move making her cry even harder. She gathered the disheveled pieces of her clothing around her with shaking hands. The two young men were now engaged in an escalating fight as Nicholas tried to overcome the intruder.

"What's the matter with you? Are you crazy?" the new person shouted at Nicholas as they exchanged shoves and swinging fists.

The two of them swayed back and forth in front of Dallas, bumping into furniture and knocking things over. She was once again afraid to move, in case she got caught in the middle of the fight. But she had to get out of there. The two men fell to the floor, rolling and punching. Nicholas cursed and made vile threats to his opponent. There was rage between the two now, and Dallas couldn't help but stare. For a second she was mesmerized by the violence of their combat. It was much worse and more scary than anything she'd ever seen on TV.

Nicholas's fist caught the other man on the cheek. He retaliated with a sharp double jab into Nicholas's ribs. Nicholas gagged and doubled over, gasping. The other man came slowly to his feet, swaying and breathing hard, wiping blood from his mouth. He used both hands to smooth back his hair from his face. Dallas realized that she had to move. She scrambled up unsteadily and rushed to the stairwell.

"Wa—wait a minute . . ." the other man said, out of breath. He reached for her.

Dallas tripped over Nicholas, who was curled up and coughing on the floor. She nearly went down on top of him. The other man grabbed her wrist in the same forceful grip that Nicholas had used. Dallas fought him.

"Letmego . . . letmego!" Dallas screamed.

"Hey, stop it!"

He tried to contain Dallas's flaying arms. She tried to jerk away, and they both went down on the floor. Dallas slapped and hit and swung frantically at his head.

"Dammit! I'm not going to hurt you . . ."

She was too tired to fight anymore. Whatever was going to happen she could no longer stop. She lay crying as he trapped her arms on the floor next to her head.

"You fucking bastard!" Nicholas coughed and groaned from the floor several feet away.

He crawled and stumbled halfway up and headed for the small bathroom in the corner. Dallas could hear him being sick to his stomach in great gasping purges that sounded like someone was choking him to death.

The other man was still on top of her, holding her

wrists. Dallas twisted beneath him, but his body felt nothing like Nicholas's had.

"Calm down," he commanded. He repeated it again more firmly until she stopped struggling and opened her eyes.

He was staring into her face. His was bloody and bruised. She watched him wearily, but Dallas could tell he wasn't trying to hold her down. There was no force. No intent. He was gauging her reaction, and she let her body relax beneath his.

"Okay . . . okay," he breathed deeply. "I'm not going to hurt you, understand?"

She nodded, watching his face.

"Come on. Get up."

He lifted himself from Dallas and stood up. He held out his hand to her, but she rejected the offer of help and stood up on her own. Her body felt like rubber, and all her limbs seemed weak and unsteady. She shrank away from him, pulling her torn blouse closed over her nearly naked breasts. He held up both hands. The retching in the bathroom continued.

"I won't touch you," the man said.

Dallas backed toward the stairs, keeping her eyes on him. Then she turned and hurried up, blindly reaching out for the landing and the open door. She tripped on the last step, hitting her knee against the ledge. Holding it, Dallas collapsed. She sat on the floor, leaning against a cabinet, and cried. Her body shook uncontrollably.

She heard heavy but slow footsteps behind her. It was him. He hunkered down next to her. Dallas could feel his body heat and his breathing, although not as labored as before. She felt his hand awkwardly patting her trembling shoulder. She shrugged him off.

"Nick didn't do anything, did he? You okay?" he asked quietly.

She didn't respond.

It surprised Dallas when he sat on the kitchen floor

as well, his back against the opposite cabinet, and stared at her.

"You can't be one of Nick's girlfriends. Who are you? What are you doing here?"

Dallas looked at him suspiciously, but she felt no threat from him at all. She could see he had thoughtful, dark eyes, a narrow face, and hair that was too long. He was as tall as Nicholas Marco but much thinner. Wiry and quick.

"I . . . I came to see Lillian," her voice warbled.

"Lillian?" he repeated blankly, his gaze taking in her appearance again. He looked around needlessly. "She's not here."

"I know," Dallas sniffled, wiping her face with her hands, feeling less scared now. But he continued to stare at her.

His gaze took in her condition, the torn blouse and her exposed torso. He frowned and stared at her chest as if he could see her breasts behind the crossed arms that tried to cover herself. Slowly he brought his attention back to her face. Dallas cringed when he reached out a hand, but he only tried to push back her hair from her face. He fingered the texture for a second. Letting go, he slowly stood up.

"You'd better get your things and get out of here. Nick is going to be pretty pissed when he comes upstairs."

Dallas looked up warily at him. But she was beginning to believe she had nothing to fear from this man, whoever he was. She'd never seen him before.

Dallas didn't move right away, wondering how she could get up without exposing more of herself. Then he reached into the pocket of his denim jacket and took out cigarettes and a lighter. He calmly took his time lighting one as he continued to stare thoughtfully at her. After taking one or two puffs he shrugged and turned his back to Dallas.

"Okay. I won't look."

Dallas hesitated, and then came to her knees as she

pulled her bra back into place to cover her breasts, glancing furtively at him to see if he was keeping his word. There was not much she could do about her ruined blouse beyond stuffing the tail into the top of her jeans and putting her jacket back on. Her crying turned to sniffles.

Dallas heard the toilet flush downstairs. It spurred her into action. She hastily crawled across the tiled kitchen floor, reaching for her schoolbag. She stuffed as much of her things in as she could find and then stood up.

"Alex! *Alex!*" Nicholas shouted from the lower level of the house. "I'm going to kick your ass, you hear me! I'm going to fuckin' *kill* you!"

Dallas stared at the one called Alex. He didn't seem to have heard the threat, or maybe just didn't care. He carefully laid his cigarette on the edge of the sink and, turning on the faucet, cupped water into his hands and splashed his face several times. He used one of the floral dish towels to dry his face and hands.

Dallas looked at the open basement door, fearful that Nicholas would burst through. She began making her way around the other end of the kitchen table and toward the door.

Alex's voice made her jump.

"You got all your stuff?"

She wasn't sure and she didn't care, but Dallas nodded anyway.

"Come on. Let's get out of here." He picked up his cigarette, took a drag.

Dallas stared at him warily again and didn't move.

He became impatient. "Look, I already told you I'm not going to do anything. I could have walked away like Nick said and stayed out of whatever was going on between you two down there."

He took two strides across the space of the kitchen and pulled the door open. Then he waited for Dallas to precede him out.

Dallas rushed past him, not realizing until he'd

closed the door behind them that she'd been holding her breath. They were halfway down the block when the realization that she'd just escaped something really terrible finally hit her. The awareness made her quietly cry. She tried to covertly use her hand to wipe her face.

"Hey . . . don't do that," Alex pleaded. "Look, it's over. Nothing happened."

But Dallas knew he didn't understand. Because she was only just starting to realize how powerless she'd been. She heard him curse in annoyance under his breath, but then he nevertheless started to murmur words of reassurance and comfort.

"Come on . . . you're okay." He briefly rubbed her shoulder.

Dallas nodded and tried to get a hold of herself. But she was recalling more than just the oppressive weight of Nicholas on top of her, or his brutal attempts to control her. Dallas was also mourning the death of a romantic fantasy she had nurtured since she became a teenager, about what it would be like to be with a boy . . . a man. Nicholas had destroyed it. She was *never* going to let a man touch her again.

She kept taking deep breaths of air and finally stopped crying. She hazarded a surreptitious glance at the thin young man next to her and felt like she was being childish. Dallas sighed thankfully and hugged her book bag to her chest.

"Where do you live?" he asked.

"Two blocks from here. The other end of Chatham."

He frowned at her thoughtfully. "Oh, yeah? Since when?"

"Since I was about six or seven."

His frown deepened, and he squinted at her through the cigarette smoke. "You're not with that black family Nick and Vin used to talk about, are you?"

Dallas nodded and stared straight ahead. "Nicholas hates me," she said simply. She couldn't believe she was having this conversation with this man. She heard him chuckle. He shook his head and threw away the rest of his cigarette.

"Nicholas is just being a jerk. Vin doesn't hate you or your family, either. He just doesn't understand you. And he doesn't like change or surprises. Anything too different."

"Lillian isn't like that," Dallas offered.

"No, she isn't," he agreed. He glanced at her, puzzled. "So, you're a friend of Lillian's. How did that happen?"

Dallas shrugged but remained silent as they continued to walk. It began when she was about seven. But Dallas had never told anyone about that, and she didn't intend to make an exception now.

"I take it Vin and Nicholas don't like the idea."

"I don't think Vin minds so much. He once told me he didn't. But I still get a little nervous. He's almost never there when I go to see Lillian."

Alex frowned at her and shook his head. "Lillian would be real upset if she knew what Nick tried to do." He blinked at her and lightly touched her right cheek, where a distinct rosette blotch was rising under her tan skin. "He do that?"

Dallas nodded.

"Asshole," he muttered.

"Who are you?" Dallas asked shyly. "Are you family?"

The corner of his mouth where Nicholas had hit him was turning purple against his pale skin, as was a spot near his temple. She winced involuntarily when she recalled the sounds of fists hitting flesh and bone. This man had taken a beating for her.

"Am I family?" He carefully considered. "In a way. Depends on who you ask."

Dallas thought about that for a moment. She didn't know what he meant, and she wasn't about to ask. "Oh."

"Mostly they like to pretend I don't exist. Except for Lillian," he said.

He hadn't answered her question, but Dallas knew she couldn't ask for more information. She stopped at the first corner. Suddenly she didn't know if it was such a good idea to be seen in this man's company. Not if he was in some way connected to the Marco family.

"You don't have to walk me all the way. I just have another block to go."

He looked around. "Afraid people will see us together? Doesn't bother me. I've been slammed for a lot worse things than for being with a black kid. I got hang-ups, but I'm not prejudiced. Besides . . ." he began, frowning thoughtfully at her, "what's the big deal?"

Dallas sensed her whole body loosening up. She was no longer holding herself as if she expected to be attacked again. She felt she could trust him. He had a kind of invincibility, like someone who didn't care. Or like someone who couldn't be hurt.

He didn't look much older than Nicholas. About twenty-one or so. She stole another quick glance, thinking he was much better-looking than Nicholas.

"I've never seen you before. You don't live around here, do you?" she asked.

"Nope. Brooklyn."

Dallas waited for him to say more, but he didn't. He was lighting another cigarette. He glanced briefly behind them, and she wondered if he expected Nicholas to come after them.

They approached a two-level Cape house situated in the middle of the block. There were no cars in the driveway and Dallas knew her parents hadn't gotten home yet. She stopped in front of the house and faced her escort.

"Are you visiting with Vin and Lillian?"

He raised his brows and looked at her. "You ask a lot of questions. Visiting?" he repeated, again testing her word. He shook his head. "Just reminding them I'm still alive. I never stay long."

Dallas became uncomfortable when she imagined him seeing Vin and Lillian later, or having to face Nicholas. What was he going to say about the bruises on his face? She gnawed her lips.

"What . . . what's going to happen when you go back there? What if Nicholas and you start fighting again?"

He lifted his shoulder indifferently. "We won't."

Dallas stared wide-eyed at him until he finally understood.

"Look, I won't say anything to Vin or Lillian, I promise. Not if you don't want me to."

"I don't. They'll think it's my fault. Nicholas might lie."

"Are you going to tell your folks?" She shook her head vigorously. "How come?"

"Same reasons. I wasn't supposed to be there anyway. It's kind of off limits."

"What's your name?" he asked.

"Dallas. Dallas Oliver."

"Dallas? What kind of name is that? Born in Texas?"

She tried to grin. It twisted, in the end, into a brief expression of sadness. "No. My mother was."

He held out a hand suddenly to her. "Alex Marco," he said.

Dallas stared at it before she tentatively put her hand in his. The handshake was quick and hard. "Thanks for—you know—helping me before. I'm sorry if you got hurt."

"Forget about it. Nick and I, we've gone at it before." He pointed at her. "*You* stay out of his way. If he ever tries anything like that again, you just . . ." He thought for a moment. "You call me and let me know."

Already Dallas was shaking her head. "That's okay."

"I'm serious," he insisted. He patted down his pockets, then gestured to her. "Give me a pen and some paper."

Dallas opened a compartment on her knapsack and dug in hastily for a pencil. She ripped a sheet of paper from a notebook and handed them to him. While he wrote something down, she looked him over again. His head tilted down at an angle, and she could see something about him that seemed familiar. Suddenly he gazed up at her and handed her the paper.

"Here. Just in case. You can always leave a message for me, and I'll get back to you."

She nodded, accepting the paper and stuffing it into the pocket of her jacket. She had no intention of ever using it. "What about you? Are you going to get in trouble?"

"I can take care of myself." He squinted at her. "You'd better comb your hair or something and change clothes before your folks see you."

She reached up and touched her hair. It was a mess. Wild and loose.

Alex slowly began backing away. He pushed his hands in the pockets of the jacket. The movement caused his elbows to stick out from his slender body. To Dallas it made him look somehow lonely and displaced.

"Maybe I'll see you around sometime . . ." he said before turning to walk quickly back up Chatham.

Dallas watched him disappear in the distance. When she couldn't see him anymore it was almost as if he'd never existed. Nonetheless, she believed that Alex Marco would keep his word and not say anything to Vin or Lillian about what happened. She believed that Alex could take care of himself if Nicholas tried to start in on him again. But Dallas also believed that there was no chance that she'd ever see him again.

Chapter One

The volume on the telephone was as low as it could be, and still its trilling sound startled her ruthlessly from sleep. Her mind, suspended somewhere in an unfinished dream, quickly shifted into semiconsciousness. She reached for the receiver before the phone could ring a second time.

Something must be wrong.

"Hello?"

"Hi, Dallas. It's . . . me," came back the deep and throaty answer.

Dallas recognized the voice on the other end. "Val, what's wrong? It's not Megan Marie, is it? Your family?"

As she asked the question Dallas pulled herself up into a half-sitting position, her shoulders supported by pillows and the headboard. She glanced at the green-illuminated digital numbers on the clock radio: 1:53 A.M.

There was sniffling and genuine distress, and the answer, when it finally came, was muffled through the folds of a Kleenex or handkerchief.

"No, no. Everyone is fine."

Dallas unclenched the muscles in her neck and thighs. Her body relaxed. She swung her legs from the bed, pulling back the covers. "Hold on a minute. I'm going to switch phones."

She put the call on hold and replaced the receiver. Once out of the bed she searched in the dark through the pile of clothing tossed haphazardly on the chair and floor. She found something large with sleeves and quickly thrust her arms into them. Dallas didn't bother to button the shirt, but wrapped it instead across her breasts as she left the room and closed the door behind her. She padded barefoot down a short hallway and into the living room, expertly sidestepping the edge of the wicker trunk that served as a coffee table. She let out a sleepy yawn and climbed onto the sofa, settling into a corner and digging her toes under a cushion. Slouching down comfortably, Dallas reached for the extension, prepared to listen to Valerie Holland's latest complaint or problem.

"You still there?" Dallas asked, fitting the phone between ear and shoulder.

"Yeah, I'm here."

"You just about gave me a heart attack, Val. I won't even remind you what time it is."

"I'm sorry. I . . . I didn't even think about the time. Did I interrupt anything?"

"Just my sleep. Not that it would have mattered to you anyway," Dallas responded.

She absently massaged her fingertips through her scalp, pulling and playing with the short, curly locks. Valerie never thought about the time. Dallas had learned that she either had to keep up with Valerie's schedule or miss half the adventure.

"What's wrong now? Did Matthew change his mind again about leaving his wife?" She heard a soft mewling sound and realized that Valerie was crying.

"Just don't say I told you so," Valerie said in a watery voice.

"I don't have to. You knew all along what could happen. You know better than to get involved with a married man. Don't you read *Ladies' Home Journal*?" Dallas teased wryly. "They always go back to their wives, and you get hurt."

"It . . . it's not Matthew. I haven't even seen him in weeks. I'm glad we don't work together anymore."

"Okay. So you're not broken up over Matthew. You

didn't wake me up at almost two in the morning to tell me what a bastard he is."

Valerie sniffed. "No . . ." She started to cry again in earnest.

Dallas's eyes opened abruptly. She stared into the dark and frowned. "Val?" she prompted.

"Nicholas is dead," Val sobbed.

For a moment the only thing Dallas could hear was the sounds of Valerie's distress. Everything else was so quiet, like a void around the crying. The confusion she was suddenly experiencing had nothing to settle on.

"Nicholas . . ." Dallas repeated blankly, as if testing the sound of the name. For a moment Dallas had no idea who Valerie was talking about. Her memory sifted through all of Valerie's boyfriends over the past several years.

"Who . . . who did you say?"

"*Nicholas!* Nicholas Marco. He's dead. He's *dead,*" Valerie said impatiently, as if it should mean something significant to Dallas.

Dallas was not fully awake. She leaned forward to grab an ecru knit afghan from a basket on the floor next to the sofa and attempted to spread it over herself. She wished she'd taken time to put on a robe. She felt a chill as goose bumps rose on her limbs. Her mind began leafing through a mental file, a chronology of childhood events, of incidents and occasions between herself and Nicholas Marco. The list was short and select. She'd actively tried to stay out of his way.

Still, there had been times, like that Tuesday afternoon, when the details remained crystal clear. Even then what most often came to mind had less to do with Nicholas and the attempted rape than with the other person so fatefully present that day.

Alex. He'd appeared out of nowhere to save her.

So, Nicholas Marco was dead.

For Dallas the announcement resurrected deep-seated feelings. Sympathy wasn't one of them. Vin must be beside himself, she speculated silently. And poor Lillian . . .

"When did it happen? How?" Dallas asked, feeling neither shock nor sorrow.

"Sometime last night, I think. I got a call from Mom. She heard from Sylvia Campbell. You remember her? That retired schoolteacher whose house is behind the Marcos'. She saw a cop car come to the house around ten o'clock. She told my mother she could hear Lillian screaming . . ."

Dallas squeezed her eyes tightly closed, and felt a strong wave of sympathy for the woman. "Bad news spreads quickly," she murmured.

"That's what happens in a neighborhood when everyone knows everyone else's business. I swear if I ever commit a crime, five people on the block will know about it before I'm booked."

"So how did he die? Was Nicholas sick or something?" There was a pause and then more quiet tears. Dallas was starting to lose patience with Val. She didn't understand all this weeping over Nicholas Marco.

"No . . ." Valerie croaked. "He . . . he was out at some party and got tanked. Then he insisted he could drive home. You know how Nicholas was. Always trying to show how macho he was. Can you believe he'd be so stupid?"

"Yes," Dallas responded flatly, although she doubted Valerie had heard or was even actually expecting an answer.

"He was with someone. Not his wife, of course. Or should I say his almost ex-wife. Some bimbo. Mom said she walked away with whiplash and a few broken nails. Can you believe that? She had her seat belt on."

"Then she wasn't a bimbo," Dallas said dryly.

"Forget her," Valerie said, annoyed. "What about Nicholas, for Christ's sake? We grew up with him."

"We lived in the same community," Dallas corrected. "Other than that I had nothing in common with Nicholas Marco. He didn't like black people."

"I don't know if I believe that."

"How could you forget the stuff that went on the year my family moved into the neighborhood, Val? The racial slurs spray-painted on our garage door? Remember your folks taking Dean and me in for a week so my parents didn't have to worry about us while the police investigated? We heard talk that Nicholas and his friends were involved."

"No one ever saw him do anything. Anyway, it was just talk. He was a kid."

"Old enough to be dangerous. And I was . . ." Dallas stopped abruptly.

Valerie made an impatient sound through the phone. "Don't tell me you were scared of him. He acted tough, but he really wasn't."

"How do you know that?"

"Look, it doesn't matter anymore. Your family was like everyone else in the neighborhood."

No, we weren't, Dallas thought stubbornly. She knew there was no way that Valerie could understand the effects of the reign of terror her family had gone through for those first months. The past was even more complicated than that because no one knew about what she alone had to endure. She got it from both sides, like working double duty: for being black . . . and not being black enough. As if it were her fault that her mother was white.

Dallas suddenly realized that her body was tense. She was a little surprised that she still harbored an intense dislike of Nicholas. It had been years since she had seen him, years since he had even remotely been a threat to her, and now he no longer existed. But that didn't offer much relief. There was always going to be someone like him. Different people . . . same issues. There was a lot Valerie didn't know or understand.

Valerie blew her nose. Dallas grimaced and shook

her head. "I don't understand what you're carrying on about. You never had much good to say about Nicholas, either."

"He wasn't so bad."

"You're only saying that because he's dead."

"Dallas, don't be that way. He was kinda cute. I thought he was funny . . ."

"He was a jerk."

"You don't understand," Valerie said, no longer crying but her voice still husky with emotion.

"No, I don't."

"We used to tease each other. You know. He'd try to come on to me and say things like, is your father sober this week. And I'd tell him he smelled like garlic. He'd say, for someone Irish I was pretty. And I'd say, for someone Italian he was smart."

"Which one of you was telling the truth?"

Valerie reluctantly laughed.

It did no good, Dallas realized, to attack the dubious character of Nicholas Marco. Maybe it was easier for Valerie to remember Nicholas more fondly because they were both white.

"There's going to be a wake Friday night. What time can you get out here?" Valerie asked.

"What?"

"There's probably going to be two viewing times. I'd rather go to the early one. More people will be there."

"I'm not going."

"What do you mean, you're not going?"

"I mean, I'm not going. I don't want to be there."

"Come on, Dallas. You can't *not* be there. It'll look strange. Everyone will notice."

"And no one will care. Especially not Nicholas's family."

"I don't want to go alone. I can't just walk in there, look at him laid out all stiff and everything, and . . . and not . . ." Valerie's voice quavered.

"Valerie, look . . . it's obvious that Nicholas's death

has really shaken you up. I'm sorry. I didn't know you had that much feeling for him."

"It's just that Nicholas was always there, you know? He was part of our lives, good or bad."

"Well, I think the best way for me to respect his memory is to stay away."

"Look, everyone knows you're friendly with Lillian. If you don't come, people are going to wonder why. You don't have to stay long, just please come." Valerie's urging ended on a plaintive note.

Dallas knew Valerie was attempting to manipulate the situation. But of course, she knew she had to go. Lillian was her friend, and she cared about what she might be going through. Lillian deserved the respect accorded her as a grieving mother.

"All right . . . I'll come . . ."

"Good."

"Just don't expect me to cry and say anything, Valerie."

"I won't, but you'll feel different once you're there. Are you going to take the train back into the city or stay over?"

"I don't know. Depends on how late this is going to last."

"Why don't you stay with me?"

Dallas chuckled. "Not if you're going to spend the night wailing about Nicholas Marco."

When Dallas got off the phone, it was almost three a.m. but she was not inclined to go back to sleep. She felt strangely wired. Not the kind that comes from shock or bad news, but the kind born of speculation. She hardly ever went back to the old neighborhood anymore. Despite having been raised there for some fifteen years, it was not a place she remembered with fondness.

Dallas stretched out completely on the sofa and wrapped herself thoroughly in the afghan. It would have made more sense to return to the bedroom, but she couldn't. She listened to the silence of her apartment, letting both a sense of disquiet and pensive reflections engulf her. No matter how far she tried to get away from the past, she was irrevocably tied to it. Everything from the past was the foundation for who she was in her life, even in that very moment.

Dallas remembered vividly that she had been six years old the first time anyone ever called her a nigger. Nicholas Marco had been the one. She understood the power of the slur in the way it had been said, and the way it made her feel. Very small. Almost invisible. It put her in her place, and made Nicholas feel strong and righteous.

Dallas sighed. She hadn't supposed that her family moving into North Lakewood, a predominately white middle-class neighborhood on the southern shore of Long Island, was going to mean being scared all the time. There were people there who hated them.

She remembered her father sitting at the window all night staring out into the dark street. It made no sense when they returned home from shopping one Saturday to find that every single window in their house had been broken. Dallas didn't understand why anyone would put sugar in her father's gas tank or set fire to their garbage. But she remembered the names of certain people being whispered, Nicholas Marco among them. Dallas recalled her father's stern warning to stay away from the Marco house. She could still hear the way her father had answered in frustration and anger when she'd asked why.

"Because they don't like black folks, that's why."

She hadn't understood what that meant when she was six years old. She didn't realize she was black until then.

The next year when she was seven was the first time she'd met any of the Marco family. It happened because of the mail. Several pieces addressed to Vincent C. Marco had been mistakenly delivered to their house. Coming home from school one afternoon, she'd been informed by her stepmother, Eleanor, that she had to take the mail back to the Marco house.

"Me?" she squeaked, her eyes huge and round.

"Yes. Just put it in their mailbox in front of the house. Then come on back," Eleanor instructed her.

"But I'm scared of them," Dallas whined.

Eleanor was a little impatient. "You walk past that house every day on the way to school. Those people are not going to do a thing to you. You're a child."

Dallas was not reassured. She wanted to ask Eleanor why she couldn't go instead. What if she went over there and never came back?

"Can Dean come with me?"

"No, he can't. I don't have time to get him dressed to go outside. I want you to go straight there and come straight back."

Dallas hoped that if she dallied long enough, Eleanor would get impatient and decide to go herself. But instead, Dallas was given a gentle push through the open door, and it was closed behind her. On the two-block walk to the Marco house, she wondered if she could throw the mail into the front yard and run. Could she leave it with someone next door? She even thought of just throwing the mail in the trash. Who would know? But then she was standing in front of the house.

It was a large ranch made with red brick. It had white accents and moldings and double wide front doors. There was an ornate black wrought-iron fencing neatly enclosing the property. There was a white statue of a kneeling lady on the front lawn. Dallas stared at it, wondering if it was supposed to be Mrs. Marco. She walked up to the fence and peered over the top at the still figure. There was a small cap of snow on the top of its head and shoulders.

"Hey! Whatta you want? Who are you?"

Dallas jumped so violently at the voice behind her that she bumped her chin on the top of the fence. The mail fell from her hands to the slushy snow at her feet. She turned to face a boy. A big boy. She pressed her back against the fence.

"Who are you?" he demanded again.

"Dallas Oliver," she said softly, her heart pounding in fright.

"Dallas Oliver?" he repeated as if she were lying. "That black family? You one of them?"

Dallas stared at him, wondering what she had done wrong. She nodded.

He looked closely at her face, doubt and confusion passing fleetingly over his pale features. And then the full power of his age gathered force within him. His mouth curled derisively.

"Nigger . . ." he muttered. "This is my house. What the fuck do you want?"

More than anything else, Dallas remembered what he'd called her. She couldn't even think how to answer because she was just hearing that word hurled at her and she felt as if she'd just been punched in the chest. It sunk in and gripped her heart and tried to squeeze the life out of her. It was the first time Dallas had ever come face-to-face with someone who disliked her on sight. For no reason.

She retrieved the soiled and wet mail and held it out to him. "Here," she said in a small voice.

He continued to look at her calmly, perhaps waiting for her reaction to his words. But Dallas just stared back, trying to decide what she would do if he hit her or called her more names. Then a door opened behind her.

"Nicky? What's going on? Who is that child?"

The boy looked beyond her, and Dallas turned her head as well. Half of the double front doors to the brick house was open, and a lady stood squinting out at them. Nicky walked past Dallas and through the gate.

"One of those black kids. She had our mail . . ."

Dallas watched as the woman said something admonishing to the boy. He swept past her into the house.

When the woman turned her attention to her, Dallas froze, expecting more terrible things to be said to her. But the woman smiled. She stretched out her hand and beckoned.

"Come here, will you?"

Dallas didn't move. She imagined that she was going to be dragged inside and something awful would happen to her. She kept her eyes on the woman but began to walk along the fence, back in the direction of home. The woman stepped out of the door. She laughed lightly.

"It's all right, child. I'm not going to hurt you. I want you to take something home with you. To your parents."

Dallas stopped, considering the quiet and pleasant voice and words. Cautiously she approached the gate. She took a hesitant step through the opening and stopped again. The woman waved her hand furiously.

"Hurry! It's cold out here." She turned and walked into the house, but left the door open.

Curiosity propelled Dallas forward. The woman had told her not to be afraid. She was inviting her into what had previously been a mystery. It made Dallas feel special.

When she reached the door, the woman had returned. Close up Dallas realized that she wasn't very tall. And she didn't look very old. Her hair was a dark blond, pulled back into a bun, and made her skin look very white. The woman reminded her of someone. Her smile and pale skin. The kindness in her eyes. She smiled again and held out a stack of papers to Dallas.

"I'm so glad you came over. Did your mother send you?" she said.

"She's not my real mother," Dallas found herself responding.

"Oh . . ." the woman said in surprise. "Well, anyway, I have some mail for your family, too. I was going to send Nicky, but he—well—never mind. Here . . ."

Dallas recognized her father's name on the top envelope. And she could see that the house numbers were close enough to easily confuse on a quick glance. 469 as opposed to 496 Chatham Street.

"And this is for you, for being nice enough to bring the mail over."

She held out her hand, and Dallas stared at the blue-wrapped candy. She wondered quickly if her father's instructions to never take anything from people she didn't know extended to this woman who lived just three blocks away.

"Go on, take it. It's mint candy."

Dallas made her own decision and took the three pieces from the woman's hand.

"Nicky said your name is Dallas. Is that right?"

"Yes." Dallas nodded softly, finally seeing a similarity between this woman and the one kneeling in front of the house.

"Well, I'm Lillian Marco. Nicky's mother. Now you and I know each other. The next time, you just come on up to the door and ring the bell, okay?"

Dallas nodded, although she wasn't sure she would ever return. But she did feel better. She felt acceptance in the warmly spoken words, even though she herself was still afraid to say anything. The woman suddenly reached out. Dallas flinched as the woman's hand cupped her chin and lifted her face. She blinked as the woman continued to stare into her face with a frown. For a moment Dallas wondered if she was going to repeat that word her son had used and push her away. But instead the woman smiled at her before releasing her, then hugged herself against the cold. "You better get on home, now."

Dallas slogged through the snow back to her house. She squeezed her gloved hand tightly, so the blue-wrapped mint candy wouldn't fall out. She wasn't going to tell Eleanor about it, certain that she would take them and throw them away.

* * *

"Dallas? Hey . . . what are you doing out here?"

Dallas frowned, disoriented by the voice. She rolled toward the sound but was slow in opening her eyes. When she did, she saw a handsome face close to hers, its brown features still soft from recent sleep. The well-shaped mouth under the trimmed full mustache was grimacing in confusion.

"Everything okay?"

"I'm fine," she sighed, closing her eyes briefly.

Burke stood up but continued to look down on her. He had pulled on his slacks over white jockey shorts. He zippered the front and hooked the tab, but it caused the loosened belt buckle to clink together noisily, further disturbing the morning.

"I didn't know where you'd gone off to," he muttered.

Dallas yawned as she slowly sat up. "I don't have any clothes on. How far did you think I'd go?"

"All I know is when we went to bed and I fell asleep last night, you were right next to me. Why'd you get up? Was I snoring?"

Dallas pushed aside the afghan and levered herself up from the sofa. Her back was stiff and her left arm was asleep. She cranked it back and forth from the elbow to get the circulation going again.

"The phone rang and woke me up. I took the call out here."

"I never heard a thing."

"Then you didn't miss me," she murmured. Dallas glanced up at him. "Don't worry about it, Burke. I couldn't get back to sleep after the call, that's all.

She stood up and he reached out for her, slipping his arms through the opening of the overly large shirt and pulling Dallas into a loose embrace. He grinned complacently and bent to kiss her briefly. It was teasing and conciliatory. The feel of her bare breasts against his warm brown skin was instantly titillating.

"I appreciate you not waking me. I was pretty knocked up by that three-day trip."

"Not so much that you wanted to go home," she observed with a slight smile. He playfully ruffled his hand through her short curly hair. It had always irritated her.

Burke moaned quietly in the back of his throat. "Three days was a long time. I wanted to see if you missed me."

"You could have called to find that out."

He chuckled. "I believe in full frontal attack."

Dallas watched his face and let him caress her. His broad grin was seductive, lighting his features with a masculine charm. She had never been able to tell how much of his actions were calculated, how much was a true gauge of his feelings for her. He had skilled hands. A knowingness of her body that spoke of extensive experience with other women. Dallas closed her eyes as Burke's hands lightly explored the smooth expanse of her back, sliding down to her buttocks. He gently pulled her forward until their groins met. Dallas instinctively recoiled as the chilled metal of his belt touched her skin. She didn't resist, although she placed her palms flat on his chest to maintain some distance between them. Dallas could sense the slow rising of heat in Burke as he rested his chin against her temple.

"I'd love for you and me to throw down one more time, but I have a meeting this morning . . ."

Throw down . . .

Dallas disengaged herself from his arms. She looked into his face before leaning forward to plant a perfunctory kiss on his mouth. There was no point in encouraging a delay. Dallas yawned again and stepped around Burke as she headed for the bedroom.

"What time is it?"

"A little after six."

Dallas groaned. She had not had a restful night. In her bedroom she shrugged out of the white shirt and went to a drawer, opening it to pull out fresh underwear. She heard Burke enter behind her and held out the shirt to him.

"It's a little wrinkled . . ."

"I can't go into my office like this," he complained, accepting it and putting it on. "I'll stop home and change."

"Ummm," Dallas murmured, picking up a brush on the bureau to rake through her hair. The bristles along her scalp was stimulating and forced the last remains of sleep out of her.

Dallas concentrated on her task, ignoring Burke's presence. But he stood behind her, reflected in the mirror. He was smoothing the slightly wrinkled shirt into the waistband of his pants and buttoning the cuffs.

Dallas watched him. She didn't stop what she was doing when he touched the back of her neck.

"Dallas, about last week, before I left . . ."

She stopped brushing her hair and stared at him in the mirror. "Don't say it. Don't start explaining. It was my fault, too."

Burke relaxed and stroked her cheek with the tip of his fingers. "I should have understood that attending that reception was important to you. But all those rich white people make me uncomfortable."

Dallas fought back an instinct to say anything defensive. "That's not even funny, Burke. It was about business. Let's face it. If someone had something you wanted, you wouldn't care what color they are."

He grinned at her. "You're right."

There was a thoughtfulness to his good looks that had always attracted her. Even when he made her mad or disappointed her, Dallas had always believed that it wasn't deliberate. But her smile was forced. "I just wish we didn't use sex as a way to make up every time we have a fight."

Burke raised a brow. "Works for me. Last night I was pretty sure you thought so, too."

Dallas nodded. "It was consensual . . ."

"And damned good," he added with a growl of satisfaction.

He shouldn't have said anything. Dallas didn't want to be reminded that it had been the wrong decision. Her annoyance grew and she again pulled away from him.

"Look, we only made love last night. That doesn't mean I forgive you for standing me up."

Burke pursed his mouth. "Why not?"

"Because it's just not that easy, that's why. And I don't have time to explain it to you. You have to go to work and so do I. I have to put some things together if I'm going out to the Island tomorrow night."

"Your family?"

"No, it's not family."

"Does it have to do with the phone call you got?"

"It was Val. Someone we both knew growing up died yesterday. I have to go out for the services and pay my respects," Dallas informed him. "I can at least offer you coffee and orange juice."

The look Burke gave her almost made Dallas regret the offer. As if he was considering other options. She was trying not to rush him out the door. She was trying not to negate what had happened between them the night before . . . but it was over.

"Sounds good." Burke nodded, gathering up the rest of his things as Dallas donned a sweatshirt and leggings and headed out of the bedroom.

In the kitchen she had a sudden sensation of déjà vu. A feeling of unease settled on her spirits. Dallas thoughtfully filled the coffeemaker with water and placed the filter in its proper canister. She was doing this for Burke as she used to do for Hayden. She didn't drink coffee.

Dallas heard Burke's soft whistle from the living room as he turned on the television low and listened to the early morning news. He was getting comfortable, making himself at home. Apprehension welled up so quickly in her it lodged in her throat until she felt as though she were suffocating. But she wasn't even sure why. Dallas was just pouring the juice when Burke came into the kitchen.

"I like waking up with you," he said behind her.

Dallas did not turn around to acknowledge his observation. She didn't want to encourage his fantasy. And yet there was a sense of the familiar. It made her nervous. It reminded her of Hayden.

"The muffins are in the toaster . . ."

"When are you getting back from the Island?" he asked, putting the warmed muffins into a small wicker basket.

"I don't know. I might stay at least overnight. Maybe longer."

Burke sat and began peeling a banana. "Call me when you get back."

Next week was a long time away. It would take care of itself, she thought uneasily. "I hope everything works out with that contract you talked about," Dallas said, not encouraging any discussion that remotely opened up an opportunity for more intimacy between them.

"It will," he responded. He began talking knowledgeably about a new record deal he was negotiating for a client, then a new promotional tour he was organizing. He never asked her to go along.

But Dallas only half listened. It was a good distraction. The desultory talk allowed her to relax over the orange juice and the muffins. She felt completely comfortable with him for the first time since he'd arrived at her apartment the night before. Or maybe she only felt this way because he was about to leave.

At the door, Dallas let Burke kiss her lightly. And once he was gone, her attention shifted abruptly from his concerns to her own. She absently cleaned the dishes from breakfast, showered, and made her bed. Then Dallas sat at her computer to write a commentary about death. It was not what she'd promised her editor, but she was able to keep the tone thoughtful and questioning. Exploring whether or not someone's passing away was a time for sorrow, reflection, jubilation, guilt, or forgiveness for those left behind. She resolutely kept her mind away from the inappropriate anticipation that developed at some time during the morning as she made her plans for attending Nicholas Marco's wake and headed into her office.

Dallas recalled that she had only been to two funerals in her life. One for her mother when she was only five years old. The other for her paternal grandmother. Both occasions had seemed dark and scary. One because of the sense of having been left behind. Abandoned. At the other she'd felt lost in a sea of unknown faces. She was a stranger to everyone. But Friday was going to be different. Not because of death . . . but because life went on.

Dallas couldn't help herself, and she wasn't going to apologize. She was not going out to Long Island to pay final good-byes to Nicholas Marco. For if the truth be known, she had a sense that the death of Nicholas Marco, childhood nemesis and unrepentant bigot, had set her free. His wake was going to be more than a closure on the past. Unconsciously Dallas was also wondering if it would generate a new beginning.

Chapter Two

Dallas was sorry she'd come.

She had forgotten that funeral home parlor rooms were small and crowded. Narrow and dim, brightened only by the profusion of floral bouquets that only made the room seem more claustrophobic. Chairs were arranged in a theaterlike fashion, all facing front with the expensive coffin placed center stage complete with soft lighting overhead. It seemed a bizarre setting, as if everyone were waiting for a performance to begin.

Standing just inside the entrance, Dallas took a brief cursory glance around. She noticed that the family of the deceased was seated on one side of the room, and on the other side was everyone else. She noticed that people sat whispering in clusters. Some were reminiscing about their pasts with Nicholas, but as she turned to sign her name in the guest book, she caught snatches of conversation that had to do not with life or death but personal problems. Someone was going over the itinerary for a planned trip to Bermuda. Someone else was discussing the results of a recent surgery. And still another was offering opinions on a friend's recent divorce.

No one seemed particularly broken up by the tragedy that gathered them, Dallas guessed. No one was crying. Not even Lillian Marco, Dallas observed as she walked down the center aisle toward the gathered family. In a way she wasn't surprised by the amount of strength and control the middle-aged woman displayed. She would have to have a certain amount of fortitude to have had a son like Nicholas. Lillian seemed more dazed and tired than anything, but even in mourning Dallas was amazed at her graciousness and her ability to put other people at ease with their awkwardly uttered condolences. Lillian smiled and thanked them for coming to say good-bye to her Nicky.

Then Lillian saw her, and Dallas felt put on the spot. Suddenly she didn't know what to say to this woman, who'd always been a special friend, about the loss of her only child. Given her feelings about Nicholas, Dallas was sure Lillian would see right through her, and she'd be caught in a lie if she tried to express something she didn't genuinely feel. No matter what she said, it wasn't going to be the right thing, and it wasn't going to be enough. And it wasn't going to be the truth.

She was conscious of the body of people seated around Lillian who watched her approach. Vincent Marco was somber and pensive as he sat next to his wife. He turned his attention on her, and acknowledged her by a small nod of his head. Unlike his son, Vin Marco didn't dislike her, but nevertheless he maintained a certain distance between them. Lillian had once told her that Vin didn't like change. Then Dallas could well imagine that a black family moving into North Lakewood might have set him back on his heels a bit. Yet one winter afternoon when she was returning home from Valerie Holland's house, he'd stopped to give her a ride.

She had done the twenty-minute walk before by herself, sometimes encountering her father or another neighbor for a ride. But this time when a car had driven parallel to her, slowing its speed to pace her, someone had yelled out the window, "Hey, you." She had been taught not to respond to "Hey, you," and she didn't even turn to look at who the driver was.

"Aren't you that girl, Dallas? You know my wife, Lilly."

Dallas stopped abruptly and swiveled her head. It was Vin Marco calling out to her. She couldn't even answer him. Dallas was just trying to remember if Vin had ever spoken to her in the five years she and her family had lived on Chatham.

He stopped the car and gestured toward her impatiently.

"Don't you know who I am? Vin Marco."

Dallas nodded. "I know."

"Where you headed?"

"Home."

He beckoned. "Get in. I'll give you a lift."

She hesitated.

"What's the matter? You don't like me or something?" Vin asked with a laugh. "Lilly says you're scared of me. What did I ever do to you?"

Dallas shrugged. She couldn't say. It seemed like he was teasing her, and she finally got in on the passenger side next to Vin.

The inside of Vin Marco's car smelled like flowers. She glanced over her shoulder and saw a wrapped bouquet of purple irises on the back seat.

"For my Lilly," Vin said proudly. "Every week I bring her flowers."

"They're pretty," Dallas murmured.

She looked at Vin's profile now, studying him closely. She didn't know why seeing the flowers made such a difference, but it changed everything she felt and believed about him. Suddenly she no longer felt wary of him. What was there to fear in a man whom Lillian loved . . . and who brought her flowers to show it?

Lillian stood up to greet her, and for the first time since entering the room Dallas could genuinely smile. Lillian was a small lady and when they hugged affectionately her head was somewhere near Dallas's chest. She had to bend down to kiss the older woman's cheek and be kissed in return. Her small, cool hands framed Dallas's face, and her expression became soft and concerned, her smile sad. Dallas was surprised at the sudden welling of tears within herself, though her sympathy was for Lillian and not because of Nicholas.

"Honey, I'm so glad you could come. You didn't have to, you know. That trip from Manhattan . . ."

Dallas took Lillian's hand and squeezed it gently, looking into her hazel eyes and admiring her strength. She felt herself struggling, nevertheless, to say the right thing. She cleared her throat.

"Of course I had to come. I . . . I'm so sorry for you and your husband . . . for your family," Dallas said.

Lillian made a kind of gesture, as if accepting the formality of the sentiments, but not wanting to know anyone's feelings about her son.

"Thank God he didn't suffer. He was killed instantly. The doctors say if he'd lived he would have been paralyzed. Nicky couldn't handle that." Lillian shook her head, with a telling knowledge of her son's limitations. "Look at how many people came today for him," she sighed.

It made Dallas wonder if perhaps Lillian knew, and had always known, the effect her son had on people. Lillian patted the back of her hand and, still holding it, turned Dallas to face the rest of the family.

"This is Dallas. She's the little girl I talk about all the time from the neighborhood. Isn't she pretty?" Lillian boasted.

A few people murmured hello, but Dallas was more aware of the awkward silence and stares of appraisal. Her gaze quickly swept the faces of the family members. There was no one here that she really recognized. Vin had turned away, facing forward again to stare at the open coffin of his son. His silence was understandable and seemed like a signal to Dallas that she should retreat. She turned to Lillian again.

"I'm going to sit across the room and say hello to some of the others. I'll be here for a while."

"Thank you for coming, hon."

"If there's anything I can do . . ." Dallas mouthed automatically.

"Call me sometime," Lillian whispered as she looked at Dallas. "I haven't seen you for so long. You kids grow up and move away and forget about all us old people."

Dallas grinned. "I don't know any old people." She was gratified when Lillian blushed and smiled briefly, shaking her head.

"You're a good girl," Lillian murmured and then gave her attention to another group arriving to pay their respects.

Dallas turned in relief to the opposite side of the room, where she immediately saw Valerie raise a hand to get her attention. Dallas slid into the row of chairs and sat next to her. They greeted each other with cheek air-kisses.

"I thought you were going to stand me up," Valerie said.

"I didn't come out here to see you," she countered dryly. She peered into Valerie's face. "Have you been crying again?"

Valerie shook her head. "No. But I haven't slept well since I called you. I'm just tired. What about you?"

Dallas raised her brows. "Do I look like I've been crying?"

Valerie looked her over critically and grimaced. "You look wonderful, as usual. Are you over the shock, yet?"

"Sorry, but I was never in shock," Dallas answered truthfully.

"He looks terrible," Rosemary Holland stage-whispered as she took her seat again next to her daughter. "Hi, Dallas. You just get here?"

Valerie glared at her mother. "The man is dead. What do you expect him to look like?"

"He looks too fleshy and puffed out. They put too

much of that stuff in him. You know what I mean," Rosemary continued, speaking her mind as always.

"Embalming chemicals," Dallas helpfully supplied with a grin. She'd always liked Rosemary Holland, who had learned in her life not to take anything too seriously.

"Yeah, that's right." Rosemary nodded. "Don't you think so, Dallas?"

"I don't know. I didn't go up to view the body," Dallas replied.

"You should," Valerie admonished. "This is the last time you'll get a chance."

Dallas wisely remained silent.

"You know, when your father passed, it looked like they glued his lips together so his mouth wouldn't drop open. You remember how Daddy used to sleep with his mouth open and you kids were always dropping things in?" Rosemary reflected, her ample bosom heaving in silent laughter.

"Ma . . ." Valerie whined in annoyance.

"Remember how Aunt Bea got drunk and started singing at the wake, and telling dirty jokes, and then she passed out?"

Valerie's exasperation grew. "Do you mind?"

"Well, it's true. I think they put too much pancake on Nicky."

"Pancake?" Dallas asked.

"Yeah. Makeup. To cover up the scratches and bruises from the accident."

Valerie groaned and covered her face with her hands. "I should have disowned you years ago," she sighed.

"I feel sorry for Lillian," Rosemary continued, ignoring her daughter. "Nicky was a boy only a mother could love. Maybe his mother knew that. Lord knows Lillian and Vin tried."

Dallas turned with a frown to Rosemary. "What do you mean? Lillian *did* love him."

"Oh, sure . . . sure," Rosemary said quickly. "What I mean is that it didn't help."

"I didn't know you didn't like Nicholas," Dallas said.

Rosemary shrugged. "It's not that I didn't like him, but he was so full of himself. Vincent Marco spoiled that boy, and look what it got him. And I didn't appreciate how he treated people."

"Was he ever rude to you?" Dallas asked.

Rosemary glanced at her. "No, not really. But I know the way he acted to you and your brother. Tate used to tell me." She shook her head and tsked sadly. "I never understood it. Vin and Lillian are decent people. They deserved better than Nick."

Dallas turned her attention again to the woman seated on the other side of the room.

Lillian was now in conversation with her estranged daughter-in-law and grandson. Dallas didn't know much about them except that Lillian almost never saw the boy and had never been able to form a relationship with him. Dallas had also not known much about the brief marriage of Nicholas Marco to Theresa Cicone, other than it had been born in lust and forced into a ceremony when Theresa, the youngest daughter of a local politician, got pregnant. Doomed to failure because they both wanted their own way, they had separated shortly after their son had been born. Acrimony between the two became legend, the fights and disagreements growing to include both families. Theresa got the upper hand, however, keeping her son Justin as far away from his father and grandparents as she could. Nicholas retaliated by not caring . . . and taking up with a string of other women.

A boy of about nine, Lillian's grandson was overweight and sullen, as if he would rather not be there for his father's service. Again Dallas was struck by the lack of sorrow and loss that anyone, other than Lillian and Vin Marco, was feeling or expressing for the dead man.

Dallas recalled the funeral when her grandmother had passed—her father's mother. The neighborhood Baptist church in Philadelphia was jammed with people from Mother Oliver's community. Ladies in their extraordinary hats and veils, the men in their good suits, sitting stiffly and respectfully until the service began. The church choir sang, and the lead mezzo-soprano put the spirit of God into everyone in the congregation. "Amen, Jesus" and "Yes, Lord!" and "Sing it, Sistah" jumped out during the eulogy. Everything about the church, the ceremony of death, the energy of the parishioners, had a deep, soulful poignancy. All of that was missing for Nicholas.

Dallas felt a pair of thin arms circle her from behind, and small hands lightly covered her eyes. She smiled and reached for the young body standing behind her chair.

"Hey, Megan! I didn't know you were going to be here."

The child giggled and then hugged Dallas around the neck. They were pressed cheek to cheek.

"I wanted to surprise you." Megan laughed, coming around the seat to sit next to Dallas and hug her again.

Dallas playfully pinched the little girl's nose and patted her knee affectionately. "Well, I am." She turned to Valerie. "Why on earth did you bring her tonight? There are only grown-ups here."

"No, there isn't," Megan was quick to correct, her gray eyes wide and bright in her face. A cascade of light brown hair was pulled back into a ponytail that trailed down her back almost to her waist. She pointed across the room. "I was talking to those kids before."

Dallas followed the pointing finger and spotted three children among the Marco adults.

"See," Megan said.

"Okay, you're right," Dallas conceded. "But you don't even know the man who died."

Megan began playing with the heart-shaped pendant

around Dallas's neck. "Mommy said she grew up with him. Did you grow up with him, too?"

"Well, I knew him," Dallas responded honestly. "But he wasn't a friend of mine."

Megan nodded but then frowned at her. "Then, how come you're here?"

Dallas was amused by the child's perfectly reasonable question. "Good question. I'm a friend of his mother's. I was sure your mom and grandmother would be here. And now I get to see you."

"Can I stay with you tonight?" Megan asked.

"Not tonight, sweetie. Let me check my schedule and I'll talk to your mom. Maybe next weekend, how about that?"

"That's cool." Megan nodded agreeably. She reached for Dallas's purse and opened it. "Did you bring something for me?"

"I didn't know you were going to be here, remember?"

"Megan Marie, don't do that," Valerie ordered her daughter as she began to rummage around in Dallas's purse.

"Aunt Dallas told me I could . . ." Megan said, continuing her search and withdrawing a thick white envelope from the bag. "What's this?" she asked, holding it up to Dallas.

"I almost forgot," Dallas said, taking the envelope. "It's a mass card for the Marco family."

"Do you want me to take it over to them?" Megan asked.

"No, I think I'd better do it," Dallas said, standing up. "I'll be right back."

But a quick glance showed that Vin and Lillian were no longer among their guests on the other side of the room. For a second Dallas thought of just handing the envelope to anyone from the family still sitting in the parlor. And then she realized that everyone was very quiet, that several people sat staring at the floor or at one another, and others were looking toward the door. Finally, Dallas sensed it, too. The subtle shimmer of conflict.

"I want to see, too," Megan announced, getting up to accompany Dallas.

"No, you don't. You stay right here and sit still," Valerie told her daughter in no uncertain terms. "This doesn't concern you."

Dallas headed toward the voices in the outer hallway. She heard Vin's voice first when she reached the door. Strident and clear, but laced with emotions other than grief. There was great pain . . . and anger.

"What are you doing here? Don't you have no respect?" Vincent Marco complained.

Dallas heard Lillian, pleading and anxious. She walked into the foyer, the card clutched but forgotten in her hand. Vin stood facing off with someone.

It was a man who was turned partially away from her. Vincent spoke angrily at him, while at the same time attempting to maneuver Lillian out of the way, who'd insinuated herself between the two men to keep them apart.

Dallas gasped. "Lillian, be careful . . ."

The tall man turned his head quickly in her direction. Their gazes met and held for a mere second before he turned his attention to Vin Marco again. But Dallas stood momentarily rooted as she stared at his profile.

"Vin, stop it. You're acting crazy," Lillian said urgently.

He tried to put her aside. "Get out of my way."

"I don't want to start anything, Vin. Get a hold of yourself," the man said firmly but calmly. "Look what you're doing to Lillian."

Vincent's face flushed deeply with his rage and frustration. "I bet you're glad Nicky is dead. Is that why you came?"

"I came because I'm really sorry. No matter what you want to believe, I didn't hate Nick."

"No . . . but you couldn't leave things alone. You couldn't stay away and just let it be!"

Vincent started for the man again, and Lillian tried to throw herself against her husband's chest.

"Don't, Vincent, please . . . you don't know what you're saying . . ." Lillian cried out, her voice breaking with the strain of her loss, finally cresting into tears.

Dallas felt a stab in her chest as she watched Lillian fall apart and cry. For several seconds all that could be heard was Lillian's deep pain. In the background was the low volume of recorded organ music that only seemed to increase the drama of the moment.

Vincent, finally losing control, struck out. But the man was quicker and grabbed Vincent's arm, pulling it back as Vincent lurched forward.

"Don't make me do this. I don't want to hurt you . . ." the man gritted as he momentarily struggled with Vincent Marco. "Vin, calm down."

"Oh, my God . . . *they're going to kill each other*!" Lillian cried.

Dallas moved on sheer nerve and instinct, and a desire not to see Lillian get hurt if the two men really began to fight. She forced herself between the two of them and grabbed Lillian, pulling the woman out of the way.

"Vincent, you have to stop," Dallas pleaded. "You're scaring Lillian . . ."

Dazed, Vin stared at her. She placed a protective arm around Lillian. Vin turned his attention to focus on his wife, who stood sobbing into her hands, her shoulders heaving with emotion. A crowd had gathered in the hallway, in a semicircle looking on but not daring to do anything. Vincent stumbled haltingly to Lillian, and Dallas released her as he gathered his wife's quaking body into his arms.

"I'm sorry. Don't cry, Lilly . . . don't cry." He glanced up at his opponent, sadness and frustration clouding his eyes, but he'd come to his senses. "Nicholas is dead," Vincent murmured emotionally. "Can't you have a little consideration for what my family is going through . . . for how Lilly and I feel?"

Boldly, the man stepped forward to touch Lillian's shoulder. He gently and briefly massaged her back in comfort, and then let his hand drop.

"More than you realize, Vin," he said. "But I'll leave if Lillian wants me to."

Lillian made an attempt to compose herself. She reached back over her shoulder to pat the man's arm. But she didn't say anything. Vin, still holding on to his wife, began to maneuver her back into the salon, past the gaping and embarrassed onlookers who slowly followed them.

Dallas was alone in the foyer with the man. He was looking toward the entrance of the salon, as if trying to decide whether or not to go in.

Her heart was thudding quietly with shock. It was Alex Marco. But he looked very different. He had changed. Still, even now there was a fearless impregnability that seemed only to have gotten more solid since she'd last seen him.

He sighed, and Dallas knew that it was not with relief but disappointment at the awkward encounter with Vin. Alex put his hands into the pockets of his jeans. He was wearing them with a black crew neck sweater and a short leather jacket. Cowboy boots finished the picture. It was a distinctive, individual style that suited him.

Something on the floor caught his attention, and he bent to retrieve a white envelope.

Dallas hadn't realized that she'd dropped the mass card in the melee and it was now bent and dirtied. He stared at the envelope, turning it over as if looking for some identification. And then Alex looked at her.

The memory she'd held for so many years had stayed exactly the same, but Alex had not. His hair was now cut in a short and more orderly style. Military length. And it was mostly prematurely gray. It was startling and she couldn't help staring. It made his skin the same shade as her own. It emphasized his countenance, the dark brows and faint five o'clock shadow. His face had filled out and was not so thin, but his prominent jaw and cheekbones were more clearly defined. He was more muscle and tone. What Dallas remembered most about Alex had been lost somewhere in his youth. He was a mature man now.

She felt bewildered and excited and let down. She couldn't count the number of times she'd thought about Alex Marco over the years, imagining what he was doing and what he had become. Wondering if he ever thought of her. Now it all seemed so foolish and pointless. Why should he have?

He stared at her, but Dallas couldn't tell if Alex remembered who she was. Or if he did, he thought better of saying so.

He held out the envelope to her and looked closely at her.

"Is this yours?"

The sound of his voice made her start. That, at least, was exactly the same. "Yes," Dallas mumbled, lowering her gaze and hastily accepting the card. Now she only wanted to minimize her contact with him.

She only had two choices. She could go around him and return to the salon. Or she could leave.

"I forgot to get one."

Dallas frowned at him. She tried to keep her gaze politely inquisitive, impersonal. She tried not to examine him too closely. "What?"

"A mass card. Not that it would have made any difference," he said.

She nodded, aware that he was looking closely at her. Suddenly she didn't want him to place her, to remember the where or when. "You could mail one," Dallas found herself suggesting.

"Is that what you're going to do? Or just forget it and throw it out?"

She shook her head. "I'll leave it by the guest book."

"Afraid to go back in there?" he asked.

Dallas arched a brow at him. "Are you?"

He laughed lightly, and for Dallas the sound spiraled up from the past. It was ironic and deep, and the amusement was wry. It was very familiar.

"No. But this is bad timing. Vin was right. I shouldn't be here," he said. His mouth shaped into a curious smile as he gazed at her. "So, what are we going to do? Stand here like outcasts, go in and risk another fight? Or leave?"

Dallas smiled grimly and shook her head. She slowly walked over to the side table against a wall and placed the mass card on the opened pages of the guest book. "I don't think I'll go back in. I shouldn't have come to begin with, either."

He stared at her for a moment, his gaze assessing her. "Then, why did you?"

For the first time Dallas realized that for all she recalled about Alex Marco she really knew very little. Her adolescent memory died, and she was left facing a man who was, in essence, a stranger. In a way that made it easier for Dallas to talk to him.

"What if I asked you the same thing?"

Surprisingly, he shrugged. "I don't know. Curiosity, maybe. Sympathy? I don't know." His face briefly registered a tight, dark flash of emotion that clenched his jaw.

"Well," she sighed, "it's your turn. I've already been in there. I'm going to leave."

"I've already had my turn," Alex said cryptically. "You saw what happened." He put out his hand toward her. "Look . . . let's forget that. Don't you know . . ."

Another voice interrupted from behind them. "Dallas? I wondered what happened to you. I heard Vin screaming. What's going on out here?"

Valerie started toward them from the salon. Although she was directing her questions to her, Dallas could see Valerie's interest focused on the man she was standing with. She turned to Alex once more, to find him watching Valerie's approach with equal interest.

Valerie turned to Dallas with concern. "You okay?"

"I'm fine."

"It was my fault," Alex spoke up.

Valerie stood protectively next to Dallas, but she acknowledged Alex's presence with a wry grimace. "Nick's been dead for only three days and people are still getting into fights because of him."

Alex shrugged, amused by her comment. "Can't blame him this time. It was me and Vin."

"Why were you yelling at each other?" Valerie directed to him.

"I'm an easy target," Alex said.

"Who are you?"

Alex glanced briefly at Dallas before responding. "Alex Marco."

The verbal confirmation felt as if it were ricocheting through her body, but Dallas kept her expression blank.

Unexpectedly, Valerie chuckled. "I thought so."

"Do I know you?" he asked.

"We've never met, but Nick used to talk about you. Mostly rotten things." Alex grinned. "I'm Valerie Holland. I used to live in the neighborhood. Nicky probably never talked about me."

"I would have remembered," Alex murmured.

Valerie's smile accepted the implied compliment. Dallas witnessed the interplay between Valerie and Alex. Val was in no way trying to gain Alex's attention, but it was happening nonetheless. She began to feel superfluous but stood still. It was a trick she'd learned to do when she was just a child and she was made to feel invisible by the presence of others. She began to back away.

"Val, I'm leaving," Dallas said. "Say good night to your mother for me, and tell Megan I'll talk to her next week about a visit . . ."

"Wait a minute!" Valerie said as Dallas turned to the exit.

Dallas already had her hand on the door, pushing it open to the cool March night air. Yet, she felt much colder than was warranted.

"Are we going to see each other this weekend?" Valerie asked.

Dallas shrugged. "I'm staying at my parents'. Give me a call."

"Aren't you going to introduce me?" Alex interrupted.

It was a second before Dallas understood the question. Alex was watching her, his expression interested.

"I . . ." Dallas began hesitatingly.

"That's Dallas Oliver. She's a friend of mine," Valerie filled in.

Alex held out a hand to Dallas.

"Hi, Dallas," he responded clearly.

Dallas had no choice but to walk back to where they stood and to accept Alex's outstretched hand of greeting. She realized suddenly that he remembered exactly who she was. And he knew exactly what he was doing. For Valerie's sake the moment successfully established a reason to acknowledge one another. He didn't actually shake her hand but held it, silently communicating.

Dallas had a jarring sensation of being swept through time. It wasn't like going back to when they'd first met. It was as if having met they were rushed forward to the present. They got to start over again.

"Hi," Dallas said smoothly.

"Dallas and I also grew up together," Valerie explained. "We've been friends since we were little kids. Her family was the first black family to move into the neighborhood," Valerie informed Alex. "We practically adopted her into the family . . ."

Dallas turned to her in annoyance. "That's not a distinction anyone needs to know, Val. Anyway, he didn't ask you for my life story."

Alex regarded Dallas. "I bet it's an interesting story. It's nice to meet you," he murmured.

Dallas was aware of the double meaning of his words. And she was grateful. "Same here. I'm sorry about the death in your family," she carefully added.

He shook his head. "I'm not a part of it. You saw what almost happened."

"What are you talking about?" Valerie asked.

"Dallas stopped Vin from trying to punch my lights out."

"No, I didn't. I tried to stop Lillian from getting upset."

"I'm glad he didn't turn on you," Valerie said to Dallas.

Alex slowly shook his head. "I wouldn't have let that happen," he said firmly.

Dallas wondered if she imagined the protective edge to his comment. Still, for the moment the less said the better.

Valerie touched her shoulder. "I wish you'd stay a little longer. I'm going to hang around here with Mom before I take her home." She gave Dallas a brief hug. "I'll call you."

"I probably won't stay the whole weekend. I have a deadline . . ." she said, heading for the exit once more, not sparing Alex a parting look but aware that his attention was still very much on her.

She was again through the door and it was about to close behind her when Dallas hazarded a glance over her shoulder. There was just enough time for her to glimpse Valerie and Alex turn their attention back to each other.

Alex had been pulled up short by the appearance of Dallas Oliver. He was surprised to see her again. And stunned at how different she looked from that last time. Fifteen years will do that. He needed to adjust to the encounter with her, but there wasn't any time. For the moment he gave his attention to the bright interest in Valerie Holland's eyes.

"Sounds like you two had plans. I should be the one to back off," Alex began.

"She didn't want to come tonight to start with. We'll see each other before she goes home."

"Where's home?" he asked casually.

"Manhattan. Upper West Side. She has a great apartment overlooking the Hudson, but I don't know how she stands all the noise and not owning a car."

"And you say Dallas is your best friend?"

Valerie nodded, smiling. "She really is. Sometimes we fight like cats and dogs, but I know I can always count on her, and she can say the same of me.

"When we were kids we used to tell people we're sisters. Not that Dallas looks white," she rushed to correct.

"No, she doesn't," Alex agreed too quickly.

"But she doesn't really look black, if you know what I mean."

Alex frowned at Valerie. "No, I don't. I don't know what you're talking about."

Valerie blushed in confusion and shrugged. "Never mind. Dallas's life is pretty complicated."

"Isn't everybody's? I bet there are things about her you don't know."

"Maybe," Valerie conceded. "So what's your big secret? How come Vin wanted to go for your throat? Where do you fit into the family?"

"I'm the black sheep," Alex said flippantly.

Valerie grinned. "Nick told me about you when you were going into the service. He was glad you were leaving. The navy or something like that."

"That's right." Alex looked beyond Valerie toward the salon. He didn't want to keep standing there. He didn't want to talk about what he'd been doing.

"Wanted to see the world? Have a girl in every port?"

Alex pursed his mouth. "Wanted to stay out of

trouble. The chances of surviving where I grew up were not good."

"Really? That sounds interesting. I'd like to hear more about it sometime."

Alex again looked at the very attractive and confident woman in front of him. He forced himself to ignore the activity beyond the open salon door, but he could peripherally make out the coffin at the front of the room. The encounter with Vin was a bad start, but he had to be here. Staring at Valerie he considered other options.

"I'm not planning on staying much longer. How about coffee or something after this?"

Before Valerie could respond, someone appeared suddenly next to her, and stood quietly staring up at Alex. Valerie put her arm around Megan's shoulder and squeezed her to her side.

"Mommy, can we go now? Where's Aunt Dallas?"

Alex looked down at the little girl, and he was riveted. He let his gaze examine her face, her approximate age. She didn't have the characteristic pale skin or coloring of her mother's Irish descendants, but she had the features and prerequisites of someone who was going to become, easily, at least equally as beautiful.

"Dallas went to her parents', sweetie. Yes, we're going to leave soon and take Grandma home, but I want you to meet someone first."

Alex couldn't take his eyes from the little girl. And he knew that his surprise, his fascination, showed clearly on his own face. He looked at Valerie, who waited, staring at him, for his reaction.

"Is . . . is this your daughter?" Alex asked, awed.

Valerie nodded.

"Are you another friend of my mother's?" Megan asked guilelessly.

Alex glanced questioningly at Valerie, who shrugged. "She knows that Nick and I grew up together."

"But he wasn't a friend of Aunt Dallas," Megan added. "She told me so."

"I just met your mother. But I guess you could say I wasn't a friend of his, either. My name is Alex."

Megan pointed blindly behind her to the salon. "He's dead, you know. I don't understand why everybody came to see him if he's dead."

Alex chuckled.

"Megan," Valerie admonished. "We come to pay our respects. It's sad that he's dead."

Megan looked confused and lifted her shoulders. "But nobody liked him."

Valerie and Alex remained silent and just exchanged looks.

Alex was reminded that he and Dallas Oliver had very good reasons for feeling the way they did. There was a kinship that was always going to tie them to Nicholas.

He stared at Valerie's daughter and he saw the future. But seeing Dallas Oliver again, and to some extent meeting Valerie Holland, had plummeted him into the past. He had a feeling of the inevitable, of not so much history repeating itself as just not being finished yet, for any of them.

Chapter Three

I saw this kid sprouting a head full of dreadlocks. He was Asian. I stared at his head, wondering how he had done it, knowing that the texture of his hair was pin straight, slick as seal skin, and fine as rain. I wondered if he'd applied some sort of gel or cream to clump the strands together, or did he roll bunches of it between his palms to get the twists started? I wondered what his parents were thinking and praying when he came home at night, a different species than the child they'd given birth to. But most of all I realized that this kid had accepted something that didn't naturally belong to him. And yet, by doing so he had validated it for some other black kid. He had not taken away something that wasn't his, but had copied it. I had to smile at his guts and his humanity. I applaud him. Imitation is still the best form of flattery.

"Megan? I *know* you've already gone to bed, just like I told you to twenty minutes ago. Right?" Valerie called out loudly as she stood in her kitchen pouring two glasses of wine.

Low and aggrieved, Megan's voice came from somewhere on the sofa in the living room. "But Aunt Dallas is helping me with my homework."

"The idea of homework is that you're supposed to do it yourself. Dallas doesn't need to learn about chlorophyll in plants, and she's already graduated from school. If you hope to do the same, I suggest you pay better attention in class."

Dallas was slouched next to Megan, and she watched the girl mimic her mother's complaints.

"That's not nice," Dallas admonished her. "It's disrespectful, and you know she's right."

"But I just don't understand why I have to know this," Megan whined.

Dallas pulled on a lock of her hair and then sat up, gathering the textbooks in a neat stack. "Because someday you may discover a way of growing better broccoli or cabbage using artificial light . . . or maybe no light at all."

Megan shuddered dramatically. "Ugh," she said, sticking out her tongue. "I hate broccoli."

"You should keep that in mind," Dallas said, chuckling. "If you don't want to be stuck growing it, you'd better study real hard to become something else."

Megan began putting her schoolbooks back into her knapsack. "I'm going to be a writer like you."

"You're not going to make a lot of money that way," Dallas said.

Valerie came from the kitchen carefully carrying the two wineglasses. She set them down on the glass-topped coffee table and glared at her daughter.

"Good *night,* Megan."

"I'm going . . ." Megan sighed pettishly, and slowly headed toward the hallway leading to the back of the tiny house. She glanced back. "Aunt Dallas, can you come and put me to bed?"

"You don't need anyone to put you to bed," Valerie said, impatience with her daughter's delaying tactics creeping into her voice.

"You go on. I'll come in to say good night," Dallas answered, careful not to usurp Valerie's authority.

Megan seemed satisfied with that promise. She nodded and then disappeared into her room. Valerie sat down heavily in a roomy armchair, prepared to relax, but then grimaced. She awkwardly heaved up her rear end and reached behind her back. She extracted a beaded hair crunchy belonging to her daughter. Shakng her head, Valerie tossed it onto the table. Dallas smiled at her expression.

"You can't believe where I find her things sometimes," Valerie muttered as she lifted one of the wineglasses. "One morning last week I nearly went crazy trying to find a sweater she was supposed to wear that day to school. I gave it to her, she put it down somewhere and then couldn't remember where. You'll never believe where she found it."

Dallas shook her head.

"In the pantry. In the middle of dressing for school she'd gone in to get a box of cereal for breakfast. She probably got distracted. Twenty minutes we spent looking for the damn thing," Valerie said, bemused.

Dallas took the second glass of wine and took a sip. "Why didn't you just get her another sweater?"

"That's not the point."

"The point is kids have short attention spans and she has other sweaters. It's a good thing she didn't misplace something that could rot."

"If her head wasn't attached to her shoulders . . ." Valerie began. "Getting her to bed at night is becoming another test of wills . . ."

Dallas chuckled quietly. "This conversation should be taped. I wish you could hear yourself."

"What?" Valerie asked defensively.

"Don't you remember how your mother used to threaten us when I slept over, because we wouldn't settle down and go to sleep? We'd always find some reason to get out of bed. Remember how she used to yell to us from the living room . . ."

Valerie rolled her eyes and nodded as she joined Dallas in mimicking the voice: " 'If I have to come in there, you girls are going to live to regret it . . . I am going to tan your hides!' "

Valerie pointed to Dallas. "And you used to whisper, 'My hide's already tan.' "

"I can't believe I said that," Dallas murmured with a grin.

Valerie's eyes widened, and she gasped as another memory came to her. "Remember the night we snuck into the bathroom after Mom had gone to bed, and we polished our finger- and toenails?"

"And then went back to bed before it was dry and got Tropical Melon Glow all over the sheets," Dallas added. "What did your mother do when she found out?"

"I don't think she ever noticed. You know Mom. She wasn't exactly the best housekeeper."

Dallas didn't comment. It was true that the Holland household had tended toward the haphazard. The breakfast dishes would still be stacked in the kitchen at dinnertime, and the daily papers could collect in the living room for several weeks. The two family cats had the run of the place.

But Dallas also recalled that the casual atmosphere was precisely the reason she'd always loved spending time at the Holland house. The rules of order were geared toward treating family members fairly. No hitting below the belt. Unlike at home, no one in Valerie's family judged her. Or expected perfection. In their chaotic house she could just be herself.

That was not to say that fights didn't break out. And there were reminders to Dallas that she was an interloper in Valerie's family. Like when she was thirteen and Valerie's sixteen-year-old brother, Tate, had cornered her in his bedroom and kissed her. Dallas remembered the alien invasion of his tongue in her mouth, swishing about like a snake and making her gag. She'd punched him in the stomach . . . and never told anyone about the incident. Dallas doubted if Tate ever had.

She and Valerie got mad at each other from time to time and would break off their friendship. The incursions never lasted for more than an hour or two. And it was always Valerie who would have to come to apologize.

"We used to have so much fun," Valerie murmured.

in reminiscence, absently combing her fingers through her beautiful shoulder-length hair. She stretched out her legs and rested them on a corner of the coffee table. Opposite her, Dallas did the same. Their limbs almost touched, ankle to ankle, and simultaneously they caught each other's gaze and smiled.

"Do you know, when I was about eight I used to think that when you got older your skin would get lighter, like mine?" Valerie suddenly said.

Dallas nearly gasped as she raised her brows. "For God's sake, Val . . . you never told me that before. Why on earth did you think that?"

Valerie shrugged. "I know it sounds stupid, but . . . I wanted you to be just like me."

Dallas slowly shook her head, still capable of being amazed at the observations of white folks. Even someone she loved as dearly as Valerie. "Why didn't you think that as we got older your skin might get darker to match mine?"

"I don't know. Maybe because I always saw you as my sister. I wanted you to look like me."

"You know," Dallas began thoughtfully, taking another sip of the wine. "Megan doesn't have your fair coloring. She's a beautiful little girl, but she doesn't look like a Holland. Now how do you explain that?"

Valerie didn't answer right away. Her expression was a blank, as if she hadn't considered that other people would have noticed the difference. And then there was a hint of embarrassment.

"Megan looks like Megan," she murmured evasively. "Maybe she favors the other side of her family."

Dallas pursed her lips and gently sloshed the wine around in her glass. She knew better than to pry. For close to twelve years Valerie had kept to herself the identity of her daughter's natural father.

"Does she ever ask about her father?"

Valerie sighed. "All the time, now. It started about

a year ago. She suddenly had all these questions I didn't want to answer."

"You must have known that someday it would happen."

"Yeah, sort of."

"So, what do you tell her?"

Valerie glanced covertly at Dallas and shifted positions. She drew both her legs up onto her chair with her arms closed around her knees. "Just that her father and I had a relationship that was short and didn't work out."

"At least you didn't tell her he was dead."

Valerie stared at her. "I couldn't do that. It wasn't true," she said softly.

There was a sadness to the admission that Dallas had never heard before. Even after she'd gotten pregnant and had the baby, Valerie had always exhibited a casual acceptance of her situation, as well as being impervious to the inevitable gossip and whispering about what she'd done, and the embarrassment to her family. There had been a total shutdown of any information that would give away the identity of the father.

Dallas nodded, staring into her wineglass. Everyone had secrets. "I used to wonder who Megan's father is, but only way back at the beginning, when you were first pregnant and she was a little baby. Now it doesn't seem important."

"I used to think so, too. I thought she'd just get used to not having a father. Lots of her school friends have divorced parents, or 'uncles' that come and go, if you know what I mean. But Megan's old enough to ask questions."

"So tell her."

"I can't."

"Why not?"

"It's . . . too complicated."

Dallas slowly shook her head. "It's only going to get worse. I'm telling you. My mother never said anything to me, but I knew there was something different about me even when I was four or five. I could feel it. Then when I came to live with my father, I *still* knew there was something but I could never get any information or answers. I want to know. Megan wants to know. Sooner or later we'll both find out."

"Look, there were reasons at the time for not saying anything," Valerie said. She sat forward in the chair and pointed a finger at Dallas. "Remember that time when you thought you were pregnant?"

Dallas frowned. "You mean with Hayden?"

Valerie shook her head, continuing to look directly at her. "I mean when we were still in high school. We were juniors . . ."

It suddenly came to Dallas. Of course she remembered. She'd been scared to death, and had cried for two weeks straight when her period was late. Instantly she thought of the circumstances that had precipitated her fright.

"That . . . wasn't the same thing," she tried to argue, but Valerie wouldn't let her get away with it.

"Okay, so you weren't pregnant. But you didn't tell me who the guy was. I wouldn't even have known if you hadn't panicked later. One week you're a virgin and three weeks later you're hysterical, sure that you were going to have a baby. Do you want to tell me who *he* was?"

"That was almost fifteen years ago, Val. What's the point?"

"Well, I feel the same way. You were lucky. I got caught and you didn't," Val said, feeling vindicated.

"I don't think I'd refer to Megan Marie as having been caught. You could have had an abortion."

Valerie rolled her eyes. "Yeah, right. My father wasn't thrilled about me getting pregnant, and he didn't get on me or make a real big fuss. But he would have *killed* me if I'd even thought about an abortion."

"Are you sorry you had her?"

Valerie sighed and stared thoughtfully across the room. "No . . . I wouldn't say I'm really sorry. I just wish things had been different. I wish I'd been a whole lot smarter."

"How long do you think you can get away with not telling her what she wants to know?" Dallas asked.

"I know, I know . . ." Valerie said. Suddenly she uncurled herself from the chair and got up. She brushed back her hair. It fell back into place with a gentle bounce against her neck and cheeks. She moved around the small room, picking up stray items belonging to her daughter. "I just need the right time . . ."

Dallas watched her, knowing Valerie was putting her off. Dallas understood what Megan wanted. Hadn't she herself been trying for years to piece together her own heritage? She had strange flashbacks, images of white children she used to play with. Another house with other white people she used to know and trust. Before her mother died and she'd come to her father . . . who was black. Who were they?

"So, tell me about Alex," Dallas asked, smoothly shifting to another subject.

Valerie chuckled. "I knew you were going to ask me about him. He's related to the Marcos in some way. I think he's one of Nick's cousins. Nick never told me how, but he didn't seem to like Alex very much. I never knew why. We went out after the service for dessert and coffee."

Dallas shook her head, bemused. "You go to a funeral and end up with a date."

Valerie shrugged, "That was two weeks ago," she glanced at Dallas. "How come you're so interested?"

Dallas shrugged. "Maybe because of what almost happened between him and Vin Marco."

"You want to know something? Alex wanted to know about you, too. Asked a lot of questions."

In the process of drinking more wine, Dallas used the motion to hide her reaction. "Really?"

Valerie looked at Dallas. "What did you think of him?"

Dallas shifted positions, once again in an effort to

disguise her response. She now sat with one leg bent beneath her, and half turned to fluff the pillow behind her back. All to avoid looking directly at Valerie.

"There was no time to think much of anything," she said. "What happened after I left?"

"Alex went to look at Nick laid out," Valerie admitted quietly. "He sat with Lillian for a long time. Finally, he said good night to her and Vin, and that was that."

"Except for the coffee afterward," Dallas probed.

"It was just coffee. Megan had ice cream. She seems to like Alex. We never even talked about Nick and I can tell you this . . . if Alex starts asking me out, it *won't* be because of him, either.

Dallas drained the rest of the wine and leaned forward to set the glass on the coffee table. She wasn't surprised that Valerie was interested in Alex Marco. As a matter of fact, she wouldn't be surprised if Alex was interested in Val. But the realization made Dallas oddly defensive. And a little let down.

"Then . . . he's not married?"

Valerie stretched, arching her back in sexy abandonment. "I don't know." She yawned with indifference, getting up from her chair. "I'll have to ask him the next time I see him."

The next time, Dallas considered.

"Are you going to be okay out on the sofa tonight?"

"Do I have a choice?" Dallas asked, getting up and taking the hint from Val. "I always sleep here."

"That sofa is so old . . . I don't know how comfortable it is."

"I'll be okay. Does this mean you're not going to tell me any more about Alex?"

Valerie shook her head. "It means there's nothing more to tell, and I'm tired. I want to go to bed."

"We used to talk until three in the morning and not worry about it."

"Yeah, well . . . that's when we were young and didn't have to worry about jobs, kids, or hangovers."

"Speak for yourself. I only had one glass of wine. I better go say good night to Megan."

Dallas took the two used wineglasses and left them in the kitchen sink on her way down the hall to Megan's bedroom. The door was half-open and she knocked softly and waited to make sure her godchild was still awake before entering.

"Can I come in?"

"Sure."

It always surprised Dallas that Megan's room was so neat and orderly. Unlike her tendency to leave things about other parts of the house, her bedroom, while filled with the necessary accoutrements of any adolescent girl, had a place for everything. Most of the room was taken up with a twin-size canopy bed, draped with an eyelet lace awning that matched the mattress skirting and window curtains. There was a small desk and chair, a red-enameled trunk Dallas knew to be filled with games and unused toys, but the top of which provided another place to sit with two toss pillows for cushions. There was a bulletin board on one wall hung with necklaces, and ribbons won for spelling bees, school track meets, a science fair, and perfect attendance the year before.

Dallas smiled as she briefly glanced around and then approached the bed. Megan was sitting with her knees drawn up so that her thighs provided the perfect surface against which to balance her diary. She closed it, but didn't attempt to hide it as Dallas sat on the side of the bed. She reached out and tapped the top of the book. She had given it to Megan on her last birthday the previous August.

"I hope you're not writing terrible things about your mother or me."

"Uh-uh." Megan shook her head. "I'm writing about my boyfriend."

Dallas suppressed her surprise. She smiled in interest and pretended that her godchild had not just said something that struck fear in her heart. "You have a boyfriend? Since when?"

"Well, he's not *really* my boyfriend. But I like him a lot and I think he likes me. He's going with one of my friends right now."

"Ummm," Dallas murmured, trying to think of something constructive to say, and wondering if Valerie had any idea of Megan's interest in the opposite sex. "Is he in one of your classes?"

"He's in the eighth grade."

Worse than she thought. He was old enough to already have had experience with girls. "What's his name?"

"Jared. Isn't that a cool name?"

"Does your mother know?"

Megan grimaced and shrugged. "No. You're not going to tell her, are you? Please don't. She'd tell me something like I'm too young, or I shouldn't be thinking about boys."

"Megan, you're not being fair. You know that things we discuss I don't take back to your mother. But I'm going to tell you the same thing. You are too young."

"You think I'm going to let some boy have his way with me and then I'll have a baby, right?"

Her observation was so accurate that Dallas could only stare at Megan Marie in amazement. "It . . . it can happen," she finally responded weakly. This was not a conversation she wanted to be having. It was not her place.

"It happened to my mother," Megan said.

This was stated as a matter of fact. Dallas was a little frightened that she could be so nonchalant about it.

"Your mother was a lot older and could take care of herself. You're still a child."

"I know that," Megan said. "I'm not going to do anything stupid," she said with an impatient twist of her mouth, as if anyone should know that she knew better.

"You tell me you have a boyfriend, you know about girls getting into trouble, and I'm not supposed to worry? You're giving me a heart attack even as I sit here, Megan," she said.

"Well, when did you start dating?"

Fourteen, Dallas remembered. But she had no intention of admitting that.

"I was older than twelve," she said firmly. "Now kiss me good night and turn out the light." She began to remove to the nearby desk other items of entertainment that Megan had on the bed with her. A library book, her Walkman. The reassuring presence of two teddy bears.

"Aunt Dallas . . ." Megan began, slipping the diary under her pillow and sliding down in the bed. "Did my mother tell you about that man she was talking to at the funeral? He had funny gray hair, but he wasn't old. Alex."

Dallas didn't respond right away. Nor did she stop in her unnecessary movements about Megan's room. She didn't want the little girl to see she was nervous.

"Your mother introduced him to me. Why do you want to know?"

"I was just wondering if he was going to start dating my mom."

Dallas felt a tightening of her stomach muscles. She remembered the interest between the two of them. She had felt like an intruder.

"Would that bother you?"

"I don't know. She's not going to ask what I think anyway. But the last guy was such a creep. I didn't like him."

"What did you think of Alex?"

Megan tilted her head thoughtfully. "He seemed okay. He talked to me and was kind of friendly. I think he's going to ask her out on a date."

"Do you mind when your mother goes out with men?"

"I guess not. She's real pretty and I know men like her a lot, but . . . I guess I'm hoping she'll find someone and maybe they'll get married . . ."

"And you can have a father?" Dallas finished smoothly.

Megan didn't answer directly, but from her curled fetal position that made her look small beneath the covers, she stared poignantly at Dallas as if afraid to voice her wishes . . . or her fears.

"Do you know who my father is?" Megan asked very quietly.

Dallas was not surprised that the child would explore any avenue that would give her information, and she was relieved that she didn't have to lie. She shook her head. "No, I don't. I'm being honest with you, Megan. I really don't know."

"Mommy won't tell me."

"Did you ever think it might be really hard for her to tell you? She could be afraid to. Maybe she's trying to find the right way to tell you. Maybe by *not* telling you she's protecting you from something. There can be lots of reasons. It doesn't mean she doesn't want you to know, or that she's just being mean.

"Now, you go to sleep and stop worrying about it. Remember that your mom and grandmother, your aunts and uncle, love you. I love you, too . . ."

"Okay," Megan murmured, the comfort of Dallas's words and the safety of knowing she was loved relaxing her into sleep. "Thanks for letting me come into the city to stay with you. Thanks for bringing me home. I had a good time."

"Me, too. We'll do it again, soon. Sleep tight."

"I will. Night, Aunt Dallas. I love you."

Dallas couldn't settle down. She lay awake in the dark quiet of Valerie's house and considered how the unfortunate death of Nicholas Marco had set in motion the stirring up of everyone's past ghosts, hers and Valerie's, and brought Alex Marco back into her life. Well, maybe not exactly into *her* life.

In fleeting moments she'd wondered why, in all the years she'd known Vin, Nicholas, and Lillian Marco, none of them had ever mentioned Alex. She only knew that he was connected to the family, certainly by name . . . but how? And why had Vin Marco been ready to rip Alex's heart out at Nicholas's service?

"Dallas? Are you still awake?" Valerie whispered.

Dallas jumped. She was more asleep than she'd realized. She turned her head in the direction of the voice. She hadn't heard Valerie coming down the hall, and she was a pale ghost standing next to the large bookcase at the entrance of the living room.

"Yeah, I am. What's wrong?"

Valerie entered the room, heading unerringly back to the chair she'd occupied just an hour earlier. She hugged herself, but Dallas couldn't see Valerie's face.

"I put my foot in it, didn't I?"

"What are you talking about?"

"All that stuff before about babies and being pregnant. I just didn't think."

A heaviness pressed down on Dallas, and made her feel as if she were sinking into the mattress. She was no longer wounded the way she had been when she thought that having a baby would save her marriage to Hayden.

"It was almost four years ago, Val. I'm okay."

Valerie sighed, the sound drifting in the darkness of the room. "Isn't this funny? You were the one who was *never* going to get married, and I was the one who wanted to find someone rich who'd take care of me. Boy, were we off!"

"Surprise . . ." Dallas murmured dryly.

"Don't worry. There are lots of great black men out there. You'll find someone else. There's still plenty of time for you to have kids."

"What if he's not black?" Dallas asked rhetorically.

"Well, he doesn't have to be, but I think someone black is best for you."

"Thank you . . ."

"I'm serious. I don't want to see you get hurt. I remember what used to happen in school when we were dating."

"I *was* married to a black man. It still didn't work. Maybe color has nothing to do with love, Val. Besides, I'm not even sure I want to marry again."

"Look at the two of us. Intelligent, gorgeous"—Dallas chuckled softly—"and alone. Nothing worked out the way we planned. Don't you feel like you don't have any control over your life?"

Dallas shifted on the hard, thin mattress of the pull-out sleeper and lay flat on her back. She stared at the ceiling, absently following the shadows and distorted outlines. "All the time . . ."

There was a momentary silence as both women shifted through their own thoughts.

"God . . . I can't believe Nick's dead . . ."

"You're not going to start *that* again, are you?" Dallas asked, bemused.

"No . . . no. I guess I overreacted," Valerie admitted thoughtfully. "But Nicky dying like that just made me feel like . . . like you can't depend on anything. Anything could happen at any time. Do you realize, he's the first of our friends to die. It just feels . . . strange, that's all. Like, it could happen to any of us at any time."

"Life's unpredictable that way," Dallas responded, but she wasn't thinking about death.

"Anyway, you know me. I'm always blurting something out without thinking . . ."

"I know you weren't referring to me. If I thought you were, I'd slap you silly."

There was a pause, and then a guffaw of laughter from Valerie. It was abruptly cut off as she clamped her hand over her mouth, remembering the late hour, and that her daughter was asleep. The laughter turned to giggles, and Dallas joined in.

"And I know you'd do it, too. You did it once, and now I can't remember over what . . ."

"You said I probably couldn't go to the school varsity dance because there was no one who would take me. You said . . . none of the white boys were going to date me. You were right."

"Oh, my God . . ." Valeric moaned in horror. "Did I really say that?"

"You certainly did. I remember wondering if they didn't want to date me because I was chunky . . . or because I was black. I was afraid to ask. But it made me mad that you told me at all. I was waiting for you to say . . . well, if I couldn't go, you wouldn't go."

"And I didn't."

Dallas chuckled silently. "You were so glad that Brian Gladstone asked you to go I don't think you noticed how I felt."

Valerie got up and climbed onto the edge of the sofa bed and placed her hand on Dallas's arm. "Dallas, I'm so sorry. Sometimes I can be so thoughtless."

"Look, we were fourteen years old. What did either of us know? Anyway, as I recall you said Brian was a real shit."

"Yeah, and the party was a drag. But you still wanted to be there."

Dallas nodded. "I still wanted to be there."

She sat up in bed, and although they couldn't see each other's features clearly, Dallas knew that Valerie would understand what she was going to say next.

"It was sometimes hard being your friend, you know."

"I guess it was," Valerie acknowledged quietly. "But you know what? I don't know what I'd do if you weren't."

They impulsively hugged. Like they used to do after a fight and they'd made up, and they'd promised never to disagree again. There was no need for further conversation. Valerie got up and returned to her room for the night.

Dallas recalled that when she was a little girl she used to love her bedroom. It had always felt squirreled away at the back of the house, like a secret hideaway. It only came to her later that she may have been put there because it was over the kitchen and not as quiet as the room Dean had. Like servant's quarters, she'd once thought. But she'd found advantages.

The room was always warm in winter, and the smells from Eleanor's cooking from the kitchen below were comforting. Eleanor was a good cook, and that was one of the reasons that made Dallas feel safe in the house, although she'd never been able to figure out why. Her father played classical music, sometimes jazz, on the countertop radio, often lulling her to sleep. After a while she discovered that eavesdropping was possible if she lay in bed quietly at night, or in the early morning, when her parents were in the kitchen discussing family matters or personal business.

Nowadays she didn't bother. She was far removed from their daily lives. Dallas now saw to it, for her peace of mind, that her visits were timed to be at reasonable intervals—but brief. The weekend before, when she'd returned Megan home after a visit with her in Manhattan, Dallas had not bothered to notify her parents of her presence on the Island. But Megan's questions about the identity of her father now spurred Dallas into her own familial thoughts.

She shifted in the bed and heard the kitchen door leading to the garage close. Dallas heard the engine of one of the two family cars gun to life, idling in the cold morning air, and then slowly backing down the driveway. She climbed out of the bed that had been hers until she was eighteen and had left for college. It was the only thing in the room that was still the same. Everything else had been removed.

Eleanor had taken it over and made it into a combination library, sewing and storage room. Dallas was careful not to step into a basket filled with professional correspondence to Eleanor, or to disturb a pile of pattern magazines. It was no longer her room, but just a place to sleep when she visited. All traces of her existence as a member of the family had been packed away.

The first time she'd come home from college during a semester break and seen that her room had been stripped of her things, Dallas had felt a sensation of displacement. Like when she was five years old, and didn't know what was going to happen to her after her mother had died. Where she was going to belong, or who would want her.

Every time she visited she felt strange being back. She was careful to make sure she left everything as she found it. Eleanor would notice, otherwise. In the hallway leading to the staircase was the "mug shot" wall, or so she and Dean had called the gallery, when they were kids, of family portraits that lined the corridor. She stopped for a moment to straighten the one studio picture that had ever been taken of them as a family. Three distinct brown faces, with Dean clearly the product of the older two. And the tan face that was her own.

"Morning . . ." Dallas murmured, entering the kitchen quietly in her socked feet. She headed directly for a yellow kettle, which she filled with tap water and set on a burner of the stove to boil.

"Morning . . ." came back the distracted reply from the man seated at the table behind her. "What are you doing up so early?" he asked in that morning croak of a person who takes a long time to start to function. He sipped from a mug of coffee and turned a page in his newspaper.

Dallas, finding the tea canister empty, began a search through the cabinets for a box of new bags. "I wanted a chance to see you before you left for the campus."

Another page slowly turned.

"You missed Ellie. She left a few minutes ago."

"I know. I heard the car from upstairs."

"What did you want to see me about? Still thinking about buying the apartment you've been living in?"

With a sigh of frustration she gave up her search for tea. She turned the flame off under the kettle and walked to the refrigerator. Pulling the door open, she took out a container of juice.

"Daddy, I meant I wanted to hear about *you*. Like . . . how are you doing? What's happening at school? A father-daughter talk," Dallas explained as she poured the juice and placed two slices of bread into the toaster. She made a place setting for herself and sat at the table opposite him. He was still buried behind the news, and Dallas playfully rattled the pages. "Hel-lo," she said in a singsong tone.

Her father lowered the paper and shook his head at her. "You're determined to get in my face. It's too early to talk politics, I read your last article and it was pretty good. And I like your hair short like that. You look sophisticated and grown-up."

His response was typical. To the point and even-handed. Not too complimentary, but a bit remote. "Grown-up? I don't know about that. Sophisticated? I think the jury's still out. I want to know how you're doing. When I called last week, you said you weren't feeling well."

He grimaced dismissively and shrugged. "I was just tired. Probably fighting a cold. Old age is beginning to beat my brains out. I'm okay now."

"When are they going to make you a full professor? What are you going to be working on this summer?"

Lyle Oliver drained the rest of his coffee and sat back as he regarded his daughter across the table. He had a pleasant pecan-brown face, his features masculine but not strong. He wore glasses that made his eyes look slightly larger than normal, and very much like a stereotypical scholar, which he was.

But Dallas, waiting for her father to finish choosing his words, only saw someone that she'd spent most of her lifetime trying to understand. He was a man of little emotion and few words. He spoke quietly and with a sense of authority and wisdom. Dallas thought her father was probably brilliant. Yet she had never been able to go to him with any question or problem that he didn't weigh academically, clinically, and fail to understand the importance that a simple but reassuring response would have meant to her.

She shook her head and reached out to rest her hand briefly on his arm. "You're not going to get a score on your answer."

He had the grace to look embarrassed. "I know," he said, leaning forward again to brace his elbows on the table. "I should hear about my appointment before the semester is over. And I don't know what I'm doing for the summer. I could teach, of course. We'll probably do the Vineyard for a few weeks in July. Your mother and I talked about traveling."

She drank from the juice and considered how to respond. The toast popped up, and Dallas pulled them out and began spreading apricot jam on the slices. "You and Eleanor say that every year. And each summer at the eleventh hour she finds some reason why the two of you can't go."

Lyle Oliver shifted in his chair and cleared his throat. "The store is a big responsibility. We don't like being away from it for too long."

Dallas was thoughtful for a moment, also carefully selecting her reply. "Or Dean."

"Yeah, well . . . after what happened last year when he was pulled over and nearly arrested driving through Maryland, we want to be around if he needs us."

"Dean is almost thirty years old. Getting arrested could have happened here, and you still couldn't have done him any good. Anyway, doing seventy-two miles an hour in a fifty-five-mile speed zone is asking for trouble."

Her father made a small shaking gesture with his head, but Dallas couldn't tell if he was agreeing with her or not.

"What he needs to do is to control his tendency to act first and think later."

"Have you heard from him lately?" her father asked.

Dallas shook her head and finished the glass of juice. She was aware that her father still had not answered her question. He had skillfully turned the conversation in another direction. "Not for a week or so. He came by to install a new accessory on my computer for me. I went to hear his latest gig with his band. It was good."

"His mother thinks he's wasting his time with the music."

"What do you think?" Dallas asked.

"He's got a lot of talent, but I'm not sure he can make a living at playing bass guitar."

"Eleanor used to say the same thing to me about my wanting to be a writer."

"Yeah, I remember. But you went ahead and proved her wrong."

Dallas nodded sagely. "So, the moral of this story is . . ."

Her father raised his brows over the frame of his glasses. "Leave the boy alone. Easy for you to say. You don't have kids. But one of these days . . ."

Dallas bit into her toast and stared at her father until finally the light went on and he stopped, his mouth poised open. She heard a guttural sound from his throat as he closed his eyes and shook his head in regret.

"Sorry. I didn't mean that . . . well . . . you know what I mean. Anyway . . . being a parent is hard work."

Dallas lowered her gaze and absently counted the little bits of bread crumbs and salt crystals on the wooden table. "So's being a child."

"Dallas, you know I didn't mean . . ."

"Daddy . . . it's okay," she said flatly. "I had a miscarriage and I lost a baby. It's not a curse. I was very sad at the time. I'm okay now."

He sighed and reached out to briefly pat her shoulder. "You're young yet. There's plenty of time."

Dallas looked squarely at her father and wondered if he was making the same connection she was. Probably not, she decided. Why shouldn't he draw the conclusion that if he could start and have two families, so could she?

"You've never asked me about what happened. Aren't you curious at all?"

Lyle Oliver pursed his lips and adjusted his glasses. He didn't look her in the face.

"Sure, your mother and I are curious, but I figured it was none of our business."

Dallas looked at him incredulously. "Did you decide that *after* it didn't work out between Hayden and me? I remember Eleanor used to tell me how lucky I was to get such an accomplished, eligible man. A good *black* man. She certainly acted like she had a vested interest in my relationship with Hayden since she introduced us, and you encouraged it."

"I thought you loved Hayden. You married him," her father pointed out.

Dallas pushed her plate away. She was no longer interested in toast or a morning conversation with her father. She *had* loved Hayden. Maybe now, in hindsight, it was for the wrong reasons. At the time she'd felt relief. She was finally doing something her father and Eleanor approved of.

"I guess sometimes love is not enough. Or maybe it's not even the point," she said reflectively.

"Or maybe you expected too much of him. He's a hard worker. Everyone likes him. He comes from a good, solid family."

Dallas leaned toward her father, her voice earnest and firm. "I know that. But did it ever occur to you that maybe Hayden was expecting too much of me? We *both* failed. Not just me."

Her father was shaking his head, as if she'd made a silly observation, or her reasoning was faulty. "Look, when people get married they're supposed to compromise. He gives a little, you give a little, and you try to make it work."

"So, you think I just gave up?"

"I don't know what happened and I don't want to know, Dallas."

"You sound like whatever happened it was somehow my fault," she said tightly, as if to show any emotion would shatter her.

"I didn't say that. I don't know what went on between you and Hayden. Everything seemed to be fine, and then suddenly you call and say you're leaving him. You run off and disappear for almost a month. Okay, I admit it seemed a little childish to me and your mother."

Dallas struggled between wanting her father to sympathize, and the need to protect herself. She thought of all the times she'd wanted to confide in him and all the reasons why she couldn't.

"Compromise wouldn't have made any difference between us. We just weren't suited. We both expected too much . . . wanted different things." Dallas looked earnestly at her father, and leaned closer to him. "What about you and my mother?" Dallas asked instead.

Dallas didn't know why she was asking this question now. She'd tried to do so only a few times in her whole life and had never gotten a satisfactory answer.

In Lyle Oliver's eyes she saw the familiar withdrawal, the shutdown and closing off that clearly erected a DO NOT DISTURB sign in front of the past . . . hers and his.

"Dallas, I'm not going to do this again. You know the story. You've heard it before. Why do you keep wanting me to say it over and over again?" her father said more with impatience than annoyance.

It was always the same reaction. That's how she knew there was more to tell.

"Don't you think I have a right to know? Can't you understand that it's a part of my life I know nothing about? What's so terrible that you can't tell me? Whatever it is I can deal with it. How did you and my mother meet? How did you fall in love? You got married and had me, but . . . why didn't it work out? I know so little that sometimes . . ." She looked at him earnestly. "Sometimes I feel I might as well be adopted."

Lyle Oliver frowned at his daughter. "You're not adopted. People used to think so when you first came to me. It raised a lot of questions . . ."

"The same ones I have, probably."

"Dallas, it's all in the past. I'm for just letting it all stay there. It was a long time ago, and things were different . . ."

"Did you love each other?"

His expression didn't change. He'd always been good at that, keeping himself at a distance.

"That's personal. And it's not relevant. There are things that you don't need to know. It's *my* past, too, and it's difficult to talk about.

"You've been with me and Eleanor and Dean for more years than you spent with your mother." He finally gathered his breakfast dishes into a stack and prepared to stand. "You're part of *this* family."

"And I should be grateful," Dallas finished.

"No. I don't need gratitude. But it should be enough." He checked his watch and hastily folded his paper. He got up and carried his dishes to the sink, rinsing them quickly before loading them into the dishwasher. "I better get going or I'm going to hit traffic."

He said no more but in passing, on his way out of the kitchen, he rested his hand briefly on her shoulder and squeezed gently. Dallas reached to cover his hand, but already it was sliding away and he was gone.

"What are your plans? Are you going home today?"

She repeated the questions in her head, wondering if she was reading too much in her father's words. Dallas sighed and nodded. "I have to. I have some articles to finish."

Lyle Oliver came back through the kitchen, shrugging into a brown leather jacket. He held a cap in one hand, his car keys jangling from his fingers, and his attaché in the other. When Dallas realized that her father was gazing at her, she glanced hopefully in his direction. His expression was thoughtful but somewhat pained.

"I thought you were happy with me. You're my daughter . . ." Lyle Oliver said awkwardly.

It sounded as if he were trying to convince himself. "I know, Daddy, but . . . I wonder sometimes if you're happy with me."

"I've raised you. You had a good home, a good life. Eleanor is a good woman . . ."

Dallas shook her head wearily at him. "That's not what I'm talking about."

Lyle Oliver shook his head in mild exasperation. "Then I guess I just don't understand."

Dallas was sure that he did. But there was clearly no point in pursuing the issue, in badgering her father to say something, tell her things he obviously didn't want to say.

He patted her shoulder again. "I have to go . . ."

He opened the door from the kitchen to the garage, and cold air rushed in at Dallas. She shivered and stood up, hugging herself. Dallas followed her father into the garage and watched his ritual for starting his day as an assistant professor of math at C.W. Post.

She recalled suddenly, when she was about seven, shortly after they'd moved into the house and were having trouble being accepted into the community, she hadn't wanted to let Eleanor send her off to school, but she'd been afraid to stay home. So as her father had been leaving for his early morning classes, Dallas had hidden on the floor of the backseat of his car. A big Oldsmobile Cutlass. It had been easy for her to crouch down and not be seen. She'd waited until her father was on the Long Island Expressway before jumping up behind him and surprising him with "boo."

Dallas frowned as she watched her father settle into the driver's seat. He turned on the engine and let it run before turning on the heat to warm the car. He put on his cap and slammed the door. He nodded at her through the closed window and waved.

On that morning so long ago, he'd been very angry with her. Not because she'd startled him, although that had been obvious, but because he'd had to turn around and return her to the house. He had not thought her prank funny or endearing.

"Take care," Dallas said loudly to her father as the second family car backed out of the driveway, turned onto the street, and rolled away into traffic.

Dallas returned to the kitchen and the silence that rather than granting her a sense of peaceful solitude only felt lonely. Every time she returned to the house, she felt somehow incomplete. That she had to keep returning and keep trying, and keep reliving the past in an attempt to make it right.

If she couldn't get her father to admit that he might have loved her mother at one time, how could she *ever* know if he loved her?

Chapter Four

April 1st—
This is the second year I've been asked to write a column about April Fool's Day for the paper. What can I say? Watch out. Don't forget to duck. Count your change. Black folks have been doing these things all of their lives. I'm a bit troubled by being asked, against all the odds, to have faith, trust in God, be a true believer. I do . . . but cut the cards. My advice for a day like any other day? Watch your back. Keep your eyes straight ahead. Don't take for granted anything you can't see, taste, touch, hear, or smell. Fool me once, shame on you. Fool me twice . . . shame on me.

She wasn't surprised when the apartment intercom sounded at almost eleven in the evening. Still, the short buzz made Dallas's nerves tighten. She didn't break from the task of putting away dishes she'd finished washing and drying. The buzzer rang a second time and, more urgently, a third. She had it in mind to ignore it, but suspected that Burke would continue persistently until she relented and let him in. He knew, obviously, that eventually she would.

"Dammit," Dallas muttered in annoyance.

She pressed the button next to the door to release the lock that would let Burke enter the building. The process was repeated when her doorbell rang. She wasn't going to make it easy for him. Delaying was her revenge. But when Dallas opened the door, she stared at Burke with an indifference she didn't feel.

"Man, I'm dead," he said as an opening, aware of her mood.

Dallas turned away, returning to the kitchen. Burke closed the door and slowly followed her. His desultory movement annoyed her even more. Nothing so far indicated that Burke was apologetic. At least, not enough to satisfy her. Dallas gathered the handful of silverware from the drainboard and began putting them away, noisily, into a utensil drawer.

Burke cupped his hand around the column of her neck and gently massaged. His fingertips rubbed upward into her scalp sending a rush of warmth that began to soften her tension. But she leaned forward to break the contact. She turned around to glare at him, and found Burke regarding her with an expression that was like the one he was wearing when she'd first met him. Filled with cocky self-confidence, interest, and quick appraisal. He was not, in Dallas's mind, exactly handsome, but he did have an undeniable physical magnetism, combined with a quick wit and assertive personality that made him hard to ignore. His background and street smarts were sometimes betrayed through the facade of urbane sophistication; when he got angry and didn't get his way.

He had an elegant build, narrow in the hips with long legs and hands and feet. His skin was a warm sienna brown, and he wore a mustache. In a suit Burke carried himself like a CEO, and was always treated like one. Out of it there was something sort of unfinished about him. Oddly undistinguished.

Dallas lowered her gaze. There were other things to commend him. He knew how to get things done. He didn't seem to be afraid or uncertain about anything. And he was a good lover. Dallas was sure of that because she'd had the other kind, thank you. Having Burke make love to her for the first time had been a revelation. He had introduced himself to her while she'd waited for security clearance as a member of the press into a concert and reception for a fifteen-year-old black singing sensation. Burke had targeted her, cleared the way through the process, and sat her with the record label VIPs.

But Burke had not exactly pursued her, she admitted. He built on her curiosity, contacting her just often enough for her not to forget him. Cooperating and offering contacts for her interviews and articles. Inviting her to concerts and press events. Popping up at her office for surprise lunches, or meeting her after work for drinks. Dallas had enjoyed the attention, but from the very beginning Burke had been in control. The timing of their relationship had been right for her. Dallas had been close to the finalization of her divorce.

By the time Burke even hinted at consummating their relationship, she was ready. She hadn't been with a man in almost two years. Dallas recalled thinking at the time that she also felt like she'd been stalked and trapped by Burke. As if he had a specific purpose or agenda in mind for the two of them.

"Did you get my message?"

"Yes," Dallas answered flatly.

He tried to put his arms around her waist. Dallas made an impatient tsk with her teeth and twisted away.

He chuckled. "You're going to punish me, right?"

She turned and pointed to the door. "You can leave, if you want. You didn't even have to bother coming."

He shrugged, putting his hands into his pants pockets. "Tonight couldn't be helped. I didn't plan on standing you up. Look, you want me to say I'm sorry? Okay, I'm sorry," Burke said grudgingly.

Dallas glanced at the wall clock over the refrigerator.

"You're five hours late," she said. "I canceled an interview because you said you wanted to have dinner early. I sat for two hours at a busy restaurant, not ordering and getting nasty looks because I told them you would be there. I was embarrassed when they finally asked for the table. And you get annoyed with me because I'm annoyed with you?"

"Don't you think you're carrying this too far?" he asked patiently.

He used a tone of criticism that Dallas had always been susceptible to. Eleanor had perfected it to an art form. It wasn't angry, but it had a kind of condescension that suggested that *she* was behaving badly and *she* was being unreasonable.

Dallas trained on Burke what she hoped was the full extent of her ire. "Your time is *not* more important than mine."

"It couldn't be helped. I told you that in my message . . ."

"That message was an afterthought . . ."

"I ran into the vice president of marketing and I had his attention then and there. He's been out of town. I had a couple of ideas to pitch and I went for it."

"For more than five hours? There is no excuse for not taking five minutes to call the restaurant and let me know something had come up."

"All right, all right . . ." Burke said. "I guess I was wrong to think you'd understand what it's like for a black man in this business."

"Burke, don't start. That excuse is so tired. What is it that's so hard? You have a great job."

"It wasn't easy. I had to fight my way to where I am. I don't have an MBA or a mentor. No special privileges."

"Neither do I . . ." she said, walking past him and out of the kitchen. She went into the living room. Burke followed behind.

"Black men still have to work twice as hard as any white guy to get a chance."

"Oh, please," Dallas said impatiently. She sat on the sofa and turned on the TV, clicking through the stations until she found the local news. "*What* has this got to do with you standing me up tonight? I'm supposed to forget what happened because life is hard for a black man? What about me?" She glared at him.

He stood over her, speaking without hesitation or thought. "Dallas, all you have to do is show up."

"Excuse me?" Dallas asked quietly.

"I mean, you're a woman, and you don't have to work at making white folks feel comfortable around you."

"No. Only my own. I guess I should be grateful that you didn't come right out and say I'm not black enough. Is that how you see me?"

Burke sighed and sat on the wicker trunk to face her. He sat right in her line of vision. Taking the remote from her, he aimed over his shoulder and pressed the mute button. Burke tossed the unit on the sofa next to Dallas. His expression went from petulant to regret.

"I didn't mean it the way it sounded . . ."

"Didn't you?" Dallas questioned softly.

He shook his head. "Look, I don't want to stay in visual marketing. That's MTV stuff. The shift is going to be from screens to computer monitors in the future." Burke leaned toward her. "I have a shot at a major new position, Dallas. It's a new division opening up that *I'm* inventing. All the artists that are hot and selling are black. It's created a whole generation of wiggers. Wannabes in white teens. We're flavor-of-the-month, and I want to make the most of it while I can. It's a window of opportunity that's not going to last. I know exactly where the audience is and how to reach them," Burke said excitedly. "There is a lot of money involved, and I want to control how it's used for marketing. And I want to make sure I get credit and some of the action from sales. The VP I ran into is *the* decision maker in the company."

Dallas didn't disagree with Burke's assessment. His thinking was clear . . . and focused. None of this was about her. Or them. She felt apprehension take over all other sensations within her, even the justified anger. It was going to happen again. Her feelings were going to get mixed up until they didn't amount to anything more than ill temper. Being . . . *unreasonable.* Burke had done everything he could to apologize. Just like Hayden had tried. She was the holdout.

Dallas closed her eyes briefly. She felt tired. "I hope you get the job. You probably will," she predicted sincerely. "You're very good at getting what you want. But I don't see why I should have to make all the concessions so that this relationship can work. I'm not as important to you as your job. Why should I put up with the way you take me for granted?"

He sighed, shaking his head. "Baby, that's not the way it is. But tonight was real important. Forgive me?"

She regarded Burke steadily. She wasn't sure he'd heard a word she'd said. "You don't want forgiveness. You expect absolution."

Dallas tried to get up and he took hold of her arms to stay her. Then he shifted his position and sat next to her on the sofa.

"Dallas . . ." He put an arm around her waist. He kissed her cheek and encouraged her to rest against his chest. "I'll make it up to you. I'll do whatever you want."

He was going to put it all back on her. What did she want?

It bothered Dallas that in that moment Hayden came to mind. Maybe not so much him as what she thought they'd have together when she'd married him. When she'd wanted then was to be loved for herself. Nothing had changed.

"If you have to ask what I want, then what's the point?"

"Okay. I'll play that game," he said smoothly, rubbing his hand along her arm. "You want me to understand when you go to your folks' or when you and your girlfriends hang out and I don't see you. You want me to understand when your godchild is over. You want to be able to cut me off with an hour's notice when you get a last-minute thing to write or someone to interview . . ."

"You *know* that's not the same thing. You *know* what I'm talking about."

"No I don't. Tell me what the difference is?"

She felt foolish. It was a hairsbreadth, but it was also about attitude. And intent. "Canceling is not the same as ignoring. You're deliberating twisting what it is I'm upset about. I didn't like being stood up, but that's not it. It was"—she searched for the exact words—"it was like, I'm the second choice."

Burke considered her conclusion. He again pressed his mouth against her face. He pursed his lips into a kiss that tickled. "I could have gone right on home. I didn't have to come and have you rag me like some high school date who did you wrong."

"Burke . . ."

"I'm trying to do the right thing. And I wanted you to see I wasn't afraid to come here tonight. We missed dinner, okay. But at least I'm here now."

Dallas didn't hear concern in Burke's voice, or an apology. Burke bent his head and kissed teasingly at her mouth. His hand burrowed under the loose-fitting sweater she wore and curved to her side, his thumb stroking her skin. The appeasement was coming too quickly, faster than she was prepared for.

"I didn't have any dinner."

"Neither did I," she whispered, beginning to respond to the cajoling play of his hand and mouth.

"I owe you." The tip of his tongue brushed against the slight parting of her lips.

The hand under her sweater slid to her breast and covered it with a warm and gentle pressure. The telltale contractions of her stomach muscles made Dallas sigh. She didn't discourage Burke's skilled seduction. He'd never been sexually aggressive with her. He never had to be. She wondered if it was really vindication she wanted. She was being subverted by the erotic invasive kisses, the hand exploring the surface of her breast and stimulating the puckered nipple through her bra. Dallas shifted slightly, trying to stay focused on the issues. They had not been resolved yet.

"Burke . . ." she murmured.

His only response was to open his mouth over hers and let his tongue explore at leisure. The affect was soothing. He handled her carefully. She wanted to protest, but Burke gathered her properly into his arms. Dallas complied, floating against the rising desire and sense of well-being. He kissed her until the sounds they made included ragged breathing and moans of pleasure. She raised an arm to circle around his neck.

Burke broke off the contact of their mouths.

Dallas opened her eyes and looked at him with confusion. She could see the longing in his slumberous gaze, but he shook his head. "You still pissed off at me?"

"Yes."

Burke nodded, and then stood up, pulling Dallas with him. He grinned charmingly and put his arms around her. He had a way of aligning their bodies so that they met from rib cage to thighs. In between them Dallas could feel the hard bulge of his erection. He slowly rotated his hips against her.

"There's nothing I can do to make it up to you?"

She shook her head, even as her eyes closed again. "You can't. The moment is gone. This . . . this is something else."

He chuckled and then kissed her. There was a guttural sound in his throat as his hands went under the sweater and unhooked her bra. "If you're going to give me a hard time, then let's do it right."

She grimaced at his pun. "Make sure the door is locked," Dallas murmured, in a tone halfway between resignation and anticipation. She turned from his embrace and headed for the bedroom.

Dallas had removed the sweater and bra, peeled off the leggings by the time Burke entered the room behind her. He silently undressed. The process had already been set in motion for reconciliation. But Dallas understood that it would not solve their problems.

"Baby . . ." Burke growled, slipping his arms around her from behind. He nibbled at her neck. His penis surged against Dallas's buttocks as he maneuvered a hand into her panties.

Dallas sighed and relaxed, letting her physical need take over from the emotional dissatisfaction that kept her in doubt.

"Ummm, baby," Burke moaned, his excitement at full throttle.

She didn't like being referred to as "baby." It was a kind of generic male tag she remembered from high school, when all the boys were interested in was getting off. It didn't seem to focus on her as a person.

Burke turned her around to kiss her deeply. His hand continued its exploration of her lower body, nestling between her legs as his fingers searched out the delicate opening to her body. Dallas undulated herself against his caressing until there was no other choice but gratification. She climbed on the bed and Burke quickly settled on top of her when she raised her knees. His languid kisses and his hand between her legs were making Dallas feel safe, but she didn't want to rush through their lovemaking.

"W—wait," Dallas moaned, screwing her eyes tightly closed and fighting against her body flying out of control too quickly. She wanted to slow down the gathering wave. She was on the brink of the crash when Burke made his entry and thrust with an electrifying determination right through the middle of the cresting storm within her.

She held her breath, held onto Burke as the driving force of his body ricocheted the climax within Dallas. Burke's limbs stiffened, his buttock muscles flexing and tightening until his own release made his body press her into the mattress with the intensity of it. Finally Burke relaxed his full weight on her.

"Jesus H. Christ . . ." he murmured, his mouth pressed on her shoulder.

The throbbing left Dallas limp. But there was little contentment, and as the physical euphoria faded she knew a sense of betrayal. The veil of doubt seemed to drift over her again. Burke had arrived less that an hour ago.

A new world's record.

He had won again.

Dallas heard Burke's slow barefoot stride out of the bedroom to the bath. The door closed. She heard running water. First it was Burke. Then it was the toilet flushing; and then the shower being turned on. Only then did Dallas let her body unwind from her curled-up position on her side. She was reluctantly, fully awake. She lay, letting her mind float up into consciousness.

The shower spray sounded like rain. Just the way she used to hear it when she was little. Someone had once told Dallas that rain meant the angels were crying because she'd been a bad girl. She wasn't going to buy into that. And yet, there was a sense of having made a bad decision.

Dallas pushed the covers aside and climbed out of the bed. She glanced down and could see that her nipples were still prominent and distended . . . that little hickey marks discolored the skin on her stomach, chest, and thighs. For a second there was a distinct memory of her and Burke making love. After their argument but before anything had been resolved. After she'd been worn down with excuses, but before she'd been willing to forgive him.

And yet she'd surrendered.

The sounds they'd made together during the night came back to Dallas. She had been completely open and Burke had filled her, found ways to hold her captive with pleasure as well as an urgent need for release from the tension that made her want to scream at him. But it had also seemed less like making love than a battle of wills, physical and emotional. As if Burke was trying to prove something. Or wear her down.

Dallas recognized that she wanted to be made love to. As if the deeply physical contact—intimate and electric, breathtaking and, *yes,* satisfying—would demonstrate that he really cared about her. Except for now, when she was left feeling like she had just had a one-night stand.

Slowly, Dallas raised herself from the bed. She didn't want to be in it when Burke came out of the bathroom. She knew what was likely to happen.

The phone rang as she was halfway to her closet to retrieve a robe. She turned back to pick up the receiver, sitting naked on the edge of the bed.

"Hello?"

"Good morning, honey. Did I wake you up?"

A dozen thoughts swept through Dallas upon recognizing Lillian Marco's voice, not the least of which was guilt. She knew that she had not called Lillian since the funeral for Nicholas nearly a month earlier. Spring had come in the meantime. Dallas thought it might have been too soon to call Lillian, but she had no guidelines. What was the protocol? How long does a mother need to grieve over the loss of her child?

"Hi, Lillian." She glanced at the clock radio: 7:43. "Of course you didn't wake me. I have to get ready for the office. Are you all right? How have you been?" she asked awkwardly. Stupid questions.

Lillian sighed. "I'm fine, I guess. They say these things take time. A lot of time . . ."

Dallas leaned over the phone so she could hear. Lillian's voice was so low, so soft.

"I'm sorry I haven't called sooner. I just thought that . . ."

"No, no. Don't worry about it. I know you were thinking of me. There was so much to do. You know, after we put Nicky in the ground. Vin and I thought things would quiet down. It's over and done and time to move on. But then friends kept calling and stopping by, and flowers were still delivered, and the mass cards kept coming. If I didn't have so much cooking to do to feed all those visitors I don't know how I would have gotten through it."

"I should have called, then. There must have been something I could have done," Dallas responded.

From the hallway the sound of the shower suddenly stopped. And Lillian chuckled.

"Oh, you helped quite a lot. You stopped Vin and Alex from making fools of themselves. They should have been ashamed to carry on like that, with Nicky lying just in the other room . . ." Her voice faded.

Dallas still had no clothes on, and the air was starting to raise gooseflesh on her bare legs and arms. The bathroom door opened. Burke had come back into the room, but she wouldn't turn around to look at him.

"This has been *very* hard on Vin, Dallas. In a way, he's having a worse time than I am getting used to Nicky's death. He loved that boy . . . maybe too much," Lillian murmured absently.

"I can imagine," Dallas crooned. She wasn't unsympathetic. "His only son."

When Lillian didn't answer right away Dallas feared she'd said something insensitive. After all, Nick was her only son as well.

Dallas sensed Burke's presence as he came to stand next to her and toweled himself dry. In her peripheral vision Dallas could see his knees, his ankles and feet. Brown and damp and roped with veins. But she wouldn't look up, because she didn't know what she would say.

"Dallas, hon . . . I have a *real* big favor to ask. Now, don't you be afraid to say no. I know you're busy and—"

"What can I do?" Dallas interrupted.

"Well . . . it's just that . . . I have to do something about Nicky's things."

Dallas blinked. Of course. There would be a lifetime worth of things.

"I understand," she murmured.

Dallas still ignored Burke as he gently kissed her on the back of her neck. She didn't respond to his attempt to bridge the gap between them. His hand brushed briefly through her hair, making the curls spring about. Then Burke secured the towel around his waist and left the room.

"I know this is a terrible thing to ask of you, but . . . do you think you could come out to help me, Dallas?"

She couldn't answer. It was the last thing in the world she wanted to do. Not because she didn't want to help, but because of what had happened between herself and Nicholas. To help with his things seemed like forgiving him for all he'd put her through. But his mother didn't know that, and she didn't need to.

"I don't mind helping, but are you sure? Going through his things is so . . . personal."

Lillian made a scoffing sound. "They're just things, hon. They don't mean much anymore now that Nicky's gone. I'll keep a few items. Vin won't give up his high school football uniform, or the bars and ribbons he earned in the service. I'm glad now Nicky didn't take everything with him when he and Theresa got married. But I don't want to have the rest of it around. She doesn't want anything . . . you know, that was becoming a nasty divorce."

Dallas got distracted by the sounds coming from the kitchen. Burke was putting on the coffeemaker. He was still trying to make up for the night before. He was being domesticated and cooperative.

"When do you want me to come out?" Dallas asked, the sound of Burke's presence beginning to irritate her.

"How about this Saturday? I talked Vin into going out to my brother and sister-in-law's for the day.

They're building a house in Wayne, New Jersey, and Vin is helping them move some shrubbery. I'll be home alone."

"Saturday is fine. Do you want me to bring anything?"

"Nothing, hon. You just come on out and keep me company."

"I'll be there early. Maybe we'll go out for lunch or something."

"We'll see. Oh, Dallas . . ." Lillian sighed, her voice starting to quaver. "I'm *so* glad you can come. See you on Saturday."

Lillian hung up, but Dallas held onto the receiver for a moment longer, even after the dial tone began to buzz again. She wondered if a parent losing a child was anything like a child losing a parent. Lillian had memories, and things belonging to her son that she could keep, that she could touch from time to time if she wished to. When they were ready Vin and Lillian could reminisce about their son. But what was a child left with when she had not lived enough years to accumulate any memories?

Dallas absently hung up the receiver. She had a flash of standing in a steamy rain with other people, around a hole in the ground. On the other side was a very large brown box that looked like it was going to be put into the hole. Someone held her hand and an umbrella over her head. But it wasn't her mother. Dallas didn't know where her mother was. When she'd asked, from the vacuum that children occupy where they're too young to know what's going on and aren't being told very much, the only response she'd gotten had been "She's gone away" or "Sshhhh . . ." Both answers had only left her confused and frightened.

Her mother had never returned.

Worse still, Dallas recalled being sent away somewhere by herself. On a train. Someone had hugged her and given her a doll. Someone had cried and kissed her cheek. A piece of paper had been pinned to her coat with her name and an address written on it. She hadn't said a word the whole time she was on the train, until at the other end someone had met her, hugged her again as she'd gotten off. Dallas frowned as she relived the sequence of events. Whatever had happened to that doll?

There had been no things for her to go through later. Nothing to pick and choose from that would bring back the face of someone with dark hair and gray eyes. Whose skin was pale and whom she knew to be her mother. There was only what was left in her memory. Almost all of it now faded and dim.

Dallas envied Lillian Marco in a way she could never explain.

Burke appeared again in the bedroom doorway. Steam curled from the rim of two cups he held. One gave off the strong aroma of hazelnut coffee. He silently passed the second cup with herbal peppermint tea to Dallas. She hesitated but finally took it.

He sat down next to her on the bed, but far enough away to not be a threat. They said nothing as they drank the hot morning liquids. This was the no-man's-land, the time-out to regroup and either continue their differences, or get over it. A Mexican standoff.

Dallas looked sideways at Burke and fought to meet him halfway. "Thank you for the tea."

He nodded. "How are you this morning?" he asked smoothly, drinking the coffee and keeping his attention focused on her.

"The same as I was last night," Dallas quietly responded.

"Even after last night?"

"Especially because of last night."

Dallas put her mug down and stood up. She felt cornered sitting between him and the headboard, naked and vulnerable. She was relieved to see him putting his clothing on. He was all out of excuses and persuasion. She was out of patience and forgiveness. Last night with Burke had not reassured her but had only served to point out to Dallas that perhaps there wasn't enough between them worth agonizing over.

Alex couldn't see a thing.

He had down vision on the full-face mask, but he still couldn't see more than ten or twelve feet. Alex thought he should be used to it by now. The impure water evolved into something murky and sinister. Bits and pieces of bottom silt and algae, rotting debris of God knew what, and filth flowing around him.

Alex breathed easily, nonetheless, because he knew better than to fight the apparatus. He had been trained for much worse than this. He didn't have a redundant air supply, but counted on not needing it. Of course, things could go wrong. And the unknown was still a scary thing.

The air bubbles released from the open circuit respirator rising to the surface above him were reassuring, as were all the functioning components of his gear. He had fifteen minutes of air left but knew he should start to ascend in half that time. He checked his oxygen mix for the third time since he'd been down, and checked the buoyancy compensator, which was lightweight and not really meant for tech diving. But he'd put himself at a slight disadvantage on purpose. It was impossible to challenge his ability to handle the unexpected if he knew that everything was perfect and as it should be.

Alex let his body tilt forward into the current, the cold water molding the black rubber protective suit against his skin. He needed an extra effort kicking with his fins to move forward, and he was careful of his footing, hoping not to discover any sharp metal edges, sheared and dangerous, that could cut into his suit, his air line. Alex didn't try to actually go against the tidal current as much as try to use it and his body to maneuver.

He got into position to check on the test sites. They weren't supposed to be too close together. None were supposed to be easy to find, but he'd planted a few in deceptive areas to test the thoroughness of the NYPD Scuba Unit search and recovery team.

To his left, about fifteen feet away, Alex could make out the dim, broadly dispersed beam from Ross's underwater light. He could detect some of the slow black motions as together they finished the course that had been plotted for training of the eight men from the unit. It was a given that he and Ross were never to get more than fifteen feet apart, but Alex knew he could no longer make even the simplest dive without remembering how even thirty seconds apart could mean someone's life. And did.

Alex turned his focus back to his own position. He double-checked his landmarks to keep the area tight and controlled. Their task was pretty specific and not meant to be difficult. But still . . . things sometimes went wrong.

For a brief second Alex was back on the Kuwaiti border, part of the team to seize the island of Qaruh occupied by the Iraqis during the Gulf War. His SEAL team never assumed success, but they had yet to fail at any mission directed to them. Until the one with the surprise ship attack. He'd fielded the signal from the second two-man team that they were to retreat back to base. He'd turned to relay the message to Crosby, his dive partner, and couldn't see him. This was not supposed to happen. It didn't help that the LAR V, a closed-circuit rebreather, was designed not to release the bubbles that would have pinpointed Crosby's position. But worse was just the fact that they had gotten separated at all. Crosby was in trouble.

The other two teams also realized something was wrong. And against the drone and vibration of a fast-approaching craft, they'd tried to locate their SEAL member. The most immediate concern was whether Crosby had dropped below the ten-meter limit of their equipment. Alex knew it was bad enough that he had lost sight of his partner, but he also realized it only took a heartbeat for the moment to become tragic. That's exactly how long it had taken.

Crosby's safety line was spotted first, leading Alex and the other team to the spot where the depth suddenly dropped off into a black hole. The end was still attached to Crosby's weight belt around his waist. His limp body was below them, swaying gently in the underwater current. His regulator had been displaced. There had been no time for any other reaction except to claim the body and get them all out of harm's way.

For Alex the flashback always failed before he got to the part about his buddy being carried to the surface as dead weight. He still wondered where his shock and pain had gone to. All he could ever recall, could still feel, was the guilt.

He was breathing too deeply.

Immediately Alex slowed his down and gained control. He concentrated on something else, counted the time between each breath through his regulator. He needed to hear that sound to reassure himself that he was okay.

Alex could recite whole passages from the official investigation summary. It was as if he were hoping that he'd missed something in an earlier reading, and would miraculously discover anything that would absolve him. The report had concluded that the LAR V rebreather, a closed-circuit unit that doesn't release telltale bubbles, had functioned as intended; that Crosby may have gone below the depth limit for a sufficient period of time to suffer oxygen toxicity, a build-up of too much oxygen in the body, which affects blood and body tissues. But it might have been induced anyway by a combination of the cold water and the strenuous activity the SEAL team was engaged in at the time. A number of symptoms but probably the most likely, a grand mal seizure, would have caused him to release the mouthpiece. He would have drowned, never realizing what was happening to him.

Sometimes Alex was close to believing that it was an accident and wasn't his fault. Maybe. But he could have done something. If not prevented it, then at least help Crosby to keep his breather in place until he could be taken to safety. They were the best special forces team ever trained. For Alex it had been like losing Crosby to "friendly fire." And *he* had held the gun.

It was time to go up. In the final minutes Alex used his light to signal Ross. His heart lurched and he knew that, once again, he'd pushed it far enough. It was going to be hard to make it to the surface. Not in the physical sense. He wasn't that deep and this was easy. But in the psychic sense. He hadn't for one moment gotten rid of the nightmares. He'd only learned how to control them and fight back.

Alex gritted his teeth so tightly on the mouthpiece to stay focused that his jaw started to ache and cramp. He sculled in place, waiting for Ross to catch up to him. Then he began to rise and head for the light above him, pacing his partner. He broke the surface and there was a sudden rush of city sounds: lapping of water, engines and motors on the river, aircraft, traffic, birds, horns, and sirens. Ross was helped aboard the waiting converted crew boat. Alex reached the entry platform from the craft, and got a hold. With a free hand he pulled off his mask and breather. He took off the fins and tossed them onto the deck. A pair of hands braced the side of the boat just above his head.

"You okay?" Ross asked, water dripping from his face.

"Yeah," Alex responded and then hoisted himself aboard. He said no more, not wanting to sound breathless. It was poor form. Only neophytes felt that way surfacing.

But he'd just made it. His heart had began to thud and his adrenaline was pumping hard, ready to flood his system. He took deep breaths.

"How much time?" he asked, releasing the buckles on the weight jacket, removing the protective booties.

"We got little more than an hour before the scuba team arrives. I think everything's ready for the demo," Ross said, beginning to remove his equipment.

"Good," Alex muttered.

He pulled the hooded rubber headpiece off, and his hair, matted and wet, spiked up and out in all directions. It looked like silver in the sunlight, a startling contrast to the black outfit he wore.

"You're doing good, buddy," Ross said casually, slapping Alex on the shoulder as he passed him. "I'll take the group down. You can do the talk through and answer questions."

"No. I want to go down again," Alex said firmly. He stood up, gathering the hood and boots, the buoyancy compensator, and headed for the hole below.

The boat rocked with the current, but he held his balance free-hand, finally grabbing a hold of the door frame before stepping through and out of sight.

"Come on, man. You're pushing too hard . . ."

"I'm going back down," Alex shouted up.

Ross Manning, two years Alex's senior and at least two more inches in height, and stockier, stopped what he was doing to wobble his way to the door and stare down.

"What for? You're not the one being tested. You're up to a full hour on your dives. It took you two months to get there. What's the deal today?"

"I want to," Alex informed him.

"Let this go until next time, Alex," Ross suggested.

"Where's the other tank?" came back the response.

"Alex, lighten up. Give yourself a break. Some guys never would have bothered at this point. You've been off the team for six fucking years already . . ."

Alex came back up. He was stripping almost down to his skin, wrapped in a thermal blanket and sipping from a mug. The breeze off the water quickly dried his hair. He gestured with the cup, ignoring the wisdom of his friend.

". . . I want you to tell the unit about some of the new search techniques. I got one or two surprises for them. I want to see how they respond." Alex turned away from the silent exasperation in Ross's expression and then quickly turned back again. "Another thing. I want to set a time limit. Let's pretend this is critical. We'll tell them when they get here."

Ross Manning frowned and shook his head. "You're making it too hard, man. It could take a while to find all the tracks down there. This isn't war. This is only a demonstration."

Alex drank from the cup, staring out to the harbor. "Here they come," he said, indicating the slowly approaching boat.

The air temperature was barely fifty degrees. The water was closer to freezing. But as Alex stood, the blanket falling from his bare shoulders, he didn't notice.

"I want to go down again."

After a moment Ross nodded, giving in. "Goddamn, fucking . . ." he muttered under his breath. Not cursing Alex, but the something else that made Alex want to do this. "Okay. Okay. We'll do it your way. Just remember where the limit is, Alex. I *don't* want to fish your ass outta there." He pointed to the choppy waters.

Alex nodded, but he wasn't listening. "How much did you say one of those boxes down there weighed?"

"I don't know. 'Bout one twenty-five or so."

"We should have made it heavier."

Ross kept his patience. "Alex, you don't need it any heavier. There's no one keeping a score on this. It doesn't matter."

"It matters to me. I want to make it about one eighty . . ."

"No way, man. I won't agree to that. What the hell do you think you're going to do?"

Alex tossed the rest of the contents of his mug over the side and turned back to the cabin below. "I want it carried up this time."

"You're crazy."

"Probably," Alex conceded.

"Alex . . ." Ross began, ready to argue and yet knowing he didn't have any argument that Alex was going to accept. This was one time when knowing someone really well was a disadvantage. You understood *exactly* why they did what they did. "Alex, that's a hell of a lot of dead weight."

Alex's head appeared briefly through the doorway. He was already half suited up again. The police crew cut its engines and glided into a parallel position. Alex waved to the team. "No different than a dead man," he responded flatly.

Ross stared at him for a moment and had no response. He seriously doubted that if he'd found himself in similar circumstances he'd do any differently. He wouldn't want to be stopped, either.

They were not trained to give up.

Ross stood with his hands on his hips, swaying with the momentum of the rocking. He had firm footing, too, even though he'd given up long ago maintaining optimum weight and conditioning. He no longer cared. He had done his job and done it well, and was proud he'd been there. And he hadn't forgotten that it wasn't about being perfect and infallible. It was about being persistent. Ross relaxed and began to grin. He shook his head as if to say, *What am I going to do with you?*

"Hoo yah . . ." he murmured.

Alex nodded. "Hoo yah," he returned.

He finished dressing as Ross shouted over the noise to the men getting ready on the other boat. "Okay, ladies . . . anybody here afraid to open their eyes underwater?" he teased dryly.

* * *

"Valerie, I want you to meet a friend of mine. This is Ross Manning. Ross, Valerie Holland."

"Hi," she murmured with the right amount of feminine reserve.

"It's a pleasure," Ross responded with a big smile and an appreciative sparkle in his eyes.

Valerie was friendly and gracious, smiling at Ross in a way that acknowledged him as a friend of Alex's. Ross Manning was a big man, good-looking in a rugged way. This was a man who spent time outdoors. Very physical. And Valerie noticed that his movements were easy and graceful. His presence had the peculiar affect of making her feel uncharacteristically vulnerable. The way he was smiling at her made her uncomfortable.

Valerie turned to Alex. "You didn't tell me you were bringing a chaperone. Or that we were double dating," Valerie tried to joke.

"You're not," Ross reassured her. "I'm on my way up to the north shore. I wanted to see who Alex has been spending his time with. Besides, you don't need a chaperone. Alex can take care of himself."

"So can I," Valerie parried sweetly.

"I'm ready . . . hi, Alex . . ."

Megan ran down the hallway toward them, stopping by Alex to hug him briefly. She was dressed in the full but parentally approved regalia of a preteen. Earrings but no lipstick. Blue nail polish on her stubby tips instead of the currently fashionable glue-on plastic extensions.

"My daughter, Megan Marie," Valerie said to Ross.

He held out his hand, giving the same smiling attention to her. "Hey, Megan." He raised his brows at Alex. "You're going to be escorting two good-looking women, buddy."

"I'm not going," Megan said, blushing at the compliment. "I'm going to my girlfriend's house for dinner."

"Why can't she come with us?" Alex asked Valerie.

She stared blankly at him, then shrugged. "Well, I thought . . . when you said let's go out together . . ."

"I meant all of us. Megan, too," Alex corrected easily.

"Really?" Megan asked, delighted by the idea.

"Unless you don't want to come along," Alex said.

Megan glanced covertly at her mother, uncertain. "Well . . ."

"What would you like to do, Megan?" her mother asked lightly.

Megan shrugged. "I want to come with you and Alex."

Ross winked at Valerie. "Looks like you get that chaperone after all."

"Sure you won't join us?" Alex asked Ross.

Ross took a long moment to consider the invitation, but he shook his head. "I don't think so. Three's still a crowd. And I'm not counting Megan. Some other time, maybe," Ross said, backing away toward the door.

Alex put out his hand to Ross. "Thanks, man. It was a good exercise today."

"No need for any thanks. You know that."

"Bye," Megan said shyly. She'd pulled her hand up into the cuff of her oversized denim jacket, and merely waved the empty end of the sleeve at him.

Ross waved at her, and turned his attention once more to Valerie. "Have a good evening."

"Yes. It was nice meeting you," she said politely.

"Same here . . . I'm sure we'll see each other again."

Chapter Five

I sat next to a young black woman on the crosstown bus the other day. We got to talking and she asked me my name. First names are okay to give in New York for chance encounters. A full disclosure is an invitation you might not have intended. I told her my name was Dallas. "Like the football team?" she asked. Then she told me her name was Clinique . . . like the cosmetics. She was serious. I started making a list: Corolla, Toyota, Keisha, T'Keisha . . . Modisha. All actual names of women or young girls I've met. I can't help but wonder, what does it mean when, in an effort to have an identity—unique, historic, individual, ours—black folks resort to total invention? Ultraviolet, Sahara, Tiffany, Ebony, Kenya. We invent ourselves by going down a list of consumer products and picking one from column A, two from column B. Dallas . . . because my mother was sentimental about her hometown. Why not Deborah or Diane? Is it because they are of European origins? Too white? Which is still better than being called a "Ho," a bitch, a *black* bitch, zebra, oreo, pinky, high yellow . . . nigger. What's in a name?

"I think we're almost done . . ." Letty Daniels said absently as she once more leafed through her agenda and checked off items already discussed.

"I'd like to know if anyone has any other ideas for future leads. And I'm telling you all up front I'm not interested in another 'what's wrong with black men' thing," the assistant editor, Peggy Rice, said.

"Damned if we know, anyway," came back the caustic response of Nona Talbot.

There were knowing cackles from the twelve people crowded around the conference table for the Monday morning editorial meeting.

Letty, the managing editor, shook her head and glanced around the table. "I agree with Peggy. I'm serious. It always comes off as an indictment against them, no matter how objective we try to be."

"Then to me that just means they don't want to listen to the truth," the ad exec commented.

"Let's not bring the truth into this . . ."

Everyone laughed in amusement.

Dallas smiled. Around the table there was a healthy level of teasing and bantering, made possible by acceptance of one another.

"Well, as the only man here, I feel I should put my two cents in and say something . . ." Matthew Curtis, the staff photographer, spoke up.

Nona snorted. "Don't even go there. You're one of *us* and you know it."

"Better-looking . . ." Matthew murmured.

When the ensuing laughter threatened to disrupt the rest of the meeting, Letty calmly rang a little bell she kept at hand. "We love you, Matty, but you're not an example of what we would have in mind of black manhood," she said.

"We can come up with a better idea than another article about men," Brenda, the styles editor, said.

"You just say that 'cause you got a man."

Brenda merely smiled complacently as a few of her coworkers again chuckled. "At least I'm doing something right."

"Okay, okay. Let's not throw down right here and start pulling hair. We're getting off the track," Letty said, regaining control of the meeting with the firm tone of her voice. "We'll table that one. Dallas, do you have any thoughts?"

Several of them glanced thoughtfully at her, and she

was aware that there were people she worked with who were waiting for her to fall flat on her face. To make a fool of herself. But Dallas had learned the hard way not to give anyone the chance. It had happened before, including the very first time she'd come for an interview as a staff writer at *Soul of the City.* She'd overheard someone say, "What does *she* know about being black?"

She'd had to prove that she knew quite a lot. But first she'd had to learn.

"I have a few," Dallas responded. "If we're talking about the July issue, how about something about freedom . . ."

There was a groan from the other side of the table. Several people shifted restlessly.

". . . and how we keep reinventing ourselves."

Dallas could tell by the polite stares that no one was following her line of thought. But she was not unprepared. She'd already given this subject some thought.

"For example, blacks opting to develop their *own* businesses as an economic base and keeping their money in their communities, rather than working for someone else. How there's a trend toward more ethnic sensibilities, from Afro-Centric styles and accessories in clothing, to how we do our hair . . ."

"Excuse me? *We*?" Nona questioned with raised brows.

There was nervous tittering. She'd expected that, too. Her curly hair did not lend itself to the styles that some of her coworkers adopted for themselves.

Dallas nodded easily and arched a brow at Nona. "Exactly. Not all of us wear dreads or extensions or Marcels or relaxers. Some of us go natural." She ran her hand through her soft hair.

After a bare second the table broke out into appreciative laughter, and several people applauded Dallas's quick comeback.

"That's what I mean by freedom of choice. How do each of us use that choice?"

"That's not bad," Letty said slowly, adding a note to her page. "See if you can flesh it out in more details, Dallas. Any other thoughts on her suggestion?"

"Yeah. I think we should lighten it up a bit. Freedom of choice sounds so . . . serious. So political, like abortion."

"Well, it is." Brenda shrugged. "Everything in our lives is politicized."

"But this doesn't have to be," Dallas urged, glancing around the table. "We can have some fun with it. Getting back to the hair thing, because it still is a hot button issue for some of us, one article could be called . . . 'Girl . . . *what* did you do to your *hair*?' "

The laughter began this time when Dallas did an on-target imitation of Nona, complete with her dramatic mannerisms.

"Now, let's see you do Dallas, Nona," Matty said with a smile.

The room erupted into more laughter.

Nona grimaced at him, ignoring the challenge. "If it comes to that, we can have Dallas write the one on skin color."

There was an uneasy pause.

"I could," Dallas agreed smoothly. "But it might make for better copy to have someone write a piece on that who has a problem with it. I think we all know that some of us do."

Dallas knew she'd scored her second point when several pairs of eyebrows shot up. But Letty jumped in before the focus was lost again in escalating personality conflicts.

"Let's keep this idea on the list. I want everyone to think of other areas to explore that would fit the theme. Anything else?"

"How about a July issue on children? We can include . . ."

Dallas let her body relax as the conversation carried

on without her. She scribbled notes and continued to follow the line of ideas that went around the table for discussion. Despite what some of her colleagues felt, this was a job made in heaven for her.

Soul of the City was a small magazine for women. It had a relatively young staff willing to challenge traditional thinking of black women about their lives, presenting new ideas for thought and a reaction. When she considered that she'd started out in an enviable position at a publication with an international reputation and readership in the millions, Dallas asked herself, how did she get *here*?

She still sometimes wondered if she'd made a mistake. She didn't make as much money at *Soul*. The magazine was still not high profile, but it had a talented and dedicated staff. What Dallas liked about it was that there was a lot of energy, and a willingness to experiment. Still, she had not been universally welcomed. She'd come from a better-known magazine, risking her future because of a need to write honestly about things no one else was talking about.

The voices in the conference room were like a background buzz in her head while she considered that wanting to be a writer had all started with a journal when she was twelve years old. And then somehow had lost it when she was fifteen. Of course, that conjured up a house several blocks from her own. She had written about it in her journal. About Lillian Marco, Vin, and Nicholas.

"Isn't that blackmail? They'll give us two comp tickets to the benefit if we write a story about it?"

"That's business," Letty corrected. "It's done all the time. Besides, I think we should cover the event. Other than the Mother Hale House, I don't know of another group that's doing noticeable work for pediatric AIDS in the black community. This gala is a fundraiser, so the organization could use the press, and our readership needs the information."

"Where is it being held?" Nona asked. "The Studio Museum?"

"No. It's downtown . . . I think the Public Library on Fifth Avenue is giving the space."

Dallas made another note, and went back to her reflections.

She wondered sometimes what her life might have become if she'd stayed with the other magazine. They had accepted her from graduate school. They had trained her, published her regularly . . . but mostly subjects suggested by editors. Her father had been so pleased, and Eleanor had been so impressed.

She'd stayed nearly three years. When she'd quit, her father had become silent on the subject, but obviously disappointed. Eleanor had told her she was out of her mind. And ungrateful. All of which was probably true, Dallas was willing to concede. Except she had known instinctively that had she stayed at the other magazine, she might have suffocated.

"Before we end the meeting I have to say something about that last piece that Dallas wrote . . ."

At the mention of her name Dallas blinked out of her reverie and glanced at the speaker, Peggy. The assistant editor was observant and quiet, hard to get next to. Dallas had never been sure if Peggy liked her very much although she was pleasant enough when they were together.

Peggy idly jangled the half-dozen heavy silver bracelets on her wrist before comfortably clasping her hands together and letting her gaze move slowly around the room.

"You know which one I'm talking about."

"Ummm—humm," Nona said, nodding. "Probably the one about big butts."

"It wasn't about people's butts," Dallas responded quickly.

"My mother read it and she got real upset," Matthew said.

"My sister thought it was hilarious. I don't know . . ." someone else said.

"It *wasn't* about anyone's rear end," Dallas insisted again.

"I wasn't sure. But I read it several times, and I realize that Dallas had a point," Peggy said.

"It was insensitive," a voice murmured.

"Maybe because we're all so sensitive to begin with about our bodies. Especially women. But that's not what I wanted to say." Peggy shook her head. "I figured out that I believe Dallas was writing about how we walk and carry ourselves. It was more about carriage—attitude—than it was a criticism about any part of the body. Now you have me staring at everybody's behind," Peggy said ruefully and without any sign of humor, but everyone chuckled.

Dallas nodded.

"I have to admit, after I read it a second time I saw more in the piece, too," Letty added. "Did we get any mail on it?"

"We sure did," Janine, the executive assistant, said. "But it was about half and half. Some people agreed with Dallas, and the rest wanted her fired."

"If we get mail pro and con, then Dallas is doing her job. Anything else? No?" Letty answered her own question before anyone else could.

People pushed back chairs and stood up. Dallas exited the conference room in front of Nona, and she could still feel her coworker's displeasure at having been used as the brunt of teasing in front of others.

The dispersing staff passed by the receptionist's desk to pick up Express Mail envelopes and packages. Dallas was moving with the flow of traffic toward her desk when the receptionist called out, "There's a delivery here for you, Dallas."

She was about to respond when she saw someone sitting at her desk. He was engrossed in an issue of *Soul.* The other women, recognizing him, greeted him with familiarity as they passed by and settled down to the day's routine. For herself, Dallas felt wary. It was rare that her brother didn't want something from her.

She was not pleased as Dean put aside the magazine and then turned to play with her keyboard, altering the image on her computer screen.

"Dallas, wait a moment."

She stopped short and turned to the assistant editor. Peggy was tall and statuesque. Intimidating, actually, because of her size. Her mouth was full and large. Her nose was a broad flattened pug shape, showing her flaring nostrils. Her brows were naturally arched, but drawn together so as to make her appear constantly impatient. The severity of Peggy's features, however, were relieved by two things. A surprising set of dimples in her cheeks that appeared and disappeared as she talked, and her beautifully modulated voice that was both calm, clear, and commanding.

"I hope you don't think I put you on the spot in the meeting," Peggy began.

Actually, she had. "No, it was okay. I . . . I just assumed you were trying to make an editorial point."

Peggy shook her head. "I wasn't. It was personal. We don't like to be criticized. The *we* I'm talking about is black folks . . ."

Dallas felt excluded. She considered that it might not be deliberate, and tried not to give her reaction away.

"I guess I'm not different," Peggy confessed openly, "except that I really do think you raised some good questions about how we see our bodies, given our history and our heritage."

"Maybe my point was too subtle," Dallas said.

"Maybe. When you're subtle, sometimes people don't get it. It's confusing. I guess that's really my comment. But it's probably better not to tiptoe around the thing. If you have something to say—even if people take offense—just say it.

"I probably really didn't like how you made your point. But I applaud that you did," Peggy finished.

"Well . . . it helped that you would print it despite that," Dallas said.

With a brief nod Peggy walked away. Dallas's gaze followed her, understanding full well her editor's ambivalence. The thought occurred to her that maybe she should write something more toned down for her next piece. Being controversial more than once a month was more than she could handle.

"What are you doing?" Dallas asked irritably, coming up behind her brother. Her presence did not deter him in the least from interfering with her things. It never had.

"Dilly-Dally . . ." he drawled in greeting, concentrating on the screen.

Dallas could see that he'd gotten into her games program, something she never did, and was playing solitaire. She no longer went into a huff when Dean referred to her by the nickname he'd given her when he was about four years old.

"I have work to do. Get up," she ordered, looking over his shoulder to see the indicator light on her phone flashing. Messages waiting.

"I'm almost finished . . ." Dean complained, and proceeded with his game until he had. With a few deft clicks he got back to her main menu. "All yours," he said.

He got up from her chair and transferred himself to the edge of her desk. He picked up a framed newspaper photo of her and Burke at a media conference the year before. Next to them stood the mayor and the governor.

"Hey," Dean began thoughtfully, "I ran into Burke just a couple of weeks ago. He was . . ." He stopped.

"Did you?" Dallas asked, distracted. "Where?"

Dean didn't answer right away. He shrugged, pursing his lips. "I don't know. A club someplace maybe. He was . . . er . . . with some folks. He didn't see me, so I didn't say anything."

"Probably some clients," she suggested.

"Yeah, probably," Dean murmured, looking at the picture in his hand. "You two still tight?"

Dallas sighed. She was still feeling angry at Burke. "Depends on when you ask."

"As of right now."

"I guess. We have our differences. Good days and bad days."

"So you're not interested in any other man?"

"There are no other men to be interested in." *Or who are interested in me*, she almost added. She turned on Dean. "What is this? Why are you asking about me and Burke?"

"No reason."

The question had, nonetheless, made Dallas uncomfortable. Probably one of the calls on her machine was from Burke, calling to monitor her mood. Good. Let him wonder. Dallas looked at Dean. "I can't lend you any money, so don't even ask."

"That's not why I came," Dean responded, putting the framed photo down. He stretched out his long legs and crossed his arms over his chest. "I'm serious," he insisted as he returned his sister's skeptical glance.

After a moment she was willing to believe him. He was good at convincing people of anything. Five years younger than Dallas, he was tall, athletically proportioned, and very fit. His skin was a rich smooth brown. He'd never actually had to shave very often, and Dallas knew that as he aged he would always look young. Dean had inherited the best from his parents. He was a very good-looking man. And he knew it. Worse yet, Dean had always known just how to play on it. And yet . . . Dallas could honestly admit that she liked Dean.

He was irrepressible. He was funny. He was very talented, both as a computer guru and as a bass guitarist on the side. It used to seem grossly unfair to Dallas that Dean had been given the best of everything, including the unconditional love of his parents. She remembered how Eleanor was always holding up her son to her as a model, as if Dallas had nothing of her own to commend her. But all things considered, Dallas thought it was somewhat of a miracle that Dean had not grown up to be insufferable as well. He was smart, and he had charm to spare. It went without saying that his success with the opposite sex was guaranteed. All his strong points were not unjustified, but Dean certainly wasn't perfect.

Dallas finally sat down at her desk. "I don't get it. You're not here asking me for money. What is it, then?"

Dean tried unsuccessfully to look insulted. "Man. You don't have to be so suspicious of me. You better watch it, or you'll get wrinkles on your forehead."

"Dean," she began patiently, looking pointedly at her watch.

He put up his hands in surrender.

"Okay, okay. What are we gonna do for Mother's Day?"

She stared at him, then sighed and shook her head. They went through this every year. But honestly, she also knew that if Dean didn't remind her she would probably forget each year.

"I don't know," she said, shrugging. Dallas automatically went into her Windows program and clicked into Eudora to check her E-mail box. More messages.

"Dallas, don't forget this package . . ." the receptionist called out again.

"Okay," Dallas responded. She frowned at her brother. "What did we do last year?"

He shrugged indifferently. "Damned if I can remember. I think you, me, and Dad took her to the Water Club . . ."

"The Hudson River Club," she corrected, looking for a pad to jot down the information from her screen.

"Right. And Dad had found that autographed copy of a book by what's-her-name . . ."

"Zora Neal Hurston. You and I got her tickets for Andre Watts at Carnegie Hall."

"I can't stand Andre Watts," Dean offered.

"Doesn't matter. The tickets weren't for you." Dallas paused, glancing at him. "What have you got against Andre Watts?"

Dean didn't answer directly. He fiddled with her perpetual desk calendar, shifting around the movable block of dates until it didn't make any sense. She took it out of his hands and silently raised her brows. He stood up.

"All right. I'm leaving. Why don't we get her a piece of jewelry? Earrings or something."

"We? That sounds like, you lay out the money, Dallas, and I'll pay you back."

He grinned. "I always do."

"You take too long. I should start charging interest," Dallas muttered, focused on the blinking red light on her phone. She had to get going with her work. "Eleanor doesn't need more earrings. She could give Cartier's competition. Dean, I just can't think about this right now. Why don't you call me on the weekend. Maybe something will come to mind between now and then."

"Fine. I was going out to the Island anyway Friday night. Maybe I'll try to scope out some ideas from Dad."

When her brother began to move finally in the direction of the door, Dallas got up to accompany him.

"I'm going to be out there myself on Saturday."

"Oh, yeah? Mom didn't say anything to me about it."

Dallas stared down at her suede boots as she walked slowly next to Dean. "I hadn't planned on going to the house or staying out there. I'm going to visit a friend."

Dean shook his head. "If you're going out there, you gotta stop by the house. Besides, I might need you to keep the folks off my back."

She raised her brows at him. "Why? What are you up to this time?"

"No big thing. I'm doin' a gig at a club in D.C. the weekend after . . ."

"And you want to borrow one of the cars," Dallas surmised.

"Just for the weekend."

"So ask. When have they said no to you recently?"

"*Don't* ask," he said dryly.

"What else?" she wanted to know.

"I'm taking someone with me."

She looked at him. He was being evasive. "Jeanette? Or is it Holly?"

Dean looked away. "Naw . . . neither of them. This is someone new."

"So what's the mystery? They already know you're working your way through the entire black female population under thirty." He laughed somewhat nervously. "Daddy thinks it's funny. Eleanor wants you to settle down with just one. She'd like to make the choice, of course."

They had reached the elevator and reception area where traffic moved adroitly around them. They faced each other, and Dean smiled enigmatically at her.

"Yeah, I know. But I'd like to make the decision by myself about who I'll marry."

"Who is she?"

Dean put his hands in his pockets. To Dallas he looked like the adolescent he used to be, keeping secrets and running harmless scams to get his own way.

"Someone I met at a computer show a few weeks ago."

Dallas nearly chortled in disbelief. "You found someone at a computer show you want to date?"

"Yeah, that's right," he said a bit defensively. "She's a software designer."

"Then she must be pretty."

"All that and a bag of chips . . ." Dallas laughed.

"Owns her own business," Dean responded, needlessly pushing on the elevator call button.

Dallas chuckled. "I don't think there's going to be

a problem. Your mother is going to love her. She won't think this is a woman who's after you for your good looks *and* your money. So you want me to run interference again, is that it?"

He gave her the most charming smile. "You may need me to return the favor someday."

"Don't hold your breath. You're too full of yourself. Someone's going to knock you down to size someday."

He pecked her cheek. "Long as it's not you. That would break my heart." Dean dramatically covered his chest as the elevator arrived and he stepped on board. He was gone with a brief wave.

"Dallas, don't forget . . ."

She turned to the receptionist. "Where is it? I wasn't expecting anything."

The young woman merely pointed to an oversized, awkwardly wrapped item sitting on the floor. It was clearly a large arrangement of flowers.

Dallas stared at it for a moment before approaching and starting to tear away the paper. She drew in her breath when the flowers were revealed. The floral design was exquisite. Exotic and out-of-season flowers had been used to create an impressive display.

"How pretty," the girl behind Dallas gushed.

Tucked into the top was a small white envelope. Dallas grimaced as she opened it and extracted the enclosure.

The flowers were from Burke. The card said simply, "Thanks for the other night."

Dallas watched in amusement as Maureen Benton finally entered the restaurant, and hip-wiggled her way through the crowded space to where she sat waiting. Maureen gave vague smiles of apology to those she grazed with her oversized leather shoulder tote, but otherwise ignored the interested glances and curious stares from those around her. She could not be missed. She was not pretty, but she was very striking. Maureen was two inches taller than Dallas and, to put it in the vernacular, had a body that wouldn't quit. Her hair was cropped short and dyed a blondish brown. She wore expensive clothing that flattered her figure rather than emphasized her attributes. She carried herself with the regal bearing of someone who had supreme self-confidence. But Dallas knew that while Maureen was not unaware of her effect on people, neither was it calculated nor staged. Her ability to draw attention was just Maureen being Maureen.

Maureen made her way past a booth, and someone called out her name. Pleasantly surprised, she acknowledged the acquaintance, a middle-aged black man in a dark suit, seated with several other men. They had *important* stamped all over them. Dallas could tell instantly from the sly movement of the man's eyes, his casual gestures and smile, that he'd probably tried hitting on Maureen at some point in the past. But he also wore a wedding ring. Maureen was too smart to waste time on relationships with no place to go.

"Sorry I'm late," Maureen said in a breezy, careless tone as she took her seat.

Dallas only smiled patiently. Maureen had *never* been on time in her life. "Who was that you stopped to talk to?" she asked, passing her friend one of the menus.

Maureen sighed indifferently as she glanced over the laminated card and put it aside. "Oh . . . some counsel with the attorney general's office. Federal, not state. I met him six months ago at a press conference. He's been working overtime to get under my dress."

Dallas raised her brows but wasn't shocked. She'd known Maureen too long. She pulled no punches . . . and took no prisoners. She had the firm intact ego of a survivor, of poverty, rape, a dysfunctional family, and social agencies that had nearly let her fall through the cracks.

"But guess what?" she murmured, leaning her elbows on the table and clasping her hands.

"What?" Dallas questioned, taking the bait. "You got a new position? They're sending you to Europe? You're starting your own firm . . ."

"I'm getting married."

Dallas couldn't respond. Her tongue was suddenly plastered to the roof of her mouth.

It wasn't that she wasn't happy for Maureen. Dallas wasn't even all that surprised. Maureen, with her pecan-tinted features and stylish hairdo, had never been without male companionship. Not all of her choices had been wonderful, to hear her tell it, but she'd had plenty to pick and choose from.

"Did you hear what I said?" Maureen inquired across their too small table.

Dallas smiled belatedly. "I heard you. I'm trying to say something else besides congratulations and I'm-so-happy-for-you."

"How about, when? Am I sure? What made Nathan ask, and you thought I didn't want to get married?"

Dallas chuckled. "Okay. All of that."

"Last weekend . . ." Maureen put out her slender hand and displayed her glittering engagement ring. It was an unusual setting. A blue sapphire surrounded by small white diamonds.

"It's gorgeous."

"It belonged to Nathan's mother. I'm getting a real heirloom. Hey, if it doesn't work out we can always split the blankets and go separate ways."

"You haven't even said 'I do' yet, and already you're calculating the chances of being sorry you did? Why bother?"

"Because I'm ready. I told him if he didn't ask me I had no more time to waste on him."

Dallas laughed, nodding her head. "Now, that sounds just like you."

Maureen looked her straight in the eye. "I wanted to get married because I want to have a baby. And I *don't* want to do it the other way around. Or alone. My mother had three kids by two different men and wasn't married to either one of them. My sister is off doing the same thing. I'm sorry, but I want the old-fashioned setup. Men can be a pain in the ass . . . but there's no substitute for the real thing."

Dallas's amusement died away. What replaced it shocked her. It was sorrow and envy. Deep, pure, unadulterated envy.

"And what can I get you today?" The perky waitress stood in front of their table, pencil and receipt pad poised.

"Chicken salad on rye. No mayo, and a Diet Pepsi," Maureen recited.

"Me, too," Dallas said, returning her menu.

"Want to share an order of fries?" Maureen asked. With Dallas's consent it was added to the order.

"I like Nathan. I think he's lucky to get you," Dallas said carefully when the waitress had walked away.

Maureen reached across the table to grab Dallas's arm and gently shook her. "Stop that. I know what you're thinking."

"No, you don't."

"Oh, yes, I do. I know you, girl. That is exactly what I said to you when Hayden proposed. And when you had to leave him I also said you were doing the right thing."

Dallas was furious with herself. She felt as if she were going to cry. Maureen had always been able to read her, even better than Valerie. Maureen had always understood better the ambiguousness of her family and situation.

"Maybe you two got together for all the wrong reasons. It's over. Don't beat yourself up about it," Maureen said airily.

Dallas absently nodded. Easier said than done. She stared at her girlfriend, wondering where Maureen had learned to cut to the chase and not bother with the self-doubt. There was no questioning of fair or unfair or hysterics or indignation about bias and racism and being held back. Things are what they are and you simply deal. Maureen kept her eyes open, her soul guarded, and her legs closed, as she often joked.

"You know what I'm going to ask," Dallas warned. "Do you love Nathan?" She sat back as the waitress returned with their sodas and placed them on the table.

Maureen shrugged. "Sure. And you know why this will work? Because Nathan loves me more than I love him. The reality is, if any man thinks you need him too much, you've just given him power over you."

Dallas was taken aback by this bluntness. "When?" she asked.

Maureen grinned at her. "When did he ask me, or when are we getting married? Last night. And we're planning mid June. I want you in my wedding party. We're doing something small and intimate. I don't want to lay out for hundreds of people," she said without sentimentality. "We're getting married in Hampton, Virginia."

"Why there?"

"His folks are from there, and most of his close friends still live in the area."

"Does this mean I'll have to buy some dress I'll only wear once?"

Maureen arched a brow. "You only wore your wedding dress once." Dallas conceded the point. "Burke can be your escort. He'll come, won't he?"

"Probably," Dallas said, remembering the recent tensions between them because of his continual habit of breaking dates when he found something else better to do. Or just not showing up. The flowers were not going to let her forget that.

"Now we have to find you a good black man. Burke, maybe?" Maureen teased.

"I had a good black man. He apparently wasn't very sure about me."

"He was a damned fool. What? Did he suddenly

wake up one morning and find a white woman in his bed?"

Dallas leaned toward her and narrowed her gaze. "Don't forget how you treated me when we were kids. You felt the same way."

"I didn't know any better. I knew someone who was passing, and it got on my nerves. I thought you were going to do the same thing."

"Pass for what?"

Maureen looked closely at her. "Something exotic. Latina. Greek. I don't know. Hayden should have known better, too."

"Doesn't matter, does it?" Dallas said, sitting back. "So, what about Burke?"

Dallas hid her response momentarily in the sipping of her drink. "He's okay, I guess. For now."

"Doesn't sound like love to me," Maureen observed.

"I don't think we want the same thing in a relationship."

"What kind are you looking for?"

Dallas raised her brows. "Honest. A good man. Someone who respects me. Loves me."

"Well, maybe that's where you go wrong. Next time remember what Tina Turner said about it . . ."

Dallas sat staring at the floral arrangement. The fragrance was rich and overpowering, disguising the office smells of machines and furniture, paper and dust. The presentation was impressive but reminded her of two things. Weddings and funerals. Both occasions made her anxious. In her mind, one was not much different from the other.

At Mother Oliver's service Dallas recalled wondering why people would send so many pretty flowers to a dead person. She didn't remember if there had been flowers for her own mother. It had rained, and she'd been more concerned with finding out where her mother was. Even after she'd been told her mother was dead, it hadn't meant anything. There'd been no body.

The arrangement from Burke was quite beautiful. But so unexpected and overwhelming as to make Dallas uncomfortable with them. They felt like a payoff.

Thanks for the other night . . .

When Burke called her at five-thirty that afternoon she understood better why she'd felt strange about the bouquet.

"Did you get a delivery today?" he asked.

"Yes, I did. There was no need to do that. Way too expensive."

"You deserve it," he said. "I'm not taking any chances this time. I'm telling you up front I probably have to cancel tomorrow night."

"Is that why you sent the flowers? Getting ahead of yourself? Covering all the bases?"

"I sent the flowers first. Then I found out about tomorrow," he corrected.

"Please don't sent any the next time."

"I thought you'd appreciate them."

Appreciate . . .

Dallas was overanalyzing, but she couldn't shake the feeling of being set up. "I would appreciate the forethought better than the apology," she murmured.

"Ummmm. They sure smell good. How're you going to get them home?" Brenda asked, buttoning her coat as she prepared to leave the office an hour later.

"I don't know," Dallas responded flatly.

"Have Terry call you a cab. I can't see you getting on the subway with that."

"I don't want to take them home with me."

"Well, you could always leave them here. I'll see you people tomorrow. Night," Brenda said, leaving.

"Night," Dallas answered.

She looked at the small white card again. The message still made her frown.

"Dallas, I'm going to ask someone else to cover that

Pediatric AIDS gala next month. If you don't mind, I'd rather have you take on the lecture at NYU Film School with Cosby and Lee. I know it's a little beyond what you normally write about, but . . ."

". . . a writer should be able to write about anything," Dallas finished for Letty Daniels. "That's okay," she sighed. "I'd like to write about something that's not going to get me slammed for a change," she said, turning the white card facedown on the desk.

"I hired you to write what you believed in. You're willing to take more chances than some of the other writers. It's okay that people don't agree with you."

"I know," Dallas agreed. "But some of it comes across as personal attacks."

"You mean like the piece about butts. I liked it. It was different." Letty nodded, putting the best spin on the controversy.

Dallas let her lips curve grimly. She wasn't going to repeat again that the essay was not about anatomy but self-image. And perception. "Thanks," she said.

Letty touched the flowers with gentle fingers. "How pretty . . ."

"Go ahead. Take some," Dallas offered. Letty pulled out two roses, a daylily, and baby's breath.

"Burke was sweet to send you flowers. It's so romantic. If we do a piece on black men, we *have* to interview him. See you tomorrow."

"You staying late?" Terry, the receptionist, called out as she closed and locked the doors to the inner offices, and returned to her desk for her coat and purse.

Dallas shook her head. "No. I'm leaving, too." She turned off her computer and stood up, picking up the little white card again.

"Well, good night, Dallas."

"Would you like these?" she asked suddenly.

"Me? You mean, the flowers?" Terry asked, incredulous.

"Yes. Go on, you can have them."

"Well . . ."

Dallas opened her bag and took out her wallet. "Here . . . why don't you take a cab home. My treat." She held out a twenty-dollar bill to the receptionist, whose face showed a combination of astonishment, suspicion, gratitude, and delight.

"How come you don't want the flowers?" the young woman asked, examining the floral arrangement as if she really had to think about it carefully.

"I'm not going right home," Dallas improvised. "And they'll dry out and die overnight here in the office."

"Nobody ever sent me flowers." Terry shook her head.

Dallas chuckled. "Then pretend they're from a secret lover."

"Yeah, right," Terry snickered. She took the money. "If you're sure you don't want them."

"I am. You enjoy them."

Terry lifted the vase carefully, her head hidden by the stalks and greens of the arrangement. "Thanks a lot."

"I'll leave with you," Dallas said, relieved to have gotten rid of them. No guilt. No remorse. No obligation.

No failure.

Dallas crushed the card in her hand and dropped it into the wastebasket as she and the receptionist boarded the elevator.

Chapter Six

Dallas realized that this was the first time she'd felt totally comfortable in Lillian Marco's house in almost fifteen years. It was the first time she'd ever been to any other part of the house beyond the kitchen and basement, the first time she didn't sit stiffly and alertly, monitoring the time and knowing when she had to leave. The reason was that Nicholas was dead, although she knew she could never admit that to anyone. Least of all to his mother.

As a child, once she felt safe with Lillian's friendship, it was easy to see her just after school, or sometimes on the weekend or holidays, with careful planning. After that incident with Nicholas, she *never* wanted to risk being there in case he walked in.

There was something eerie and surreal about being in the room that had belonged to Nicholas Marco. She, of all people, was aiding in the disposition of his belongings. Shifting through his life, piece by piece, getting to know him in a way not possible when he was alive.

"I think this will make up the last box," Lillian murmured from inside the open closet.

"Here, I'll take those," Dallas said, getting up from the floor, where she knelt in front of a corrugated box, half-filled with Nicholas's old clothing and other accessories.

Dallas relieved Lillian of the armful of hangers with shirts and jackets and pants, and laid them on the bed for sorting and folding. The clothing had more than just a musty smell. They were limp with age and many of the colors faded. You could mark the changes in Nicholas's size and age by the kinds of things she found.

"Some of these are very old, aren't they?" Dallas couldn't help commenting. "You're very sentimental."

Lillian shook her head as she joined Dallas again in removing hangers and separating the clothing into piles by category. "No, it was Nicky. He never liked to get rid of anything. You give him something, he wanted to keep it forever. I can understand, in a way," she said cryptically. "One year he had so much stuff in this room I came in while he was away at camp and got rid of whatever I could. Only things I knew he couldn't wear anymore, that I hoped he wouldn't miss."

"Did he?"

Lillian chuckled. "I almost got caught when he couldn't find some special shirt from one of the school teams. I told him, maybe you left it someplace. Look around again. He did, over and over again, getting very upset. My goodness, he carried on. He didn't want anybody fooling around in his things."

Dallas was a little stunned, both at the degree of Nicholas's self-absorption, and the kid gloves with which he had been handled. As if he could do no wrong.

Dallas looked at the older woman, but saw only love and sadness in her eyes as she handled her dead son's things. Lillian didn't look like a mother who had been afraid of her own child. So how had Nicholas become the kind of person he had?

"What are you going to do with all of his things?" she asked.

Lillian stopped for a moment and looked at the already packed boxes in the middle of the floor. "Father Cirelli said he'd take everything and give them away to needy families—oh, for heaven's sake! Look what's in here . . ."

Lillian bent and retrieved something from the box. She shook it out, turning her face from the dust that billowed out. It was a tank top of navy blue with faded yellow print. It was very wrinkled, but Dallas could make out the words "Long Beach Swim Club, South Shore" forming a circle in the front.

"This doesn't belong to Nicky," Lillian murmured, bringing the shirt close to examine it, running her fingers on the cracked and dried-out acrylic ink that formed the lettering. She held it against her nose briefly. She slowly smiled. "It still smells like the ocean. Salt water." She glanced at Dallas, her eyes bright and the gaze slightly distant. "This is Vin's shirt."

"Do you want to keep it? Or should it go into the bag with the other things?"

Lillian didn't respond right away, and seemed to have drifted back in time as she stroked the blue cloth. She held it with a reverence that indicated it held very important memories for her. "No. I want to keep this . . ." she finally whispered.

Feeling like a voyeur, Dallas returned to the closet to check if anything else needed to be removed. There was nothing but dust and scraps of papers on the floor.

"I think that's it," Dallas said. "We can seal the boxes and . . ." She turned around to find herself standing alone in the room. "Lillian?"

After a minute Lillian returned. She held the shirt in one hand and a small piece of paper in the other. She held it out to Dallas. It was a yellowed and faded black and white photograph, the old kind with the serrated edges. In the center of the image was a couple. Teenagers. A young boy and a younger-looking girl. The girl was sitting on a blanket or towel in the sand, squinting against the sunlight. He was kneeling behind her, his hands on her shoulders. And he was wearing a shirt just like the one Lillian held.

"That's me and Vin," Lillian said.

Dallas regarded the picture intently. She could see

it now. A very young, shy-looking Lillian, her hair surprisingly blond, pulled back into a ponytail. She didn't look older than fourteen or fifteen. And Vincent, perhaps eighteen. Sturdy and muscled and *very* handsome. So close together in the picture, Dallas could also see the obvious ethnic differences between them. She'd never considered that before. That Lillian might not be of Italian heritage. She was very fair, and Vin an olive tone, with dark thick hair.

"Did I ever tell you how Vin and I met?" Lillian asked, her voice lilting and a bit dreamy.

"No," Dallas responded.

Lillian took the picture back. "Let's go downstairs and I'll tell you."

Lillian said no more for a while, even after they'd reached the kitchen and begun their comfortable ritual of preparing coffee and tea to go with the plate of biscotti. Lillian added a bowl of strawberries taken from the refrigerator.

"I remember when I was growing up, you had to wait until the summer for fruits like strawberries and melon and peaches. Now you can get anything you want all year long. That's too bad," she said, sitting down.

"Why? Don't you think it's great that you can get them anytime you want to?"

Lillian shook her had. "Then there's nothing to look forward to. I'd wait all year for the summer to come so my mother could buy fresh watermelon. When you can get it anytime, the surprise is gone. The fun of going to buy the first of the season. My mother would cut up a melon into chunks, and we would take it with us to eat at the beach."

"We almost never went to the beach when I was small. My parents didn't like sitting in the sun and getting sand in everything," Dallas said as they settled down together at the table. "I went with Valerie Holland's family, her sisters and brother."

Lillian picked up the small photograph and looked

at it once again thoroughly. "I met Vin at the beach. He saved my life."

Dallas stared at Lillian and waited for the details, wanting to know the story of how someone as gentle and kind as Lillian came to marry a man as tough and taciturn as Vincent Marco.

"I was just standing on the edge of the water, no deeper than my knees. I didn't know how to swim. My mother didn't want me to learn how. She was afraid I'd get out in a pool somewhere or go too far out in the ocean and drown." Lillian chuckled silently at the irony of her mother's logic. "She said girls didn't need to know how to swim. They need to find a husband who was going to take care of them." She shrugged when she sensed Dallas's smile. "Well, you know . . . in my day that's what a girl did. She got married and had kids. None of this career stuff. A little part-time job was okay. But it was supposed to be temporary."

"How did Vin save you?"

"I was standing there when all of a sudden this wave came rushing in. I turned my back thinking, well, I'll get wet a little. Instead, it washes right over me. Pulled me clear off my feet. I felt myself being dragged along the sand, and water was going into my mouth and nose. I couldn't even scream. Then suddenly my head came out of the water and I was lying in wet sand and the water had rolled back. I was gasping and choking, and before I could catch my breath or get up, here comes another wave. *Bam!* pulls me down again.

"Well . . . I finally did hear someone start to scream. I'm thinking, my mother is *never* going to let me come near the ocean again as long as I live." Lillian chuckled at her own humor. "Then I felt something grab me real hard, and hold my arms real tight. I couldn't stand up, so I was lifted and carried out of the water. I thought it was my father, except he couldn't swim either. When I opened my eyes, there was this young guy bent over me. And he was whispering that I was going to be okay. And he was touching my face. I started to cough up water, and he pulled me up and told me to put my head down. The water ran out of my mouth and nose.

"My mother was crying and my father was crying, and there were all these people around me, but he, this boy—this man—he kept holding my hand and telling me I was fine. That was Vincent Marco."

In Lillian Marco's expression as she retold the story, Dallas could see a light reflecting the magic of that moment. She could really see a young, virile Vin coming to the rescue. But Lillian had seen something more. Her hero.

Lillian was pensive for a few moments, and then sighed and shook her head. She absently sipped her coffee, and nibbled on the fresh-cut strawberries. "I thought he was the most handsome man. My folks were very grateful, of course, but they wanted me to stay away from the beach after that. I think it had less to do with my almost drowning than it did with the fact that I wouldn't stop talking about how wonderful and strong Vin had been. I didn't understand, at first, why they weren't as impressed. But I knew I wanted to see him again, and I knew I couldn't tell them. So, for the first time in my life I started lying to my parents about where I was going, and getting my girlfriends to cover for me. And when I could I'd go to the beach when Vin was there on duty as a lifeguard. And later, after school, when he worked at a garage his uncle owned. He was so sweet to me. But we *never* did anything . . . you know . . ."

When Lillian's voice faded, Dallas took one look at her suddenly blushing face and could figure out the rest. She didn't have to hear the details of how Lillian had fallen in love with a handsome young lifeguard with strong arms and gentle hands . . . who'd saved her, in more ways than one.

"Of course, our families found out. My parents didn't want me to get involved with someone who was

Italian. And Vin's family wanted him to stay away from me because I wasn't. Can you believe that?"

Dallas chuckled to herself. She certainly could. Lillian took one of the biscotti, broke it in half, and extended a piece to her.

"Vin's sister taught me how to make these. Poor girl. She died many years ago. A real tragedy . . ."

Dallas was instantly intrigued. She waited for Lillian to explain. But she didn't.

Lillian suddenly began to laugh merrily as some memory bubbled up within her. She waved her piece of the cookie at Dallas.

"I remember the first time I gave one of these to Nick. What a mess he made, dipping it into his milk. As a matter of fact, he wanted to dip everything he ate into something else."

She continued to laugh, but it began to make Dallas uneasy. When Lillian couldn't seem to stop, Dallas hesitantly reached out to her.

"Lillian . . ."

"He was so funny when he was small. And so strong-willed. I used to tell Vin that Nicky learned that from him, but . . . but . . ."

"Lillian, don't."

Lillian shook her head. The laughter stopped abruptly and she fought for control. She didn't cry, but sat and covered her face with her hands.

"I failed him, Dallas. I failed Vin. And Nicky . . ."

"No, you haven't. You're a wonderful wife, and Vin adores you. You're a wonderful mother," Dallas insisted, sliding out of her seat and reaching out to hug Lillian, to comfort her.

It felt strange. Dallas was so used to Lillian being the one to comfort and care for everyone. "What happened to Nicky was no one's fault."

"I know. I'm just being silly."

Lillian gave Dallas a gentle little shove, urging her to take her seat again.

Dallas shook her head. "I wouldn't ever call you silly."

Lillian took a deep breath. "I'm sorry," she whispered.

"You don't owe me an apology," Dallas said sadly. "It must have been really hard to go through your son's things like that. But now you're finished."

"Oh, no. There's more stuff in the basement."

Dallas stared at her blankly.

The Basement.

Why hadn't she considered that things might be stored there? That's what basements, attics, and garages were for. Depositories of family stuff. But Dallas had not gone down to the basement of the Marco house again since that day with Nick. An instant apprehension gripped her in the pit of her stomach.

Already Lillian was opening the door leading to the lower level of the house. "Vin put those boxes down here for me. To get them out of the way once Nicky left home," she said. She turned on the wall switch just inside the door, and a glow of light came up the stairs. "I don't know what's in them . . ."

Her voice faded as Lillian descended the stairs. Dallas watched her disappear. Finally, she got up from the table, taking her things to the sink. She washed out all the dishes that had been used. She could have put them into the dishwasher. Delays. Just killing time. Trying to adjust.

There was the trilling of the bell from the outside door. Dallas turned to look and could make out the shape of a man standing on the step.

"Will you get that, please? It's probably the mailman."

"Sure," Dallas acknowledged, unconsciously sighing at the reprieve.

She was annoyed with herself, however, for her reaction. Lillian's announcement had caught her off guard. And she was behaving badly. Like a kid. But that's all she had been back then, she considered defensively as she opened the door.

"Hi. Mrs. Marco is down . . ."

That's as far as she got. The man, looking down the block where some boys were playing street hockey, quickly turned to face her. It was not the mailman but Alex Marco. There was a quick light of recognition in his eyes.

Alex's scrutiny of her was immediately focused and direct. A look that saw her and nothing else. It made Dallas feel self-conscious knowing that he was quickly bridging the past to the present. She'd thought about something like this happening and then suddenly here it was. There was so much between them.

Dallas and Alex stood like that for perhaps ten seconds, but it felt like in that time they'd covered the entire span of years it had taken them both to grow up.

"Hello," Alex opened first. His tone held just a slight lilt of surprise.

Dallas opened her mouth to respond and couldn't even get out a simple hi. Speculation aside, after all those years, she had never been prepared for this moment.

"I thought I'd better come back up." Lillian's voice came over Dallas's shoulder. She sounded slightly winded from the climb back up the stairs. "In case I have to sign something. Did he leave any packages?"

Dallas stepped back and turned to Lillian, who still hadn't detected that it wasn't the mailman at her door. It was only as Alex came into the kitchen, the heels of his boots making a sharp thump on the floor, that Lillian took him in fully. She didn't seem surprised to see him. She smiled and held out her arms to him.

"Alex! You're here," she said.

He stepped forward and bent to give the diminutive Lillian a light hug, swallowing her in his long arms and lifting her onto her toes. He kissed her cheek and pressed his against hers briefly.

"Hey . . . sorry I'm late," he murmured.

So, he *was* expected, Dallas saw, as she witnessed the warm greetings between the two. It was evident that there was an enormous amount of affection between Lillian and Alex, and it was also obvious that it was long-standing. But after all . . . he was family.

"Oh, you know I'm going to forgive you," Lillian scoffed playfully, pushing him away to gaze into his face.

Alex arched a brow. "Yeah, I sort of counted on that. But I'm not going to push my luck. You might change your mind." He spread his arms. "I'm here to do whatever you want me to."

Finally, Alex turned to Dallas again, and his look said many things. It tested *her* response. It apologized for the intimate moment with Lillian. Dallas was also certain that his gaze questioned her. As if to ask, *Are we ready now?*

For what, she wasn't sure. That is, until Lillian remembered her presence and reached out to take her hand.

"Alex, I want you to meet a very dear friend of mine. I never mentioned her to you before, but I've known her since she was a chubby little girl." Lillian chuckled, squeezing her hand.

Dallas felt herself blushing. She glanced somewhere over Alex's shoulder rather than directly at him.

"Now she's a famous writer," Lillian enthused. "This is Dallas Oliver. Dallas, this is Alex."

He didn't extend his hand and neither did she.

Alex spoke up. "We already know each other."

Dallas felt a sudden sinking in her stomach, like an elevator stopping short. Though looking at him, she was aware of Lillian's surprise.

"Valerie Holland introduced us at Nick's wake," he said smoothly.

"Oh . . . yes," Lillian murmured.

Alex gave his attention once more to Dallas, his expression merely friendly. "We didn't get a chance to do more than say hi. Dallas had to leave. You didn't mention that she was going to be here."

Lillian shrugged. "I don't know why I didn't think to tell either one of you. Don't mind me." Lillian waved her hand in a vague dismissiveness. "You know what I've been through . . ."

"It's okay, Lillian . . ."

"Don't worry about it . . ."

Alex and Dallas spoke simultaneously to put Lillian at ease. They exchanged brief glances.

"Anyway . . . I'm glad you two are finally getting a chance to meet. I care so much for both of you . . . Oh! there he is . . ."

Lillian rushed back to the door. Finally, coming up the walk, was the mailman. She stepped outside the door and engaged in conversation with the postal worker, leaving Dallas and Alex alone.

He was still staring at her. It was beginning to make her nervous. And irritated. She met his gaze squarely. He took a step back and leaned against the counter, his arms crossing his chest.

"Did you think I was going to say something else?" he asked quietly.

Dallas stood on the opposite side of the kitchen and leaned back against the edge of the sink. Their positions reminded her of that other time in this kitchen, when he was trying to calm her down and get her away from Nick.

"I wasn't sure," Dallas admitted with a slight shrug.

"Then I would have to explain more than either of us would want. Right?"

The blush returned. "Right."

He gnawed on the inside of his jaw. "If you'd known I would be here, would you have come?"

"Would you?"

"Absolutely." Alex nodded without hesitation.

Dallas's attention faltered from his inquiring gaze. "I . . . I don't know."

Then they heard Lillian say good-bye to the mailman and the door closed as she returned with a handful of envelopes, flyers, and newspapers. She placed them on the table.

"Mr. Cavannagh just told me he's retiring at the end of this year. He wants to move closer to a son who lives in Denver. He hardly looks old enough. But then, he's been on this route for as long as Vin and I have lived here . . . twenty-five years. I wonder who'll replace him . . ." Lillian chattered mostly to herself.

Alex and Dallas were, in the meantime, engaged in a silent communication, staring at each other and trying to come to an understanding of how not to betray what they knew.

"So, what do you want me to do?" Alex interrupted Lillian, refocusing her attention.

"Oh . . ." She rubbed her forehead, thinking. "The basement. Dallas and I were going down to the basement . . ."

Alex didn't look at Dallas. "Maybe we should start first in his room. There used to still be things in his closet . . ."

"We've . . . already done that. Just before you arrived," Dallas informed Alex. Her voice held a note of appreciation that Alex might try to spare her the trip to the lower level of the house.

"I didn't want to wait," Lillian said softly with a shake of her head.

Dallas and Alex exchanged glances again fully appreciating what the work of the afternoon was costing Lillian, and that to delay it was both unnecessary and cruel. It was best to be done with it.

Alex swung his arm out toward the basement door and looked at Lillian. "Okay. Lead the way."

Lillian went down the stairs first and Dallas went right behind her. Alex brought up the rear, sandwiching her in between. In a way Dallas felt buffeted, protected. It kept her initial panic at bay as the three of them reached the floor below. There was a flash of memory, a sweeping play of images and sensory responses to the smell, size, and details of the room. Dallas's stomach heaved and then settled down. She experienced a chill over her skin, and then was warmed by her own flow of blood. After a moment Dallas knew she was okay. She was not going to be swallowed up whole by the past. After all, when it mattered, she had not been alone.

The basement was exactly the same as it had always been, Alex saw. The same furniture in the same place. The same pictures on the wall. It served to conjure up the past with the same images and the same details of things that had happened here. It evoked the same feelings. Rage and disappointment. Only now he was old enough to deal with it.

Alex glanced over at Dallas. She sat quietly and apart on the stone ledge of the hearth. Her head was bent over a stack of papers balanced on her lap. Her expression was pensive, but he would bet that she had the same thoughts that he had about this room. Lillian always referred to the basement as the playroom. But only he and Dallas knew the truth about things that had taken place here.

Dallas hesitated in her sorting and suddenly turned her head and glanced at him. Alex didn't pretend that he hadn't been staring. Her eyes had a soft light of defiance, as if to question his interest in her. Just as quickly Dallas backed down, looking away to the work at hand. But he continued to watch her. He was very aware of her presence even though she was mostly silent while the three of them worked. Hers was the silence of someone used to being an observer rather than a participant. She would be careful of having any expectations, and would be selective in accepting either friendship or love. Which gave Alex every reason to feel pleased with himself, because of the trust Dallas had once placed in him.

He wasn't even thinking about the first time they'd met, right here with Nicholas trying to force her into sex with him. Instead, Alex was remembering the second time. It had been almost a year after the incident with Nicholas. Alex wondered if Dallas was thinking about it, too.

When the three of them had reached the basement, Lillian had crossed the room to a storage area that was a tiny space next to where the hot-water heater was housed. Dallas had hung back, unconsciously hugging herself as her gaze swept quickly around the room, blinking at the dim corners as if expecting Nick to jump out at her. Alex had stepped up right behind her.

"Are you okay?" he'd whispered so that only Dallas could hear.

She hadn't started, hadn't looked back at him. She'd merely nodded her head.

Alex's attention narrowed and settled on the spread of dusty rose over her cheeks. It suddenly reminded him of something else from that day the first time. Dallas had told him that Nick didn't like black people. And when he had returned after walking her home, one of the first things Nick had done was to spew forth accusations that it was her fault what had been going on. That she knew she'd wanted him to . . . and she'd changed her mind. Nick had dismissed the incident and Dallas, calling her just a nigger.

A *nigger.*

Alex didn't know what to make of that. He understood it even less now when attached to Dallas. Black guys he knew routinely called each other nigger. A kind of insider's joke. A bold and provocative affirmation of self, turning a hated stereotype and insult around, pointing it toward themselves and claiming ownership. But Alex didn't think it could be dressed up and made acceptable. It was still . . . ugly.

Dallas was not ugly.

Alex was surprised, as a matter of fact, to discover that she had grown so attractive. He averted his gaze and frowned down at the things in his hand. School notebooks, mostly. Had Dallas not been so pretty before . . . or had he not bothered to notice? Alex hadn't really thought about it back then. She was just a kid. Too young. Too scared. But . . . the next year . . .

Math. English. Another math . . . health ed. He leafed through the pages. Half-finished work, mediocre marks.

"Lillian, do you want any of the notebooks from junior high?" Alex asked Lillian.

"No, I don't think so," she replied after a moment's thought.

Alex chucked several of the composition-style books to the floor in front of him. Dallas automatically retrieved them and added them to the black garbage bag. He noticed she had pretty hands. They were slender and pale. No, not pale. Tan.

His attention went back to her face, bypassing the casual clothing Dallas was wearing. Khaki slacks and a navy-blue sweater, sneakers. Yes, she really was much prettier. She'd lost all the young-girl roundness and soft flesh. The last stage of baby fat . . . or whatever you wanted to call it. She now seemed taller. Her mouth fuller in her thinner face. She had cheekbones and a narrow chin. Alex didn't remember a thing about her hair, except that there had been a lot of it. Wild. Dallas had cut it all off. What was left was still curly, but short and looser with a fullness about her face that added feminine softness.

"Oh, look . . ." Lillian murmured.

Both Alex and Dallas turned to her. She had a leather certificate holder. Lillian opened it, smiling softly in memory.

"It's Nicky's diploma . . ." She ran her hand over the surface of the gilded paper, her fingertip testing the ridges of the embossed seal.

"You have to keep that," Dallas advised quietly.

"Yes, yes." Lillian sighed. "It's a miracle that boy ever got out of school with one. I really wanted him to go on to college. He tried for one semester but . . . he didn't stay."

"What did he go for?" Alex asked carefully.

Lillian sighed. "Oh . . . I thought he should go into something practical. Like accounting. Vin always hoped that Nicky would take over the business someday. But he wasn't interested." Lillian chuckled and shook her head ruefully. "He wanted to be rich and famous, I know that, but he never said how he was going to do it."

Alex shrugged. "Some people aren't meant to go to college."

"You should have," Lillian admonished. "You're a smart man. You're smarter than Nicky was," she ended.

Dallas was surprised that Lillian would admit such a thing. She looked at Alex for his reaction, but he seemed to have not heard Lillian, or chose to ignore it. He'd heard, Dallas decided. Alex had always struck her as someone who paid attention and noticed things.

"What is Vin going to do about the business?" Alex asked Lillian. He silently handed the rest of the notebooks to Dallas and she disposed of them in the black bag.

"I don't know," Lillian sighed. "You know it's a family business. Vin's father started it, but Vin has really made it much bigger and more successful."

"I didn't know that," Alex said in a low voice.

"Vin would hate to lose it but . . . when he retires he might have to sell it. I don't know. He doesn't talk about it too much, but I know he's concerned."

Dallas happened to glance at Alex again, and found his features intent and thoughtful. He sat on the edge of the sofa with his legs slightly spread and his elbows braced on his knees as he looked briefly through each book.

She reached into the bottom of her box. It was empty.

"I'm finished with this one," Dallas announced. She

stood up and sealed closed the top of the garbage bag. She then took the bag and the box and placed them closer to the foot of the staircase for removal upstairs when they were all done.

"I'm almost done, too," Alex said.

He lifted the next notebook in his stack and wasn't even going to bother leafing through it until he noticed that the handwriting on the cover was different than what he'd been reading so far. He looked closer. In the small white space on the front of the composition book was written "My Journal." Alex opened the cover and on the inside of the jacket was printed in the same hand, "this belongs to Dallas Kristin Oliver. *Private.* DO NOT READ! The last three words were carefully written in capital letters.

A quick glance through the book showed the text was written in a neat block print tilting forward. The book was only three-fourths filled. When Alex lifted the last page another folded sheet fell out. He quickly retrieved it, putting it back in place. Out of his peripheral vision he saw Dallas returning.

"Lillian, I think you should take another look through these. You may still want to throw out some of it," Dallas said, getting down on her knees to straighten the stack of Nicholas's things she'd put together.

Alex quickly thumbed through the pages, only catching a word or phrase here and there. His initial reaction was to return it to her. Then he rejected the idea. For one thing, announcing that he had found it in one of the boxes belonging to Nick would require an explanation. Lillian would want to know how it got to be there. Since Lillian knew nothing of what had happened, there was no point in bringing it to light now. Dallas had had her reasons for remaining silent, and so had he. Instead, Alex decided to remain silent about the notebook.

Covertly, Alex slid the notebook into the inside

pocket of his leather jacket, which was lying over the back of the sofa, just behind him. He stood up.

"I'm going to start taking some of this garbage upstairs."

"I'll help," Dallas offered, getting up from the floor.

Alex was going to say that he could manage, and then he changed his mind. He picked up the two heavier garbage bags and started up to the kitchen. Dallas followed behind, maneuvering three corrugated boxes up the narrow passage. She waited while Alex opened the kitchen door and stepped through with the bags to put them among the other outgoing trash in the bins along the side of the house. Dallas stepped outside into the cool night air and stacked her boxes. Suddenly she and Alex were facing each other. She couldn't see his expression, but she knew that he was watching her. The silence was okay. It didn't make her feel defensive the way she used to when someone stared at her too long. She took a deep breath. She had to say something.

"I appreciate . . . you know . . . that you didn't say anything to Lillian about . . ."

He shifted restlessly, hitching up his shoulders so that he could stuff his hands into the front pockets of his jeans. "I couldn't do that to you. I *wouldn't* do it to Lillian. She doesn't need to know that Nick was . . . anyway, I promised you a long time ago."

"And you're a man of your word?" Dallas found herself teasing in a quiet, curious tone.

"All I have is my word. I'm short in other areas."

It seemed an odd thing to say. In any case, she didn't agree with him. It felt so surreal to be standing there talking to Alex Marco like this.

He chuckled. "We're not really strangers. I feel like . . . we should hug each other or something. You know. Great to see you again, and all that."

But he made no move to do so, and Dallas did nothing to encourage him. It would have been too awkward.

"How did you feel when you heard about Nick?" Alex asked.

He stepped closer to her and the light from the kitchen window highlighted half of his face. Dallas shrugged.

"I was sorry for Lillian, of course. But . . . I really didn't feel anything else for myself. I just remembered what he'd tried to do to me."

"Men are pigs," Alex said forthrightly.

The statement was so outrageous that Dallas couldn't help but laugh, albeit a little uncomfortably. "Are you speaking for yourself, too?"

But Alex apparently didn't find it amusing. He didn't respond for a long moment. "You tell me," he drawled.

Then it hit her. Her amusement vanished as well. This had nothing to do with Nicholas, but just her and Alex. Dallas suddenly felt stripped bare, as open and exposed as it was possible to be before another human being. Yet Dallas knew that Alex wasn't making light of the past or of the memories. She had been right about him. He did remember everything.

"Do you know what I'm talking about?"

Now it was her turn to nod. Of course she did. More than the circumstance that had first brought them together, there had been another time a year afterward that had had an even more profound effect on her.

"Valerie never mentioned what happened," Alex said.

The statement confirmed that they'd been seeing each other, and talking about her. Dallas felt like her life had been invaded and it made her wary. "I . . . never told Val. I never mentioned it to anyone."

Alex pursed his lips thoughtfully and stared down at his boots. The light made his hair look like silver. "She and I have been out together a few times."

"You don't have to tell me that," she said quietly.

He shifted restlessly. "I know, but . . . I wanted you to know."

"Why?"

He shrugged. "I feel like, I always want to be honest with you. We're friends, and I won't do anything to hurt you."

Dallas was surprised by his confession. And ambivalent. It was none of her business who he or Valerie dated, but there *was* the question of how she felt about it. Nothing more was said on the subject. She and Alex continued to stand together in the dark.

The suburban quiet was very different from the constant noise and underlying buzz of the city that she had grown used to. She liked the vitality and bustle of Manhattan better. It was easier to be anonymous in the city, blend in.

"What are you thinking?"

She sighed. She had a suspicion that Alex knew what she was thinking. But she wanted to stay away from . . . the other thing. "I feel sorry for Lillian."

"Why?"

"I guess because . . . I think she deserved a better son than Nicholas," Dallas hesitated. "She loved him so much. I bet he could have had anything he wanted from her and Vin, but he was so . . . so . . ."

"Yeah, I know." Alex slowly nodded. "It didn't work out the way they'd hoped at all."

Another strange thing to say, Dallas thought. She hugged herself against the chill. "I hope she's going to be all right . . ."

"She will. What about you?"

She stared at him, trying to see his expression. "What do you mean?"

"Valerie said your life is very complicated."

Dallas felt annoyed. "She shouldn't have said that to you."

"Is it true?"

"Isn't everyone's life confusing? Isn't yours?" she countered. "I don't know anything about you, either."

He chortled, reaching for the door. "You know more than you think you do."

Alex said it with such certainty that Dallas looked quizzically at him.

Alex pulled the door open again, and held it while Dallas preceded him back into the house.

"You care a lot about Lillian, don't you?"

Dallas stepped back into the kitchen. The bright overhead light made her squint after the absolute darkness of outdoors. "Yes, I do. Lillian is like . . . a surrogate mother to me. She's special."

"Yeah, she is special," Alex agreed reflectively. "She's a lot like . . ."

Alex suddenly stopped and turned his head partially in the direction of the open basement door. When Dallas started to ask a question, he held up his hand for her silence, his expression alert and focused. And then she heard it, too. Crying. Soft, but heartbreaking sobbing from the basement. Alex moved quickly and started down the stairs. By the time Dallas responded and followed him, he had already reached Lillian. He was kneeling in front of her, and had gathered her against his chest. Lillian's body shook with her tears.

Alex did nothing more than to support and hold Lillian. Over her head Alex caught sight of Dallas, and stared at her. In an instant of déjà vu she recalled Alex's comforting her. He hadn't held her the way he was holding Lillian, but he'd been there for her. Dallas quietly retraced her steps, leaving the two of them alone.

She stood alone in the kitchen for no more than a minute when she heard footsteps on the path leading to the side of the house. The door opened, and Vincent Marco stepped inside. He carried a small bouquet of flowers. Before she had time to gather her wits, he was shrugging out of a jacket and pulling off a baseball cap and calling out for his wife.

"Lilly? I'm ho . . ."

Vin's eyes widened with surprise when he spotted Dallas standing behind one of the kitchen chairs.

"Dallas. How you doin'?"

"Hi, Mr. Marco," Dallas greeted him a bit awkwardly.

His initial surprise quickly faded and Vin Marco placed the flowers on the counter, his cap and jacket on a chair.

"I told you, you don't have to call me Mr. Marco. Vin is okay. Where's my wife?"

Dallas was trying to detect whether or not Lillian was still crying. She gestured vaguely with her hand in the direction of the basement.

"She's, er . . . downstairs."

Vin nodded. "Oh, yeah. You were helping her with stuff that belonged to Nick. Did you finish?"

He was heading toward the door. She was not unmindful that there might still be some tension between him and Alex. "Yes. I . . . I just put out some garbage. I was on my way down again to see if Lillian wanted me for anything else . . ."

There were footsteps behind her now. Voices and murmuring. Vin also waited, his stocky body poised comfortably. Dallas saw the frown gather between his brows at the sound of another man's voice. Lillian came first into the kitchen. Dallas watched her face carefully, looking to see if there was any evidence of crying. Her eyes were a bit pink, but she merely looked tired. When Lillian spotted her husband, her eyes brightened and she smiled, happy to see him.

"Oh, Vin. You're home already." She turned her cheek to him so that he could briefly kiss her.

He looked over his wife's shoulder. "Who else is here?"

Alex appeared next.

"I asked Alex to come out, too. I had no idea how many boxes I'd find, or how heavy they'd be. I didn't think Dallas and I could move them around."

"Vin . . ." Alex nodded in greeting, appearing with his jacket slung over his shoulder. He entered the kitchen, which was becoming overcrowded. The atmosphere was charged with additional tension now that Vin was home.

"I didn't know he was going to be here," Vin said a bit gruffly, referring to Alex, but not addressing him. "I coulda stayed and helped if you wanted."

"No," Lillian said adamantly. "You needed to get *out* of the house. I needed to stay *in.* Besides, it gave me a chance to visit with Dallas and Alex. I didn't think you'd mind," she said reasonably, patting his arm.

Vin grunted. "Hi," he finally mumbled to Alex. "Thanks for helping Lillian."

"Anytime," Alex responded.

"Yes," Dallas also voiced.

"And it gave Alex and Dallas a chance to meet. How is Larry and Marilyn? How did the work go?"

Vin turned and picked up the flowers. "Okay. They want you to come out. Stay a few days. Here, these are for you."

Lillian was delighted, and accepted them with a smile as if it were the first time her husband had ever brought her flowers. Dallas knew it wasn't. She was charmed by Vin's thoughtfulness.

"I'd better get going. You two probably want to be alone, have dinner and some peace and quiet for the evening," Alex interjected. He reached out and stroked Lillian's shoulder, and she smiled up to him with an assurance that she was fine now.

Dallas also took advantage of the opportunity. "I have to leave, too."

"Alex, maybe you can give Dallas a lift back to the city . . ."

"Oh, no . . . I'm not going back tonight. I'm staying with my family. I can walk the two blocks." She got a purse from where she'd left it, under the kitchen table on the floor, and Lillian got her jacket from a closet next to the basement entrance.

"I'll drop you off. It's on the way," Alex insisted in a voice that brooked no debate. He crossed the kitchen as he put on his coat. He stood a foot or two away from Vin addressing him. "I don't know what else you might need a hand with, but let me know. I can come back out."

Vin turned around. Dallas had always considered Vincent Marco to be a giant of a man. Perhaps because he was stocky and always seemed so aggressive to her. But he was about three inches shorter than Alex, and the difference to Dallas made Vin suddenly seem less intimidating.

Vin cleared his throat. "Yeah. Sure. Look, I appreciate you coming out to help Lilly." He awkwardly offered his hand for Alex to shake. "Dallas, you, too," he said again.

"Good night, darling," Lillian crooned and she reached to hug and kiss Alex. "Thank you for everything."

Dallas noticed that Vin averted his eyes. And then Lillian turned to her with the same words and expression.

After a moment of repeated good-byes, Dallas and Alex left the house. They said nothing as they walked to Alex's car, and he opened the door and held it for her to get in. But she didn't right away. She turned to Alex, sorry that she couldn't see his face.

"Can I ask you a question?" Dallas opened softly.

Alex let the door go and preceded to walk around the front of the car to the driver's side. "Go ahead," he instructed, unlocking his own door.

Dallas hesitated. She hoped she wasn't getting too personal. "What are you to the family? What was your relationship to Nicholas?"

Alex opened his door before he looked at her again. "I don't have any relationship to Nicholas or Lillian . . . Vin is my father."

Chapter Seven

Alex pulled up in front of the house and put the car in neutral. He stared out the windshield onto the dark street. Dallas did the same. Someone's dog barked mournfully from a backyard. A gruff "shut up" quickly silenced the animal. A car turned into a driveway down the block ahead of where Dallas and Alex sat. Getting out of the car, the driver cast a long and curious look at them and finally headed into the house. When the door closed it became very quiet again.

The ride from the Marco house took less than three minutes. Neither she nor Alex said a word to each other the entire time. They exchanged brief glances and grinned, looking away.

"You lost weight," Alex observed awkwardly.

Dallas grimaced. "You're not supposed to tell a woman that. You're supposed to say . . . you've changed, or you look great."

He chuckled. "Yeah. That, too."

"You stopped smoking. And your hair . . ." Her gaze roamed over him. "What happened?"

Alex looked at her. "Life. Does it make me look old?"

"No . . . it's kind of interesting. It looks good on you."

It made him look, oddly, more like Vin.

Vin Marco was Alex's father.

Now Dallas realized why, even when she'd first seen Alex, he'd seemed familiar. But now that she thought of it, now that she'd actually seen Vin and Alex side by side . . . now that Alex had said so himself . . . of course Alex was Vin's son. Another son. The *other* son.

Dallas gazed at his profile. He seemed lost in his own thoughts. He didn't seem in a particular hurry to leave.

Alex waited for the questions to begin. It made him uneasy. Not because he wasn't prepared to tell about himself, but because it also meant talking about his mother. Vincent Marco being his father was more her story than his. And Alex had always been more protective of her than himself.

He caught Dallas's intense gaze upon him. He couldn't see her whole face. Just the places where the shadows created from the streetlamps didn't fall directly on her.

"You probably had guessed," Alex said quietly.

Dallas shook her head slightly. "No, I didn't. Not *that* way. I never would have thought . . . Vin seems to be so in love with Lillian . . . I . . ."

"He is in love with Lillian. I don't think Vin has ever loved a woman as much as he loves her." He looked out the front windshield again and shrugged. "Vin and my mother . . . it wasn't about love. It was a whole lot of other things."

"Oh . . ."

He laughed softly. "You don't really understand. That's okay."

"Look, I don't think it's any of my business. It doesn't matter."

"It doesn't?" he asked cynically.

"No, why should it? Not to me or to anyone else, I bet. I mean, it's not as if it doesn't happen and . . ." She sighed in annoyance. She looked at him squarely. "Why am I trying to make it sound better?"

"I don't know. Why are you?" Alex asked.

Unexpectedly, he put his car into park and turned off the engine. The humming sound of the motor died, and they were left in the small space of the vehicle with the sounds of their own breathing. Alex swiveled in his seat and reached out to touch her shoulder. "Okay, let's forget it. I was just answering your question. I'm not anything to the Marcos."

"But you just said that Vin is your father," Dallas said, confused.

"That's right. He and my mother met and *bang*! That's where the connection ends. He made a shot in the dark, and I was the bull's-eye. Vin didn't know I existed until I was almost fifteen. I knew who he was. I used to think that he'd come to look for me. But he really didn't know. So, I went to him."

In the dark, Dallas could see the tightening in Alex's jaw. The fingers that just touched her shoulder slid away and curled unconsciously into a loose fist. She knew exactly what had happened between Vin and Alex and how Alex must have felt. Her stomach muscles clenched as she had a vision of herself at five, facing a black man with glasses and a mustache, with a black woman beside him, telling her he was her father. It didn't fit. It didn't make sense. But it was true.

"He didn't believe me. He denied it. But Lillian . . . she took one look at me and knew." Alex shifted to a more comfortable position in the seat and sighed deeply. "If Lillian hadn't stood up for me and tried to calm him down, I would have left and never gone back. She was crying and, man . . . I was so scared I was shaking. But I was also mad as hell. Nick was there, too. He just kept yelling and shouting, 'Get outta here. You don't belong here . . . *I'm* his son . . .' "

Dallas stared blindly into the night, the story coming to life before her eyes. A skinny kid with dark hair standing for the first time ever, alone before the formidable angry shock of his own father. And being rejected.

"You were so brave." Dallas shook her head in wonder. "I don't think I could have done that."

"I had to. I had to know."

"But . . . it . . . didn't work out. Did it?" she asked carefully.

Alex shook his head. "He had Lillian. And he had Nicholas. I didn't compute. I didn't fit. Hell . . . I wasn't supposed to happen."

Alex looked at her, touched her shoulder again. "You know, Vin is not a bad guy. He's honest. He works hard. He's good to Lillian. When she fell in love with him and agreed to marry him, I think Vin couldn't believe his luck."

"What do you mean?"

"Lillian once told me her parents didn't much like the idea. They didn't think he was good enough for her. He wasn't one of them, if you know what I mean."

Dallas did. She remembered the photograph. She knew about Lillian's background and family. Her father owned a number of successful neighborhood businesses where she'd lived. She had an older brother who had also done well, who lived in New Jersey.

"Vin getting Lillian to marry him was a big deal. She was the best thing that could have happened to him. Lillian made him feel like more than he thought he was. When I showed up, it was like I blew his cover."

"And Lillian?" Dallas asked.

"Lillian . . ." Alex murmured in consideration. And then he sat there slowly shaking his head, as if he couldn't find the right words to say it all. He raised his left hand and then let it drop to the steering wheel. "She didn't hold it against me or Vin. She tried to bring us all together. She wanted Nick and I to get along. That didn't go over big, but . . ." He sighed deeply. "Lillian probably saved my life. I'd do anything for her. *Anything.* Next to my mother, I love her more than anyone else in the world."

Dallas was deeply moved, but she wasn't surprised at all by Lillian's part in the drama. All she had to do was remember standing outside that fence when she was seven years old, with Lillian urging her to come closer.

"You know what I'm talking about," Alex suddenly said. Dallas turned her attention sharply to him. "Lillian is exactly the same way with you as she is with me. So, what's your story?"

Already Dallas was shaking her head, denying that there was anything remotely as significant as Alex's relationship to Vin and Lillian. Not willing to share her history, and not sure she could explain it to someone who never had to worry about race first.

"I was just a little girl. My family was new on the block . . ."

"I know. The first black family, or something like that. That's what Valerie said."

"Lillian was just very kind to me. I don't know why. But I've always liked her. She's . . . one of my favorite people," Dallas confessed shyly.

Another car came down the street behind them, its headlights shining and growing larger like spotlights. They ignored the slow-moving vehicle until it continued down the street and turned the corner. It was quiet again. He waited for her to continue.

She waited for him to ask. Dallas knew he was going to. She could almost feel the question forming on the tip of his tongue. She felt like her heart was beating faster. She held her breath, waiting.

"Do you remember that time? Not with Nick. That other time?"

Oh, my God . . .

Dallas closed her eyes briefly as her stomach heaved. It was an odd kind of giddiness. She nodded.

"Me, too," he murmured with a nervous chuckle. Dallas remained silent. Alex gently shook her arm. "Hey. You aren't ashamed, are you?"

Again she merely nodded.

"Why? Don't do that."

She templed her hands and fingers, hiding her mouth behind it. "I can't believe I did that. I can't believe I actually had the nerve to call you and . . ."

"Yeah, well . . . I couldn't believe you did it either . . . it's okay," Alex rushed to reassure Dallas. She shifted in the seat and uttered a slight moan. He stroked her arm and squeezed it gently. "I'm not complaining but . . . it was the first time anyone had just asked me to . . ." He made a helpless sound, unable to find the words for how incredible it had been.

"Please . . . I can't talk about this," Dallas said, nearly out of breath.

He took hold of her arm again. "I don't want to upset you, but I have to ask you something. I mean . . . afterward, I nearly went crazy wondering . . ."

"I don't want to . . ."

"Dallas . . ." He said her name with a sudden urgency. "I have to know. Were you all right?"

She stared at him. She hadn't been at first. After they'd made love and she'd gone about her business and Alex had just gone. She'd never found out where to. Dallas thought now, as they sat facing each other discussing one of the most important moments of her life, fifteen years ago, that she had no idea what she would have done had things worked out differently.

Her gaze shifted out the car window. Her hands were locked together in her lap. She could feel the firm grip of his hand, and the absentminded way his thumb rubbed along the material of her coat. The pressure went through to her skin.

"I was two weeks late with my period," she said in barely a whisper. Alex uttered an oath under his breath. She could tell, however, that it wasn't in anger but rather a confirmation of his worst fears. "I can't begin to tell you how scared I was. I didn't know what to do. I couldn't tell anyone. I . . . I thought . . . I thought I was pregnant."

Just saying it evoked in Dallas the total panic she'd

felt several weeks after the evening spent with Alex. She'd cried to Valerie. To Maureen. But she'd never told either of them a thing about him.

Dallas had wanted to have sex. That's all it had been to her at the time. She had hoped that it would one day be romantic and tender, like true love . . . sacred and pure. But the boys she knew only wanted to get into her pants. For them it would have been a conquest. For her, it was the ultimate surrender. The first time had to be with someone she could trust. And the only person she could trust, because he'd never tried to take anything from her, had been Alex Marco.

Dallas had *asked* him to.

"But I wasn't pregnant," she finished. Alex squeezed her arm again. Relief? Understanding?

"Man . . ." he drawled with feeling, rubbing his hand over his short springy hair.

"You worried for no reason," Dallas said.

"You're wrong. It was more than that, Dallas. It was . . . you know . . ."

Slowly, she found herself smiling and she glanced at him in the dark enclosure of the car. "You mean . . . was it good for me?" She laughed. "I can't believe we're really having this conversation."

"Okay. So my ego wants to make sure I wasn't a failure."

After a moment Dallas shrugged. She felt herself hedging. "I . . . I don't know. At the time I didn't know anything. I guess I didn't know what I was supposed to feel. I didn't have anything to compare it to."

Alex sighed. He slid his hand down her arm and closed it around one of hers. "I'm sorry."

"Alex . . . I'm not. I know I wasn't any good"—he curved his lips and shook his head at her judgment—"but I'm not sorry and I don't blame you for anything."

Alex remembered how he'd felt that there was something personal at stake in taking Dallas Oliver to bed. First of all were all the myths that virgins were a great experience because they were so tight. Alex abruptly let go of Dallas's hand and once more ran it over his head. But part of the thrill, he recalled, was talking the girl into believing she was going to enjoy it, and it wasn't going to hurt, and of course that he cared about her.

Alex turned his head to stare at Dallas's profile. Her skin was smooth-looking. And her mouth had a sensuous little pout to it. Her chin small and pointed. He hadn't noticed any of this when she was lying beneath him, panting in fear, her body stiff and inexperienced. Alex really hadn't cared. Dallas had come to him, and he was ready to just get it on, and get off. Wondering whether Dallas had felt anything, if she had enjoyed it, was a concept that had come to him afterward. Years later, once he'd thought about it again. Because by then he knew more about women and had failed once or twice.

Of anything Dallas could have done, she'd chosen to call him. He still didn't understand why. Alex couldn't remember if he'd ever taken the time back then to ask.

Alex looked out the window in the direction of the house. "You still live with your folks?"

Dallas grimaced. "No. I'm only staying for the night. I live in Manhattan. And you?"

"I live in Brooklyn."

"Still?" she questioned.

Alex nodded. "I've lived other places."

She wanted to ask him about his family. His mother. But Dallas didn't know how to begin the conversation. Their knowledge of one another didn't yet allow for that kind of intimacy.

Another approaching car slowed and pulled up almost directly behind them. Dallas looked over her shoulder and thought she recognized the car out the back window. It belonged to Eleanor. The driver was Dean. He glanced in their direction several times and, after alighting from the car with several packages in his hands, walked to peer into the passenger side window.

"Do you know him?" Alex asked.

Dallas quickly detected the alertness with which he was assessing the man standing outside the car.

"He's my brother."

She searched for a means to open the window. Alex faced forward and started the engine again and then pressed the power window buttons. Dallas smiled up at Dean, who, having identified his sister, craned his head to get a good look at the driver of the car she sat in.

"Dilly-Dally . . ."

"Hi. Where are you just coming from?"

"The mall. I wanted to pick up a few things."

Alex got out of the car. Dean stood back so that Dallas could do the same. The three of them converged on the sidewalk. Dallas could see the close attention her brother was focusing on Alex, taking his measure. She introduced them.

"This is Alex Marco. Alex, this is my brother, Dean."

The two men shook hands. Dean was slightly taller than Alex, but he also appeared very slender and much younger standing next to him.

"Alex Marco . . ." Dean repeated, his attention still drawn to him.

"Nice to meet you," Alex said clearly. His own thorough scrutiny indicated his surprise as well.

Dallas knew what he was thinking.

"You related to that Marco family a few blocks down the street?" Dean asked.

Alex felt Dallas looking at him, wondering how he was going to answer. He put his hands in the pockets of his jeans. His arms pinned his leather jacket open. The action made Alex very aware of the notebook in the inside pocket. The one he'd found among Nicholas's things that belonged to her.

"Sort of."

"Alex gave me a ride from Lillian's." Dallas turned to her brother. He was appraising her with something approaching skepticism. "I haven't seen him since I was a teenager."

"I don't remember him. How come you never mentioned him before?" Dean asked outright.

"I never lived around here. I just come to visit now and then."

"Oh. You a cousin?" Dean asked.

Alex grinned cryptically. "Once or twice removed," he murmured.

Dean nodded thoughtfully. "Well . . . I'm heading in. Mom's holding dinner for me." Dean pointed a finger in their direction and turned toward the house. "You coming in?" he asked his sister.

"In a minute."

Dallas and Alex faced each other after Dean had closed the door behind himself.

"I didn't know you had a brother," he said.

"Once or twice removed," she repeated.

Alex nodded, as if he understood. "You'd better go in, too."

It seemed a little abrupt to have to wish him good night now. Suddenly she didn't know what to say. It was nice to see you again? Thanks for worrying about me? Thanks for not asking about Dean?

"Thanks for the lift."

He waved briefly and felt the weight of the notebook against his chest. "So you're a writer. What do you write?" He opened the driver side door, preparing to get in.

"Articles. Essays. Sometimes a short story. I write about people's behavior and beliefs, trends. How sometimes they don't make any sense. I'm paid to voice my opinion."

"Oh, yeah? Sounds deep," he said, chuckling. "I'd like to read your opinion about what love is."

He said it so offhandedly that she knew he was

teasing her. "Couldn't you pick something easier? What about you?"

"You mean, what do I think about love?" He grinned, and Dallas laughed at his quick comeback. "I don't do anything important," Alex said smoothly. "I collect garbage. Look for lost things."

The answer so surprised her that Dallas stared at him, waiting for the punch line.

"I'm kidding," Alex said, seeing her blank expression. "I do marine salvaging. I'll call you sometime," he announced cavalierly. "Maybe we'll get together . . ."

Salvaging . . . "Have a safe trip home."

"Right."

Dallas stood and watched his car pull away down the street. After a moment she could only make out the red globes of the taillights. Then he signaled to make a left-hand turn. And then he was gone.

Alex reached inside his open jacket and pulled out the notebook. *She's a writer,* he said to himself, as if that explained something. He just held it, feeling the thickness of it and trying to decide if he'd been wrong in taking it. *Private* . . . DO NOT READ was pretty specific. Alex had a sense that if he read the thoughts of Dallas Oliver written when she was just a kid, he wouldn't find anything that could be very interesting. Probably embarrassing. He glanced at the notebook in his hand. Mistake. He should definitely not have taken it. He dropped the book on the passenger seat and gave his attention back to the road.

He was going in the wrong direction.

Annoyed with himself for the distraction, Alex checked the street signs to get oriented again, and doubled back about a quarter of a mile. Soon he was heading northeast on the Seaford-Oyster Bay Parkway. He glanced at the car clock. He was going to be late. But there was nothing he would have done differently. He would have come out to help Lillian no matter what. Dallas being there was, now that he thought about it and the shock had worn off, a bonus. It had come back to him, several times since seeing her at Nick's funeral, little details and information about that first time they'd met. And the second. But Dallas was a whole different person now. Fifteen years ago she had been so damned young. Well, so was he . . . but he had known a lot more about *everything* than she did. Not that he'd been any smarter.

There was a bright prettiness to her face. When she moved and when she talked, Alex sensed a woman who was quick, smart, and strong. Not as afraid as she used to be. Dallas Oliver had come into her own, but there remained a certain reserve about her. Careful around people. He'd seen it earlier with Vin. With himself.

Fifteen minutes later, Alex was still considering the change in her. He frowned as he turned off the main boulevard onto a residential street. He suddenly realized that he really didn't know anything about her. She'd grown up a few blocks from Lillian and Vin. The one thing he really couldn't get a handle on was the fact that Dallas didn't look anything like her brother, Dean. Not even close.

Alex pulled in to the curb and parked his car again in front of another house. He sat for a moment, only beginning to wonder what it must have been like for her growing up where she wasn't welcomed. He remembered all that Nicholas had said about her. But all he had to do was think of his own mother, Alex realized, and how he was raised. He'd grown up poor, had been scorned and harassed by kids and adults who treated him as if he were worthless. Alex looked at Dallas's book again, picked it up, and frowned at the cover. My Journal . . . Private . . . DO NOT READ . . .

He remembered once thinking, if he could find his real father, prove to the other kids in his neighborhood that he had one, they'd stop calling his mother names. It had gotten to a point where Alex didn't care what they called him. What was said to him didn't make it true. But he'd wanted a father. He wanted someone there who came in the door at night, tall and steady with a deep voice and big hands. Who was strong and knew how to do things. Who could take him places, and sit at the dinner table with him and his mother and grandmother. Who could stand around the front of the building talking to the other fathers, and he could look and see him there and point him out as *his* father. The Old Man. Dad.

He had a feeling that there was a strong connection between himself and Dallas Oliver. Especially because of the relationship Dallas had with Lillian. Alex frowned as he stared out his car window. He felt a caution pull him up short. He had to be careful. He was already carrying enough of his own baggage. There was already enough in his life that was a mess.

Alex turned off the engine and put the notebook inside his glove compartment. He got out of the car and approached the door. Before he had arrived at the top step, it opened. The woman holding the door looked both a little annoyed and half amused.

"I was beginning to wonder if you were going to stand me up." She chuckled wryly.

He smiled as he noticed how great Valerie looked. "I bet no one's *ever* stood you up."

"Not more than once, and they don't get a second chance. Did you run into traffic? Saturdays out here can be god-awful, especially near the malls."

Alex stepped into the house and turned to face Valerie as she closed the door. "No, it wasn't traffic. I was with Lillian this afternoon, helping her with Nick's things."

Valerie's smile vanished. She nodded sadly and walked into the living room. Alex followed her.

"I bet that wasn't a lot of fun," she murmured.

Alex shrugged. "It had to be done."

"So . . . did you find anything interesting?" Valerie asked.

Alex hesitated. He didn't know why yet, but he decided not to mention Dallas's presence. "Nothing you need to know about."

Valerie became instantly curious and came to stand directly in front of Alex, looking up into his face. "Tell me."

"Nick liked to read pornographic magazines."

She grimaced and turned away. "You're right. I guess I shouldn't be surprised."

Alex glanced around. "Where's Megan? You get a baby-sitter for the night?"

"She's at my mother's until tomorrow. She was hoping to see you before I drove her over there. She likes you, Alex. I'm so glad," Valerie said.

"I like Megan, too. You're lucky. She's a nice little girl. Everything seems to have worked out."

Valerie looked disconcerted. "I don't know. She's starting to ask questions, Alex."

"About who her father is."

She nodded. "Yes."

Alex turned away, thinking about it. He walked about the small room until he was once again standing in front of Valerie. "I don't know what to say to you, Val. Maybe you should just tell her."

Valerie cringed and shook her head. "That's what Dallas said. I can't. Megan might get really mad at me. She'll say, if I knew all along where her father was, why didn't I say anything."

"Tell her he didn't know about her." Alex pursed his lips and stared down at the toes of his boots. "It happens all the time. One-night stands. Close encounters . . ." He glanced at her sideways. "Does Dallas know about you and . . ."

Valerie shook her head vigorously. "No, I never told her."

"I thought she's your best friend."

"She is, but . . ." Valerie hedged. "I just never did. My mother still doesn't know."

"That was a mistake."

"Yeah. I'm good at that," she said sarcastically. "Megan says she's not going to get married or have children until she's old. Like twenty-five."

"Smart." Alex grinned.

Valerie chortled. "Not at all like me, which is probably a good thing. I don't want her to make the same mistakes I did."

"Maybe they weren't all mistakes," Alex said. "You'll always have her."

"It's not like I'm ashamed or anything. But I should have done things differently. I should have said something at the time. You know?"

"Yeah, I do."

Valerie was standing in front of a large mirror that hung over the sofa. She automatically checked her reflection, fingering her hair and straightening the necklace she wore.

Alex glanced around the quiet living room. "Megan could have come with us," he murmured. "It would have been okay with me."

Valerie shook her head. "It wouldn't have been okay with me. You and I couldn't really be alone, or talk openly. She really wanted to spend the weekend with Dallas, but she already had plans."

Alex wondered why Dallas hadn't been specific about her plans to be with Lillian. On the other hand, he didn't see the need to mention that, coincidentally, he and Dallas had spent the afternoon together.

Valerie turned from the mirror. "Do you want a drink before we leave?"

"I don't drink," Alex said absently.

Valerie, in the process of heading for her purse, glanced over her shoulder at him. "What do you mean you don't drink?"

"Soda's fine. Beer. No alcohol."

Valerie's expression showed genuine surprise. "Really? You're . . . you're not an . . . alcoholic, are you?"

"No." He moved restlessly around the living room

again. The space was beginning to feel cramped. "Alcohol affects my judgment. I don't like the feeling."

"Oh, a control freak," Valerie muttered dismissively.

"Only about myself."

She laughed this time. She came close again and smiled seductively into Alex's face. "I like that. A man who's sure about himself . . . *and* who knows what he's doing."

Alex looked down into Valerie's face. Her makeup only enhanced a natural beauty that he would bet had been apparent since she could crawl. She was in the prime of her looks and allure. She was the kind of a woman who drew men so effortlessly that he was surprised that she had never married or moved away from Long Island.

Valerie was looking back at him, waiting. He felt compelled to lean down and brush a light kiss across her mouth. She was willing, and responded. Valerie lifted her hands and pressed them to Alex's chest, leaning into him. He was glad that he'd removed the notebook. She would have wanted to know what he was carrying. Was it something for her?

Alex took her hands and pulled them down to her side. The action brought them that much closer, and Valerie smiled as she tilted her head to let him kiss her again. He did, because she was expecting it and because he wanted to. Alex had known from the moment he'd seen her at the funeral home that it would come to this. But he had to switch emotional gears. Part of him was still with Dallas, as they'd been most of the afternoon. But mostly Alex was thinking about sitting with her in his car, talking about intimate things between them. He looked at Valerie's mouth. She was extending the invitation.

Alex slipped his arms around her waist and she rested against him, her breasts like soft cushions. Finally, he felt the heat buildup, the excitement of anticipation. He kissed her and took his time to let his tongue and lips cover territory. It was every bit as heady as he'd thought it would be. And Valerie did not disappoint him. But there was another sensation that interjected into the moment, and interfered with the pleasure. A sense of being watched. It was ridiculous. He and Valerie were alone in her house. But Alex couldn't shake the feeling.

She ran her hands down his chest and stomach, boldly to his thighs searching out the evidence of her effect on him. He was relieved when Valerie stepped back with a dreamy smile on her mouth.

"Ummmmm. To be continued. Let's go. We're going to be late for dinner."

"Are you sure you want to go?" he asked, looking down into the top of a black latex bodysuit she wore that showed enough cleavage to make promises he knew Valerie was capable of keeping.

"I spent a lot of time getting dressed to look fabulous, Alex. I want to see you drool a little and appreciate it."

Alex raised a brow as she spun out of his arms and took a jacket from the hall closet. "I never drool."

"Oh, really?" Valerie said with a narrowed gaze. Her smile was wicked and playful. "Let's see if you feel the same way in the morning."

"What do you want me to do with the rest of this?" Dallas asked, holding out the serving platter that held what remained of a vegetable dish from dinner.

Eleanor Oliver gave a cursory glance over her shoulder before continuing her task of wrapping aluminum foil around a small mound of sliced pork loin.

"There's not much left. Just throw it out. You know your father and Dean hate leftover vegetables. You can take it home with you if you want," she added.

"No, thanks," Dallas murmured.

"Take the potatoes, then. There's plenty of that. I hate to see good food go to waste."

"Maybe you shouldn't cook so much," Dallas suggested.

"Well, I was raised to put plenty of food on the table for the family. You know how Dean loves my au gratin," Eleanor boasted. "Lord, that boy can put food away."

"I love your potato salad," Dallas said, scraping the rest of the succotash into the garbage. "I think you make the best salad in the world."

"Thank you, dear," Eleanor murmured. The wrapped meat was put in the refrigerator. "Hayden used to say the same thing. He *really* enjoyed my cooking."

Dallas became alert at the reference to her ex-husband. She pretended she hadn't heard and didn't respond. Her stepmother still tended to bring up Hayden's name with a kind of lingering regret. As if it was such a shame and, by inference, such a mistake that he was no longer her son-in-law. Hayden was the son of one of her good friends. The heir apparent of educated and professional parents, and the product of black middle-class upward mobility. Hayden was the recipient of everything his parents had benefited from as a result of the civil rights movement of the sixties and seventies, Affirmative Action of the eighties, the opportunities and networking of the nineties. He had everything, and accepted everything as his due.

Eleanor chuckled softly to herself. "He used to say if his mother cooked as good as I did he might never have left home. Ooooh . . . he was really a sweetheart."

Again, Dallas said nothing. She had yet to confide in her parents the nature of her marital relationship to Hayden. She had yet to express her opinion that Hayden had never really left home, even after they'd married. Dallas knew she certainly couldn't admit to Hayden's comparison that she was not like his mother . . . or other black women that he knew. That alone had been enough to reduce her to a sense of inadequacy.

"I don't want the potatoes either. I'll just put them in a container," Dallas said quietly.

"That's fine," Eleanor sighed.

What was it Hayden used to say when he thought she'd disappointed him? *My mother would never do it that way* . . . or *I don't know any black woman who would say that* . . . Hayden had found every one of her buttons and pushed them. She'd never understood why he felt he had to.

Dallas fumbled the plastic containers she pulled from a cupboard and several fell out and to the floor with a clatter. "Sorry," she said when Eleanor turned to see what she was up to.

Dallas kept her head lowered. There was the sensation of pain in her abdomen. There was the memory of the pressure, of fiberglass and metal forced against her and into her, pinning her body in a cruel twisted position. Hayden moaning next to her, bloodied and semiconscious. *Jesus . . . sweet Jesus.* She took a deep breath, remembering the details. Remembering the senseless argument between her and Hayden in their car . . . at sixty miles per hour. A moment's distraction and they'd plowed into the back of another car. Remembering the hospital visits from both families after the car accident where everyone was careful not to blame her, but showing it. Hayden had been badly hurt. He'd been comatose for three days. But *she* had lost a baby. He went home from the hospital to eventually heal. She left the hospital empty.

"Do you ever hear from him?"

Dallas sighed. "I don't want to have anything to do with him. You think he's so wonderful, but we divorced for a reason, you know. I had reasons."

"Marriage requires a lot of work," Eleanor said in that manner of careful enunciation she had that was imperial and unforgiving. "*And* sacrifice. *And* compromise."

"Yes, but it shouldn't mean that anyone has to stay in a hopeless situation."

"You just didn't know how to handle the man," Eleanor scoffed.

"I guess not," Dallas conceded easily, unwilling to get into a battle with her stepmother.

"You have to make a black man feel like he's a *man.* Like he knows it all and you depend on him. You got to flatter him sometimes, but not spoil him."

Dallas nodded. "And what about what he does for me?"

Eleanor stood leaning against the counter, her hand poised on her hip. She got people to listen and make them believe that her truth was better. She could cut you cold and make you regret ever having crossed her, blanketing your spirits with righteousness. Or she could become surprisingly generous with compliments and kisses, offering just enough, Dallas knew, to make her feel hopeful that she was wanted.

Dallas remembered when she thought she would have done anything to have Eleanor bless her with a smile even half as bright as that she bestowed on Dean, who was really her child. And she remembered when she finally gave up all of that, realizing that trying to get someone to love you was too hard.

"You are not making any sense, Dallas," Eleanor admonished. "How could it be hopeless? Hayden ran his own business. He was making good money, and you didn't want for anything. You didn't even have to work if you didn't want to. What else did you expect? Any other black woman would thank her lucky stars. Let me stop . . ." Eleanor finished.

"Any *smart* black woman would get out when the situation got bad. That's what I did."

"All right, Dallas," Eleanor sighed wearily. "I'm not going to fight with you about this. But I think you made a big mistake. And you know I'm hardly ever wrong."

Eleanor was pragmatic, and saw things for what they were. Life was very simple for her and the choices clear. But what about love? Dallas wondered. What about respect?

"I expected to be treated at least as well as Hayden treated his mother, since he wanted me to live up to her standards." Dallas felt the need to continue. "I wish he could have just accepted me without wanting to make me over in her image. I thought he knew what he was getting when he married me."

Eleanor looked impatient. "All this talk about acceptance and treatment and standards. You just didn't learn how to *manage* your man. That's what it's all about."

Dallas looked incredulous. "You believe letting someone always get their way is compromising?"

"You got to make him *think* he's getting his way."

"That's giving him permission to throw tantrums, if you ask me."

"I don't have to ask you," Eleanor said dryly. "*You're* the one that doesn't have a husband."

The barb stung. She'd wanted it to work. Desperately. Maybe that had been the trouble. She wanted Hayden's love too much. Dallas finished stacking the dishwasher and poured in detergent before closing the door. "Maybe I'm better off without one."

"Better off without what?"

Dallas turned at her father's question as he sauntered into the kitchen, carrying his empty dessert plate and half-finished coffee. His unexpected appearance caught her off guard, and for a split second she saw not her father but an aging man who seemed very tired. Dallas was not used to seeing him so distracted and slow.

"A man," Eleanor said.

"I didn't say a man. I said a husband," Dallas corrected. She took the dishes from her father and he smiled absently.

"Thanks. If there's more coffee I'll have another cup. Then I'm going to bed."

"Lyle, maybe you shouldn't. All that caffeine before going to bed . . ."

He accepted a half-filled cup from Dallas with a brief nod of thanks. "I've been sleeping like the dead lately. I don't think I have to worry about the caffeine."

"How's everything going?" Dallas questioned carefully.

"Well . . ." He sat at the kitchen table. "I'm sure glad I was able to hire a part-time manager at the shop. That and my classes are wearing me out."

"I'm sure Dean would have helped you if you'd asked him," Eleanor said.

"I didn't ask Dean because I know I'd get excuses from him," Lyle Oliver countered.

"Why don't you sell the bookshop?" Dallas asked, standing next to her father.

He peered over the top of his glasses at her. "Ask Ellie."

"You don't have to ask me anything," Eleanor said tartly. "The bookstore is making money. It's in a perfect location, and we have loyal customers. It'll be much easier to run when we retire."

"If I live that long."

"Daddy . . ."

"Ellie's right. It's a good business, and it brings in good money."

Eleanor nodded. "We'll have that and our pension, *and* Social Security."

"Great. You'll both be rich but dead," Dallas said.

"Well then, you and Dean will split everything," he murmured.

"But don't bury us yet," Eleanor quipped. "I plan on being around a long time to spend my money."

One of the qualities that most annoyed Dallas about her father was his complacency. His giving in to Eleanor. Hayden came to mind, and his domineering mother.

Dallas didn't want to be like that. She couldn't love

a man like that, not for long. She'd wanted to be Hayden's wife, his lover and friend. She hadn't wanted to be his mother. He already had one.

"What's going on in here?" Dean said, joining the rest of the family.

"We have that whole family room out there, and you all pile up in my kitchen," Eleanor complained, squeezing past Dallas to put away the plastic wrap and aluminum foil.

"We're talking about you behind your back," Dallas teased her brother.

He actually looked uncomfortable but hid it in a snickering chuckle. Dean grabbed Dallas by the hand and with a tug turned her around and pulled her playfully into a choke hold. He growled in her ear. "Tellin' all my business?"

"What's going on? What are you talking about?" Eleanor asked.

"Nothing," Dallas replied, trying to wiggle out from beneath Dean's arms. He started to tickle her and she giggled. Then he brushed his hand vigorously through her short curly hair, knowing it would annoy her. Like Burke. "Don't do that. You're messing up my hair."

Eleanor grimaced. "Dean is hardly messing up your hair. All you have to do is run your fingers through it. So what business are you talking about?"

Dean released Dallas and stepped out of the way of her attempts to punch him in the arm. "Nothing . . ."

"Must be that new girl he's seeing," Eleanor directed to her husband.

"She's a woman, not a girl," Dean corrected smoothly.

Lyle Oliver got quietly up from the table, poured out the rest of his coffee, and put the cup on the counter.

Dallas stole a glance at her brother, sensing his restlessness. He'd made mention to her of someone new. What was it he'd said?

"I called you last week, and some girl answered your phone," Eleanor said.

"Ma . . ." Dean sighed.

Dallas shook her head. For all of her brother's confidence, for all his mouth and machismo and attitude, only with his mother did Dean become differential and uncertain.

Smart black men. Stronger black women . . .

"I'm going to bed," Dallas's father announced.

"I'm not being nosy," Eleanor placated her son.

But both Dallas and Dean exchanged glances that said otherwise.

"But I have *not* been happy with some of the girls you've been dating. I remember the one who was a so-called model . . ."

"Carrie . . ." Dallas supplied, much to her brother's annoyance.

"That's right. She was cute, with her little narrow self," Eleanor characterized. "But she didn't have two sentences she could put back to back that made a paragraph, let alone a complete thought."

"I don't think Dean was interested in her thoughts," Dallas said, grinning at him.

"Well, just as long as he doesn't bring me any illegitimate grandchildren to raise . . . or some white girl."

"Good night," Lyle Oliver said as he quietly walked from the room.

"Good night," came back the chorus of replies.

For a second Dallas focused on her father's departing form. She'd wanted to say more to him, bring him into the bantering discussion of his son's love life. But it was too late. Now she was distracted with Dean's response to his mother's bold and impertinent harping.

"What have you got against white girls?" Dean asked.

"They're not black," Dallas filled in, but doubted that either had heard her.

"Not a thing," Eleanor said with a shrug. "But not with *my* son."

Dallas and her brother had been listening to this indoctrination from Eleanor all of their lives. Only as she'd gotten older and knew more about Eleanor's background and family had Dallas understood. Her stepmother had been raised in the South, with its history of segregation and miscegenation and racism, where there were strict boundaries. Black is black, and white is white, and never the twain should meet.

That's how Dallas knew that she was in on a pass. She'd always believed that Eleanor had treated her as if she were tainted. Certainly not white, but not exactly black. It might not be her fault that she had a white mother, but now she had to do something about it. Prove herself. Pick a side. Buy black.

"Hey, why are you on my case?" Dean asked his mother. "I'm not the one you should be worrying about."

"*Now* what are you talking about?" Eleanor asked suspiciously.

Suddenly Dallas saw it coming. She could feel the shift as Dean searched for a way out from under his mother's relentless probing. Dean nodded in her direction, and Dallas frowned, not having a clue where her brother was headed.

"Ask Dallas. She was the one sitting out in front of the house with a white guy."

Dallas didn't even bother getting annoyed. It was a juvenile ploy and so typical of the way she and Dean would dig at each other. Eleanor looked sharply at her, however, a look that Dallas had seen often enough growing up. It had always made her feel as if she was about to do something reprehensible that was going to prove to her stepmother that she'd been right all along about her.

"Who?" Eleanor asked.

Dallas realized she didn't have a ready answer. To say the name Alex Marco would immediately evoke all the uncertainty and horror they'd all first attached to the family when they'd first moved into the neighborhood. She couldn't think how to sum up the brief, unusual relationship she had with Alex Marco. What was it, really?

Who was he?

Dallas finally shrugged. "He's a friend."

Chapter Eight

The house was absolutely silent as Dallas lay in bed. She was thinking about Dean's baiting of her in the kitchen with Eleanor, then about sitting with Alex in his car . . . and talking about the time they'd made love. Both of the evening's encounters were oddly linked. Alex was the common denominator.

Dallas shifted in bed until she was flat on her back. She hesitated and then slowly ran her hands down her body, from the tops of her breasts to the flat plane of her rib cage and belly. To her navel and groin and thighs. Her inventory was not an attempt at self-stimulation. She was trying to figure out what men really responded to when they touched her, saw her naked. When a man desired to penetrate the soft center into her body, pump and grind until release and satisfaction were achieved, what had she achieved in return? When it was over they took their whispered words of seduction and left. Not just her body. But *her*.

Dallas remembered every single man she'd ever been to bed with. It was easy. There hadn't been that many. They could all be accounted for on one hand. She remembered the first time she'd ever had a climax. That much described, praised, and mystified sensation of the flesh that was supposed to make the effort all worthwhile. It had been, but it had not touched her heart or soul.

He was a musician she'd met. A cool and worldly clarinet player who blew jazz. Dallas recalled that she was supposed to interview him and his band at their club appearance in an East Village joint for a small weekly she worked on as an undergrad intern. He'd teased her with his sophistication, seduced her with his music. The foreplay between them had gone on for several weeks before they ever even touched. Dallas thought she was falling in love with him. But the physical euphoria that had brought her to the edge of madness and toppled her into gasping breaths and pulsing nerves had been less his skill and expertise than it was her need for affirmation and affection.

It had been great sex.

But it had been a one-night stand.

So had the first time she'd made love. She had wanted to lose her virginity. At sixteen being a virgin had become a burden. The boys in school were after her, not because they were infatuated, but because they wanted to be the first.

Valerie had lost hers at thirteen. *Thirteen!* Dallas remembered how Valerie had giggled, proud of herself. It had been with one of her brother's friends, a boy of seventeen. But what had amazed Dallas was not that her best friend had already done it, but that she had apparently really liked it. With Maureen it had been much different. Not exactly rape, Maureen had decided years late, but definite coercion. She'd been compromised by a visiting cousin when she was nine. Someone she'd always liked. Too young to know that what was happening was wrong, she'd never said anything. But neither had she been left particularly traumatized.

Dallas thought about seeing Alex Marco again, about being with him earlier for most of the day, and sitting talking in his car. Feeling, oddly enough, that same protectiveness with him she'd first experienced in the Marco basement when she was fifteen. But bringing up the delicate but bold subject of her virginity now kept her awake. The loss of it. No . . . the surrender of it to Alex Marco. Because she'd asked him to.

Dallas recalled that it was fear that had sent her to him. Fear of failure at the fumbling hands of one of her classmates, who would then naturally need to shoot his mouth off about his success, and of her incompetence as a lay.

Actually, it was Brett Percell who'd helped Dallas to make the decision. She thought they were going together. He'd started to sit with her at lunch, to ask her questions. He walked her almost all the way home from school one day rather than take the bus. When they held hands, she was aware that their entwined fingers reminded her of a zebra. She thought Brett really liked her, and maybe he really did. He'd taken his time and told her she was fine . . . he was used to dating girls with darker skin, but he liked her anyway.

She liked him because he was funny and cute. He was popular and stayed out of trouble. She'd felt nothing when he'd kissed her and even less when Brett had tried to touch her. Which is probably why, when the opportunity was there to go all the way, Dallas knew she didn't want to. Not with him. And then he had said something that had cleared up the mystery of his sudden interest in her. He had promised that if she'd let him do it to her, he'd take her to the Westbury Music fair to see . . . well, she couldn't remember who. It was then that Dallas had decided that if the only thing she had of any value was the place between her legs, then at least it should go to someone who had never tried to use her, or wanted anything from her.

She'd searched everywhere for the scrap of paper with the phone number on it. For more than a week she leafed through notebook pages, dug into the pockets of sweaters and jackets, emptied out totes and bags and wallets, and then gave up. Finding it by accident as it slipped out quietly and slowly, like a leaf falling from a tree, from between the pages of a novel she'd never finished reading. By then Dallas was having second thoughts. Until Valerie and a group of their friends had decided on an evening out together, and she had stayed home rather than go along stag, not attached to anyone. Not having anyone to hold hands with. Not wanting to be the only token in a group that never accepted her as being quite the same as they were anyway. *Not* when it came to dating. *Not* when it came to pairing off.

Dallas dialed the number the next day. A woman answered the phone. A woman with an aged voice.

"Hello?"

Dallas hadn't expected a woman to answer. She struggled for her voice.

"Hello? Who is it?"

"I . . . I . . . is . . . Alex there?"

"Alex?" the woman repeated in the absentminded squeakiness of the elderly, as if the name meant nothing to her.

"Yes. Alex Marco. He gave me this number."

"Oh, Alex . . . He's my grandson. No, he's not here no more."

"Oh," Dallas murmured, feeling a contradictory rush of relief and disappointment.

"He's got his own place. You want the number?"

Dallas blinked. This was not a dead end. Did she want the number? "Yes. Yes, thank you."

"All right, wait a minute . . . wait a minute . . ."

Dallas listened as the receiver was put down, and a rustling of noise came through the line as the woman searched around her for whatever source contained the number. There was coughing and a grunt of movement.

"Wait a minute . . ." the woman said again. "Here it is . . ."

Dallas wrote down the number that was recited, thanked the woman, and hung up. She felt a surge of victory, of accomplishment. Until she realized she hadn't gotten anywhere, yet. She still had not reached

Alex. She had yet to ask for his help. Dallas stood across the street from the high school, digging her fingers through the heavy load of coins in her pocket, which she'd collected to use in the pay phone. If she'd used the one at home, for sure Eleanor would have discovered the phone numbers on the bill and questioned her or Dean about long-distance calls into the city.

Dallas hesitated, staring off across the way at her classmates gathered casually around the grounds of the school before the start of the first period class. They engaged in what had always been to her the confusing rituals of mating, dating, and fitting in. She gnawed on her lip, trying to think if there was even one boy whom she liked well enough to encourage.

Dallas sighed and turned back to the phone. Her heart pounding, she dialed the second number. And then hung up before the phone began to ring. She waited a few minutes and then tried again. She had no time to change her mind this time. The phone was picked up on the first ring, and a brusque male voice answered impatiently.

"Yeah . . ."

"H-hi. I'd like to . . . to speak to Alex Marco, please."

"Yeah, that's me. Look, I'm running late for work. Who is this?"

"It's . . . Dallas Oliver," she whispered. Only as she said her name did it occur to Dallas that Alex Marco might not even remember who she was.

"Who?"

"Dallas. We met last year." There was no response. No recognition, and now it was too late to hang up. "Don't . . . don't you remember? It was . . . because of Nicholas, and . . ."

"Dallas . . ." he murmured. "Sure, I remember. What do you want?"

She felt the blood drain from her body. She felt lonely and confused. He didn't sound exactly pleased to hear from her. Dallas turned her back on the school and the sounds and voices of her friends and classmates. "You said I could call you. You said that . . ."

"Is it Nick again? I told you to stay away from him," he said, annoyed. "Maybe you should tell Lillian this time. Maybe . . ."

"Can I come to see you?"

There was a short pause.

"What?"

"Can . . . can I come to see you?" Her voice was thin and shaky, nervous with the audacity of what she was doing. And she was scared.

"Christ . . . what did he do to you?" Alex asked, the annoyance building.

"I can't talk about it," Dallas improvised.

"All right, all right . . ." Alex said. "Ahh . . . I can't see you until this afternoon around four or later."

"That's okay," Dallas quickly agreed. "I can take the train in. Where should I come?"

"Take the LIRR into Jamaica, and change for the train to Flatbush . . ."

Dallas hadn't really expected Alex to agree to see her. So she was unprepared to write down the directions. She memorized it all, repeating the details to herself all through school. She'd not mentioned her planned trip even to Valerie, knowing that she would be hounded for information. And Dallas feared that she herself would let something slip out that would betray her, and her intentions . . . and Alex Marco.

She never could remember anything that had happened the entire day in classes. Nothing until afterward when she'd walked to the nearest commuter station and boarded a train into the city, for the first time by herself. Dallas had had no idea how expensive anything was going to be and had only enough money for her train ticket and bus fare, and two dollars left over. She wasn't used to the city and got off the bus by mistake a half mile from the street Alex had given her. She walked the rest of the way, both frightened and fascinated with the energy of the streets, of the people and overwhelming noise. The homes here were different. Smaller and closer together, mixed in with three- or four-storied buildings with apartments above and storefronts below. She knew she must have looked out of place, too wide-eyed, because men watched her. She could feel their gazes searching beneath her clothing and exposing her. This thing of her body changing and sloughing off the rest of childhood was terrible. And now men and boys wanted her, *not* because of herself, but her body. They were constantly in season . . . sniffing about for *anyone* in heat.

Dallas reached the address Alex had given her. There was no answer when she rang the bell in the tiny vestibule of the building. She panicked. What if she'd remembered it wrong? What if he'd forgotten, or had no intentions of showing up? How long should she wait? Dallas began to experience the utter foolishness of her mission. What was she going to do . . . except to return back home?

She left the building and glanced around the strange street. Suddenly it was no longer an adventure and seemed like an awful mistake to have come. She began walking aimlessly down the street, until slowly tears filled her eyes and ran down her face, blurring her vision. Suddenly she couldn't stand the noise or the people or the city and wished she were home again. Dallas didn't know what to do. She completely circled the block. Crossed beneath an elevated train. She passed signs with the name Bay Ridge. She had no idea where she was or how to get back to the rail line in Flatbush.

The houses were right on top of each other, and she began to feel closed in and crowded. It was dusk now, and chilly. She cried as she walked, scrubbing the heel of her hand, like a child, across her eyes. Sniffling up with nothing to wipe her runny nose.

Dallas arrived back where she'd started. She entered the building and again tried the bell. Nothing.

She sat down on the two steps in the foyer and then the crying continued. She was going to have to call her father. She was going to have to . . .

Someone rushed into the door and stopped short in front of her. Dallas raised her head and through her tears saw Alex. She just stared at him, and he at her. She was so glad that he'd shown up that she cried even harder, burying her face in her folded arms.

"I know I'm late. You been waiting long?" Alex hesitated. "Jesus Christ . . . are you okay?"

She couldn't say a thing. Just shook her head and cried. Dallas heard him sigh heavily.

"Christ . . ." he repeated, a touch of anxiety in his tone. "Okay, okay . . . let's go inside."

She heard the jangle of keys, the front door being unlocked and opened. She stood up and blindly followed Alex into the building. It smelled musty and stale. She'd never known anything like it. She couldn't remember if she'd ever even been in an apartment building before. Alex was already ahead of her, taking the stairs two at a time. Dallas reached the second floor as Alex continued up the final flight to the third level. By the time she got there she'd almost stopped crying because she was out of breath. A door stood open into an apartment, and she cautiously approached, peering inside. Dallas jumped when Alex appeared again, running his hand through his hair.

"Come on in," he said awkwardly.

She stepped into the room past Alex, and he closed and locked the door behind her. Dallas slowly walked into the center of the room and realized that this was pretty much it. She glanced around at the large open studio space, but didn't really notice very much. Nothing that she was ever able to recall later when she was alone again. Except for a love seat, a table, and a floor lamp. The bed. Not really a bed. A platform base with a mattress on top. The bed was unmade. She stared at it. It had never even occurred to Dallas that Alex might have a girlfriend. A wife! What if there had been someone with him that very morning—or the night before—in that bed?

"What did Nick do to you?"

Dallas spun around to face Alex. She felt immediately comforted because he looked the same as the first time she'd met him. Only . . . there was something older about him, too. In his eyes and the set of his mouth. His face didn't look quite so thin. His mouth seemed . . .

"Nick? Nicholas?" Dallas repeated absently. She was suddenly wondering if Alex would look at her the way the boys at school did. He showed impatience, standing with his hands braced on his hips.

"Yeah, Nick. What did he do? Did he try to . . ."

Dallas blushed and turned away. She shook her head.

"Did he hit you again?"

She gnawed her lip and hugged herself. "It wasn't Nick."

"It wasn't?" Alex questioned, confused. "Then who . . ."

Dallas took a deep breath and faced Alex once more. She played with her hair. "It . . . it wasn't anybody." She felt awkward. It hadn't occurred to Dallas that she'd actually have to say it to him. Ask him.

He gestured toward her with his hand. "Wait a minute. What do you mean, it wasn't Nick. It wasn't anybody? Then . . . what's going on? Why did you call me?"

Dallas looked at Alex and her heart began to pound. She couldn't say it. She couldn't even form the words.

"Answer me," he said firmly, annoyance sharpening his tone and making Dallas jump.

"I . . . I wanted . . ." She swallowed but felt the tears building up again. This wasn't going to work. What she wanted, Dallas suddenly realized, perhaps even Alex could not give her.

He sighed, shaking his head in exasperation. "Dallas . . ." He walked toward her.

Dallas stood riveted, afraid to move. Was he going to get angry with her? Was he going to shake her? Alex took hold of her arms and made her face him squarely. He tucked himself down a little, bending his head so he could look her right in the eye. His voice once again tried patience.

"I'm not going to hurt you. You know that. I'm not going to be mad at you. No matter what it is. Just tell me. What happened?"

She stared at him. She felt so guilty and so ashamed. But she'd come this far on nerve and determination.

"I . . . want you to go to bed with me." Her voice was barely audible.

Alex stood stone-still, not even blinking. "Say that again," he slowly commanded, as if he didn't understand the words, let alone the request.

Dallas took a deep breath. "I want you to . . . to . . . take my virginity."

"You want me to . . ." Alex attempted.

His features contorted into an expression of utter disbelief. He released her as if her skin burned his hands. Alex began shaking his head as he squeezed his eyes closed and began muttering, "No . . . no, this isn't happening. It *can't* be . . ."

"But I want you to . . ."

"I don't care what you want," Alex thundered, glaring at her. "Are you crazy? Where did you get an idea like that? This isn't how it's done." He combed his hands through his hair, and began to pace back and forth in front of her. "You don't go up to some guy and say . . . and . . . and say . . ." He looked helpless again, and gave up, walking away from her. "Jesus . . . oh, man . . . *fuck*!"

"I know how it's done," Dallas countered, revving herself up for an argument.

"Good! Then you also know it happens when two

people like each other, and they've been going together for a while, and . . ."

"I want you to do it."

"Stop saying that, will you?" Alex demanded. He marched over to her and took her arm. He began to propel her back to the door. "Look . . . go home. You had a fight with your boyfriend, then make up with him. Or find somebody else." He jerked open the door and stood aside for her to leave. "It just can't be me."

Dallas felt her shame spread, embarrassment creeping over her. And oddly, the more Alex objected, the more Dallas was convinced that she was doing the right thing. And she had no intention of being turned away.

When she just stood staring silently at him, Alex raised his hands in surrender. "I won't say anything about this, I swear."

"I know you won't," Dallas said, her voice stronger now, the tears completely gone. "That's one of the reasons why I chose you."

Alex snorted in disbelief. "You *chose* me? What is this? Some sort of lottery?"

"Please listen to me. I know what I'm doing. I know what I want. I know you don't really care about me . . ."

"Dallas . . . it's not that I don't care about you," Alex began slowly. "But we don't know squat about each other. You can't just go up to someone and say, will you bust my cherry . . ." She looked blank, and Alex cringed, coloring over. "You know what I mean."

"I still want you to do it to me."

"Why me?" he asked frantically. "You telling me there's not one horny guy in your whole goddamn school that doesn't want to screw you?"

"Yeah, lots of them," Dallas admitted. "But that's all they want to do. Be the first."

"Well, somebody has to, Dallas."

"I know, but . . . I want to decide who it is. And I

don't want it to be anybody from school. I thought about it, and . . . I decided that if I wasn't a virgin anymore, then they'd leave me alone."

Alex shook his head, looking both sad and amused. He reached out and gave the door a gentle push to close it again. "They won't leave you alone, I can guarantee that. You just make it easier for them to run a line on you. Guys just have one thing on their mind."

"I know."

Alex continued to look at her for a long moment before muttering some profanity under his breath. He approached a bookcase and reached for a pack of opened cigarettes. Shaking one out of the pack, he took matches from his shirt pocket and lit it, inhaling deeply and blowing the smoke up toward the ceiling. Putting one hand into the pocket of his jeans, Alex walked to stare out the window. Dallas watched him. He wasn't going to just send her home. But she was still a long way from convincing him that she really wanted him to do this.

"How come you couldn't ask someone you know in school? All those young bloods . . . If all you want to do is get rid of your virginity, what's the big deal?"

Dallas came toward him, but he didn't turn around. She stopped, and then just sat gingerly on the edge of his bed. She realized that she still had her school knapsack hanging from her shoulder. Dallas shrugged it off and let it drop to the floor at her feet.

"Because it won't mean anything to them. I'm sick of being a virgin and being treated like I have a disease. Everyone thinks I'm so different."

He said nothing for a moment, and then finally turned around. "What do you mean, you're different? How come?"

Dallas shrugged, blushing. "I just am, that's all."

Alex began to walk back to her. He stood looking down at her, forcing Dallas to crane her neck to see his face and expression. It was thoughtful. Not angry anymore. He made a vague gesture with his hand.

"Why did you call me? Why are you asking me to do this?"

"Because . . . I trust you," she said in a small voice.

"How do you know that?" Alex persisted.

"You didn't let Nicholas hurt me last year, when he tried to rape me. You didn't tell Lillian. You didn't make fun of me or call me . . ."

"Go on."

"Nicholas called me a nigger," Dallas whispered, and then looked at Alex sharply to see his response.

Alex winced and shook his head. He bent down and reached behind him, pulling up a chair to sit in front of her. He leaned toward her, bracing his forearms on his thighs. The lit cigarette dangled from his fingers, the smoke curling up between them in front of his face. "Dallas, how do you know I don't feel or think the same thing about you?"

"I don't," she admitted honestly. "But I think I would know if you did. I always know when people don't like me."

He rubbed his forehead, his gaze wandering over her face. "I don't understand why anyone wouldn't like you," Alex murmured.

"Does that mean you'll do it?"

He frowned at her. "You're serious, aren't you?"

Dallas nodded.

"Look . . . don't you understand that going to bed with a man, having sex, is supposed to be something really special?"

"What's so special about being a virgin? I bet the first time you were with a girl you couldn't wait."

He chuckled. "You're right. My balls almost turned blue, I was so ready." He caught himself and shrugged. "Sorry . . ."

"See what I mean? If you didn't care what I thought or how I'd feel, you wouldn't apologize."

"That's not the same thing as . . ."

"Please? I won't be sorry. I know it might hurt a little, but I won't blame you, honest."

"You really think it's not so important? And when your virginity is gone, things will be easier for you?"

Dallas shrugged. "How come it's so important?"

Alex shook his head wryly. "I don't know. Maybe it isn't anymore." He looked pensive for a moment, took a last drag on the cigarette, and stubbed it out in an ashtray that was on the floor by the foot of the bed. "My mother once told me that a long time ago if a girl lost her virginity before she was married, she was called a tramp."

"The first time you were with a girl, did you think she was a tramp?" Dallas asked.

"Hell, no. I was too grateful," Alex said slyly. "But you're the first girl to *ask* me to do this."

They stared at each other, and Dallas watched as Alex inventoried her face, a slight frown between his brows, his jaw tensing with his thoughts. He leaned forward again, clasping his fists together and resting his mouth and chin against them. After a moment he jumped up and walked to the window, but then returned to take up his seat again in front of her.

"It's going to hurt . . ."

"I won't mind."

"Bullshit. You *will* mind," he came back, impatiently. "But it can't be helped."

"You'll do it?" Dallas asked, not disguising her eagerness.

Alex sighed. "Yeah . . . I'll do it. But I know I'm going to live to regret this," he said, getting up. He went to the windows to close the blinds, and turn on a lamp. It was getting dark outside. Alex hesitated and looked sharply at her. "Where did you tell your parents you were going to be tonight?"

"With my girlfriend, Maureen. What do I have to do?" Dallas asked, watching him as he moved about the room. He was picking up candles.

"Not much. Just take off all your clothes and hop

on the bed." He stopped when he saw the stricken expression on her face. "That's how we start, Dallas. We get naked. Want to change your mind?"

"No."

Alex began to put the candles around the area of the bed. On a night table, and a stool. On the floor and a shelf overhead. "This girl I used to go with got these for me. She said candles made it romantic. I don't know . . . never did anything for me."

He turned and saw Dallas standing in the middle of the floor watching him with overly bright eyes. He came to stand before her, watching the way she stood with her arms crossed.

"How old are you?" he asked.

Dallas thought about lying, but knew she wouldn't be convincing. Anyway, she knew lots of girls who had been doing it with boys since ninth grade. Valerie had been younger.

"Sixteen."

He nodded thoughtfully, as if that wasn't as bad as he'd imagined. Alex slowly reached out and pulled her arms loose. "You can use the bathroom behind you to take off your stuff."

Dallas twisted her hands together. "I don't have anything else to . . ."

"I think there's a shirt or something behind the door. You can put it on. I'll wait for you out here."

Dallas nodded, her mouth suddenly dry. The euphoria she'd felt with Alex's consent quickly faded into insecurity and fear. But not doubt. She had *never* been in doubt. It was just that as she turned and slowly walked to the bathroom, she realized that this was irrevocable. She could only lose her virginity once. Only fleetingly did Dallas wonder how things might have worked out differently if Alex hadn't fortuitously arrived at the Marco home the afternoon Nicholas had her cornered in the basement. If she had been forced to give her virginity then, her body pinioned and plundered, would it have seemed any more sacred—or any less—than she held it now? She had had to persuade Alex to agree to this, but having given in did he think any more—or less—of her?

The bathroom was tiny. Dallas lowered the top of the toilet seat and sat down on it, realizing that she was trembling and her skin was cold. She sat like that, her hands squeezed between her thighs for warmth. Her knees almost touched the opposite wall and she wondered how Alex, who was much taller than she was, managed. Focusing on the wall, Dallas began to pull off her sweater. She carefully folded it and laid it across the edge of the tub. She removed each item as if she were in a trance, until she was left in her bra and panties. And then it came to her that no one had ever seen her naked before. Maybe Valerie, over the years that they'd slept over at one another's homes. But that was different. It was too late to wonder if she looked fat, or had heavy thighs, or if her breasts were too big.

Too late . . .

There was no shirt behind the door in the bathroom, and she had no intentions of opening the door and asking for one. Instead, Dallas made do with a towel from the rack over the tub. It did not cover as much of her body as she'd hoped, and there was not enough of it to also tie. So she held it closed with her hand. She stood indecisively, wondering if she should call out, or if Alex would call her. Finally, Dallas opened the door a few inches and spoke through the space.

"I'm ready," she said softly.

The lights in the room went out. What remained was dim and flickering.

"Me, too. Come on in," Alex said in a low voice.

Dallas heard the uncertainty in his tone, but did as she was told. As she stepped out of the bathroom, the wooden floor was cold under her bare feet. She kept her gaze down and clutched the end of the towel. Her heart was thudding in her chest. She glanced up covertly and saw that there were candles around the room, providing the only light. Alex had straightened the linens on the bed and now knelt in the middle of it, waiting for her. All of his clothing had been removed, too, except for his underwear. Close-fitting white shorts that covered the slight bulge of his genitals. Dallas noticed that, and his hair-covered chest. She squeezed her eyes closed and then averted her gaze to his face. But it was all in shadows. She was glad she couldn't see his eyes . . . and hoped he couldn't see hers.

"Come here," Alex said.

Dallas slowly approached the bed and, hesitating for just a moment, awkwardly climbed on to face Alex, while trying to keep the towel in place. He said nothing and did nothing for a long time, until finally she opened her eyes and realized he was waiting for her to look at him as well. And once she did, she couldn't look away. This close, his eyes were like an anchor. They gave her a focus, and helped her to remember that Alex had never done anything to hurt her, to humiliate her, and there was no reason to believe anything would change now.

Dallas had no idea what was expected of her, and she just sat there. But she began to feel less nervous, her body less stiff and tense. Her breathing became less shallow, and the warmth returned to her skin. As if sensing that she was ready to be touched, Alex finally reached out a hand to her. But it was to stroke her hair, finger it lightly. He reached farther and found the cord holding it, and tugged it off. Set free, Dallas's thick, unruly hair spread out and framed her face. She wondered if Alex thought it made her look primitive. Ethnic. He was clearly fascinated as he tested the corkscrew curls, pulling on one and watching it spring back. His concentration distracted her until he touched her face. Alex trailed his fingers down the side of her neck and to her throat.

Too late . . .

The contact was like an electric charge, sensitizing

the surface of her skin and making her nerves beneath it vibrate. Dallas kept her attention on his face and tried not to move as Alex's hand explored. What Dallas felt was a cross between being tickled, and something else she hadn't felt before. A pleasurable tingle that seemed strongest in her nipples and in her stomach.

His hand moved to the edge of the towel. Alex took hold and tried to pull it from her. Dallas held on.

"You can still stop."

"No. I won't," she said bravely.

"Then . . . let go," Alex commanded in a whisper, never taking his gaze from hers.

She obeyed, and felt the cloth slide away from her body. As each part was exposed, Alex shifted his attention. Dallas felt like she was shrinking under his scrutiny. When he did nothing but look closely at her, she was unable to resist the need to cover her breasts and the dark triangle below her groin. Alex stopped her in the process.

"Don't," he said simply, grabbing her hands. "Relax and let me look at you."

Dallas listened to each of his commands as he slowly peeled away her resistance along with anything she might have hid behind. She had never felt so vulnerable, so exposed in her life. Valerie had not told her about this part. About what it was like to be completely naked in front of a man.

"Are you scared?" Alex asked.

She nodded, feeling ashamed for admitting it.

He sighed heavily. "You know what? Me, too."

The admission put an immediate stop to the trembling in her hands. For a moment Dallas almost felt the need to comfort and reassure *him.* She wasn't afraid of Alex, but she was not prepared when he touched her breast next. His hand stroked and squeezed the roundness, lifted it, and rubbed over the nipple. Alex now was using both hands on her body. Somehow finding other parts to caress that only increased the languid melting that was in combat with her lingering shyness and self-doubt.

The tingling spiraled out. It seemed to sink deeper into the pit of her stomach and flow into the inward space between her legs. It was a kind of aching that made her feel short of breath. There was a small sound, a sigh or moan, and Dallas realized it came from her.

"It's okay if you want to touch me, too," Alex said.

When she seemed inclined not to, Alex took one of her hands and placed it on his chest, and held it there. Dallas gasped, surprised at the firmness of his skin. Surprised by the heat that came through. Surprised by the silky feel of his chest hair. Alex let go of her hand when she tentatively brushed her fingers through the dark strands. Curiosity began to direct her movements.

She was enjoying touching Alex. She was enjoying the way his hands were gliding over her body, and Dallas began to fully relax at the gentle foreplay between them. It made her feel good. It made her feel bold . . . and very grown-up. Until his hands began to rub along her thighs, his large hands curved over the sides. Dallas found herself staring at his hands, realizing that his skin color was the same as hers. Back and forth his hands moved, his thumbs pressed along the insides of her legs . . . all the way to the top to where the hair was. She stopped her movements on his chest to look at what Alex was doing to her. Her thighs were parted just enough for him to cup a hand against her private parts. Dallas gasped and stiffened reflexively when his fingers briefly explored, and sent a surprising jolt of pleasure shooting through her.

"Alex . . ."

"It's okay," he said soothingly. "I just need to be sure you're a little wet."

She'd understand the significance later, and come to love the stroking of the delicate valleys, but just then her inclination was to pull his hand away. But already

Alex was doing just that. Dallas found herself momentarily confused by the physical feelings, undecided as to whether or not she wanted Alex to stop touching her there.

"Lie down," he said, shifting to make room for her.

A shiver racked through her body as slowly Dallas stretched out on the bed, on her back. She no longer bothered to try to hide herself. She had already come too far to turn back. But the anticipation of what was going to happen again stirred up a fluttering of fear. Dallas lay waiting. Alex sat back above her staring down at her, his gaze again roaming over her exposed body. It wasn't until Alex came up on his knees that Dallas realized his body had gone through a change, too.

Alex quickly removed his white briefs and dropped them on the floor. His penis rose stiffly from his body, pointing toward her. Dallas closed her eyes and then felt his hands again on her body. His touch was slow, as if he was satisfying a curiosity. Then Alex again took her hand, this time to carefully wrap it around his penis. Dallas winced, but closed her eyes as she held him. He was very hard. The skin was warm and smooth, but taut. On her own Dallas began to explore the length of him. He said nothing as she did so. She squinted briefly at him and found Alex with his eyes closed, and his head a little back as she awkwardly stroked him. He stopped her, gently grabbing her wrist.

"Okay," Alex murmured. "This is it . . . try to relax, okay?"

Dallas merely nodded. She couldn't open her eyes. She jumped when Alex indicated with the pressure of his hands that she should raise her knees. She jumped again and he began to part them.

"Are you ready?" he asked.

"Y-yes."

"I can still stop, Dallas. But you gotta tell me now."

"N-no. Go on."

Suddenly he was resting his body slowly atop hers. Automatically Dallas put her hands on his shoulders. He was heavy and long. The pressure of his hips and thighs forced her legs to open wider. Her whole body trembled. His naked body against hers was extraordinary. It seemed that it wasn't possible to get any closer to another person than this. She was totally defenseless. She gasped and her heart started to race again.

"Take it easy . . ." Alex said soothingly. His hands slipped under her buttocks, lifting her.

Dallas felt the probing against the opening into her body.

Too late . . .

And then Alex stopped, his body poised stiffly above her. His chest flattened her breasts, but his hair was soft and his body still very warm. Dallas let her hands tentatively glide across his shoulders, feeling the muscles play under her fingers. When nothing else happened she opened her eyes only to find Alex staring down into her face. His expression was serious. But it was also very tense with his jaw flexing and his eyes a little dazed.

"This is going to hurt. I'm sorry. It can't be helped."

She held her breath, focusing on his eyes and mouth. And then he surged forward with a low grunt. It took her by surprise, and her eyes squeezed shut again. Her fingers clenched his shoulders.

"Oohh . . ." Dallas bit her lower lip, shutting off the sound.

Alex surged forward again, a little deeper.

Dallas refused to utter another sound. But her breathing became labored and deep as she tried not to wiggle away from his effort to bury himself inside her body. It wasn't so much that it hurt as it felt as if she were being torn apart. Stretched beyond bearing. All of her energy and attention was centered on the feel of Alex pushing deeper within her. But he seemed to be struggling to breathe also, and Dallas wondered if he too was in pain.

Then Alex seemed to be withdrawing and Dallas thought it was all over. She thought he was pulling out. She released a deep breath of relief. But instead Alex thrust forward again. She didn't think it was possible, but his body went even deeper until there wasn't an inch of space between them. Alex seemed to rest against her for a moment, groaning deep in his throat. Dallas held on to him around his back, and felt the deep breaths he was taking. She hid her face against his shoulder.

"Is . . . is it over?" she asked very quietly. She couldn't move. She felt as if something much too big had been shoved into the center of her, impaling her. Alex shook his head against her.

"No. Not yet . . ." he said hoarsely.

Alex slid his hands from beneath her bottom and came up on his forearms. And then he began a rhythmic in and out movement with his hips and penis against her, into her. Dallas realized his whole body was tense and straining. She could do nothing more than lie there, gritting her teeth against the repetitive pushing and stretching inside her body. Holding on to Alex with her arms clamped tightly around him, her fingernails unconsciously digging into his skin. He didn't seem to notice. For a moment Dallas was horrified at what she was doing. To be naked with a man, in his bed, under him . . . it was different from the books. Different from the movies. Different from what the girls at school talked about. Already Dallas suspected that there was also something close to magic about the way their bodies were joined. It was almost . . . sacred. The way they fit together and moved with a natural motion from which Alex seemed to be drawing some enjoyment.

Dallas also sensed that he could be exerting much more force, but was controlling his efforts. But none of it lasted for very long. Alex's whole body suddenly seemed to stiffen. He moaned and pushed his pelvis forward one final time. It was as if he were trying to squeeze right into her. He held himself rigid, breathing deeply. She felt the fluttering of his penis inside her. The pulsation of his release. His body went limp. He rested momentarily on Dallas, his weight relaxed. Dallas heard him trying to catch his breath. Her hands stroked unconsciously across the back of his neck, down his spine to his lower back. The skin was damp and hot. But she liked the way he felt. Even his hair was damp.

Finally, Alex lay still. He lifted his buttocks and his penis slid from her body. The movement still caused discomfort. It was unexpected. He was not as big as when he'd first started to make love to her. His penis was wet and soft now.

"Dallas . . ."

"I'm okay," she managed in a soft, thin voice to reassure him.

He sighed. "I'm . . . sorry. I . . . I shouldn't have finished so fast."

She didn't know what he meant. It seemed like it had taken forever for his thrusting to end. What she liked more was having Alex lie still on her. She could feel his heartbeat, and smell his skin. It made her feel dreamy. Suddenly Alex grunted and rolled away from her. He sprawled on his back next to her with his eyes closed. Without the warmth and covering of his body on top of hers, Dallas began to feel very cold. She carefully drew up her legs and hugged herself in a fetal position.

Now what?

Was she supposed to say something? Was something else supposed to happen? She looked down the length of his body and felt her initial shyness give way to open curiosity at Alex's body. Dallas had a real awareness now of how different his body was, and an appreciation of the gentleness in him, beneath the hard contours of his body. There was a stinging and tingling between her legs. Tender and very sore. She also felt wet, and warm.

Alex rolled his head in her direction and opened his eyes. He reached out a hand and lazily smoothed her hair.

"Well . . . it's done," he murmured sleepily. "You're not a virgin anymore."

"Thank you."

Alex blinked at her and then chuckled. "Don't thank me. Believe it or not, this was the easy part. I know it hurt. I know you didn't get off . . . or feel very much. You're probably thinking, so what's all the excitement about? The first time is always the worst for girls. It gets a lot better if you keep at it."

"You mean . . . do it again?" Dallas asked, her voice betraying her reluctance at having to submit to being penetrated again.

Alex lay quietly for a moment, still playing in her soft hair, his gaze thoughtful and drowsy. "Yeah. But not now. Not with me. So . . . was it worth it? Or are you disappointed?"

Dallas closed her eyes and felt the way her body was still responding to its recent invasion. There was a lot about being with Alex that she liked. But she really wasn't sure what she was supposed to feel.

"I don't know."

He stared up at the ceiling and sighed deeply. "I can tell you this. With the right person at the right time . . . it's great." He swung away from her, sitting on the side of the bed and reaching for his underwear. "I did what you wanted me to do. But find somebody you really care about next time. You'll get the hang of it, and you might even get to like it."

"Are we through?" she asked, slowly sitting up. She used both hands to sweep her hair back from her face. She looked around for the elastic band that had held it in place, but couldn't find it.

"Yep. That's it. Sorry I can't say that satisfaction was guaranteed," Alex said, almost completely dressed by the time Dallas had gotten off the rumpled bed.

His sarcasm stung. Now that the contact was over between them, now that it had finished and she'd gotten what she wanted, Dallas felt deserted. But she didn't really know what else she thought he should do. This was just what she knew the boys in school would have done, had she submitted to their demands. But what had she expected? Alex wasn't really interested in her either, and she never pretended that he would be.

Dallas resorted to modestly covering herself with her hands again, but Alex wasn't watching. He had retreated to the window again to light another cigarette. She grabbed the towel and hastily wrapped it around her body. She tried to stand up and stumbled. Her thighs began to quiver almost uncontrollably, and the center of her body felt like it was burning. Dallas walked unsteadily to the bathroom and, closing the door, began to get dressed.

She thought she'd be happy about this. She thought there would be this great sense of relief and satisfaction. But what she actually felt was confused . . . and a little empty. Dallas knew what was supposed to happen and even how. She'd read about it. But she hadn't anticipated feeling so totally open and helpless. It had been much more complicated than just sex. Alex's tenderness beforehand suggested something that was meant to be about feelings, and emotions. That if what had happened between them was all there was to it, then it seemed a wasted effort.

Dallas came out of the bathroom. The lights were back on. The candles had been blown out, the air a little acrid with the odor of sulfur and wax. It hardly seemed romantic. Alex's apartment looked sad and unfurnished. There was nothing cozy about it. He had no pictures on the walls or curtain at the window. It was bare bones.

"Does it hurt?"

His voice startled her, and she turned to face him.

Alex was standing at the kitchenette counter, drinking from a can of soda. He looked restless. Annoyed.

"Just a little," Dallas murmured. But she wanted to leave. She wanted to go home and be by herself.

"Are you mad at me?"

"No. Why should I be?"

He sighed. "I'm sorry I let you talk me into this. This is not the way it's supposed to be. I . . ."

"I wanted it this way." She walked over to him. "I'm not sorry. I'm glad it was you."

He held out the soda can to her and Dallas accepted it. She gratefully took a gulp of the cold drink and gave it back to Alex, mumbling her thanks.

Alex continued to look doubtful. But then his expression softened and he shook his head, bemused. He reached out his arm to hook Dallas around her neck and pull her toward him. It was an awkward hug, but she welcomed it, wanting to curl up against him and take whatever tenderness he had to offer.

Alex turned his mouth against her hair, near her ear, to whisper, "This is the first and last time I ever do this. I'm getting out of the business of deflowering girls."

She gave him a shaky smile. "Then . . . I'm glad I was your first."

He studied her for a moment, and touched her cheek. "You're sweet. I'm glad I was your first, too." He drained the soda and headed to pick up his jacket. "Come on. I'll drive you home."

"I can take the train. I have a ticket."

"That'll take too long. Anyway, I need to get out for a while."

She nodded and headed for the door as Alex turned out the lights. She was quiet until he'd locked the door, and she followed him back down and out of the building. Around the corner to where his secondhand car was parked. They were on the road before either spoke again. Dallas knew she had a lot to think about.

She had no idea what was going through Alex's mind. Until they were on the Belt Parkway heading east.

"What are you thinking?" Alex finally broke through the pensive silence between them.

Dallas wasn't sure he would understand. She wasn't sure if it would have mattered to Alex as much as she knew it would matter to her in the future.

"About . . . what we did."

"Didn't like it, heh?"

She stared out the window, aware that her body now was different. There was a connection, an affinity that was going to last forever. He was imprinted on her, part of her . . . in her . . . that had been absorbed. No matter what, Alex was *always* going to be the first. Dallas felt changes already that she hadn't even anticipated. More than just losing her virginity and breaking through a barrier, a physical membrane into her body. This was a whole new realm of experience and sensation. It was overwhelming. Her chest felt tight suddenly and her throat closed in, choking her. Slowly tears spilled from her eyes and rolled down her face.

She shook her head, finally finding the voice to answer Alex. "It's . . . not that," Dallas sighed. "I just . . . I didn't know it was going to be so personal."

It was a long moment before Alex responded. He swept a hand through his hair.

"Yeah. Me either . . ."

Dallas stood at the window looking out on the early morning sun washing over the neighborhood. It was Sunday. Still too early for anyone to be up.

She sipped the hot tea and noticed that the first signs of spring were finally appearing on the trees and shrubbery. She felt an odd relief. She'd always found winter rather oppressive and dark. Spring always offered more . . . hope. Dallas glanced at her watch, thinking she should leave soon. Call for a cab back to the station for the trip back to New York. When she heard the sounds of someone on the stairwell Dallas thought that it was probably her father. Even on weekends he tended to rise early. To sit with a cup of coffee and the morning papers, undisturbed by the rest of the family. But it wasn't her father.

When Dallas turned from the window she found Dean entering the kitchen. He looked half-asleep, still rumpled and not completely dressed. He looked annoyed and impatient. Then Dallas recognized the expression. It was shamefaced, reluctantly repentant.

"Morning," Dean muttered, sitting at the kitchen table and bending to put his sneakers on.

Dallas watched him warily. She drank her tea and didn't immediately respond. After a long moment of silence, Dean glanced furtively at her, and then stood to stuff the tail of his Henley shirt into the waist of his jeans.

"There's coffee if you want some," she said.

"Thanks," Dean acknowledged, heading for the counter and the overhead cabinet where the mugs were kept. He poured himself a cup, laced it with sugar, and turned to face her, stirring the hot liquid. But he wouldn't look directly at her.

"You're up early," Dallas commented smoothly.

Dean took a large gulp of coffee. He stood holding it in his jaw for a considering moment before swallowing. Then he looked at her.

"I was pretty sure you'd be up. I wanted to see you before you left for the city again."

Dallas finished her tea and walked to the sink with the empty cup. She merely set it on the counter. "What about?"

He took an audible deep breath. "To say I'm sorry. About last night. About what I said." Finally, he looked at her. "I don't know why I did."

"I don't know why you did either. You used to do stuff like that when we were kids and you wanted to get *me* in trouble. What were you trying to get back at me for?"

Dean moved restlessly around the kitchen. He

shook his head. "I don't know. Nothing. I just . . . let my lips flap without thinking."

Dallas shook her head. She didn't know what to say to her brother. "Dean . . . don't worry about it. It doesn't matter."

"Yeah, but if you're really dating that guy, then I made it sound like . . ."

"I said, don't worry about it. I'm not dating him." She said it with finality. She didn't want to discuss it anymore.

"I want to check out, too. If I hang around any longer Mom will be up and start in on me."

"It wouldn't happen if you stood up to her."

"She still wants to treat me like a kid."

Dallas pursed her lips as she looked at Dean. "Maybe if you didn't sometimes act like one, she'd stop. You're too old to be playing games, you know." Dean looked truculent and stubborn, but didn't refute her observation. Dallas sighed, and headed for the living room, where she'd left her coat. She was ready to leave. "I'm going to go now."

"I'll take you to the station," Dean offered, putting down the unfinished cup of coffee.

"I was just going to call a cab. You might want to hang around until Eleanor is up. You know she won't like it if you leave without saying anything to her."

"That's okay. I'll call her later." He hurried off to get his own things.

In Eleanor's red Camry, Dallas strapped herself in and sat silently as they pulled away from the front of the house and headed off down the street. She was suddenly feeling very tired and sleepy. She decided that when she got home she was going to go back to bed for a few hours. Then she had work to do. She closed her eyes. This, too, would come to pass.

"You know, even if you were dating that guy, it wouldn't bother me," Dean said magnanimously.

"Thanks," Dallas said dryly.

She sat considering her family, and all the men she'd

dated, the one she'd been married to. She thought of Valerie and Maureen and a host of others whom she'd considered friends over the years. Her own brother. All of whom, without exception, had hurt and betrayed her at one time or another for their own reasons, their own gain. Except for Alex, who had fought for her, worried about her, protected her. *How ironic,* Dallas thought.

Alex Marco could very likely turn out to really be her best friend.

Chapter Nine

Alex woke up with a start. His skin was hot and slightly damp. He realized that his heart was racing and for a brief moment it actually pounded like a closed fist, making him struggle for air. He felt as if he were suffocating. Or drowning.

He never dreamed about the Gulf War. He never had nightmares, although he remembered everything that had happened. Underwater, his skills and training, his equipment and swim partner, kept him alive. But on the surface his life was his own.

Alex sat up slowly, feeling too hot and throwing off the covers. The room was actually a little cool, an early spring suburban dawn chill because the sun had not risen high enough yet to warm the air. But it felt wonderful and he breathed deeply, getting his pulse back to normal. He'd awakened suddenly because it hit him that he was doing something wrong. He'd made a poor decision. It was one of those instinctive kind of feelings like a lightbulb going on, or when he got the punch line. Or when he was keenly aware of danger. It was that absolute.

When Alex opened his eyes and looked around he realized he wanted to leave. This room made him uneasy. It was a small bedroom, outfitted and lived in with a woman's things. It was too cozy, and too in need of the one thing that would complete the domestic picture. A man around the house. He glanced down at the sleeping woman next to him. Valerie was the only woman he'd ever known who looked beautiful while she slept. He swung his body out of the bed.

"Where are you going?"

The voice was slurred and sleepy, but still incredibly sexy and inviting. Alex felt her hand on his back. It lightly stroked the skin and explored the surface with incredible sensitivity. As much as he felt the need to get up, Alex also felt the quickly rising desire that made his penis surge into an erection.

"It's almost light. I better go . . ."

Valerie shifted with a sensual twist of her body until she was facing Alex. Her drowsy gaze was warm and welcoming, her abundant hair a flamelike enticement billowing out on the pillow around her. Her hand slid along his thigh, curving the fingers inward, enticingly close to his genitals.

"Megan's at a girlfriend's for the night, remember?" Her voice was throaty and seductive.

Alex glanced down at her, feeling the heat of longing. Her nightgown had thin straps that barely held it in place over her body, and a thin fabric that molded to her skin and showed the outline of her breasts and nipples. He watched Valerie's eyes and mouth, which held the kind of patience and calm of someone who knew she would get what she wanted.

He wished she hadn't mentioned Megan, but the child was the one person he was most concerned about. At twelve she was perhaps old enough to understand the practice of dating, and men and women being together. Alex wasn't comfortable with Megan finding out what was happening between her mother and himself. He and Valerie had been very careful to appear to be not more than friends in her company. He didn't want to give either of them the wrong impression.

"What about your neighbors?"

Valerie smiled. "You've never lived in a bedroom community, have you? If you did you'd know that everyone has interesting secrets behind their closed doors."

Her hand grazed against him, and Alex knew he was going to give in. Alex turned in one swift agile motion and gathered Valerie against him. There wasn't any foreplay to speak of. They just got to it.

Alex slid his hands up Valerie's thighs and hips and torso, taking the light gown with him and pulling it over her head. Her skin was very pale, and Alex found it disconcerting that she had so little color, except for her body hair. She had wiggled onto her back, arching it so that her breasts, beautifully formed and firm, jutted out toward him. Valerie boldly wrapped her hand around his hard penis, and Alex groaned as she began to stimulate him.

Somehow, though, this felt wrong. Being with Valerie gave him only some of what he wanted. He looked into her flushed face and then closed his eyes tightly, trying to hold the image. There was another face that would have taken her place. The imagery took Alex by surprise, and confused him. He settled between Valerie's legs and brought them together. Her body moved with him, and the very center of her held him fast and captive. Neither of them lasted very long. Their climax was explosive. There was no lingering euphoria or deep closeness. It didn't change one iota the way Alex was feeling.

What he wanted and what he got seemed to keep missing each other. It reminded him, suddenly, of some of the things he'd read in that journal belonging to Dallas. About her family and her relationship to her stepmother. It reminded Alex of himself and Vin. He recalled her feeling caught between two heritages but unclaimed by either. About this deep and persistent ache of emptiness that needed to be filled . . . by family. About Dallas's friendship with Valerie and all it meant to her, but also how it had disappointed her.

His feelings seemed like a betrayal, given what he and Valerie had just done together, to be lying in her bed thinking about her best friend. But strangely enough Dallas's confusion wasn't much different from his own.

Valerie was curled up next to him, her body flushed and warm. Her fingers played idly in the hair on his chest, and then went still. He knew she'd fallen back to sleep. Finally he got out of the bed, feeling both relief and urgency. Alex headed for the bathroom and the shower, hoping the therapeutic pelting of the water would clear his mind.

He had to be careful. What he wanted and what he was getting were not the same thing.

Valerie smiled when she heard the doorbell. She thought that Alex had returned. She couldn't think of anything he'd forgotten. He was very careful not to leave or disturb things in her house because of Megan. Valerie had already told Alex that he could relax. She wanted Megan to get used to the idea of Alex's presence. She wanted them to like each other and get along.

Valerie breezily headed toward the door and loosely tied the belt of her robe. She hadn't begun to get dressed yet for work and was still naked under the soft flimsy covering. Valerie chuckled as she opened the door. She was going to be late. But so what . . .

However, she stood with her mouth opened when she saw that it was not Alex. For a moment she hadn't the first idea who this tall, broad man was. Except that there was an immediate visceral response to his obvious masculinity. Then Valerie placed him. He was Alex's friend. Ross something-or-other. His alert gaze, his infuriatingly complacent smile, reminded Valerie that he made her nervous. Actually, she was sure that she really didn't like him very much. Alex spoke with near reverence about his friend, which was another reason Valerie decided she didn't like the man. She had learned enough about Alex to realize that there weren't many people he held in high regard. To be singled out was to be made special. She wasn't sure she'd achieved that status, yet.

Valerie quickly realized that she was fairly exposed in the light robe, and although he was controlled enough to keep his attention on her face, Ross was clearly enjoying the fact that he'd caught her off guard. His nonchalance, his seeming unawareness of her reaction, drove Valerie to be brusque and ungracious.

"What do you want?"

"Good morning," Ross said with a pleasant smile. "Ross Manning."

Valerie discreetly tried to wrap the robe tighter about herself until she realized it caused the material to hug her breasts and display them rather prominently. She crossed her arms over her chest.

"I know who you are."

"Is Alex here?"

Ross took a step into the doorway, forcing her back. She'd had no intentions of inviting him in, but he gave her no choice. And she certainly couldn't continue to stand in the door with almost nothing on.

"What made you think he would be here?" she asked.

"He was supposed to call me last night and didn't. We were supposed to get together this morning, now we can't. It's late." His smile widened. "I didn't have to be Sherlock Holmes to figure out where he'd be."

"Well, he's not here," Valerie said, neither confirming nor denying that he had been. "I'm sorry, I'll have to ask you to . . ."

"I think you ought to know, you can't have him."

Valerie's mouth dropped open. She quickly recovered and narrowed her eyes on him. "What did you say?" she questioned in a disbelieving voice.

Ross finally let his attention wander. But it wasn't lascivious and obvious. His gaze didn't strip her bare as other men had been wont to do. It was openly admiring, but it was also . . . polite.

He shook his head. "I can see why Alex is so taken with you. But I don't think you can write the happy ending you want with him."

Valerie blushed, something that was as foreign to her as being ignored. "Who the hell do you think you are? Who asked you?"

"I'm his friend," Ross answered easily, not the least perturbed by her indignation.

"Well, friend or no friend, I don't think Alex is going to appreciate that you . . ."

"You don't understand," Ross interrupted her. A slow smile began at the corner of his mouth. Amused. Patient. Warm. "I'm not worried about Alex. He can take care of himself . . . most of the time. I'm trying to warn you."

Valerie was totally confused. She didn't know how to respond to such a direct approach. Now, oddly enough, she did feel exposed. It was as if this man had unerringly found a way to look into her heart. Even Valerie wasn't sure what he'd find.

"I don't know what you're up to, but you have a lot of nerve coming here like this and jumping into my business. Now, will you please leave . . ." Valerie said, walking past him and reaching for the door.

"Don't do that," Ross instructed, again in a smooth, even tone. Not a demand. Not urgent or a plea. A preemptive suggestion. He wasn't finished yet.

"Look, I'm starting to get *real* annoyed with you. I don't have time for this."

Ross calmly put up his hand. He took yet another step closer to her, and Valerie stood her ground. That made him smile. He liked that. She wasn't afraid of him. "Stop playing games, Valerie. Alex is trying to clean the ghosts out of his closet. You're looking for a good man."

Ross reached past her, not touching her as he opened the door. Valerie stood back out of his way.

"How can you be so sure that Alex doesn't want

me?" Valerie found herself asking with a combination of defiance and curiosity.

"Oh, he wants you, all right. But it's not the same thing as being in love with you."

Valerie watched Ross as he stood in her doorway. He filled nearly the whole frame. "I think you're jealous. I think it annoys you that Alex wants to spend more time with me than he does with you. You're the one that needs to get a life."

He grinned. "I'm working on it."

"Well, I wish you luck. You're going to need it. You're the most arrogant, obnoxious man I've ever met. A good friend would *never* try to control a friend's life."

"You're absolutely right. But a best friend would never stand by and let a friend get hurt."

Valerie felt the blush return. She began to push the door closed on him. "Please go. I have to get ready for work."

"Okay, I'm gone. But one more thing."

She glared silently at him but waited.

"Megan is a great little girl. Don't give her a reason to be disappointed in you."

She closed the door in his face.

Alex drove into the service center and parked his car along a fence. It was out of the way, and wouldn't be mistaken as being in need of work. He turned off his engine, climbed out of the car, and glanced around.

The lot looked smaller than he remembered. Maybe because everything looked smaller once you go away and come back. But it also looked exactly the same. The large metal sign with the name of the business, MARCO MECHANICS, EST. 1947, was bent from seasonal winter winds over the years. The words were faded and peeling and barely legible. Everything about the establishment looked worn and out-of-date. And it didn't seem busy. Two cars were pulled up to the self-service pump, being gassed up. There was one car up on a four-pull rack, but no one working on it. There were no sounds of work anywhere. There were several cars in a side lot, and Alex guessed that Vin had acquired them in trade or secondhand in the hopes of rebuilding them to sell. The cars looked like they'd been there for a while. He didn't think work was going to begin anytime soon.

Alex began walking to the small brick building that housed the office. Through the glass window he could see Vin, seated at an old wooden desk and talking on the phone. Even the furniture had not changed in all these years. Alex stood for a moment, trying to sort out his feelings as he watched his father in some business discussion. As he watched it occurred to him that like Marco Mechanics, Vin was beginning to show his age as well. The realization brought Alex up short. He could see the deeply etched grooves on the sides of Vin's nose and mouth. The nose itself seemed to have changed shape with age, broadening. His hair, still remarkably thick, had very little grey. The compact body was less muscled and hard, a little more thick, but still sturdy and strong. He wore reading glasses. But there was no question that Vin was getting on.

Still, Alex could see what it was about Vin that would have appealed to women. Vincent Marco was a man's man in the old sense of the word. He was a strong and handsome man who made gentle women feel protected, shy women feel beautiful and special.

As if sensing his presence, Vin glanced up and caught sight of Alex. He didn't much like the sense of being the outsider looking in, but it accurately described his relationship with his father. Alex didn't expect Vin to invite him into the office. That would have been out of character. When Vin glanced back down at a pile of receipts in front of him, ignoring him, Alex just continued to stand there and watch. It had taken Alex years to figure out that just because Vin seemed indifferent to things didn't mean that he was. Only wary and threatened . . . and confused. The knowledge, however, did not make Alex feel any better.

He began idly walking around the lot, making note of the equipment and the extent of the services Marco Mechanics provided its customers. When he was growing up, his friend Benny Almos had gotten him an after-school job at a gas station belonging to an uncle. Alex guessed he'd had some idea that if he knew something about his father's business, perhaps Vin would hire him. They could get to know each other. It didn't happen.

Alex looked around. There were no customers. He checked his watch. It was still early yet. The place looked the same as that day when he was about fifteen, and had traveled all the way from Brooklyn in search of a man named Vincent Marco. The man his mother had finally admitted was his natural father. The man he used to think would magically show up and claim him, thrilled that he had a son.

> Sometimes I think it would have been better if I was just adopted. Then I wouldn't worry so much if my father really loved me. I would know that he was just feeling sorry for me because there was nobody else who wanted me.

Alex remembered reading that in Dallas's journal. He'd figured out that she'd come to her father when she was about five years old after her mother had died. Alex could imagine what that must have been like. Vin had stared blankly at him and said, "I don't know what you're talking about." Then Vin had walked away, and not looked back.

A knot of torment seized Alex for a brief second. He recalled running after Vin, to confront him and make him acknowledge him. Only later, when he confessed to his mother what he'd done, did he learn the rest of the story. Vin Marco had no idea he'd fathered a child with her. It would take two more attempts by Alex to get Vin's attention and to realize that Vin didn't even remember his mother.

"Excuse me. Do you work here?"

Alex turned at the sound of the female voice. There was a black woman standing outside the open door of her car, which was pulled up near one of the gas pumps.

"What's the problem?" Alex asked in response. He began walking toward her.

She closed the door, shaking her head. "I don't know. When I went to start my car this morning . . ."

Alex stopped at the hood of her car as she attempted to describe the trouble. After the woman explained, he opened the driver's side door and sat in the seat. He tried to start the engine and heard the hesitation. He popped the hood and got out to lift it open, checking inside.

"It's probably just transmission fluid. It could be low . . ."

"Can I help you?"

Both the woman and Alex turned at the approach of Vin Marco.

"Yes, this man says I need transmission fluid."

Vin quickly checked the car, repeating the same examination that Alex had. "Yep. That's what it is. I'll be right back." He walked to the open garage and disappeared momentarily inside.

"Are you a regular customer?" Alex asked the woman.

She shook her head. "No, I've never been in this station before. I usually go to one about a mile from here, even though this station is closer to where I live."

"How come?"

The woman hesitated. "Well . . . this place is kinda small and old. I stopped here 'cause I wasn't sure I'd make it to the other shop." She laughed sheepishly.

"Maybe I should give your car a once-over, just

to make sure that there's nothing else wrong," Vin suggested, returning with a gallon jug of a blue liquid. He began administering it to the appropriate spout under the lifted hood.

"No, that's okay. I'm in a hurry. How much is that?"

Alex stood back while the rest of the transaction was completed.

"Thanks for your help." She smiled at Alex before getting into her car and driving off.

"You looking for a job?" Vin asked sarcastically, heading back to his office.

"You offering one?" Alex answered, falling into step next to him.

"I have all the help I can use," Vin said, sitting back in his squeaky chair.

Alex entered the small room behind him and stood facing Vin across the desk. He was sure that the pile of manuals and telephone directories were exactly the same ones that had always been on the desk and cabinet. "Doesn't look like you need much. Not very busy, is it?"

Vin frowned. "It starts picking up around eight. My helper, Julio, will be here soon. He's usually on time."

"Whatever happened to Jimmy Halpern and George Tills?"

Vin made a dismissing gesture, as if the mention of the two names was annoying. "Jimmy went to that new place in the next town. George got old. Said his wife was tired of him coming home with grease and dirt under his nails."

"Couldn't hold on to them, eh?" Alex said bluntly.

Vin glared at him. "If they didn't want to stay, fine with me. The guy I got now is good. He's Dominican, I think. But he's okay."

Alex pursed his lips and glanced out the window onto the lot. There was not another car or potential customer in sight.

"I didn't know you were planning on coming here this morning."

Alex sat in the only other chair. "No plan. I stayed with . . . a friend last night. I'm on my way into the city. Thought I'd stop by."

Vin pretended busyness and began sorting the various pink and yellow billing forms on his desk. "How come?"

Alex studied him for a moment. He'd gotten better at being able to read Vin over the years. He was a fiercely proud man. He was a hardworking, good man, but one who was stuck in time, and having a great deal of trouble keeping up to speed with the changing world around him. He was set in his ways. Which was why, Alex thought with resignation, he no longer had hopes that Vin would ever see him as anything but an interloper in his life. Alex, therefore, no longer tried to make a place for himself there.

"I wanted to talk to you about Nick."

Vin looked at him. There was suspicion in his eyes, but also a weariness that reflected pain and anger. He began shaking his head. "I got nothing to say to you about my son."

The deliberate reference made Alex's jaw tighten, but he kept his expression blank. "You don't have to. But I have something to say anyway. That night at the funeral home . . . I'm sorry for what happened between you and me. You were probably right. I shouldn't have been there."

Vin scowled, drawing his brows together. His clasped hands lay atop the pile of papers. He nodded. "It wasn't a good time."

Alex chuckled. "It has *never* been a good time. I wonder what would have happened if Lillian hadn't been there . . ." He blinked and frowned. "Or if Dallas Oliver hadn't gotten between us?"

"I don't know," Vin admitted. "It was hard enough . . . . losing Nick like that. But Lillian crying . . ." He shook his head.

"I have to be honest with you. I didn't come that night because of you or Nick, but because of her."

Vin shrugged. "I know you like Lillian. I know you didn't like Nick."

"No, I didn't," Alex said. "But not for the reasons you think. Not because you loved him and not me. Nick took too much for granted. He only cared about himself."

"You didn't understand him."

"He didn't deserve the love Lillian had for him."

"You've said enough," Vin said.

Alex stared at Vin, seeing much more than pain in his eyes . . . and it surprised him. Vin had never struck Alex as being a vulnerable man. But he could see a level of doubt and anguish that he hadn't expected, as if Vin might actually believe there was some validity in what he was saying. Alex stood up and took a deep breath. There was no point in voicing any criticism of Nicholas to his father.

Alex swept his hand over his short bristly hair. "Look . . . the truth is, Vin, I used to be jealous as hell of Nick. But I got over it. He had the kind of life I used to dream about as a kid. He had a family . . . the way I wanted. As far as I'm concerned, he blew it."

Alex half expected Vin to rush to the defense of his son, but he didn't. Instead he sat still, staring off into space with tired eyes. Alex stopped directly in front of Vin, forcing him out of his reverie.

"You don't know everything about Nick."

Alex shrugged. "Too late to change anything, even if I did." He stared at Vin. "Do you ever think about . . . grandchildren?" He almost didn't expect Vin to answer, but he stared down at his hands and his brows lifted in an almost wistful fashion.

"There's Justin. Nick's kid with Theresa. But we never see him. Don't know him hardly." Vin shrugged in resignation. "Nothing Lilly and me can do about it. A grandson could have carried on the business. Now

I don't know what I'm gonna do when it's time to retire." Vin straightened his shoulders and withdrew, once again becoming caustic. "Anyway, it's nothing for you to worry about. I'll be okay."

"I know. I came here to tell you I know it hurts a lot. Whatever Nick's faults were, he was still your son." Alex walked to the door and opened it. He turned once more to his father. "Now you know how I always felt."

Vin blinked up at him. "How?"

"I don't think it's any different than when I realized I was never going to have a father. And you were never going to accept me as your son."

Alex had no more he wanted to say. He left the office and headed back toward his car.

"Wait a minute . . ."

Alex continued on but slowed his steps as he glanced over his shoulder at Vin.

Vin slowly approached Alex, his expression pensive and hesitant. He stopped several feet away. "I got something to say, too."

"Go ahead," Alex encouraged.

"Your mother and me . . ." He shook his head, shrugged, struggled for words. "It just happened. It was one of those things. I don't even remember her. I don't remember what she looked like. I . . . I was upset about something else and . . ."

Alex felt his skin grow warm and flushed. He'd waited his whole life to hear his father acknowledge his mother. But not in this way. This is *not* what he wanted to hear. That his mother had been nothing more than an opportunity.

Alex nodded. "I know. Like you said, it just happened. But you and Lillian were already married by then."

Vin shifted uncomfortably and didn't deny it. "Yeah, that's right. We were having some problems and . . . I made a mistake. That's all it was."

"My mother always said you probably don't remember her. She was never angry or bitter. To her it was kind of romantic. She knew you from the neighborhood . . . your family's business. She said she always had a crush on you."

Vin looked genuinely surprised. And then suspicious again. "Yeah? How come she never told nobody about me and what happened?"

"Because she never blamed you. And she never wanted anything from you."

Vin stared at him for a long moment. And then he walked closer to Alex. It was the first time Alex felt that Vin was responding to him with some emotion other than anger. Alex waited, knowing that they were both on the verge of an understanding that, for a lot of reasons, was not possible before.

"I love Lillian more than anything. She was the best thing that ever happened to me. What I did . . . I thought if she found out, I'd lose her. I would have deserved it."

"Then, why did you do it? Why did you risk everything?"

Vin's mouth clamped shut. "I can't talk about it. I know you talk to Lilly . . ."

"You don't have to worry. She's never said a thing to me about that time."

Vin narrowed his gaze on Alex. "That time when you showed up, I thought it was some kind of trick. I thought . . ."

"That me or my mother were going to try and blackmail you." Alex shook his head at the irony of it. "How? For what?"

"You could've told Lilly."

"But I didn't have to. The moment she and I met, she knew. And it didn't seem to matter."

Vin sighed. "No. She didn't ask any questions. But I . . . I told her everything."

"And she forgave you."

"Yeah . . . she forgave me."

"You didn't learn anything from her, did you?" Alex asked softly. He turned to get into his car.

"How come you're so interested in my business?"

For a moment Alex was confused. He thought he'd made himself clear how he felt about his mother. About Nick. But Vin was now referring to the service station. Alex shrugged, as if he hadn't really thought about it all that much.

"This is a good location for your business. It's on a main street and there's a lot of traffic. How come you don't have people driving in here all the time?"

"Some people go elsewhere, that's all. Competition, plain and simple."

Alex faced him squarely. "How come you're not doing anything about it?"

"Like what?"

"Like not cave in and let your customers go elsewhere. Fight for them. Otherwise you're not going to last another five years."

"Marco Mechanics has been a family business for fifty years. I was hoping Nicky would come in and keep it going. With him gone . . ."

"Doesn't mean you have to give up, Vin. Look at this place." Alex spread his arms and looked around. "It's old. I can't believe you're still using a four-pull rack for hoisting cars. How come you don't have hydraulic lift? Where's the impact wrench? Pneumatic equipment and a real diagnostic center?"

"There's nothing wrong with what I got. Everything works."

"So does that ten-year-old Cavalier in the side lot. But it doesn't have power windows or air bags. No one is going to buy it without those things. People want modern. New."

Vin shook his head. "Cost too much money . . ."

Another car turned into the lot, and their attention was drawn to the medium-priced sports car that was maneuvered into the space next to where Alex was parked. A rap number boomed from the speakers but died abruptly when the engine was turned off. A young male got out, his hair cut in a severe fashion from ear to ear, suggesting the use of a bowl to achieve the hard, clean edge. He sported a gold earring in his left lobe. These were his only concessions to his age and current fashion. He was otherwise attired in a royal blue workman's jumpsuit, appropriate to the trade of working on the innards of cars.

"You're late," Vin greeted him in an unforgiving tone.

"Traffic, man," the young man gave as a nonchalant excuse. He openly scrutinized Alex. "You a new customer, or you gonna work here?"

Alex grinned, amused. He thought he might have to change his mind about Vin. Maybe he was loosening up and becoming more tolerant. "I'm passing through. Just leaving."

"This is Julio, my new mechanic. He's good. Knows what he's doing most of the time," Vin complimented the young man.

"Hey . . . I'm the *man*," Julio announced with the confidence of a con artist. He held out his hand to Alex.

Alex automatically adjusted, grasping the offered hand in a street greeting more complicated than a mere shake. "Alex Marco," he introduced himself.

Julio caught on right away. "You related or something to the boss?"

Alex cast a quick glance at Vin, who stood waiting for his answer. Alex knew better than to attempt one. But he also wasn't going to let Vin off the hook. He pointed to Vin as he climbed into his car. "I think you'd better ask the boss."

He drove away leaving Vin with something to talk about.

"Hello?"

"Who's this?"

"I'm Megan. Do you want to talk to Aunt Dallas?"

"*Aunt* Dallas?" The male voice chuckled. "You must be the godchild she told me about. Yeah. Put her on."

"What's your name?" Megan asked.

"Oh . . . she'll know who it is. Just tell her, a friend."

Megan knelt on the sofa cushions and yelled down the short corridor leading to the rest of the apartment. "Aunt Dallas . . . there's a man on the phone. He says he wants to talk to you."

Dallas hung her robe on the hook inside the closet door and leaned toward the bedroom door. "What man? Did you get his name?"

"He said you'll know."

Dallas sighed. She hated this. What was this with people who didn't want to identify themselves? She sat down on the side of her bed and picked up the extension.

"I got it," she called out again, and heard Megan hang up from the living room. "Hello?"

"Guess we can't get together tonight."

"Hello, Burke. You should have called sooner."

"I called yesterday morning. You didn't get back to me."

"I was probably in a meeting with Peggy. Then I had an appointment I was running late for. I never checked my voice mail."

"You didn't check it in the afternoon, either."

She tried to remember. "You're right. I had to pick up Megan from Penn Station. She's staying with me for the weekend."

"See that? You can't always blame me when we don't talk," he said self-righteously. "But I won't hold it against you."

"Thanks."

"So you're not available?"

"Megan goes home this afternoon. What do you have in mind?"

"Just to be with you," Burke said disarmingly.

Dallas waited. Then she felt ashamed of herself. She expected so much from him, and then was suspicious of his offering. "That's nice."

"I was hoping to meet and catch a show at the Blue Note."

One of his clients, Dallas guessed. "I can do that. Are we meeting for dinner first?"

"I can't. I have to sit in on a taping at five. You have to get your godchild home, right?"

She shouldn't complain, Dallas realized. He was trying. "That's true."

"Meet me at the club? It'll save time, and the taping might run over."

Dallas quietly hung up the phone. She sat and waited for the crash to start. That sensation in the middle of her body that made her feel as if she were shrinking and were going to disappear. That digging into her soul to let the air out because she wasn't quite good enough and her feelings didn't matter. Except for the first time she wasn't sure they'd ever been together that it wasn't about business. Sleeping with him was private. Maybe. Either Burke didn't get it, or he didn't really care.

"Aunt Dallas! Come here, quick!"

Dallas jumped. She got up and hurried to the living room, where Megan had been watching Sunday morning TV since waking up.

"Megan? What's wrong?"

"Look!" Megan pointed at the screen.

Dallas was confused by what she saw. There was a table with what appeared to be broken items like bottles and jars, tools, what looked to be an old revolver, several pairs of glasses. A voice was talking about the things laid out, and another voice was asking questions. The TV camera pulled back, and the lens panned onto two men, one holding a hand mike, and the other, a big and husky man with the wind riffling through his light-colored hair, was dressed in some close black rubber outfit, describing and explaining everything. They were outdoors, and in the background was the blurred and out of focus shimmering of a body of water.

Dallas frowned. "What am I looking at?"

"I saw Alex. Look . . ."

The camera eventually pulled back even farther to include a third man. It was Alex, dressed in the same black garment. It was his turn to answer questions, and Dallas sat next to Megan. What became quickly obvious was that Alex and the other man were divers. The things spread out on the table in front of them had been retrieved from the rivers, inlets, bays, estuaries, and other coastal waters in and around New York.

"How did this project begin?" the commentator asked.

The first man began to answer.

"That's Ross," Megan announced.

"Who's Ross?" Dallas asked.

"He's Alex's friend. He's really nice."

". . . find a lot of stuff down there . . ."

"No bodies, I hope," the interviewer joked, but the man didn't find the question amusing and skirted answering directly.

"The rivers and ocean is a convenient place to dump a lot of things."

Dallas turned to look at Megan, who was still attired in an oversized T-shirt that served as a nightgown. Her long wavy hair was loose and tucked behind her ears. "How did you meet Ross?"

"Alex comes to see me and Mom sometimes. One time he brought that other man. Ross. They're best friends. Like you and Mom are best friends."

Dallas stared at the screen again. Alex had been seeing Valerie. Somehow, she knew she shouldn't be surprised. But she had a peculiar reaction to the news. She struggled for a moment to identify it and finally settled on a sense of loss. The TV camera panned back and forth between Alex and Ross as they answered questions. Alex was serious and thoughtful with his answers. He didn't display the easy smoothness of Ross, whom he deferred to, but he spoke with a surprising knowledge and expertise of diving. What he and Ross had salvaged from the waters was like an archaeological treasure trove of urban life.

"Can we go and see them?"

"See them? Where?" Dallas asked.

"At the aquarium. All that stuff they found is on display. And Ross and Alex are going to be there to answer questions. Can we?"

"I . . . don't know," Dallas murmured, knowing, however, that she wanted very much to find out more about what Alex did. "Have you finished your homework? I thought you wanted to interview me for one of your classes."

"I do. You answered all my questions. If I write it up real quick so you can see it, then can we go to see Alex and Ross?"

Dallas grimaced, finding herself more and more interested in what the three men were discussing on TV, but giving her attention to Megan. "We'll see. First you have to make up the pullout bed in my studio. Then we have to have breakfast. You have to finish your school report . . . I have to finish my article . . ."

Megan got up abruptly from the sofa and ran out of the living room. "I can do that."

"I didn't make any promises, Meg," Dallas called after her.

She then looked at the TV again. The interview ended, and after announcing that the special exhibit of river finds would continue at the aquarium through the end of the month, the male commentator turned the program back over to his studio.

Dallas got up and headed back to her bedroom. But she hesitated in the hall, and detoured instead to the second room that she'd converted into an office/studio cum guest room. She leaned in the doorway, watching Megan search through a pile of jumbled items of clothing in her weekend tote.

"You sure you want to spend the afternoon at the aquarium? I thought you wanted to have lunch at Planet Hollywood and go to a movie."

Megan sat back on her haunches and looked momentarily indecisive. She had a hair scrunchy on her wrist, as if it were a bracelet. She swept back her hair from her face and adroitly pulled a gathered ponytail through the elastic hair ornament. Megan nodded but looked beguilingly at her godmother.

"Yeah, I'm sure. But can we still do Planet Hollywood the next time I come to visit?"

"Fine." Dallas walked into her office and sat at her desk. She began to play with a novelty pencil, bent and shaped into an open heart, that someone had given her at a conference. "So, you really like Alex? Does he spend a lot of time with you and your mother?"

Megan thought about it and shrugged. "Um, not really. He's only been over a few times. Once Mom cooked dinner, but the other times the three of us went out to eat."

Dallas frowned at the pencil. She wasn't sure she should ask any more questions. She felt peculiar wanting to know about the visits. "Sounds like it was fun."

"It's okay. I like Alex. He's really nice. But he and my mom talk about stuff I don't understand. It's kinda boring."

"Does . . . your mom like him a lot, too?" Dallas asked uncomfortably, aware that she was pumping her godchild for information.

"Oh, yeah. She spends a lot of time getting ready when he's coming over." Megan chortled knowingly.

Dallas nodded. Valerie had always taken the position that she never knew when a date might become more interesting. "You said that the other man, Ross, is Alex's best friend?"

Megan sighed, finally stopped her pubescent toiletry, and sat cross-legged on the floor in front of Dallas. "Yeah. He's really cool. He tells all these funny stories about when he and Alex were in the war."

"What war?" Dallas interrupted in surprise.

Megan shrugged. "I don't know. I don't remember. And he thinks Beavis and Butthead are stupid, too." Her eyes brightened with excitement. "And he and Alex scuba dive! I think that would be really cool to do, but . . . I don't even know how to swim."

Dallas smiled affectionately at the little girl. "I think that's kind of important," she agreed. "So, you like Ross, too?"

Megan nodded enthusiastically. "He's really neat."

"Ross comes over when Alex is there?"

Megan scrunched up her face and tried to remember. "I think . . . only twice. I don't think Mom likes him very much."

"Why not?" Dallas asked.

Megan got up from the floor and began pulling on a pair of jeans. She became distracted halfway through by a scab on her elbow, which she proceeded to pick. "I don't know. She said he was rude and too . . . oh . . . ar . . . auda-cious," Megan struggled. She turned to frown at Dallas. "What does that mean?"

Dallas had a feeling it meant that Valerie couldn't make him do what she wanted. "There's a dictionary on my desk. Look it up," Dallas told her goddaughter. Megan groaned. "What do you want for breakfast?"

"Can we have pancakes?"

"Okay," Dallas said, leaving the office and heading back to her room. "But you'd better hurry up and get dressed if we're going out to Coney Island. You still have to get back home tonight."

Megan skipped over to Dallas, wrapping her arms around her. "Aunt Dallas . . ." she started in a crooning little girl voice.

"The answer is no. You can't stay another night. You have school in the morning, and I have work."

Megan didn't pursue the inevitable, although she sighed deeply, a martyr to youth and lack of power.

But she continued to hug Dallas, walking with her to the other bedroom, and then releasing her to bounce down on the bed, sending her ponytail flying like a glorious silk rope.

"I really love being with you. I'm glad you're my godmother."

Dallas smiled to herself, enjoying the warm regard of the little girl, and feeling a poignant regret that she'd lost her own child. She was very careful to remember that Megan was not hers. And she didn't know whether to be disturbed or pleased that the loss didn't hurt as much anymore. She hadn't been that far along in her pregnancy. Three months. She hadn't begun to picture her child yet. A little boy or girl. Dallas remembered thinking she wanted a boy. But she would have wanted him to grow up to be like Hayden. He would be handsome and bright and funny, and combine the best of her father, Dean, and . . . and . . .

She caught her breath at an unexpected thought and image, and turned quickly away from it. It made her nervous. She smiled teasingly at Megan Marie. "All in all, you're not so bad, either. I think I'll keep you."

Megan giggled.

"There they are . . ." Megan shouted, and took off toward the area set up outside the New York Aquarium for the advertised exhibit.

Dallas kept an eye on the twelve-year-old, watching as Megan Marie worked her way down the row of tables. She hung back, walking slowly, left with her godchild's weekend tote. The exhibit was free for all to see, a promotional tease to encourage visitors to the indoor facility. But it was also to show a side of sea life that most people never think about. There were nearly a dozen tables and stands, tanks and canisters, displaying the unusual finds and treasures retrieved from the waterways around the city, along with the equipment used.

Dallas spotted Alex first. From a distance of about a hundred feet, she stopped and stared at him. She frowned at the strong sense of knowing this man. But what did she really know about him? Bits and pieces. Impressions. Nothing that was tangible or concrete. And yet . . . she *knew* this man.

She noticed Megan had finally reached another man. She saw the smiling surprise greeting he gave to Megan. He then turned to Alex and mouthed something, gaining Alex's attention. Megan leaned across the table to kiss both men on the cheek. There was more exchange of conversation as Megan pointed in her direction, and Dallas watched as both men searched until they'd found her.

Ross cheerfully waved at her, as if he knew her. Dallas had to laugh. But Alex stared in surprise for a second, until a smile curved his mouth. He looked like he was glad to see her. In truth, Dallas acknowledged to herself, she felt the same way. He beckoned to her. Dallas approached the table, waiting patiently until a group of eager children had passed.

She noticed that Megan had ducked under the tables to stand next to the other man. Dallas frowned and held out her hand toward the child.

"Megan, don't! You can't . . ."

Alex reached for her hand. "It's okay. This is pretty laid-back. A guy down at the end has his dog with him." He squeezed her hand and tugged. "Come on. There's another chair."

Dallas shook her head and gently tried to free her hand. "No. I . . ."

Alex ignored her, shifting aside several large black nylon duffel bags to make room for her to step behind the table next to him. He pulled the chair out and indicated that she should sit down. Then Alex's attention was diverted to another question, from a man and his son about an item on the table.

Dallas found herself listening to Alex's answers and

grew more and more impressed. Whatever Alex did for a living was not limited just to collecting garbage.

Alex said good-bye to the departing father and son and turned back to Dallas. He stuffed his hands into the front pockets of his jeans. He squinted against the light salty breeze off the Atlantic Ocean, just off to the right of where the tables were set up. Alex let his gaze wander over Dallas. He had a sensation that she had changed, and realized it was because she was not in the company of Valerie or Lillian. He'd been thinking about her, ever since driving her home that night and meeting her brother.

"Baby-sitting?' he asked.

Dallas grinned and nodded. Her eyes were bright. "Once a month. Bonding time."

"Megan talks a lot about you. She loves you."

Dallas averted her eyes briefly. He spent a lot of time with Valerie, she surmised. "The feeling's mutual."

"Whose idea was this?"

"Megan's. She saw you and your friend on a news program this morning. So, here we are."

Alex grinned at her. "Good for Megan. I'm glad to see you again. I've been thinking about you."

She didn't answer. Instead, what went through her mind was a silent "me, too."

"I've been reading some of your articles."

She was surprised. "You have?"

He nodded and sat down next to her. "*Soul of the City,* right?"

"Yes, that's right."

His gaze wandered over her face. "Lillian was right. You're good."

"Lillian is biased. And I'm not sure if she's ever read anything from the magazine. It's not one you find at her local newsstand."

"I know it's aimed at black readers, but I like it. I find out things," he said slyly.

Dallas laughed. "Like what?"

"Like . . . about hair. And food. I always wondered what Hoppin' John was. There was a piece about Farrakhan as a father and not just a political icon. I liked the one you wrote about . . ."

Dallas sighed. "I know. Butts. That article is going to haunt me the rest of my life."

"It wasn't about butts, was it? I read into it that it was about pride, in a way."

Dallas looked at him. He wasn't teasing now. "That's right . . . that's part of it."

"Don't be so surprised. I told you I wasn't prejudiced. Besides, I grew up around a lot of different kinds of people. Black. White. Hispanic. When you're poor, you don't have a choice about where you're going to live."

She didn't know that, but Dallas had always suspected that he had an interesting history. She looked around at the setting, the things on the table. The man before her. Dallas shook her head.

"You don't just collect garbage, do you?"

He shrugged. "No, not really." She waited patiently. "I also own a dive shop with Ross . . ." He indicated him with a gesture of his head. "We keep one boat at the marina a little south of here. We teach search and recovery techniques to police rescue teams and use their craft at Earie Basin. We do some commercial diving . . . the guy interviewing us this morning called it urban archaeology. It's a fancy name for the junk we find."

"Where did you learn?" she asked.

He shrugged nonchalantly, as if it wasn't important. "The navy. Guys with money go to college. Guys like me . . ."

"Go into the service," Dallas finished. "Megan said you and your friend were in a war."

He nodded. "Kuwait. Desert Storm. We're ex-SEALs."

She stared. Navy SEAL. She understood that was special. Alex and Ross had been more than just enlisted men. Dallas had a thousand questions to ask. So much she wanted to know.

"Hey, Ross? Come here a minute," Alex said over his shoulder, but without breaking eye contact with Dallas. "Ross Manning, this is Dallas Oliver."

Dallas stood up to face him and Megan. Megan lumbered toward her, wearing a diving mask that was much too big for her face. She had her hands in a pair of swim fins, all in all looking like an overgrown insect. Dallas laughed at her.

Ross didn't shake her hand, but stood grinning and appraising her quite thoroughly.

"Hi, Dallas. Hey, that's a great name. Born there?"

"No," she responded simply.

"Another friend of Alex's, right? Man, he has a lot of pretty women for friends."

"Me, too," Megan voiced, and the men chuckled.

Dallas could see that the TV camera that morning had not done him justice. Ross Manning was not nearly as heavy as the projected image had indicated. He was big and handsome, but hardly soft. He was staring at her rather intently, to the point of making Dallas feel uncomfortable.

"You know . . . you and Megan could be mother and daughter," Ross observed.

Dallas blinked and her smile wavered. She'd been told that before many times. Dallas realized that Alex was staring at her, too, and she imagined she knew what he was thinking.

"So, who came first? Alex or Valerie?" Ross asked.

Dallas frowned, not understanding the question at first. "Oh, you mean who did I know first? Valerie. She and I have been best friends since we were kids."

Ross clapped a hand on Alex's shoulder. "Well, Alex and I don't go back that far, but I'd do anything for him. Great guy."

Alex shifted, uncomfortable with the compliment. He grinned at Ross. "Sorry I can't say the same."

Ross laughed heartily.

Megan stood in front of the two men, looking from one to the other through the mask. "I don't have a best friend."

Ross tugged at her ponytail. "Will I do for today?"

Megan nodded. "Okay."

"Well, just part of the day. Megan has to get back home."

"Alex and I will be through here in about two hours. Why don't you hang around? We'll catch something to eat."

"Oooh, can we?" Megan asked excitedly.

"We'd better call your mother and let her know," Ross said.

"I'll call her," Alex volunteered smoothly.

Dallas smiled at the camaraderie, and appreciated that both men were, in their own way, attentive and protective of Megan's young ego. She didn't know yet what part Ross Manning played in the connection between Valerie, her daughter, and Alex. She glanced at Alex and found him watching her, and then he turned his attention to Megan, listening to a question.

You could be mother and daughter . . . That's what Ross had said. But it only just now occurred to Dallas, as she witnessed the interplay between Megan and Alex, that she might make a similar observation.

Valerie heard the car pull up in front of the house and got up from the sofa, clicking off the TV with the remote. By the time she reached the front door, she could hear her daughter's voice and laughter, and that of a man. She'd been feeling annoyed all afternoon, since she'd received the call from Alex about Megan's adventure. But she was feeling a little more charitable now that Megan had been delivered safely home.

When she opened the door, Megan was halfway up the walk toward the door, calling good-bye to the man standing at the curb, about to get back into his car.

"Hi, Mom," Megan said breezily, kissing her mother perfunctorily on the cheek.

"Hi, sweetie. Did you have a good time?" Valerie responded, her voice trailing off as she looked at the idling car.

"Yeah, it was great."

It wasn't Alex. It was Ross Manning.

Valerie stopped and gazed out at him. Ross leaned over the hood of his car and stared right back. Her stomach somersaulted, and her muscles became tense. Yet Ross showed no inclination to linger. He stood up and started to open his car door.

This retreat made Valerie curious, and she continued to stare at him, waiting for Ross to give her an opening in which she could retaliate, set him in his place. But instead he smiled a slow considering smile. It was openly friendly, as if he'd never told her, in so many words, that Alex was not for her. As if she'd never told him to mind his own business.

She wanted to whirl on him, cut him cold, and slam the door in his face. But Valerie knew now she wouldn't do that. There was something she had to know.

"I thought Alex was bringing Megan home. That's what he said when he called."

"I know. I told him I'd drive her home. He took Dallas back to her place. Night . . ." he said.

Valerie didn't respond. She stood, dumbfounded, as Ross got back into his car and drove off. That he had no more to say Valerie found frustrating, and it angered her even more. But she didn't know why. She returned to the house and slammed the door anyway.

Chapter Ten

"Hello, Dallas Oliver . . ."

"Hi. It's me."

"Hey, Val. I've been thinking about you. I was going to call . . ."

"The road to hell is paved with good intentions. Is that how it goes?"

"That's right. But I wasn't on the road to hell. What a thing to say. I was just real busy. As a matter of fact, I can't stay on the phone—"

"Yeah, I know. You have a deadline," Valerie interrupted.

"Are you okay? You sound angry about something."

"Why should I be angry?"

"Megan. Is she getting on your nerves again? Wait a few years. Someone told me it gets worse. Teenagers are pretty obnoxious. Of course, *we* weren't like that . . ." Dallas chuckled.

"So what's new? What have you been up to?"

Dallas frowned. Valerie did sound formal and a bit cool. She used to do this whenever she got annoyed about something. Like when her parents wouldn't let her go to a party or concert. When a man hadn't called to ask her out.

Dallas turned to gaze at the photographs on her desk. One of them was of Valerie and Megan and herself. They were all laughing and hugging one another, with Megan in the middle—a loving demonstration of the solid relationship between them.

"Trying to keep my social calendar straight," Dallas said wryly. "I have two functions to cover this week for *Soul,* my stepmother's birthday is coming up, Maureen is getting married and I haven't a thing to wear," she teased.

"How nice for Maureen. Tell her I said congratulations."

Dallas sighed and sat back in her chair. "I will. I'm in the wedding party, so I'll probably have to buy some awful rack dress that—"

"Who's going to be your escort?" Valerie interrupted.

"Burke," Dallas murmured indifferently. "Unless Maureen's fiancé needs to partner me with one of his friends. How's Meg?" There was a slight pause that only made Dallas all the more curious about Valerie's flat tone.

"She's good. She's still talking about last weekend. Sounds like you guys had a good time."

"We did. I'm surprised that she still likes to come and visit every month. You know, she's getting to the age when her friends—"

"She told me you two went out to the aquarium to see Alex. Some exhibit or something?"

Dallas was suddenly alert to the subtle question in her friend's voice. Cautiously she responded. "Yeah, that's right. It was fascinating. I guess you know that Alex is a professional diver? Ex-navy SEAL."

"I'm sure he told me at some point when we were together."

Dallas chuckled. "He told me he collected garbage. It was fun. He had all this stuff that came from the river. Some of it very old. It was kind of interesting to see what sort of things people used and then got rid of years ago. Unfortunately by tossing a lot of it into the river."

"Did you meet his friend?" Valerie asked.

"Ross? Yes. He was very nice. Charming and friendly. He and Megan get along great. Has Megan told you she wants to learn to scuba dive?"

Valerie sighed. "She did. But she's too young for that. Besides . . ."

Dallas waited. "Besides, what?"

"I don't know. I'm not sure that I like Ross."

"Really? He seems so easygoing. He thinks the world of Alex."

"Well, if he did, then he wouldn't . . . never mind."

Dallas became impatient. "Okay, Val. What's going on? What's the matter with you?"

"I thought *you* were going to bring Megan back home on Sunday. I was really annoyed when I opened my door to find that Ross had brought my daughter home. I don't know him all that well. When Megan called to say she was on her way and was getting a ride, I thought maybe Alex would be bringing you both. You and Alex are my friends. Ross isn't."

Dallas detected a real note of possessiveness on Valerie's part toward Alex. And yet, while she felt that perhaps Valerie was overreacting to the events of the previous weekend, she understood the legitimate concerns for Megan Marie.

"Well . . . I'm sorry. I didn't think that you'd object."

"If you were going to be spending the day at the aquarium with Alex and Ross, why didn't I get invited along?"

"Valerie . . . I don't get this. You always look forward to Megan's visits with me because it gives you a day to yourself to do what you want. Besides, going to see Alex and Ross was a split-second decision."

"That's all I've been hearing about for two days."

Dallas grinned and tried to coax Valerie out of her mood with teasing. "Don't tell me you're jealous. Just because you missed a bunch of rusty junk from the ocean?"

"Ross said that Alex drove you home."

"Only into Manhattan. I was meeting Burke for a late date."

"Oh, really?" Valerie cooed. "So, how was it? What did you do?"

"Not as much as I thought we would. We went to a club act in the village."

"Nice."

"It turned out to be business, not a date. Some new talent Burke is promoting for his label. I was there to make him look good for some execs. Afterward he sent me home in a cab."

"How romantic."

"Exactly. I had more fun with Megan, Alex, and Ross."

"Sounds like it," Valerie murmured.

"I can make it up to you."

"How?"

"I have to go to a lecture at NYU this week. Want to go with me? Burke can't. There's a reception afterward."

"No . . . I don't think so. It's too much of a hassle to come into the city, and I'd get home so late."

Dallas gazed at the photo again. "Not any more so than when I come out to visit you and Megan. Or my folks. Or Lillian. And you have a car."

Dallas glanced up and saw that Peggy was standing in front of her desk. She raised her brows in question and briefly covered the mouthpiece.

"Yes?"

"I'd like to see you in my office. When you have a moment," Peggy said.

She didn't wait for an answer, and Dallas watched her walk away, wondering what she'd written now that had gotten people stirred up.

"Five minutes . . ." Dallas called after her departing figure. She turned her attention to Valerie again.

Valerie sighed. "But I'd have to make arrangements for someone to stay with Megan . . . maybe some other time."

"Are you sure that's everything? Is there something else you want to tell me, Val?"

"No. I'm just feeling . . . I don't know. I guess I'm not in a very good mood."

"PMS?" Dallas suggested. Valerie laughed. "I promise you the nest time Megan and I decide at the very last moment that we're going to do something fun, we'll let you know."

"Did I sound bitchy?" Valerie asked, slightly mollified by Dallas's offer.

"Yes."

"You have my permission to get even."

Dallas smiled. "Don't be surprised when I take you up on that offer. I gotta go. I'll talk to you later."

When Dallas got off the phone, she continued to sit for a moment thinking about the call. As much as she'd tried to convince Valerie that she hadn't missed a thing, Dallas was very aware that she'd not told Valerie everything. For one thing, it had been wonderful to find out more about Alex without the distraction of Valerie, who most certainly would have demanded his undivided attention. For another, Dallas had a sense that the things Alex had told her he had not told Valerie.

After the exhibit they'd all gone out for something to eat. McDonald's, keeping in mind the limitations of a twelve-year-old's food likes. And they'd stopped by Alex's place near Manhattan Beach to drop off equipment. He'd invited them in for the ten minutes it had taken, and Dallas had used the time to get a better sense of who the adult Alex Marco was.

He was settled. He had a place that looked like a home, unlike that grim apartment fifteen years ago. It was definitely a male domain, but orderly and comfortable. Dallas had especially liked the stack of *Aqua Corp* and *Northeast Dive* journals, right next to copies of *New York* magazine. There were even a few houseplants. A little scraggly, but their presence was reassuring.

There were photos of Alex in obvious military settings, dressed in weighty dive gear, or handsome in a uniform. He caught her examining the photos and whispered in passing, "Not very impressive, is it? Not like being a lawyer or something like that."

She'd smiled at him. "I have no complaints."

But the more Dallas thought about it, the more she felt somewhat dissatisfied with the designation of being Alex's friend. It made her feel like the second banana. The also ran. The bridesmaid. But what were the alternatives?

Dallas looked at her watch. She had to get to Peggy's office. She located a pad and pen for notes and got up from her desk. Just then the phone rang again, and Dallas hesitated, debating the wisdom of answering. On the other hand, it could be one of a half-dozen different sources she'd been trying to reach for interviews or comments. With another quick look at the time she leaned back to lift the receiver from the phone.

"Hello, Dallas Oliver."

"Hi. Is this *the* Dallas Oliver? The one who writes the column 'My Word' in *Soul* magazine?"

A rush of surprise coursed through her, making her sit down abruptly again. "Alex?"

He chuckled. "Nobody answers their phone anymore. I thought I'd get your machine or something. Is this a bad time to be calling?"

Dallas was still too unprepared to respond naturally. She realized that she was struggling to settle down and not be so pleased to hear from him. "No . . . I . . . No, but . . ."

"I know I caught you off guard, right?"

Again Dallas tried to find the appropriate reaction. Finally, she gave up and went for the truth. "Yes. You did."

"I've been meaning to."

"So you got up this morning and decided you were going to call me today?"

"That's pretty much it. Look, I know you have to go. Probably have a meeting or something . . ."

Dallas laughed. "As a matter of fact, I do. You're right. I normally would have let the answering machine pick up the call."

"Hey, then this was meant to be. We have to take advantage of it. I have to be in your neck of the woods this afternoon. Any chance we can meet for lunch or something?"

Dallas sat still and silently repeated the question to herself. The conversation with Valerie was fresh in her mind, and Dallas wondered if it would be a betrayal to accept. "Well . . ."

"I know I should have called you sooner, but . . . I guess I was afraid you'd say no."

Another surprise. "You were? I don't understand why you would think that. I mean, I wouldn't have," she answered, even though she knew that she might very well have because of Valerie.

"Do you have time today?"

No, she didn't. She hadn't counted on *anything* like this. "Sure. Today is fine."

"Great. Where should I meet you?"

The warning bells did not stop when Dallas got off the phone. She made the short walk to the meeting with Peggy feeling squeamish. But the moment Dallas walked into Peggy's office, she had to pull herself together. No more time to indulge in speculation. Nona was there, too.

Dallas looked back and forth between the two women, knowing instinctively that they'd been discussing her before her arrival. Peggy had that "enough said" look, while Nona was looking rather pleased with herself.

"Sorry. I guess I'm still a few minutes early," she said to cover the awkward moment.

"No, you're on time," Peggy said, beckoning Dallas into her office. "I asked Nona to be here for a few moments. Sit down."

Dallas took the second of the two chairs positioned in front of Peggy's desk. She glanced surreptitiously at Nona, trying to figure out what was going on. She couldn't, so she decided to take the offensive.

"Let me guess," Dallas began. "It was either the piece about hair extensions and fake fingernails, or the one I did about black fatherless children."

Nona slowly turned toward her, focusing a stare meant to make her wither. But Dallas was not intimidated. She'd come too far for that.

"I didn't like either one of them," Nona said honestly. "I wish you'd pick something else to criticize besides black styles and fashion."

"It wasn't a value judgment. It was observation."

"That's not what this is about," Peggy interjected, not taking sides but quickly attempting damage control. "If we only wrote what people liked to read all the time, Nona, we'd be no different from a dozen other publications on the newsstand. I don't think I have to play the First Amendment card to make my point.

"I'll make this brief. Dallas, I've decided to let Nona cover that film forum event at NYU tomorrow. You're off the hook."

"That's not how I looked at it," Dallas responded. She ignored the satisfaction on Nona's face. "Can I ask why?"

Nona crossed her legs, calm in her victory. "Because I asked Peggy to let me cover the program. Because I'm the entertainment editor. I don't write what you do, and you can't write what I do."

Peggy nodded. "I think Nona's right, Dallas. Not about you not being able to do a straight piece, but she does have the background and I'd like that particular angle."

Dallas met the editor's gaze straight on. As always, it was hard to read her expression. She didn't doubt Peggy's reasoning at all, but she also wondered about this turnabout.

"Fine with me."

Peggy handed a business-size envelope to Nona.

"Here are the passes for the program. That's it for now."

Dallas watched as Nona stood up, accepting the information. After final instructions from the editor she left the office.

"I hope you don't take my thinking on this personally, Dallas," Peggy began, calmly looking through several pages of letters and phone messages on her desk. She looked at one in particular and placed it in front of her, reading it through again. "Quite honestly, looking at the assignment on balance I decided that changing your voice to do a piece that was just straight reporting was not what I wanted." Peggy looked up, her broad, stern features those of a person who had to make the hard decisions. "You know you have a certain reputation as one of our writers."

Dallas nodded, feeling her stomach starting to knot with apprehension. Was she going to be fired?

"You know, I'm sure, that you sometimes cut a little too close to the bone. And I'm sure you know that you tend to open up a lot of cultural wounds that keep scabbing over but never really heal. You take a lot of heat for that. As far as I can see, you handle being on the hot seat well enough. That's why I'm going to ask you to think about doing a piece on being biracial."

Dallas stared at her editor. Throughout her entire career at *Soul of the City* she had been controversial, but she had never written about something so personal. Peggy's request struck Dallas now as being asked to cut open a vein. She was being asked to write not what she thought, but how she felt.

"What makes you think I should do that?" she asked.

Peggy merely smiled. "What makes you think you shouldn't? I'm not going to tell you how to write it, of course. But I bet you've given it some thought. You certainly have shown that you're not unwilling to go toe to toe with other sensitive topics."

"No, I haven't been afraid," Dallas conceded cautiously. "But I've also paid the price."

Peggy shrugged, not particularly sympathetic. "That's what happens when you ask hard questions and expect people to think. That's why you're a journalist."

Dallas couldn't tell if Peggy actually supported the idea or was simply making an editorial decision. But if nothing else, Dallas always sensed that Peggy was fair. She nodded in consent. "I'll work up an outline . . ."

"I don't need one. Just do it," Peggy said, indicating that the subject was over and she wanted to move on. "Now," she said, still holding the single sheet of paper and looking at Dallas. "No good deed goes unpunished or unrewarded. However you choose to look at things. You've been on the firing line on more than one occasion, and people have been taking notice. Some people might have trouble with you, but lots of others, apparently, admire what you do. That means opportunities for you."

Dallas frowned. This was sounding too much like a buildup to being given *very* bad news. "You . . . you don't think I fit in here? Am I being asked to find another publication to write for?"

Peggy chuckled, and her dimples appeared briefly. "I just asked you to write a very up-front article. Why would I then turn around and let you go? Don't worry. Your job is safe. This is a letter of intent, Dallas, from an editor who contacted me a month ago. He'd like you to write a book. I'm not asking for your resignation. You're being offered a book contract."

Alex had two thoughts as he watched Dallas walk toward the restaurant where he stood waiting for her. One was that he was glad she'd shown up. Two . . . was the unexpected observation that his mother would like her.

Every time he saw Dallas, Alex realized, he felt not

only comfortable but a certain rightness. It felt natural to him, like family or close friends he'd grown up with. He didn't have to pretend to have qualities far beyond the reach of mortal man. Unlike with Valerie, he didn't have to be anyone but who he was.

Dallas suddenly saw him. For a moment Alex could detect the uncertainty that made her blink, and then look down at the ground to hide her expression. He'd never thought of Dallas as shy, but that's what it was. That, and an awkwardness based on what they still did not know about each other. When she looked up again, Alex waved briefly and smiled and was rewarded with a smile in return. She slowed her steps several feet from him.

"Hi. I, uh, I'm sorry if I kept you waiting."

He glanced at his watch. "You're five minutes early. I think you're the first woman in history to ever make a date on time."

She grinned. "I'm used to working under deadlines."

Alex pulled open the door to the restaurant and held it for her. "This isn't a business lunch, so forget about deadlines."

They entered and were seated at a tiny square table. Their knees were pressed together beneath it, but neither of them bothered to move their chair back to make more room. Dallas ordered the soup and salad lunch combo while Alex went for the traditional burger with all the trimmings. With that out of the way, they faced each other. Alex felt uneasy, and he noticed that Dallas also seemed so. But she spoke first.

"I want to thank you for Sunday afternoon. It was real nice. Megan had a ball."

Alex smiled. "I feel like I should thank you. It was going to be a *very* long day. You were better company than Ross and a lot better-looking."

Dallas arched a brow. "That doesn't sound like much of a compliment."

"Well, if it helps, Ross thought so, too." Alex sat back as the waiter put down place settings with napkins and glasses of water. "Did you, uh, hear from Valerie?"

Dallas slid the napkin from beneath the flatware and spread it over her lap. The action allowed her to keep her head lowered so that he couldn't see her face.

"Yes, I did. I never thought to invite her to meet us. I guess I should have. She missed all the fun."

Alex listened to the carefully worded explanation. It made him want to smile because it was typical of what he'd come to know about Dallas; she was protecting someone else's feelings. "What you really want to say is that she was pissed off, and took it personally." Dallas stared at him. "I'm sorry if she gave you a hard time."

"I'm used to Valerie. Sometimes I think she's really insecure, and she hides it behind wanting everyone's undivided attention."

"You seem to understand her well," Alex said with a nod.

"She and I go back a long way. We've been through a lot together. I guess I know her a little better than most people. She can probably say the same about me."

Alex placed his elbows on the table and leaned across the space toward Dallas. "And do you tell her everything?" He was fascinated to see the slight flush that colored her cheeks. She knew what he was talking about.

"No. Not everything. But then, Val has secrets, too. Even Lillian and Vin had secrets, remember?" She found that he was studying her very closely.

Alex lowered his gaze and nodded. He knew some of Dallas's secrets. He was not at liberty to talk about Val's. He was not prepared to talk about his.

"I was surprised when I got your call. Was there . . . any special reason?" she asked.

"How about, I just wanted to see you. I said I would call, and I usually keep my word."

Dallas remembered very well, but she still felt uneasy. She was sure that Valerie had staked a claim on Alex Marco, and for all Dallas knew it was reciprocal.

She tilted her head at him. "Okay. What else?"

He chuckled in surprise. "Man, you've gotten tough. Don't you believe me?"

"I guess that's the reporter in me. People sometimes have ulterior motives."

"Okay, I confess." Alex reached into an inner pocket of his sports jacket and extracted a small bundle, wrapped in red tissue paper. He held it out to her.

Dallas stared at it, looked at him, and finally accepted the offering. She slowly peeled away the paper until the object was revealed. It was a small round bottle of cobalt blue, about the size of a tangerine. The top was gone, and the glass surface had a muted frosty appearance instead of being shiny the way it must have appeared when new. It was also embossed all over the outside with stars.

Alex paid close attention to her response. He could see by the subtle smile that played around her mouth that Dallas was pleased. He had guessed correctly that she would appreciate the bottle. That had been important to him.

"This is . . . beautiful," she breathed. She rubbed here fingers over the bottle, slightly roughened from the elements of salt water and sand. Dallas frowned. "Are you giving this to me?"

"That's right."

Her eyes widened. "Why?"

Alex should have known that she would ask. "Because I knew you'd like it. You seemed to really get into the things in the exhibit last weekend. I wanted you to have that."

"But . . . isn't it valuable? Shouldn't it be in a museum?"

He laughed. "The person who chucked it overboard is going to be real upset if that's true. No, I don't think it's worth very much that way. Ross and I find stuff like that all the time. A lot of it we don't even bother bringing to the surface."

Dallas didn't know what to say. It was an unusual gift. But it was a gift nonetheless, and she felt peculiar about accepting it. Doing so would somehow change the boundaries of their relationship, much of which was still undefined.

Alex could see the hesitation. "I have an old-fashioned rubber kewpie doll for Megan. She doesn't have to worry about dressing it. The clothing was painted on."

Dallas laughed, still examining the blue bottle . . . and inordinately pleased with it. "What about Valerie?" she questioned carefully.

Alex pursed his lips. Should he tell her that he hadn't found anything that he thought would satisfy Valerie? Or should he lie and make something up? "I have this little ceramic cat with a real bell attached around the neck. Think she'll like it?"

Dallas wasn't sure. Valerie wasn't terribly sentimental. She was the kind to equate collectible with junk. She might not see Alex's gesture as romantic but odd.

"It has a Tiffany stamp on the bottom," Alex added.

Dallas grinned. "She'll love it." She began to re-wrap the bottle. "I don't know what to say besides thank you."

"That's enough. I'm glad you like it."

"You didn't have to meet me for lunch just to give me this."

Alex reached inside the other jacket pocket. This time he withdrew a magazine. "Wait . . . there's more." He placed it in front of her.

Dallas put the wrapped bottle in her purse, and turned her attention to the magazine. "This is a copy of last month's issue of *Soul of the City*. This is my article."

"Will you autograph it for me?" Alex asked.

Dallas was again caught off guard. He'd purchased

the magazine. He'd actually read it. "You want my . . . autograph?"

"I really enjoy your style and what you have to say. It's really interesting."

Dallas chuckled wryly. "Is that a euphemism for you don't understand what I'm talking about?"

"You think because you write for a black publication and maybe a black audience that I won't understand? What's the difference between black women who wear fancy hairdos with braids and the women in Bensonhurst who still wear big hair? What's the difference between black women bringing up kids alone and white women bringing up kids alone?"

Dallas could only stare openly at Alex. Not because he'd questioned her point of view, but because he had seen that in many cases there was a very slim line of differences separating people . . . beyond cultural ones we make up.

He leaned across the table again. "You know what I think? You and I are a lot alike. We're both trying to figure out where we belong, but we also just want people to accept us, no questions asked, no judgment passed. When someone calls me a bastard, it's true. But that's a technicality, isn't it?"

"What do you mean?"

He lifted a shoulder. "Someone calls you a nigger, is that true?"

Dallas shook her head slowly, watching him. She heard him say the word and wasn't offended. Perhaps because she knew with a deep certainty that Alex would never refer to her in *that way*.

"There is a difference. No one has to know that you're . . . illegitimate. Someone looks at me, and they immediately have an opinion. They draw a conclusion because of the way I look."

"I know that's been a problem . . ."

She frowned. "How do you know that?"

Alex realized at once that he'd almost tipped his hand. He wasn't ready to do that yet. But if he wanted her to continue to trust him, he had to give her something she could feel comfortable with. "For one thing, what Nick used to say, and the way he treated you. For another . . . Val."

Dallas blinked at him. Of course, Val. But how much had she said to him about her? Dallas didn't get a chance to ask. Alex seemed to be able to read her blank expression.

"I know about your family and when you moved into the neighborhood. I . . ." he hesitated. How far should he go? "I know about your parents . . . your real mother."

Dallas averted her attention. But it's not as if any of it needed to be a secret. Still, Alex's knowing so much made her feel naked. There was nothing for her to hide behind beyond her pride, and the hope that, unlike other people, what he knew he wouldn't hold against her.

Alex looked down at the table suddenly, using a fingertip to smooth out a crease in the white tablecloth. He glanced up at her finally from beneath the hood of his eyes, through the dark lashes. "I, ah, I also know that you were married." He hesitated. "That . . . you had a miscarriage."

Dallas blushed and let her annoyance come to the surface. "Valerie had no right . . ."

"I asked her. Valerie is your friend, and she'd never say anything that she thought was out of line."

"Well, if you wanted to know, why didn't you ask me?" Dallas questioned him.

He conceded with a nod. "You're right. I should have. I guess I wasn't sure how you'd feel about that."

Dallas could find no real reason to fault either Alex or Valerie. While she wasn't sure of Val's reasons for revealing so much, Dallas hoped that Alex's interest wasn't just superficial. That the discussion about herself between them didn't amount to mere gossip one evening.

"Look, I wanted to cut to the chase. There was a lot

I didn't know about you," he confessed. "Which seemed sort of strange, after all we've been through . . . together. You know what I'm talking about."

His voice had become soft and quiet. His gaze drifted past her, not focusing on anything except his own thoughts. "I went into the service not to see the world, but because I thought I had to prove something. To Vin. To myself. He probably never even thought that my mother would get pregnant when they were together. So when I showed up out of nowhere, it was like . . . how could this have happened? He didn't want it to be true. I didn't blame him for what happened, and my mother didn't either. But *I* wanted him to accept me. I really wanted him to be my father."

"So you thought you could make yourself . . . worthy of his love?" Alex nodded. "I guess it hasn't worked?"

He smiled grimly. "Not really. Maybe Vin thinks that if he accepts me he'll have to acknowledge my mother. Maybe he thinks Lillian won't be *that* understanding. Maybe . . . maybe he just really doesn't care."

Dallas looked at the bowed silver head. She could hear in Alex's voice the regret of that possibility. "I don't know, Alex. I don't get it, either. You're so much more of a son, more of a man, than Nicholas ever was. Vin should be so proud of you. Lillian loves you very much . . . as if you were her son, too. Vin should be thanking God for you . . ." She stopped when she saw first surprise and then amusement in his eyes.

"Do you really believe that?" he asked.

"Yes," she responded, and looked up to meet his pensive stare.

"I'll take that," he said cryptically. "I could do a lot worse."

"What about Valerie?"

Alex stiffened imperceptibly. "What about her?"

"Doesn't she agree with me?" She watched him relax again, knowing that she'd come dangerously close to asking about their relationship. It was none of her business.

Alex shrugged. "Valerie sees . . . something else in me. If she thinks I'm wonderful, she's keeping it to herself. She's more concerned with how I feel about her . . . and Megan."

Dallas became uncomfortable again. "I don't think I want to go there," she murmured.

He shook his head. "No, you don't. So . . . what are you going to write next?"

She smiled shyly. "A book, apparently."

"For real? That's cool. What's it going to be about?"

"Anything I want. The editor wants my articles expanded and given more depth. About what life is like from where I stand."

"You mean, being half white and half black?"

Dallas was taken a little aback. It was unsettling to have Alex speak his mind so bluntly. He wasn't judging her. And *what* she was didn't seem to matter as much as *who* she was.

"Yeah, that's right."

Alex gnawed the inside of his lip. He looked furtively at Dallas, quickly assessing the moment and her. "You're going to need this, then. It might give you some ideas . . ." Once again Alex reached into his pocket and pulled out one more item. He silently passed it to her across the table.

Dallas recognized the notebook immediately. She looked at Alex. She had no idea what to say to him. How did he get her journal? How long had he had it? Had he read it?

"I found it the day we helped Lillian in the basement of the house. It was with Nick's things." He continued to hold the book out, but Dallas made no move to take it. Alex sighed. "I started to give it back to you, but . . . when I saw what it was, I decided to hold on to it for a while. I read it, Dallas. I'm . . . sorry. I shouldn't have. But at the time it seemed the way to find out more about you. Stuff I knew Valerie might not know, or wouldn't tell me. I took advantage of the opportunity."

Dallas still couldn't find her voice. She had wondered for years what had happened to her journal. Had Nicholas found it . . . or had Lillian? No. Lillian would certainly have said something. She had lived with knowing that her adolescent concerns were somewhere out there in the world for a stranger to see. Dallas didn't know what to make of Alex being the one to have found it. To have read it. He wasn't a stranger. But she couldn't help feeling a profound vulnerability that threatened to reduce her to that adolescent insecurity once again. She just sat there.

"Go on. Take it," Alex whispered, wishing Dallas would say something, even if she got really angry at him. "I figure you were about thirteen or fourteen when you wrote this. Even then you were a good writer. I learned a lot, Dallas. I really understood where you were coming from. I could relate."

"Sorry it took so long," the breathless waitress said, arriving with two plates balanced on her left forearm and holding a third in her free hand. She unceremoniously leaned in between them to put the dishes down. "Excuse me . . ."

Dallas quickly took the notebook, ignoring the chatty waitress's apologies. When she'd finished serving, she stood looking back and forth between them.

"Can I get you anything else?"

Alex merely shook his head.

Dallas put the notebook in her lap. She picked up her fork to start on the salad. "Thank you," she quietly murmured.

The waitress nodded with a smile and walked away.

Alex carefully lifted his burger. "You're welcome," he answered with great relief.

* * *

Maureen sucked her teeth. "There're no more seats," she muttered as she glanced around the filled auditorium.

"That's because we're late. They probably started with all kinds of introductions anyway. We didn't need to sit through all of that. You would have gotten bored," Dallas said in a whisper, also glancing around as she looked for empty seats.

They stood just inside the doorway of the theater. There were several people on the stage that included the director of the film department at NYU, and four of the currently hot new black directors who'd produced successful screenplays in the past six months.

Dallas leaned toward Maureen. "I think we're going to have to split up, unless you don't mind sitting way in the back on the side."

"That's okay. Then if I don't like the program I can sneak out."

"I was lucky to get these tickets. You will *not* sneak out on me. I had to give up my passes to another writer from the magazine. She should be here to cover this.

"Besides, if we hadn't stopped to buy you shoes . . ." Dallas reminded Maureen. She hated to be late, but had accommodated her friend as they'd finished dinner and headed toward the university campus across Third Street.

"They'll be perfect with my wedding dress. I can't believe my luck. I *had* to get them . . ."

"Ssshhh!" someone nearby voiced at their whispered conversation.

Maureen sucked her teeth again. "It's so dark I can't even see anything."

"Let's just stand here for a moment. I think these are introductions and they should be over soon. They'll put the lights up for a few minutes before starting the film. We'll look for something then."

Maureen sighed. "I'm going to find someplace where I can have a quick cigarette. I'll come back . . ."

Dallas nodded as Maureen left her. Sometimes she didn't know why she bothered. She would never have heard the end of it if Valerie had come with her to the evening lecture and Maureen had found out. It had never been so much jealousy as competition between Val and Maureen, Dallas knew. But she still hated being in the middle as they vied over being her best friend. She had asked Dean to attend the lecture, but he had claimed a prior date with his new girlfriend. So Dallas stood alone for the next fifteen minutes, until the opening comments had been made and the next part of the program was about to get under way.

The auditorium lights went up as the panel left the stage and the tables and chairs were removed. Some people took the opportunity to shift about. Dallas located two empty seats and commandeered them for her and Maureen. She looked around, now seeing and recognizing any number of people she knew.

"What are you doing here?"

Dallas turned at the question and found herself facing Nona.

"Are you spying on me?" she said flippantly.

Dallas ignored the bait. "I was able to get more tickets. How's the program so far? I just got here with a friend."

Nona grinned. "Not with your boyfriend?"

"You mean Burke? No. He couldn't have made it anyway."

"Is that what he told you?"

Dallas frowned. "What do you mean by that?"

"I'm not trying to start anything, but some men you have to keep on a short leash."

"Dallas . . ."

The two women turned their attention to Maureen as she reappeared, pushing her way through the milling crowd to reach them.

"Maureen, do you remember Nona? She works with me at—"

"Yeah, hi. Dallas, did you know that—"

Nona chuckled. "I don't think she does. Excuse me. I don't want to be around to see the fur fly on this. Bye."

Dallas watched Nona walk away, and then frowned at Maureen. "I don't get it."

Maureen sighed and looked helpless. "You will. Are you sure you want to stay for this? If it's all the same to you, Dallas, I'd rather go find someplace to have a drink . . ."

"Hi, Dallas. I was just asking . . . ooops."

Dallas turned her head to the new person next to her. He was an actor she'd met through Dean, who'd tried to set up a date between them. Until Dean had found out that Bruce was gay.

"Bruce . . . hey," she said. "I knew you'd be here. I just saw . . ." and she stopped.

Maureen sighed in annoyance. "Oh, shit."

Dallas glanced over Bruce's shoulder because she saw someone who was familiar. The body language and tilt of the head. The hand gestures. It was Burke. And suddenly Nona's sly comment, and Bruce's utterance, and even Maureen's suggestion that they do something else began to make sense.

He was seated near the front of the theater with a very attractive black woman next to him. He had his arm around the back of her seat, his fingers amorously stroking her neck. They were in private conversation, unconcerned with others around them.

Which is what hurt most of all, Dallas decided. Not that Burke was obviously involved with the woman, but that he didn't even have enough respect for her to be discreet among people who would know both of them.

Bruce cleared his throat. "Well . . . it was, er, nice to see you. I'll be in touch," he said, turning away into the crowd.

"Come on. Let's get out of here . . ."

Dallas grabbed Maureen's arm. "No. I want to stay."

"Dallas, everyone is going to—"

"I know. And they're going to do it whether I stay or leave. So, I'm staying. I have to show that this doesn't matter. Burke and I don't belong to each other. There was no commitment, no promises."

"Are you telling me that you don't care? The man is acting like an asshole," Maureen exclaimed.

She did care, but that was not the point. "I know a lot of people here. Many of them also know Burke. If I leave, it looks like he won. I'm embarrassed. Put down. If I stay . . ."

"You win?" Maureen asked skeptically.

Dallas refused to look in Burke's direction again. Sooner or later before the evening was over, someone was going to point out to him that she was there. She shook her head and prepared to sit down and finish out the program. Maureen reluctantly sat down next to her.

"I don't win. But I don't lose anything, either."

Chapter Eleven

On the news recently there was a report of a woman who had been arrested for the death of her four-year-old daughter. The mother was accused of having locked the little girl in a room for almost a year, denying her food and water until slowly, the child starved to death. We were spared accompanying photographs of the little girl, but I envision a child curled up on a floor, alone and neglected with no idea of what was happening to her. Or why. Unwanted and unloved, wasting away because her mother might have hoped that she would just disappear. We were shown the mother being led away in handcuffs; calm, blank, silent, and unremorseful. And we are told she has five other children and is pregnant with another. When asked how could she mistreat her own daughter the mother answered, because she didn't like the child. That was the reason. That was enough to make her feel righteous. I couldn't help but wonder why killing her little girl was so much easier to do than giving her up to someone else who might have cared for her. Why wasn't *this* child worthy of love?

Dallas had already figured out this was *not* a date. It was more like she was just along for the ride to even out the numbers. Ross was one of the most even-tempered, good-natured men she'd ever met, but he didn't seem the least interested in her beyond pleasant dinner companionship. Dallas felt exactly the same way. And she had never dated a white man before.

In any case, for the moment she wasn't interested in dating anyone. Dallas swiveled her head from one person to another as the conversation was carried on around her. But she did not participate and knew she was probably terrible company. Her mind kept drifting back to earlier in the week and the revelation of Burke with another woman. Dallas had no idea how she felt about it. The only thing she knew for sure was that she was tired of trying to figure out what Burke wanted from her.

Dallas realized that she'd been studying the pattern around the edge of Valerie's dinnerware. She glanced up quickly to see if anyone had noticed her silence, and met Alex's steady gaze. After a brief second of looking at one another, Dallas averted her eyes. She forced herself back to the moment

Dallas turned her attention to Ross, who was in the middle of one of his anecdotes of a dive adventure with him and Alex.

"Well, the instructor waited until my partner here had an armful of these weights. Then he comes up behind Alex, cuts the air hose, and pulls off the face mask. Now, I figure I could buddy-breathe with him until we hit the surface. But I check my gauge and see I don't have enough air for both of us to make it. So what does Alex do? Does he head topside? No. He grabs the instructor and arm-wrestles with him for *his* mouthpiece." Ross chuckled at the memory.

Dallas couldn't help smiling. Ross told funny stories. She hazarded a surreptitious look at Alex, who sat with a grin on his face.

Valerie's smile was uncertain at the punch line. "I don't think that was so funny. My God . . . you could have drowned," she said to Alex, turning to look at him with concern.

Alex shrugged. "If I drown it's because I panicked. If I panic under tough conditions, then I deserve to. It was called 'pool harassment.' It's part of the training. We can't expect perfect conditions all the time when we're underwater. We have to be able to think fast and come up with alternative solutions. Our lives depend on it. Or someone else's," he added quietly.

Dallas noticed that his jaw began to tighten reflexively and the smile slowly disappeared. She turned to see Ross's reaction and found him thoughtfully rubbing his thumb on the side of the wineglass.

"Maybe it wasn't so funny after all," he conceded wryly.

"I think it's stupid and cruel," Valerie complained.

Ross nodded at her, his smile amused but understanding. "Stupid? No. Cruel? I suppose. Because your enemy is going to be cruel and worse. He's going to do his damnedest to take you out. A lot of guys never make it past the first week of SEAL training. Alex went the distance."

"And you," Dallas included him.

"It was a great challenge," he admitted.

"Just to show how macho you are?" Valerie asked.

Ross turned his attention to her and paused for a long moment before answering. He shook his head slowly. "It's not about being the best or the toughest. It's about determination and teamwork."

"Then how come you quit? Why did you leave the service if it was so great?" Valerie asked Alex and Ross.

Neither answered right away, and the hesitation caught Dallas's attention. For the first time since she'd met Ross, he didn't have a quick and irreverent answer. And Alex just seemed pensive, as if he was considering a response, but wanted to be careful how he did so.

"I outgrew my usefulness," he murmured cryptically.

"We'd served our time," Ross added. "After a while, the losses and victories didn't add up."

"Have you lost many friends?" Dallas asked.

"Even one is too many," Alex admitted.

Ross cleared his throat. "Alex's swim buddy,

Crosby, bagged it when we were in Kuwait. He blames himself."

"How did it happen?" Valerie asked.

"The technical term? Oxygen toxicity. Simple language? He drowned," Alex explained.

"The ability to breathe is inhibited and there's an onset of dizziness, tingling in your limbs, blurry vision."

"The body starts to convulse, like a seizure," Ross picked up. "What happens is the diver can lose control of his mouthpiece under those conditions. He simply drowns."

"But I thought SEALs are so highly trained," Valerie commented.

"We are. Sometimes"—Ross exchanged glances with Alex again—"things go wrong."

"This doesn't help, I know, but I'm so sorry," Dallas murmured.

"We had to move on. Get a life."

"So you start a business dragging the river for junk?" Valerie questioned.

Ross slowly shook his head. "That's not all there is to it. Besides . . . I do other things."

"Megan said you both teach diving, and I remember Alex said there was a dive shop. Actually"—Dallas let her gaze sweep around the occupants of the table—"it sounds kind of exciting."

"I like the way you put it. You ever been snorkeling or scuba diving?" Ross asked her.

Dallas chuckled. "I don't know how to swim."

"You don't?" Alex asked in surprise.

"No, I never learned how. It wasn't one of those things my parents thought I needed to know."

"It's not hard to learn. I could teach you," Alex volunteered. "What if I take you out in the boat this summer and throw you overboard?" he teased.

Dallas sensed that Valerie too was waiting for her answer. She felt she had to sidestep the issue. "What makes you think I have any intentions of getting on your boat?"

"Oh-oh. Sounds like a challenge to me, Alex," Ross murmured.

Valerie wrapped her arm possessively around Alex's and leaned against him. "I don't think Burke is going to be so hot on the idea. But a boat ride would be great. Maybe you'll take me across the channel to Connecticut. Mystic has some wonderful seafood restaurants. We can go over for the day, or overnight."

"We could do that," Alex agreed. He looked at everyone. "We'll all go. Take Megan and some of her friends, if she wants."

"Alex," Valerie whined. "I meant just you and me."

Alex looked at her but didn't respond. Ross emptied his wineglass. Dallas pushed her chair back. Now was *definitely* the time to cut out. "Valerie, why don't I bring out dessert?" Dallas suggested into the awkward silence. She got up from the dining table and headed for the kitchen.

Valerie did not discourage her, and Dallas was glad to escape. Watching Valerie in action was starting to get on her nerves. She had obviously targeted Alex. But this time Dallas wasn't sure she wanted to be pushed off to one side.

Dallas went into Valerie's small kitchen and automatically started the coffeemaker. The evening had been more stressful than she'd imagined, with the need to pretend that she and Alex didn't know one another very well.

Dallas was slicing a small chocolate torte when she heard someone come into the kitchen behind her. She looked over her shoulder expecting to see Valerie. It was Ross, with the stack of dinner plates and clattering silverware.

"Need a hand?" he asked, putting the plates down and starting to scrape the uneaten food into the garbage.

Dallas smiled at him. "No, I'm fine. You don't have

to do that. I can take care of it. Go back and talk with Val and Alex."

He chuckled. "That's not what you and I are supposed to do. Don't you know this is the point in the evening when we make ourselves scarce so they can have some time together?"

Dallas turned to stare at Ross. She was embarrassed by his insight, as if she somehow had been party to Valerie's plans.

"I'm sorry. It's pretty juvenile of Valerie."

"That's okay. I'm not really cooperating."

"You're not?"

Ross placed the dishes in the dishwasher and came to stand next to Dallas, casually watching as she carefully arranged slices of the cake on the dessert plates.

"No. Alex doesn't need me to help him with his affairs, and you shouldn't let Valerie use you to distract me."

She winced. "I'm not happy about it either. If I'd known what Valerie had in mind, I would have stayed home. No offense, Ross . . ."

He nodded. "None taken."

He narrowed his gaze on her. "I'm going to be perfectly honest with you, Dallas," Ross said seriously. "I think you're very attractive. But there is someone else I'm interested in."

Dallas nodded. "Valerie," she stated flatly.

Ross arched a brow. "How did you know?"

"What man isn't?" she responded. "I just wish she'd stop playing us all like chess pieces. And that we'd stop letting her."

He signed. "You're a smart woman. And a better friend than she realizes."

"Are you mad at her?"

He crossed his arms over his broad chest and frowned at what she was doing. Slowly he shook his head. "No, I'm not. Just . . . disappointed."

Dallas glanced at him. "Disappointed. Why?"

Ross pulled himself together, as if realizing that he'd

spoken out of turn, or had said too much. Dallas was surprised to see the veil of annoyance that crossed his normally calm and open features. But it was quickly gone and he shrugged easily.

"I don't like playing games. I'm getting too old for it. But I'm willing to wait a little longer for her to figure out that she's on the wrong trail."

"What if she's not?" Dallas suggested.

He shrugged. "Then I get over it. I move on."

Dallas took a deep breath and pursed her lips. "What about Alex? Does he know how you feel? Do you know how he feels about Valerie?"

Ross sighed. "Does Alex know how I feel? I hope not. I don't want to stand in the way if he feels he really wants her. I'm not sure of Valerie's motives."

"You sound like you don't think they're pure," Dallas surmised. Ross laughed lightly.

"I gotta be careful around you. You're very observant. Alex said you're a really talented writer."

"Did he?" she said in surprise, and then quickly recovered. Talking about herself and Alex was dangerous. Dallas looked openly at Ross again. "Look, Valerie is my best friend. I don't know what it is she wants, but I certainly won't say anything to her about—you know—what you said to me."

He reached for the dessert plates, balancing two in each hand as he headed back to the dining room. "I know."

"How do you know?" Dallas asked, forestalling his departure.

"I'm very observant, too. I think you can be trusted. Okay . . . I think they've had enough time alone, don't you?"

Dallas made up a tray with the cups, sugar, and cream. She thought about the brief conversation with Ross and wondered if Valerie had any idea how he felt about her, let alone Alex. And she wondered, once again, what was she doing in the middle of Valerie's concerns when her own were in such terrible shape.

"Do you want to talk about it?"

She stiffened at the sound of Alex's voice, but she gave him only a cursory glance, feeling the need to maintain a distance more appropriate to their circumstances. She could hear Val's and Ross's voices from the dining room. "What do you mean?"

"Something's bothering you. You were pretty quiet during dinner," he said, coming toward her.

His cowboy boots thudded softly on the tile floor. He stood just behind her left shoulder, watching her prepare to pour the coffee.

Dallas shook her head. "I'm okay."

"No, you're not."

"Okay," she conceded, "then it's something I don't want to talk about. I'm sorry if I'm spoiling the evening."

He dismissed the idea. "You're not spoiling anything. I just wanted to know if I could help in some way."

"Thanks for asking, Alex. But I don't think so."

"Would you tell me if there was?"

Dallas turned to face him. "I appreciate you asking, but I think it's about time I handle some of my own problems. Besides . . ." She glanced toward the direction of the dining room and the other voices. "You have other things on your mind."

Alex looked a little uncomfortable. He sighed and leaned toward her. "I'm not going to push. But you remember one thing."

She searched Alex's face, his dark, steady gaze and the flexing in his jaw as he talked.

"I know you, Dallas, and I don't want you to ever forget that we're friends."

She shook her head, and her voice dropped to a quiet, firm tone. "Sooner or later we're going to have to put it behind us. No one else knows we've met before. How do you think Valerie is going to feel if she finds out? Or Ross?"

He didn't answer, and they continued to regard each other silently.

"Dallas, what are you doing? Where's the—"

Valerie stepped into the kitchen and stopped dead when she saw Alex and Dallas so close. She laughed uneasily.

"I came to see what happened to the rest of dessert." She came over and looped her arm through Alex's. "And where you were." Valerie smiled up at Alex. Then she focused her attention on Dallas, her smile fixed. "What's going on here?"

Dallas was aware of the real question that Valerie was asking, but knew that her suspicions were unjustified. "Alex came in to see if he could help. Especially since Ross cleared the table and you did all the cooking."

Alex reached in front of Dallas and picked up the heavy tray. "And Dallas brought dessert. Let's go to it. This looks good."

He disappeared through the door, and Dallas carefully placed the remaining cake back into its box and put it into the refrigerator. She licked a glob of frosting from her thumb. "There's plenty left for Megan."

"She'll probably eat the rest of it," Valerie said absently, watching her.

"Better her than us. Come on. I'll help you clean up later."

"Dallas?"

Dallas was already at the kitchen entrance. She looked at Val askance. Valerie caught up to her at the doorway.

"Alex means a lot to me. You don't understand how important this is."

"I think I do, Val," Dallas said honestly. "Why do you feel you have to tell me that?"

Valerie frowned. "I don't know. He's different from

any other man I've ever known. You can see that, can't you?"

Dallas looked at the uncertainty in Val's green eyes. But there was also a determination and, she was sure, a little bit of fear. Dallas knew that no matter what, she and Alex could never let Valerie know anything about their past. Ross would have to fend for himself. She nodded with a smile, and lightly shook her friend's shoulder.

"You don't have anything to worry about. He seems to feel the same way."

"Will you listen to them?" Eleanor muttered with displeasure as she glared at the three young women seated near the performance area. "Don't they know any better than to talk and laugh while the band is playing?"

"Ssshhh," Lyle Oliver whispered to his wife. "You can't hear a thing they're saying, and neither can anyone else. The music's too loud."

Eleanor narrowed her gaze on her husband. "I don't think they came to hear the music anyway. I've never seen such a shameless display in my life."

"They're here to have a good time. Just like *you're* supposed to be," Lyle reminded his wife.

"They're pretty," Dallas observed, leaning forward to see past her stepmother. She also guessed that they were not at the club to hear the band but to check out the men and the musicians. And to be seen. They had a certain nonchalant boldness that Dallas envied and which she herself had never been able to master.

"I don't think any of them is Dean's type," Eleanor said to no one in particular.

"Ellie . . ." Lyle said patiently. "You don't have a clue what Dean's type is. Now leave those girls alone and just enjoy the music."

Eleanor sighed in exasperation and tried to give her attention to the four musicians and one female soloist in the spotlight in the darkened club. But her stepmother was less interested in the new age jazz than she was in seeing her son perform.

Dallas had been surprised when Dean had included an invitation to hear his group as part of his mother's birthday celebration. Ever since Dean had become interested in the guitar at age sixteen, Eleanor and her father had indulged him. He'd taught himself to play, learned to read music, and formed his first band at eighteen. They'd called themselves Toxix. Dallas didn't think her parents had ever heard their son play before, but even if they didn't like the music, they were proud to see Dean perform for an audience.

She remembered the first time she and Burke had come to hear her brother play. He'd teased her that she was angling for a record deal for Dean. The thought had never entered her mind. In any case, Burke had not liked the music. It wasn't mainstream enough.

The memory reminded Dallas that Burke had left several voice-mail messages for her that she had yet to answer. But sooner or later she would have to. And she would have to decide what she wanted from him.

The audience broke out in applause as the number ended. One of the young women got up and walked to the edge of the stage. She leaned over to get Dean's attention and whispered in his ear. She was dressed, and moved her body, as only someone who was self-conscious but fearless could. To get attention. Dean nodded and smiled and whispered something back. Out of the corner of her eye Dallas caught Eleanor nudging her husband's arm.

"Thank you. Thank you very much," Dean said graciously into the mike. "We're going to take a little break and return in about ten."

There was more applause as the group put aside their instruments and chatted with people coming forward to ask questions or comment on their playing.

Dean searched across the room until he spotted them, and he nodded and waved briefly, acknowledging their presence. Dallas watched as Dean and the drummer stepped to the table with the three young women and were greeted with light hugs and kisses.

"I told you so," Eleanor said under her breath.

"Ellie, I think I'd like to get started home," Lyle said to his wife. "Do you mind if we skip the rest?"

"Do you have a headache?" Dallas asked.

He nodded his head, rubbing his left arm. "Yeah, a little bit. And I'm feeling cold."

"Maybe you shouldn't have had that second beer," Eleanor suggested. "I think I have some aspirin." She opened her purse and riffled through the contents. "I really would like to stay for the rest."

"I'll ask Dean how long the next set is," Dallas offered.

"Your father's okay," Eleanor decided. "I'll order him some club soda. That should help."

"I don't think so," Lyle Oliver said firmly. "I'd really like to go home. It's a long drive anyway."

"Well, let's talk to Dean, first," his wife persisted.

"Ellie, this doesn't have to be discussed."

"Oh, good . . . here he comes," Eleanor said as they watched Dean approach.

Dallas was ready to compliment her brother on his performance, but she detected a hesitancy in him. He was rubbing his hands together, as if he had sweaty palms.

"Hey, Mom. Dad," Dean said, kissing his mother's cheek and shaking hands with his father. He squeezed Dallas's shoulder. "I hope you're enjoying the show. Happy birthday."

"Thank you. You and Dallas were so good to me last weekend. But I'm enjoying this. You play so well." Eleanor beamed.

Dean and Dallas exchanged amused glances. They both knew that given the kind of music he played, it was doubtful his mother could really tell.

"Can you sit with us awhile?"

"We might not stay for the rest, Dean," Lyle interrupted his wife. "I'm not feeling well . . ."

"Lyle . . ." Eleanor began.

"I just wanted to warn you that we may slip out early," Dallas said to Dean.

"No problem." He nodded, again glancing over his shoulder.

Dallas followed his gaze. To the three young women, waiting to speak with him again. To the two couples.

"There's someone I'd like to introduce you to," he said. "I'll be right back . . ." Dean retreated to the front of the room.

"I told you so," Eleanor said quietly, pretending to be looking for something else in her purse.

Dallas watched as Dean held out his hand to one of the women as she stood up.

"Ellie . . ." Lyle Oliver said quietly to his wife. As she looked at him, he pushed back from the table and stood up to face his son and the pretty black woman next to him.

Dallas stood up, too, and smiled at the woman with understanding and encouragement. And then she looked at her stepmother. Dallas was surprised and impressed. If Eleanor had any particular feeling she hid it very well. She sat regally and calmly, like a queen granting an audience. Like a mature woman meeting a younger one. Not like a mother who could be disappointed, disapproving, disbelieving.

"This is Alikah Daru," Dean introduced, placing his hand possessively on the woman's waist. "This is my mother and father."

"Hi," she said, nodding at them and smiling. Her eyes were bright and inquisitive.

"Nice to meet you, Alikah," Lyle Oliver murmured politely.

"And this is my sister, Dallas."

The woman turned a knowing, almost amused smile

on Dallas and held out her hand. "Dean has told me about you."

Dallas arched a brow at Dean.

"You're the writer."

"That's me," Dallas said wryly, accepting the cool slender hand.

There were two silver bands on her thumb. A dozen bracelets on her wrist. The woman's hair was locked and dyed a light brown. Most of it was gathered in a ponytail, but tendrils fell over her forehead. Her double-pierced earlobes were fitted with a pair of gold hoops and rounded studs. She wore a deep burgundy lipstick on her beautiful mouth that made her look as if she'd been eating berries. She was dressed all in black. And Alikah Daru also wore a very thin gold wire nose ring.

"You're the computer genius," Dallas said.

Alikah glanced with warm and admiring eyes to Dean. "He tell you that? I'm not a genius."

"But she knows more than I do," Dean said. His glance bounced back and forth between his parents.

"Sorry to interrupt the celebration. Dean said it was your birthday, Mrs. Oliver. Congratulations."

"Thank you," Eleanor managed.

"I didn't know Alikah was going to be here," Dean said, as if that explained anything.

Dallas could see from her stepmother's stiff back and lifted chin that it did not. Her father looked less astonished . . . more resigned. Tired again.

"Dean's been inviting me to come and hear him play for a while. I brought some friends along. We all work together."

Dallas couldn't tell if Alikah was aware of the tension, but her brother's nervousness faded away.

"I'm going to hang out for a while when we're done. I might not see you . . ." Dean announced.

"No, you won't," Eleanor spoke at last. Her voice was dead calm and flat. "We're going to leave before you start again. Your father doesn't feel well."

Dallas sighed in relief. She knew from experience that her stepmother's silences were the worst. With them she censored and sat in judgment. Her controlled responses were preferable. At least then, Dallas had learned, you stood a chance of surviving them.

"Oh, I'm sorry," Alikah said solicitously.

Dean frowned at his father, finally shifting his concerns from himself. "Your okay, Dad?"

"Thank you," Lyle murmured. He was exhausted. He turned to Dallas. "Are you staying or leaving with us?"

Dallas didn't think either option was particularly attractive at the moment. But she turned to Dean. "I'm going to walk them to their car. Then I think I'll head uptown." She smiled at the young woman. "We'll see each other again."

"Yes. I hope so."

Dallas didn't say a word to her brother. And she knew she didn't have to. The arching of her brow and slight smile as she turned to follow her parents said it all.

"Is it serious?" Ross asked out of the blue as he noisily slammed the locker door.

The sound was like a gunshot, and reverberated through the large tiled room. It was empty now of students. The advanced dive class was over. Ross turned from the locker and quickly pulled a black T-shirt over his head and his broad, hairy torso.

Alex knew exactly what the question was about. No, not what. *Who.* He was seated on the end of a long, narrow bench carefully packing his black rubber suit into an oversized duffel bag.

Alex closed his eyes tightly for a second and brushed his hands over his cropped hair. "I don't know."

Ross tucked the tail of the T-shirt into the waist of his jeans and then finger-combed his hair. "Why not?"

Alex gestured helplessly before returning to the task at hand. "It's . . . not what I expected, that's all."

Ross squatted down to help speed up the process of packing their gear. "Why not?"

Alex glanced up in annoyance at his friend. "I just told you."

Ross zippered one bag and pulled over a second, dumping in their fins and masks. "You know the reason, Alex. You're bullshitting around it. Come on. Why not?"

Alex wanted to tell Ross to back off and let it be, but that wasn't going to help. The fact of the matter was, he wasn't really sure what he felt for Valerie. He only knew he felt more himself with Dallas Oliver. It was the same . . . only different.

"Maybe . . . it's just happening too fast."

Ross took a deep breath. "So then, you don't know if you're in love with Val? Or just with the idea of being in love with her?"

Alex considered the question for a long moment, flexing his jaw muscles anxiously. He gave up and shook his head in defeat. "Am I crazy, or what? Valerie Holland is gorgeous, she's sexy, she wants me in her bed. Megan likes me, and I know how important that is to Valerie. Is there a problem?"

Ross lifted the two duffel bags and carried them to the exit. He propped the door open with them and returned for one of the oxygen tanks. "In answer to your first question, no, you're not crazy. Everything you said about Valerie is true and then some," Ross conceded. "About the second question . . . I suggest you pay attention to your gut and stop thinking with your johnson."

When the lobby buzzer sounded Dallas knew it was her brother. It had been several days since that uncomfortable meeting at the club with Alikah. Eleanor had not been so considerate. Dallas was still smarting from the fact that her stepmother had called her the next morning to express her displeasure at Dean's current choice of girlfriend.

"Dean knows how I feel about *that,*" Eleanor complained.

"About what?" Dallas baited her stepmother, forcing her to say exactly what she was thinking.

"About dating these women with their back-to-the-motherland thing. I know it's fashionable, but did you see her hair? How does she keep it clean? Ridiculous. She might as well be wearing a bird's nest. And that name. What kind of name is Alikah? And that ring in her nose! Lord, have mercy."

"Eleanor, all Dean did was to introduce us to a woman he knows who happens to dress Afro-Centric. As far as I recall Dean did not confide in us that he was in love, in like, just passing through, or hadn't decided yet."

"Maybe they're just messin' around, but did you see the way she looked at him? She's got 'looking for a husband' stamped on her forehead."

Dallas sighed patiently. "Did you see the way he looked at her? I think the admiration went both ways," Dallas suggested.

"Well, I won't have it."

"Dean is a grown man. This isn't about what you want."

Eleanor hung up on her.

And Dallas had yet to call and apologize, because she knew that she would have to.

The door buzzed again.

Reluctantly Dallas put aside her laptop and slowly got up from her sofa. She went over to the intercom next to the apartment door and pressed the talk button.

"Yes?"

"It's me, Dilly-Dally."

"I don't want to talk to you, Dean. Come back when you grow up."

"Come on, Dallas. Let me in. I want to explain."

"You can't explain away your thoughtlessness."

Having gotten her knock in, Dallas stood by the door, holding it open for his arrival.

Dallas had to admit that Dean did look more contrite than usual. But if he was going to try to get over with her again, she was going to toss his butt out of her apartment.

"Hey, how're you doing?" he asked as he stepped into the foyer and wandered into his sister's living room. "Did I interrupt your work?"

Dallas sighed. "Have you spoken to your mother?"

"No, not yet."

"Then you'd better. I'm tired of being a sounding board for you and Eleanor."

Dean paced the room. "Why should I have to hide the fact that I like Alikah. But it's not like I'm engaged to her or anything. We're just seeing each other."

Dallas unconsciously began pacing parallel to her brother, in the opposite direction. She had one fist braced into her waist, the other hand rubbing her forehead. "You don't have to explain to me, Dean. But I'm not your mother. I don't know what's going on with you and Alikah and I don't care. I don't care how she wears her hair, who she votes for, or who she prays to.

"If *she* was smart she wouldn't have anything to do with you. But at least have the guts to stand up for what you believe in and stop always looking for the easy way out," Dallas nearly shouted.

Dean stared at her. "Man, you really got worked up over this."

Dallas was reluctant to admit it was much more than *this*. She was feeling edgy and impatient. Valerie had been testy with her. An eruption of that's-not-fair was circulating through *Soul* because she'd been offered a book deal. She still didn't know what she was going to say to Burke when and if they ever talked again. Her father had been withdrawn and aloof lately . . . and Eleanor was on the war path.

"I have my own problems to deal with."

"You mean Burke? Man, kick that dude to the curb," Dean advised.

"You should talk."

He grinned ruefully. "You mean with Alikah. I know I have to deal, or cut loose."

"Tell your mother that," Dallas suggested dryly.

"I'm gonna. I know Mom. She shoots first and asks questions later. But it's going to be different. For one thing Alikah is hip to how Mom feels. Her own mother did a number on her, too. Especially when she changed her name from Alicia to Alikah."

"So I'm hearing that you're willing to go to the mat for, er, Alikah? Is she worth it?"

Dean splayed his hand on his chest and leaned toward her. "*I'm* worth it. Mom will have to deal with me."

Dallas grimaced. "I'd buy a ticket to see that."

The phone rang.

She went to answer, talking to Dean over her shoulder as she reached for the receiver. "You do know about condoms, right?"

Dean cackled at her audacity.

"Hello?"

"Hey. It's Burke."

Dallas was caught off guard and felt her emotions crashing together as she quickly tried to regain her balance. She'd somehow expected that Burke wouldn't try to call her if he was seeing someone else. But why shouldn't he try to burn his candle at both ends if he thought he could get away with it?

"Hi."

"I thought I'd call and see how you're doing. Check when we could get together."

Dallas frowned. "Get . . . together?"

He laughed. "Hey . . . I know you saw me the other night."

"That's right."

"You want to know who she is."

"Not particularly."

"I knew her a long time ago. You know how that goes. I couldn't act like I didn't know her."

Dallas was tempted to laugh. "No, I guess not. That would be rude. So is that what you wanted to tell me?"

"I was hoping we could make a date . . ."

"You're kidding, right?"

"Come on, Dallas. At least I didn't try to lie."

"That's supposed to make it okay? I don't have time for this anymore, Burke." She hung up.

"That was the man himself."

Dallas looked at Dean with a frown. "Do you know something I should know about?"

He pursed his lips and shrugged. "I don't really . . ."

Dallas sucked her teeth. "For Christ's sake, Dean . . ."

"I'm pretty sure I saw him a few months ago with someone else. A singer I know. I didn't want to say anything, but . . ."

Dallas felt peculiar knowing that her brother, maybe a lot of other people, had known that Burke was seeing other women. She felt so foolish. She had a lot of nerve advising Dean on the state of his affairs when her own were such a mess.

When the phone rang yet again, her anger at having been used had risen to the level of resentment. Dallas snatched the receiver up and spoke before listening. "Burke, I can't tal . . . who is this?"

Her eyes widened and Dallas turned to stare at Dean.

"What's wrong? What? Okay . . . okay . . . Yes, he's here with me."

"What's going on?" Dean asked.

Dallas waved for him to remain quiet as she listened. She squeezed her eyes closed and placed a hand over her mouth. "Oh, my God . . ." Dallas moaned. "All right. I'm on my way. Yes, I'll tell him." She hung up.

Dallas looked dazed for a moment before rushing past her brother toward her bedroom. "That was Eleanor. It's Daddy. He had a heart attack."

Chapter Twelve

The nuclear family is dead. Due to wars, attrition, evolution, domestic violence, divorce, and lack of interest. What remains is a mishmash of orphan souls desperately seeking safety, a home, validation, love. We pick and choose and discard, starting with one and moving on to another if it doesn't work out. Families are disposable. We cross cultures, mix races . . . and genders, or make it up as we go along, so confusing the issue that we are numb when we lose someone we care about . . . because we learn too late that we care about them deeply. What we need to do is find them all, gather them to us and hold on tight, because loneliness is pointless. Life is already too short to spend it looking for the perfect mom and dad, the right husband or wife, the ideal kids. There is no such thing. There is only us; you and me and everyone else in need. We have a lot in common. Maybe we can join forces, combine our energies, share our lives . . . and be a family. What a novel idea.

Dallas quietly opened the bedroom door several inches and peered into the semidarkness. The bedside reading lamp was on, but her father was perfectly still. He lay with his upper body slightly elevated. A hand was draped over the edge of the bed, and a book had slid from his grip, threatening to drop to the floor. His glasses were perched on his nose. Watching him, she felt a stab of fear. Dallas approached the bed, looking down at her father's calm and peaceful face.

"Daddy?" She barely whispered, afraid that she might disturb him and wake him up. Afraid that he wouldn't. She touched his hand. It was cold. "Daddy?"

Lyle Oliver responded with a weak sigh. His head rolled on the pillow, and he drew his hand up to lay on his chest.

He was only sleeping. Dallas breathed in relief.

She carefully removed the book and her father's glasses and put them on the nightstand. She touched his cheek with the back of her hand. He *was* cool. She didn't know what that meant. Should she call the doctor? He looked okay. Youthful almost. Not nearly as drawn and tired as he'd appeared lately, that they all had not noticed. Until it was almost too late. Dallas turned out the light and left the room. She stood in the hallway just outside the door and hugged herself. And listened.

She used to love the absolute quiet of this house. It used to seem so safe. She'd feel grateful that she had a home. Until her father's attack she'd never fully realized how much she'd taken for granted. Eleanor was sometimes difficult and domineering. Dean was irreverent and often maddeningly irresponsible. Her father was reserved and gentle. But they were good people. In their own ways they cared about one another. They were a family. This was *her* family.

Dallas absently rubbed her hand along her temple and forehead, fingering the soft curly hair. She headed toward the stairwell to the first floor. She passed through the mug shot gallery and, as always, glanced over the framed faces, many of people whom she'd never met. But they were her family, part of her heritage too.

Dallas started down the stairs, pensive and confused. The thought occurred to her, if her father had another attack and died, would she still belong here?

The phone rang, sounding much louder than usual. She realized it was because they were all oversensitive to sound these days.

"I'll get it," Dallas called out softly, and then hurried to the extension in the living room. "Hello?"

"Dallas? It's Peggy."

Dallas perched on the arm of the sofa. "Hi, Peggy."

"How's your father?"

"Fine, thank you. He's upstairs taking a nap."

"Any more word from the doctors?"

"Just that he take it easy. They want him to stay home for a few weeks. Which will probably drive him and Eleanor crazy. They're still running tests, but he might eventually need surgery."

"And what about you?"

Dallas wasn't prepared for the question. She had to actually think about it. "I'm okay. Just a little tired."

"And scared, I bet. Listen . . . this is your father we're talking about. The thought of losing your parents will definitely make you sit up and take notice."

"Yes, it really does. By the way, thank you so much for the flowers. That was very thoughtful."

"It's from all of us. Even Nona . . ."

Dallas had to smile.

"We just wanted you to know that we're thinking of you, and you and your family are in our prayers."

"Thank you, Peggy. I appreciate that."

"Take as much time as you need. Don't worry about the column . . ."

"I'm already done for the next issue."

"You didn't have to. And that's not why I called," Peggy said in exasperation. "You can always do another column, but you can't replace your father. You need to be with him right now."

"That's really kind of you," Dallas murmured. "There's not much more I can do. I think I'm probably underfoot. I'm going back home on Friday, unless something else comes up."

"Well, let's pray that it doesn't. We all get to a point where we are on crisis overload and running on empty. Keep in touch and let me know how things are going."

"Thanks again, Peggy. I'll let my stepmother know you called."

When Dallas got off the phone, she wasn't inclined to face Eleanor just yet. She could hear low voices in conversation in the kitchen. Eleanor and Dean. Were they talking about her? Were they rehashing the terrible scene in the hospital when she and Eleanor had argued while her father was being stabilized? Even thinking of it was enough to plunge Dallas into despair and embarrassment.

Eleanor's voice suddenly rose, followed by Dean's. Dallas stayed where she was. She was glad that her brother was here, even though it was more time than he could afford from work, he had been the buffer between her and his mother. The voices hovered in the background, and she shifted her attention to the dozen or so get well cards sent to her father from coworkers, neighbors, distant family. Lillian Marco had signed both her and Vin's names to one, and she had ventured over one afternoon with a cooked covered dish, as had Rosemarie Holland and the family across the street.

Deciding she had delayed long enough, Dallas got up and made her way back to the kitchen. When she walked in, Eleanor's voice faded away in midsentence.

"How's it going?" Dean asked.

"Fine. Daddy's sleeping."

"Was that the doctor calling?" Eleanor asked stiffly, not favoring her with even a glance.

Dallas took a seat at the table. "No. My office. Peggy sends her regards, and I thanked her for the flowers."

The ensuing silence was strained, but then the phone rang again. Dean quickly responded.

"I'll get it," he said, gesturing for Dallas to stay seated. He got up and went into the next room.

Eleanor continued to ignore her, listening to her son's voice in an attempt to figure out who he was talking to. Dallas thought this was as good a time as any to penetrate the wall of silence between her and Eleanor. It had to start somewhere.

"He fell asleep reading. I took off his glasses and turned out the light."

Eleanor examined her manicured nails. She said nothing.

"He looked very peaceful," Dallas added.

"Umph!" Eleanor uttered. "I'm surprised you didn't say his *color* looked good."

Dallas stared at her. She realized the stress her stepmother had been under. "That was uncalled for," she answered stiffly.

"So were the things you said to me. Your father could have died, and all you did was worry that *I* was making a scene at the hospital and yelling at the doctors."

Dallas sighed. This was not going to be easy. "They were doing everything they could. Accusing them of doing less wasn't helping Daddy."

"Just don't forget how *you* insisted on seeing him."

"I wanted him to know I was there."

"Oh, Lyle knew, all right."

Eleanor clamped her mouth shut. She rubbed her hands together anxiously.

"He worries about you all the time."

"Over me? Why?"

Eleanor hesitated. "You know why. Because of your mother and having you. He never was sure he'd done the right thing. You are a constant reminder."

"Are you saying his heart attack was my fault?"

"As long as you're blaming someone I guess I did my share," Dean said, strolling back into the kitchen. He had his jacket on. He looked at his sister and mother. "Let's face it, I got away with stuff a lot of times. I did things"—he exchanged a glance with Dallas—"that were dumb. Mom, I know you aren't thrilled about Alikah."

"No, I am not. I thought I made myself clear on that issue."

"You did," Dean said wryly.

"I never thought you'd let yourself be influenced by all this black nationalist stuff," Eleanor scoffed.

"I didn't." Dean shrugged. "I just met Alikah. I like her. That's all it is. I seem to recall something about judging people by their character. Works both ways, Mom."

"Are you leaving?" Dallas asked, communicating with Dean with her eyes.

He nodded. "That was Alikah. She wanted to say how sorry she was to hear about Dad," he said to his mother. She pretended not to hear. "She's going to pick me up at Penn Station. I called for a taxi to get me to the station."

"Your father is seriously ill and you have the nerve to leave for a date? What is wrong with you?" Eleanor said, in that parental voice developed to quell children. It no longer worked.

"Hanging around here isn't going to help Dad," Dean said with an edge to his voice. "The doctors said it wasn't serious, but a warning. If anything happens I'll come back out."

"If anything happens, it will be too late."

"And it won't be *anybody's* fault," Dallas added.

Dallas could see Eleanor's pained expression, and her slumped shoulders indicated a sense of defeat. Dean rubbed his mother's shoulder and bent to kiss her cheek. But Eleanor was going to punish him by being unresponsive, unwilling to forgive his lack of loyalty.

"You said he has to see the doctor on Monday," Dean began. "You want one of us to go with you?"

"That's not necessary," Eleanor said, being more reasonable. "I'll let you know what the doctor says."

"Okay. I'm going to wait out front. The taxi should be pulling up any minute. I'll call when I get home," Dean said to his mother, kissing her again. He turned to wink at Dallas. "Be cool, Dilly-Dally. Talk to you later."

Dallas and her stepmother remained seated as Dean departed. When the front door closed behind him they were plunged once more into an uneasy silence.

"Is there anything I can do now?" Dallas asked, risking further argument.

"I don't think so. I have to fix Lyle something for lunch. You can do what you want."

Dallas let the dismissal pass. She got up and began to clear the table. "Then I'm going down to the basement . . ."

"Are you finally going to do something about the stuff from your room?" Eleanor asked.

"Yes." But Dallas did not mention the box her father had told her about the night before.

She'd sat in his room while Eleanor had run over to their bookstore. Dallas had watched him as he slept, making a mental list of all the things she would say to him when he was stronger, that she'd been afraid to say before. About being his daughter, and about her mother. But as it had turned out there had been no need.

Lyle Oliver had awakened and found his daughter watching over him. Without his glasses Dallas wasn't sure that he could see her clearly. But she sat still, in case he quickly drifted back to sleep. Her father, however, finally spoke.

"You look a lot like your mother . . ." he croaked, but his voice was stronger than it had been.

Dallas didn't answer right away. He could be dreaming. She had a feeling that if she asked him if he was okay, it would interrupt his train of thought. She wanted to keep him talking.

"Do I? I don't remember her very well."

"Your face is shaped like hers. You have her smile. When you were small it reminded me of her. Now that you're all grown, I can see some of the Oliver side in you. People used to say you were another man's child."

"I once believed I was adopted," Dallas confessed.

"No. No . . . you're mine. I was there when you were born. Caused a little bit of an uproar in the hospital. Black man. White woman . . ."

"Mixed child," Dallas said. She got up and moved her chair closer to the bed, next to her father.

He closed his eyes and sighed. "If I'd stayed down there, they would have killed us all."

"They?"

"The local whites. I got along fine as long as I was going to graduate school, and working and staying out of trouble. I knew lots of people, was well liked. Meeting your mother, and then getting married, changed all that. Returning north made more sense. My family would have accepted Delores. I could find work, a place to live . . ."

"Daddy . . . you don't have to tell me everything right now. Rest. We'll talk later."

"We should have talked a long time ago. You always wanted to know the details. You're right. I should have told you. I didn't desert your mother or you, Dallas. Terrible things happened down there. Terrible . . . we came back to Philadelphia to live. But your mother didn't like the city. People said and did terrible things. She was scared all the time. Then you got sick, and she wanted to be with her family."

"So you just let her go and take me with her?"

"You needed to be with your mother. We were all just trying to survive, Dallas. It was hard."

"But I was your child, too."

"I couldn't protect either of you. It was better . . ."

Dallas felt astonished. How could he have made the decision that she was better off without him? How could her father really believe that she wouldn't want and need him? How was she supposed to react to having been thought a mistake?

"It's all in that box. It's somewhere. Read the letters."

She was desperate to question him more, but knew she couldn't. He was getting tired. "Go back to sleep,

Daddy," she said quietly. "Don't worry about that now."

"It's somewhere . . . in the basement . . ."

"There's a box," Dallas said distractedly now to Eleanor, repeating her father's words.

"There's more than one," Eleanor confirmed. "I'd like to get rid of them."

"I'll go through them so you don't have to worry about them anymore."

"You know, you're wrong about me, Dallas. I've tried to be good to you. I've *never* mistreated you or resented you like you think I did."

Dallas was surprised that the conversation had turned to their relationship. The timing seemed fortuitous. She nodded, being careful not to escalate the tension between herself and Eleanor. "I know. You gave me a home. I know you hadn't expected to raise me."

"And I never complained," Eleanor emphasized. "You are Lyle's child, and no matter what I think about that I made you a part of this family. I didn't see anyone else claiming you when your mother died."

The reminder of being sent back to her father stiffened Dallas's spine.

"It hasn't always been smooth and easy, but I never felt like you accepted me, either. You always called me Eleanor. You always let me know I was just your stepmother."

Dallas was stunned to hear Eleanor's point of view. It was not that she believed that Eleanor had never cared about her, but Dallas sensed that her stepmother's feelings were tempered by her background. It *had* been held against her.

"I guess because you never made me feel like your daughter. So we both missed out. There are some things you can't control. And if you're not careful how you feel about Alikah Daru, you're going to risk losing your son."

* * *

Going through the boxes reminded Dallas of that afternoon at Lillian's. She realized now that she too had a lot of stored memories to examine. She read through dozens of papers that were like watching a movie of her parents' lives. Their involvement had been star-crossed.

Dallas heard footsteps on the basement stairs and looked up when Eleanor called her name.

"Dallas? Valerie is here. You want her to come down?"

"No . . . I'll come up," she said, laying aside a large envelope.

She found Valerie and Eleanor chatting about her father when she reached the kitchen. Valerie looked her over and grimaced.

"You look terrible."

"Thanks."

"Eleanor told me your father's going to be fine."

"This time," Eleanor sighed, and wandered away into another room.

"How's *she* been?" Valerie referred to Eleanor as she gave Dallas a hug.

"Concerned but strong. You know her."

Valerie arched a brow. "That means she's been driving everyone crazy." Dallas grinned. "Comb your hair and grab a jacket. I thought we'd go somewhere for coffee. Get you out of the house, and give us some time together."

"You know I don't drink coffee," Dallas quibbled good-naturedly.

"Ice cream?" Valerie countered.

Dallas sighed with gratitude. "I'll get my things."

Alex listened to Lillian's warm voice, and noticed that Vin was not edgy or impatient with his presence. But decided that the time was not right to tell them.

Since arriving at their house he'd gone through a half-dozen different openings, trying to anticipate their reaction to what he had to tell them.

"Alex? I know you said you were eating later, but just a little more?"

Alex came out of his reverie and focused on Lillian. She stood poised with the salad bowl, ready to serve him more, but he declined with a slight shake of his head.

"I'll take some," Vin said, sitting back so that his wife could put more on his plate. "Lilly didn't tell me you were coming over tonight."

"That's 'cause I didn't tell her. It was a last-minute decision. I didn't think she'd kick me out, and I wasn't planning on staying long."

Vin grunted. "It's not Lilly you have to worry about."

"Vin! What kind of thing is that to say to Alex? I'm glad he comes. With Nicky gone we should be kind to the family we have."

Alex looked in surprise at Lillian and grinned. He turned to see Vin's reaction, but his father was studiously digging into his lettuce and tomatoes. But at least he hadn't rejected Lillian's claim.

He wondered again if this was the right moment. Could he tell them now that . . .

"You know what you told me? About my business and the future," Vin opened gruffly.

It took Alex a moment to figure out that Vin was referring to his last visit to the shop. "Sure, I remember."

"How much would it cost?"

Alex knew that Lillian was keenly listening to her husband's questioning of him. They both knew this was an important moment. Vin never asked for help if he could avoid it. He was too proud. He was careful. "How much would what cost?"

"You know. To make the business do better. Bring in more customers."

"Well, you first need to decide what kind of business and service you want to offer. Then you figure out if it means new equipment or more staff. What do you want to charge? Do you need to advertise . . ."

"Okay, okay. I get it." Vin waved his hand to make Alex stop.

"It's not going to take a lot of time, Vin. Offer something at your shop that nobody else in the area can do. Then people will come to you first."

Lillian looked back and forth between them. "Vin . . . is Alex .. is he going to help you?"

"I didn't say that," Vin pointed out to his wife. "Don't get excited. I only asked a question," he murmured.

"Stubborn," Lillian accused him without rancor.

She didn't ask or say more, but her gaze on Alex was filled with hope. Vin's goodwill was hard to come by. And Alex didn't want to build up Lillian's hope for a full reconciliation between them if Vin was going to turn difficult about accepting his help.

Alex glanced to Vin. "The offer stands," he said casually. "If you want to go ahead with new plans for the business, let me know."

"Ummmm," Vin murmured.

Alex stood up. He'd tell them another time. "I gotta go."

"I wish you could stay longer. I didn't even tell you Vin and I are going to California for our anniversary. I've always wanted to. It'll be good for us, especially since Nicky. And did you know poor Dallas had quite a scare this week. I'm thinking of turning Nicky's room into a . . ."

"What was that about Dallas?" Alex asked, trying to keep his tone mildly curious. But he was surprised by the jolt of concern. Distinct memories flashed through his mind of the past.

"Her father had a heart attack," Vin said. "Lillian cooked up something and took it over. You know. Trying to help out."

"Dallas has been at her parents' house since it happened. I just saw her this morning. We ran into each other at the corner market."

Alex listened thoughtfully. He was remembering things he'd read in her journal. About her father and stepmother. Her sense of not being wanted. He looked at Vin and Lillian, glanced at the wall clock. "Can I use your phone?"

"Of course." Lillian nodded.

Alex excused himself and went into the kitchen. He picked up the phone and punched in a number. He felt relief when the line was finally picked up.

"Hey, it's me. I figured you'd still be there. You got any plans for tonight? . . . No, nothing's wrong, but I need you to do me a favor . . ."

When Dallas opened the door and saw Alex standing there, she felt an odd displacement of time. She was suddenly sixteen again. When she'd needed someone to turn to, Alex had been there. Like now. She didn't even question his presence, but seeing him brought her perilously close to tears. Only this time there wasn't anything he could do to rescue her.

Dallas's mind was still reeling from the contents of the box her father had told her about. She'd expected something big, packed with mementos and books, albums and sentimental heirlooms. It was only a shoe box tied with string. But it held the entire story of her father and mother's relationship, the beginning, middle . . . and end.

The letters had been painful enough to read, the ones between her parents expressing fear, doubt, love, and finally regret. Years later there had been letters from cousins, relatives of her mother who'd tracked her down, tried to communicate with her, to let her know she had more family. And they wanted to know her. The letters had all been addressed to her, all had been opened and read . . . and she'd never seen one of them before that afternoon. The last one had been written ten years ago.

They'd given up.

Far worse, however, were the news clippings reporting the brutal attack on a young black man who was known to be married to a white woman. Her parents. The details had been so horrifying that Dallas couldn't adequately respond. She'd gone numb with shock, reading them over and over again with the realization that people really were capable of doing such hideous things. Her parents had endured atrocities because they loved each other. And decisions had been made to protect her, Dallas realized, because they loved her, the child of their union.

She stood staring blankly at Alex, and hoped that he would speak first, so that she wouldn't have to. She was afraid of what would come out.

"How's your father?" he asked without preamble.

"Fine. He's . . . fine. It wasn't serious," she said in a thin voice.

"Lillian told me what happened. Are you here alone?"

"My stepmother is upstairs with my father."

"Good. Go get a coat or something."

"Why?"

"We're going for a walk."

It reminded her of Valerie's visit the day before. But this time she shook her head. "I don't think . . ."

"I'll wait out here for you," Alex said, turning away.

Dallas was too flustered to offer excuses, and too tired to argue. Her mind felt crammed with too much information, too many feelings to be able to make decisions. Right now it was much easier to let someone else tell her what to do. She went to the hall closet and reached in for a coat. She extracted a denim jacket belonging to Dean. Way too big, but it didn't matter.

She stepped outside and closed the door. Without a word they fell into step together and began slowly walking. Dallas expected Alex to ask her questions about her father, or to express sympathy or offer advice. But he didn't look like he felt there had to be any conversation. That was okay. She was comfortable with him and the silence. And she was grateful.

Alex knew full well that there was nothing he could say that would make a difference. Besides, that was not the point. He just knew he had to be here with Dallas. They got to the corner and made a left turn. He admired her smooth, graceful walk. No matter what was happening to her, she'd always had a certain strength of spirit.

Dallas was so glad that Alex knew he didn't have to say anything. She was still preoccupied with those grainy newsprint images, and their graphic details.

Her father had been attacked.

Dallas felt her throat clog. Her ears were ringing. She felt like she was having trouble breathing. She didn't jump when Alex put his hand on the top of her shoulder and squeezed gently. His fingers curved to the side of her neck. She felt a quiver at his touch.

They turned at the corner again. They had no real destination. She just kept moving. She was thinking of her parents, split apart by ignorance and bigotry, and their love destroyed.

She and Alex walked around the entire block without a word said between them. She slowed her steps when she realized they were almost at her parents' house again. It had been like coming full circle. She stopped, and Alex stopped with her. His fingertips were rubbing at her nape. Dallas didn't know for sure if Alex knew exactly what he was doing, or what this was doing to her. But it certainly seemed right. Knowing that there was no place else to go, Alex made it easy for her to turn into his chest. He held her gently and easily and for a long time she just cried.

"I don't believe you," Megan scoffed. "You never jumped out of a plane."

Ross nodded while smoothly turning his car at the corner and driving slowly down the darkened street.

"Oh, yes, I did. Ask Alex if you don't believe me. He's done it, too."

"Well, what else can you do? I bet you don't know how to roller blade . . ."

Valerie sighed. "Megan, please. Can't you sit still and not talk so much?"

Ross glanced at Valerie's stiff profile. "I don't mind. It's nice to have someone to talk to," he hinted broadly, and Valerie tightened her mouth impatiently. "No, I gotta admit I've never been on them, Megan."

"Well, I can. It's easy. Aunt Dallas got me a pair for Christmas."

"Maybe you can show me sometime."

"Yeah, that would be cool," Megan readily agreed.

"Well . . . here we are. Home again, jiggity-jig."

Megan giggled as Ross parked the car in front of the house. "You're a lot of fun. Just like my godmother."

"Why, thank you, Megan. I consider that a great compliment. I think your godmother is pretty neat myself."

Valerie didn't wait for Ross to turn off the engine, and had already gotten out of the car by the time Megan had thanked Ross for taking them to dinner.

"Megan, please go on in and turn on some lights. It's getting late."

"I know, I know . . . go get ready for bed. I'm almost thirteen. Can't I stay up another hour?"

"When you're thirteen we'll discuss it," Valerie said firmly. She tugged her daughter's hair and gave her a brief hug. Megan sighed and turned to flounce toward the house.

"Night, Ross," she called out as she opened the door. "Thanks for dinner."

Ross waved to the young girl, and walked slowly around the front of his car toward Valerie. She stood her ground, waiting for him. Not an ounce of the annoyance she felt that he'd taken her and Megan to dinner in place of Alex had abated during the whole evening.

"Now, admit it . . . that wasn't so bad, was it? Nice dinner, so you didn't have to cook. Good company . . ."

Valerie averted her gaze briefly and smiled, despite herself. "Okay. I appreciate it. You didn't have to fill in for Alex," she said, trying to be gracious, but finding that being around Ross seemed to make her testy.

"Nice of you to say so, but I bet you're pretty ticked off with Alex for standing you up."

Valerie turned on her heel, ignoring the comment, and walked to her door. She turned and faced Ross as he followed her. "I don't suppose you'll tell me who the sick friend was?"

Ross shook his head. "Alex didn't say, and I didn't ask. If he thought it was important for me—or you—to know, he would have said something."

She regarded Ross with open speculation. "You know, you have the wrong idea about me."

He raised his brows. "Do I?"

"You think I'm calculating, and trouble. And you probably believe that I'm not good for Alex, or he's not what I want . . ."

"Most of that is true," Ross conceded. "But I guess it never occurred to you that Alex might want someone else."

Valerie just stared at him. Ross could see that the idea clearly had not occurred to her.

"How do you know that?" she asked in a strained voice.

"I don't know. But it might be something to think about."

Valerie was dumbfounded. She had it all worked out. She'd made plans. When Ross reached out to hold her arm, however, she didn't perceive it as a threat but, oddly, as comfort. She wanted to rail at him, but she didn't know about what. She'd never met anyone like him before. She decided on the spot that it wasn't dislike she felt for Ross Manning so much as fear. He was overwhelming. He knew entirely too much. He had strange powers.

Valerie looked into his eyes and saw something else. She thought she'd seen it the first time they'd met, and had found it so impertinent in him. Now . . . it seemed different. She narrowed her gaze and shook her head. She put a hand on his chest to maintain the distance between them.

"You wouldn't dare," she said in a whisper.

Ross smiled warmly at her, and his hand on her arm tightened. He took a step closer to Valerie, towering over her. "Never say that to a man when he's got your back against a door."

He didn't give her a chance to say anything else, but bent to kiss her. Ross didn't attempt to take Valerie in his arms. There was no need. They were as close as he wanted them to be. His lips knew what he wanted, and immediately forced her mouth open to his tongue and warm breath. The surprise was that he only felt an infinitesimal resistance in her. But he didn't give her a chance to reconsider her options, or the kiss. He explored her mouth sensually but briefly and gently ended it, releasing her lips slowly.

Valerie hadn't closed her eyes, and was staring at him. Then she blinked at him rapidly. Finally, she pulled away.

Seeing her startled features, he lifted a corner of his mouth. "Now's your chance," he murmured.

"Wh-what?"

"To slug me, knee me in the groin . . . or kiss me back."

Valerie did none of those. She turned abruptly to open the door, went inside, and closed it.

Ross sighed and turned away to his car. But the smile and amusement were gone from his mouth. He realized that if he was wrong about Valerie, Alex, or himself . . . he was in deep trouble.

Dallas stared at Valerie across the table.

Valerie glanced at her watch for what must have been the hundredth time since they'd sat down to breakfast. Either Valerie had other things on her mind that distracted her, or she was being deliberately obtuse. Dallas decided it was the latter.

"I want another muffin," Megan announced, pushing back her chair from the table.

"Go ahead," Dallas encouraged.

"No. Sit still, Megan. You've already eaten too much." Valerie looked at her watch again. "We have to leave soon anyway for home."

Megan gasped in surprise. "How come?"

"I thought we were going to take Megan to Central Park so she can skate on Wollman Rink?" Dallas said.

"Yeah, and Aunt Dallas said we were going to the Motown Café for lunch."

"I don't think so. Not today."

"Mom . . ." Megan started to whine.

"I'm sorry, Meg. I need to get home. I have things to do."

"What things? You said we wouldn't go home until tonight. We have all day . . ."

Valerie lost her patience and pointed a warning finger at her daughter. "Megan, don't argue with me. I said I need to go, and that's the end of it."

Dallas could feel Megan's stunned surprise at her mother's hard tone. For a moment the only sound was the Saturday morning TV program on the set in the living room.

"It's okay, sweetie." Dallas smiled calmly at her godchild. "I'll give you a rain check. That means we'll do this some other time. Maybe next month when you come in, okay?"

"But . . ." Megan tried again.

"Do me a favor and go turn off the TV. Did you make up the futon in my office?"

"No," Megan pouted.

"Well, go do it now. Get your stuff together and get dressed," her mother commanded.

Megan looked beseechingly at Dallas, hoping for her to run interference. But Dallas knew better than to counter any orders from Valerie to her daughter. Besides, she had her own reasons for wanting to be alone with Val.

Megan, deeply aggrieved, slid from her chair. Then she bent to cup her hand to Dallas's ear and whisper, "Can I have another piece of bacon?"

"Just one."

Having won this small victory, Megan was satisfied. Munching on the crisp bacon, she left the kitchen.

Dallas sat in silence. She was going to give Valerie a chance to speak first. There was something that had strained their visit ever since Valerie and Megan had arrived the night before.

"I'll clear the table," Valerie said.

Dallas put her cup down. "You were very hard on Megan. And I don't understand why you're cutting the weekend short. We made plans months ago."

Valerie silently scraped her food remains into her daughter's empty plate and stacked them.

"What's the matter, Val?" Dallas asked calmly.

Val's mouth tightened. She shook her head as she reached to gather the silverware. "I don't know what you mean. I need to get home, that's all."

Dallas reached out and grabbed Val's wrist. They stared at each other. Now Dallas could see it clearly. Suppressed anger made Valerie's eyes sparkle, heightening the color in her cheeks.

"Talk to me, Val," Dallas whispered uncompromisingly. "You've been unusually quiet and distracted and, quite honestly, not very good company. You've snapped at Megan for the littlest thing, and treated me as if I were invisible. What is the matter with you?"

Valerie didn't hold back any longer. "It's not me, it's you. You've been seeing Alex Marco, haven't you?"

Dallas didn't betray her feelings of guilt. Her immediate response was to deny Valerie's claim. But it wouldn't have been true. She wasn't sure what she and Alex were becoming to each other, but she did sense they were moving beyond friendship.

"What are you talking about?" Dallas asked.

Valerie pulled her arm free, setting the plates back on the table. "Alex broke a date with me last week. I know he was with you."

"I don't know about any plans he had with you, Val," Dallas protested. "But he did stop by my parents' house to see how my father was doing. He was visiting Lillian and Vin. They told him what had happened."

"How come you and Alex didn't tell me?"

Dallas was nonplussed. "I can't speak for Alex, but I don't see why I should have."

Valerie leaned across the table toward her. "He hardly knows you. Why would he care about your father?"

Dallas stiffened. This was territory she had avoided for so long. "Why don't you ask Alex why he did? I only know he was kind and sympathetic."

Valerie got up impatiently. There was not enough room in the kitchen for her to place enough distance between her and Dallas. Dallas watched her friend closely. She knew, of course, exactly what this was all about. But she was going to make Valerie say it out loud.

"I think it's more than that. He's always asking me questions about you. I mentioned you were divorced, and he wanted to know about you and Hayden. He wanted to know about Dean and your parents. Were you dating anyone now . . ."

"He's just curious. Just like Ross is so curious about you."

Valerie blushed, momentarily surprised. "How do you know that?"

"From the day Megan and I went to the aquarium."

Valerie made an impatient sound and averted her eyes. "This isn't about Ross . . ."

"And it's not about me," Dallas said firmly. "I

know you like Alex. You've made that clear. I . . . know he likes you . . ."

"I want to marry him," Valerie blurted out defiantly.

Dallas felt a peculiar tumbling in her stomach at this announcement. She didn't know how to answer.

"Alex wants me," Valerie said.

"Well, if he wants to marry you, then it doesn't matter what happened last week."

"He hasn't asked me yet," Valerie corrected, annoyed. "I just don't want you to do anything to mess this up for me."

"I don't think I like you telling me that. I resent you thinking that I'd do anything to get between you." Dallas stood up to face her.

"Remember when we were in high school? You used to work overtime to make sure that any white boy you wanted didn't notice me. Is that what this is about? You making sure that I remember my place?"

Valerie flushed deeply. "That's not true. I didn't want to see you get hurt, that's all. Going with white guys would have caused a lot of trouble."

"I don't need you to decide that for me. I can choose for myself who I want."

"As long as it's not Alex," Valerie said succinctly.

Dallas shook her head as she and Valerie faced one another. "We've been friends all our lives. You know more about me than even my parents. But don't make the mistake of believing you know what's best for me. I don't need your approval, permission, or advice to conduct my life."

"I'm just telling you, Dallas, to stay away from Alex Marco."

"Why? Because he was kind to me? Or because he's white?"

"I've already told you."

"And I'm telling you I don't like it."

"This isn't about you! This is a chance I've been

looking for since Megan was born. I don't want anything to ruin it."

"What can I—"

"Can you do this for me?" Megan asked, suddenly appearing in the kitchen again.

By silent agreement the conversation ended between Valerie and Dallas. Megan presented her back to Dallas.

"What do you want me to do?" Dallas asked quietly. Valerie resumed the clearing of the table.

"Could you French braid it? Mommy doesn't know how to do it like you."

"Are you almost ready?" Valerie asked her daughter.

"Yeah. What were you talking about?" Megan asked.

"What?" Valerie frowned at Megan.

"You were talking real loud. Were you two fighting?"

Valerie turned to the sink and began rinsing the plates. She didn't respond.

"Of course not," Dallas said. "Like you said, we were just talking loud. Do you have a barrette or something to hold the end of this?" she asked, finishing the style in an extended braid that hung down Megan's back. She took the offered rubber band and secured it around the tail of the hair.

"I wish I could wear extensions like some of my friends in school," Megan observed, facing Dallas.

"Do you?" Dallas asked.

"Why?" Valerie added, genuinely curious.

"Because it stays one way for a long time. It's really cool that you don't have to comb it every day," Megan answered simply. "Thank you," she said to Dallas when she was done, and then quickly left her mother and godmother alone again.

Dallas and Valerie exchanged glances. Dallas wondered if they had crossed a line, if something was changing between them.

"If Alex Marco is in love with you, Valerie, if he wants to marry you, then your suspicion about me was uncalled for," Dallas said in a soft voice. "I don't think we should say any more, or we're both likely to say something we're going to regret later. I don't want to do that."

Valerie looked stubborn and began shaking her head. "I'm almost thirty-two years old. I already have a teenage daughter, but I've never been in love. I've met so many guys who were immature or dishonest. I could have a real chance with Alex. I really want this."

Dallas shook her head sadly. "If it doesn't happen, you can't blame me."

Valerie stared at her for a long moment, indecisive and conflicted. Then her expression hardened. "Megan?" she called out. "Are you ready? Let's go . . ."

Valerie walked out of the kitchen, leaving Dallas alone. She remained, considering all the ways their friendship had been tested over the years. How ironic, Dallas thought as Valerie and a bewildered Megan left her apartment, that when push came to shove, friendship couldn't hold out against the overpowering need for love.

Chapter Thirteen

Alex squinted through the wet windshield, trying to keep on the alert for any nearby craft. Rough waters rocked the boat, adding to the task of keeping it on course. He gripped the wheel, holding the boat steady as it plowed through the choppy waters at the mouth of New York harbor. He used a hand to wipe excess water from his face, only to be immediately splashed over with rain.

"There's a coast guard cutter on the way," Ross shouted from below, his voice bellowing to be heard over the engine and the sound of the rain.

"How bad is it?" Alex shouted back as the bow of the boat bounced up sharply on the crest of a wake. It came down heavily, the boat displacing a wall of water on either side.

"It's down. A bird with two on board."

"How long do we have?" Alex asked rhetorically.

"We don't. In this weather as soon as it went in the drink the passengers were in trouble. Unless they got lucky and got out in the first thirty seconds, we're talking bodies."

In the distance could be heard the eerie whine of a siren. The urgent sound faded in and out as it was carried on the wind. Alex glanced in the direction of the signal, trying to spot the boat, but visibility was cut by the sheets of rain. It was late in the day. Already under cover, the sun would set in another twenty minutes. What would have been a difficult rescue even under optimal conditions was going to become extremely difficult.

"I checked the tanks. We're okay. See anything yet?" Ross asked, joining Alex at the controls.

"Not yet."

"I think they'll get there before us. We probably won't have to go in," Ross said.

Alex nodded shortly. "Yeah, we do."

Ross slapped him on the shoulder in reassurance. Alex wasn't concerned about taking part in a rescue, but that he would fail, and someone's life would be lost again. For the past six years there had not been a single dive that he did not think of Kuwait and the mission that had gone wrong.

Alex was soaked under the slicker. Not from the rain, but from nervous sweat.

The boat pitched up again, matching the roil of tension in Alex's stomach. He'd never been seasick, not even his first time out on a boat. He wasn't going to let it happen now. But he was gripped by the need to redeem himself.

"There she is," Ross called out, pointing beyond the windshield.

A peculiarly twisted clump of material appeared to be floating on the surface. It looked like a giant insect that had been swatted into the water, a main rotor blade broken at an odd angle, another torn off completely. It wasn't going to stay buoyant for long. Slowly circling the downed copter was a tugboat, and a recreational craft with two young men looking for adventure.

Alex cut the engine and let his boat drift to within a hundred feet of the chopper.

"I'll get on the horn and see if the other boats found anything."

Alex held the boat steady as Ross got on a bullhorn and communicated through the wind and rain.

"You got anything?"

"Yeah," came back the amplified voice. "We got the reporter. The pilot is still out there."

"Still on board?"

"Can't tell . . ."

The copter was partially submerged with the main fuselage upside down in the water. The tail rotor had snapped off. It was hard to tell what was still inside. The siren grew louder, but the hulking gray cutter was still not visible. The police marine boat had also not arrived, although one of their Bell 206 helicopters was positioned overhead. It stayed to the side, about a hundred feet up to cut down on the angle of rotor-wash near the downed craft. Alex anchored their boat.

Protocol dictated that in lieu of a police presence, the coast guard was in charge. But Alex and Ross knew there was no time to play top dog. There was still a man missing. They were already preparing to do down. They were donning the rest of their equipment when the coast guard arrived with two ready divers of their own. There was quick assessment, and a decision about using a pattern line for searching. And then, one by one, the divers dropped into the water.

The four divers swam around the copter before signaling to pair off. Then they disappeared below the surface.

Dallas stepped out of the small room that served as a lounge, dunking a tea bag in and out of a cup of steaming hot water. The hum of office activity seemed a strange anecdote to the inner turmoil that had plagued Dallas for the past week. Her anxiety had not been helped by her father's insistence on returning to work. With only two more weeks to the spring semester the doctors had given permission. But there would be no summer teaching, he had been told.

Matty abruptly rushed in front of her, heading into the conference room, where Peggy, Nona, and several other staffers were watching the TV.

"Sorry 'bout that," Matty apologized as he adroitly avoided a collision.

Dallas smiled vacantly at the others in front of the set. "News flash?" she asked.

"A news helicopter crashed in one of the rivers," Matty responded.

At first, Dallas was only mildly interested. She watched the reporter, huddled under an umbrella, relating the known details of the crash. But she was too distracted by the recent events in the lives of people she knew to care much for perfect strangers. The journalist in her couldn't be objective. Until the reporter mentioned that the rescue teams searching for the pilot consisted also of two area tech divers recently featured on the network. Dallas, curious at last, drew closer to the screen. She looked closely at the indistinguishable black forms bobbing about in the water. But she didn't have to hear names to know that Alex and Ross were somewhere out there.

"Has anyone been hurt?" she asked.

"I think they got the reporter who was on board," Nona said. "At least one other person is missing."

It wasn't the kind of story *Soul* covered, and after another ten minutes with no new developments, the staff drifted back to their own routines. But Dallas stayed behind, watching the screen until the segment ended and the news went to another story. She went in search of Peggy, finding her and Letty in conversation outside the conference room.

"Peggy, I'm sorry to interrupt, but is anyone using the car tonight?"

"Not that I know of. Matty just got in from his shoot. Did you put in a request to use it?"

"No. But I just need it for tonight."

"Is this business?" Peggy asked.

Dallas sighed. "No, it's not."

Peggy hesitated, finally nodding. "Please return it tomorrow."

* * *

Alex knew they weren't going to find the pilot alive. That meant the task was just to recover the body. In the opaque river water Alex could barely make out the other divers, huge black monsters with snouts attached to hoses and tubes of the Aga masks that allowed them to breathe. Lights affixed to their heads helped minimally as they each tried to cover an area where the body may have settled. There was a possibility that, weighted down, the body might have sunk and drifted with the current.

Alex had a sudden adrenaline rush as a remembered moment, not similar in circumstances but with the same results, made him feel a sense of panic. He had made a deal with himself. He wouldn't surface again until the pilot was found. Alex knew that he would be found, but he also only had about twenty minutes of air left.

Ross signaled with his light, and Alex swam to meet him. Ross had located the broken-off rotor blade. Nearby was what looked like a camera bag with the logo of a local network on the side. A cap floated by. Together they circled in a widening area.

Then they heard what sounded like a crunching, stretching grind of metal. It was like a great moan. The water whooshed around them, and Ross glanced up and saw what remained of the fuselage of the downed copter, hurling down at them. Bubbles gurgled geyserlike to the surface as the cockpit cavity filled the rest of the way with water.

Alex tried to swim quickly out of the way of the falling object. The water displacement created a wave that jostled him, flipping Alex onto his side. He flailed about, trying to steady himself. Below him, the beam of light from Ross's handheld searchlight seemed to go crazy before it disappeared. The copter landed in the riverbed, sending out a cloud of thick silt and mud. Through the murk, Alex saw Ross topple over, struck by what remained of the tail boom.

Orienting himself, Alex and another diver swam downward. They found him on the far side of the flooded copter. Ross had just avoided being crushed, but Alex could see he was having trouble with the full-face mask. Probably a leak. He favored one leg in his kicking movement to swim above the wreckage.

Alex used a hand signal to ask Ross if he was okay. He got back a thumbs-up, but he also indicated something below them. Alex kicked several feet deep and came to a sudden halt as some sort of growth seemed to appear before him. It wasn't marine life but a pair of legs swaying upward at him. His stomach heaved at the discovery. He started breathing too fast again, but only for a moment. He got over it. He got back in charge, because he was missing that sense of horror and blame that had trapped him six years ago with Crosby's death.

The pilot was still strapped to his seat. There was nothing that could be done for him beyond recovery. Alex returned to Ross, who was now exploring his equipment with his hands. Alex grabbed hold of his weight belt and pointed up. The other two divers also came to assist. They began to rise upward. They broke the surface and found themselves surrounded by emergency marine craft and blinding searchlights. Another team of divers were ready to relieve them, having just dropped from a 412 NYPD copter. The hovering craft clattered deafeningly overhead with the crew chief perched and tethered to the open hatch as he directed his pilot and divers. Its lights showcased the rescue team. Hands reached out to help Ross aboard one of the boats, but Alex sculled away.

"We found him," he communicated through hand signals to one of the relief divers. Once submerged, Alex used the buddy phone in the front of his mask to give the police divers the location of the body. They followed his lead.

There was no sense of victory. They'd accomplished what they'd started out for, but the end to the story was anything but triumphant. The best that could be said was that it was a mission well done. Somebody's loved one had been found. Out of the tragedy there had also been found resolution. And peace.

Dallas stood back behind the cordoned-off police lines and watched through the hurricane fencing as a stretcher was hoisted into a waiting ambulance. It held a zippered body bag. She experienced an immediate primal fear and dread. Her gaze followed the departing vehicle. But there were two more waiting. The injured news reporter had been the first to be removed, but Dallas couldn't tell yet if the other EMS teams were there just in case or if there was a real need. There was still a lot of activity and manpower around the dock where the rescue efforts had ended. But she had yet to actually see any of the divers. Or Alex.

She caught sight of several men headed slowly toward the remaining ambulances. One was wrapped in a gray thermal blanket and was supported on either side as he limped forward toward a waiting ambulance. A second man walked with him, also with a blanket around his shoulders. The pier lights clearly illuminated his silver hair. She felt a tremendous rush of relief.

Dallas approached the police barricades, prepared to flash her press pass, but no one stopped her. The rescue was over, and most of the personnel had cleared from the area. By the time she'd reached the ambulance, the limping man had been helped inside. She didn't have to call out Alex's name. As if sensing her presence, he turned his head in her direction, finding her in the dark. Dallas stopped, and Alex separated himself from the group and walked over to her.

She couldn't see his face, but Dallas could tell he was physically exhausted. Alex stopped in front of her and let his gaze wander over her before speaking.

"Hey. What are you doing here?" His voice was a deep croak.

The truth came without hesitation. "I was worried." Dallas glanced quickly around. "Maybe . . . I'm not supposed to be here."

"No, no. This is . . . great. Really great."

"Ross?" she questioned, to cover her nervousness.

"He's okay. That's him." Alex indicated with an inclination of his head. "They're taking him overnight for observation. He banged up his leg a bit."

She blinked at him. "And you?"

"Beat."

"What happens now? Do you have to hang around or . . ."

"No, I'm through. They have our preliminary report. I can give the rest tomorrow. I can't move the boat tonight . . ."

She swallowed, hesitating. "How . . . were you going to get home to Brooklyn?"

Alex kept his gaze on her face, still riveted by her intense concern. Her being there. He shook his head and shrugged. "I hadn't thought that far. You have something in mind?"

Dallas felt her stomach contract as she stared at him. She felt herself on the edge of a great precipice, with that strange sensation of being both afraid she would fall . . . or that she would hurl herself forward into the unknown. It was a breathtaking and scary feeling.

"You can stay at my place."

"Are you sure that's okay? I can go with Ross and crash with him at the hospital."

"But I'll throw in *real* coffee and a hot shower."

He laughed, and then slowly sobered. Alex took hold of her hand and squeezed it. "No contest. I'd rather go with you. It's really good to see you, Dallas."

She smiled, feeling somewhat fortified by his confession. "What are friends for?"

"Right." He nodded, wryly. "Wait for me? I'll be right back."

Alex returned to the standing rescue workers and handed them the gray blanket. He accompanied the emergency crew to a temporary triage setup for further conversation before climbing on board his boat and going below. Dallas waited and watched, wondering about her actions, and steadfastly refusing to address the dozen or so questions and what-ifs her mind created.

Alex reappeared in just ten minutes, fully dressed. There was another moment of conversation with the rescue crew before Alex shook their hands and came back to Dallas. She led the way to the parked car. They were headed toward Broadway and uptown before either spoke again. Dallas questioned him about the accident, and the remainder of the ride was spent talking about the rescue efforts. It was a safer subject than exploring the instincts that had brought her to him. The moment felt charged with anticipation that stayed with them until the car was parked once more, and they entered her building. Dallas covered the awkward silence by looking for apartment keys. Under the ceiling light of the elevator she could see the stress on Alex's face. He seemed slightly dazed, now, but he only stared silently at her as she babbled nervously.

"They should have kept you for observation, too . . ."

"I'm fine," he said quietly.

"Come on in," Dallas murmured once she'd unlocked the apartment door.

Alex followed her into the dark foyer, and she flipped the light switch. She was immediately aware that his presence altered the space, shrank it in a way that seemed to make him larger . . . or her more vulnerable. It brought them closer together. Alex stood awkwardly as Dallas maneuvered around him to lead the way into the apartment.

"This is the living room. Here . . . let me take your

coat." She held out her hand as he slowly shrugged out of the jacket and handed it to her.

"I have a foldout futon in my office," she explained. "Or you can sleep on the sofa. It pulls out, too."

"It doesn't matter," he said, his eyes slightly red and bleary as he continued to stare at Dallas.

"The office. You'll have some privacy and quiet." She moved sideways, heading into the hall and beckoning him after. "It's through here. Do you want anything to eat?"

"I think I'm too tired to eat. I'd like to take a shower," Alex responded, stretching his shoulders and rubbing his eyes. He was done in.

Dallas nodded, pushing open the door to her office and letting Alex precede her in. "Across the hall . . ."

He stepped into the room, and turned around once to survey it. Alex faced her again and shook his head wryly at her. "Sorry. No change of clothes. No toothbrush. I bet I look funky and smell worse," he murmured.

She grinned at him. "Don't apologize. I'll look around and sec if I can find anything my brother might have left here." She turned away.

"Dallas?"

She hesitated at the sudden gentle urgency in his voice. "Yes?"

Alex slowly approached and stood right in front of her. She stared up into his face, and all the things she'd ever known about him—or him about her—seemed to spring up between them. There was a peculiar familiarity, yet her stomach warned her that something was very different. Alex wrapped his arms around her lightly, and she responded naturally. She squeezed her eyes closed to vanquish an image.

Valerie . . .

It was a slight embrace, however, and when Alex released her again, Dallas sighed.

"Thank you," he murmured.

She averted her gaze. She felt not so much shy as careful.

"You . . . you're welcome. I'll hang up your coat. If you need anything, let me know. If you want to call anyone . . ."

Valerie . . .

He wearily swept his hand over his head. "The hospital. I want to know how Ross is doing."

She pointed to the phone. "Go ahead."

Dallas pulled the door partially closed as she left the room and retraced her steps back to the hall closet, where she hung up their coats. Then she had to stop for a moment to catch her breath. Guilt made her feel warm and flushed. Her invitation to Alex now began to seem foolish . . . and hypocritical in light of her discussion with Valerie. She had offered Alex her hospitality in a truly spontaneous moment, but Dallas knew that the gesture could lead to more.

What had she been thinking? What was going on? And what was it she felt that made her so nervous and confused around Alex suddenly?

Dallas put on fresh coffee and searched for something she might prepare to eat. It was after ten o'clock. She couldn't help but notice that having Alex in her apartment felt very different from any other visitor. She'd only entertained one other man since her divorce, and Burke's presence had never been a comfortable one.

Dallas heard movement down the hall. She leaned out of the kitchen entrance. "Let me know if you need anything," she called out.

Alex appeared briefly in the bathroom doorway. He'd already stripped to the waist, had removed his shoes and socks. The shower water hissed in the background, and steam began to waft around him. He leaned against the door frame, one hand casually in the front pocket of his black jeans. The motion forced the waistband down to expose his navel. Dallas remembered suddenly when she was sixteen and she had boldly sought Alex out at his apartment. She had a vivid flashback of what had happened that night between them.

"I . . . I can make something to eat . . ."

He shook his head. "Not for me. Is that coffee I smell?" She nodded. "That's good . . ."

But then they stood staring at one another down the length of the hall. Finally, Alex pushed upright, entered the bathroom, and closed the door.

When the phone rang, it made Dallas jump. She hurried into the living room to answer. Under the circumstances, the first person that came to mind was Eleanor calling about her father.

"Hello?"

"Hey, I figured you'd be home about now."

Dallas sat on the arm of her sofa. "Hi, Dean. I just got in."

"I tried calling you at the office. I need to talk to you, Dallas."

She frowned, apprehension rising quickly. "Is it Daddy?"

"No, no. It's about Alikah. Mom is seriously getting on my nerves."

"Well, what do you want me to do? She won't listen to me either right now. We're in the same doghouse . . . or at least adjoining rooms."

Dean chuckled. "Yeah, I know. I just need some advice."

"There's nothing I can tell you that you can't tell Eleanor yourself. Don't judge a book by its cover . . . stuff like that."

"Mom is a proud black woman, but she doesn't understand that Alikah is, too. It has nothing to do with her hair, her clothes, or anything."

"See, you know what to say. Stick to what you believe, and be prepared for the fallout."

He sighed. "Man, I've been feeling the fallout ever since I tried to introduce them."

"I ask you again. What do you think I can do?"

"I don't know, but I thought maybe . . . can I come over? I'll only stay a few minutes."

Dallas heard the bathroom door open again. She looked toward the hallway, expecting Alex to appear. But of course he didn't. Not without clothes. "I . . . I can't tonight." There was a momentary silence.

"Got company?"

"Yes," she admitted smoothly.

"You and Burke made up?"

"It's not Burke," Dallas had to clarify, if for no other reason than she didn't want her brother to think she wasn't on to Burke and how he'd treated her.

"Yeah? Who?"

"Dean . . ."

"Okay, okay, it's none of my business."

"So, what are you going to do?"

"I think I'll lay low for a while. Maybe if she doesn't hear from me she'll figure out that my life doesn't belong to her."

"What if she doesn't come around?"

"I love Mom, but . . . that's her problem."

Dallas chuckled in disbelief. "You're willing to risk excommunication for Alikah?" He laughed. "Wow."

"Well, if it wasn't Alikah, it might be some other woman. What if she had been white?"

"Well?" she prompted.

"Okay, I get it. Same thing. I'll let you know how things go with Mom."

"Night, Dean. Good luck."

She hung up and wondered about the call. Dean had never been one to seek advice from her about his love life. Maybe this woman was going to be the real thing. Or close enough that he had the strength of his own convictions.

Dallas poured a mug of coffee before she went to the office. She was making up the futon for Alex when she heard him behind her. She turned to find him standing with a towel wrapped around his waist. Another was draped over his shoulders. She noticed that

Alex's chest, like his eyebrows, had almost no gray hair in it. Alex lifted the towel and began to briskly rub his head, causing the strands to spike on top. There were fresh black and blue contusions on his shoulder and arms. More on his rib cage and thigh. Probably from the rescue, Dallas guessed.

His bone-deep weariness made his movements slow and lethargic. She didn't feel any embarrassment or discomfort from his naked state. After all, this was not the first time. She silently pointed out the mug on her desk. Alex lifted the cup and took a long swallow.

"Thanks," he murmured, his voice hoarse and thick. "I needed that."

"Or a shot of whiskey. But I don't have any," she teased quietly.

He grinned tiredly at her. Alex glanced down at himself. "Sorry. I should have pulled my pants back on at least."

"I don't mind," Dallas said smoothly.

"I wasn't trying to be fresh or anything." He shook his head. "Maybe I should just shut up before I say something really out of line."

"Maybe you should just go to bed and get some sleep."

He nodded. While she finished the bed, he glanced over the papers and things on her desk and bookcase. He found a bracelet made of plastic multicolored hearts and held it up with a questioning rise of his brows.

It was a painful reminder to Dallas. "It belongs to Megan. She left it on her last visit."

He turned it over thoughtfully, drank more coffee. "Did Valerie stay, too?"

Dallas opened a closet and pulled out a pillow from the top shelf. She fluffed it and threw it casually on the futon. "Yes, but they left early." She looked at him. "Do you want to call her? Let her know where you are?" Alex stared back at her, but she wasn't uncomfortable under his scrutiny.

He shook his head. "No, I don't. I want to tell you something."

"You're tired. It can wait until tomorrow."

"It can't."

Dallas stood with her arms crossed as Alex sat on the edge of her desk and wearily rubbed his hand back and forth through his damp hair. She focused her attention on the center of his chest. "What is it?"

"I'm breaking it off with Valerie. I'm not in love with her."

Oh, my God, Dallas thought. "Why are you telling me this now?"

"Because you need to know. Right now."

Her gaze raised to his, and she felt her heartbeat jump. "Have you . . . told her this?"

Alex flexed his jaw and shook his head. "Not yet, but it's coming."

The way he was staring at her was beginning to make Dallas nervous again. She felt as if Alex was drawing her to him with an invisible power that, nonetheless, felt inexorable. She felt no resistance. "I . . . don't think I want to . . ."

"There's someone else." She didn't respond. "Don't you want to know who?"

She shook her head. "No . . . no, I . . ."

"Dallas . . ." he interrupted.

"I'll get you some more coffee." She took the cup and quickly left the room.

Her heart was racing, and she felt too hot. Alex was too close. But the emotions that coursed rapidly through her were a mixture of light-headedness and anxiety. As if she knew this moment was coming but had ignored it. She took her time to pour the coffee. Dallas was afraid to return to the room. She was afraid *not* to.

By the time she got there, however, Alex had discarded the towels and gotten into the makeshift bed. He still had Megan's bracelet banded around the four fingers of his left hand. And he'd fallen asleep.

Watching Alex, Dallas felt a constriction in her chest. She admitted to herself that what she was feeling for Alex Marco was significantly more than mere friendship. Perhaps it had been there for as long as she'd known him. But that didn't mean that all was right with the world. There were still more questions than answers, not the least of which was, would she and Alex have to redefine what their relationship was?

". . . There was a dramatic rescue this afternoon, when a news helicopter went down in New York harbor with the pilot and a local reporter on board. Unfortunately, the pilot is being reported as dead, drowned, apparently, when he was unable to release his safety belt. Several teams of divers from the police department and the coast guard were aided by two ex-navy SEALs who operate a dive shop and sometimes conduct advanced training to police scuba-diving units. Mark Mackenzie was on the scene near the East River heliport when the body of the pilot was brought ashore. Mark . . ."

Lillian gasped, and her hands covered her mouth as she saw the hazy camcorder image of men in black gear. They were being assisted with their equipment as the reporter attempted to interview them.

"Oh, my god! Vin . . . wake up. Look. *Look!* It's Alex . . ."

Vin started awake next to his wife as Lillian placed her hand on his shoulder and shook him.

"For Christ's sake, Lilly. What's the matter?" Vin turned over and struggled into a half-sitting position. "You sick or something?"

"Vin, it's not me. Look. There's a report on TV about a rescue. It's Alex, Vin. Alex was there . . ."

"What are you talking about?" Vin muttered. Still dazed, he watched the quickly changing images on the screen. "I don't see Alex."

She nudged him in his arm. "There! Did you see him?"

A shot of Alex appeared on screen as he pulled off his mask and breathing apparatus. He still wore the hooded top, but there was no mistaking him.

"Listen to what they're saying about him. He was in some special team in the navy, Vin. He never said anything about that before. Alex helped with some crash in the river today . . ."

Vin squinted and stared. Finally, he reached blindly for his glasses and perched them on his nose.

". . . dangerous attempt under adverse weather conditions. Again, there is one confirmed death, that of the copter pilot, and two men hurt and removed to area hospitals, although we haven't been told how serious the injuries are. Reporting live from the East River Pier on Thirty-fourth Street, I'm Mark Mackenzie. Now back to the studio . . ."

Lillian burst into tears.

Vin sat up. "Lilly, what? Why are you crying?" He tried to comfort her.

Lillian rejected him as she covered her face and sobbed. "He could have been killed today. I can't stand it. I couldn't take it if . . . if Alex . . ." She turned on Vin, her eyes watery and blazing with anger. "I want you to stop, you hear me?"

Vin gestured helplessly. "Lilly . . ."

"You listen to me, Vincent Marco. When I fell in love with you, I didn't ask you first if you were Italian. I didn't ask your sister who fathered her son before I said we'd raise Nicky like he was our own. I didn't hate you when I found out that Alex was your child. You don't ask those things, and you don't place blame when you love people. Alex is your *son*!"

Vin collapsed against the pillows, looking bewildered and tired. He shook his head. "I know . . ."

"Well, you don't act like it. When are you going to stop blaming him for your mistake? When are you going to see that Alex is a good man? He doesn't want anything from you but for you to accept him as your son."

"Lilly, please . . ." Vin whined, unable to defend himself against the truth. "You're right."

"I love you, Vin, and I'm sorry to say this to you. I know you adored Nicky. I know you adored your baby sister . . . but . . . but . . ." The tears rolled down her face. "Nicky wasn't half the man Alex is. You know that. You *know* that. Maybe if I . . I could have had children . . ."

Vin took his glasses off and sighed wearily. He pulled Lillian into his arms and absorbed her anguish. "Don't say that. You know it doesn't matter to me. I love you. Please don't cry, Lilly. I'm sorry."

"Alex could have been killed today. Oh, Vin . . . we could have lost Alex, too."

Vin stared at the screen. The anchors had moved on to another report, but he wondered if they would repeat the story about the rescue mission in the river. He wanted to see it again. Not because he didn't believe it, but because it confirmed what he would never allow himself to admit. Just like Lillian had said. Alex was, in every way, a son to be proud of. The kind of son he'd always hoped for.

Dallas was irritated when the doorbell sounded early the next morning. She was already awake, but that didn't make it okay for Dean to show up.

There was no time to get dressed. She hurriedly donned a silk floral robe from behind the bathroom door. Dallas went barefoot down the hallway to the front of the apartment. The doorbell buzzed a second time as she reached it. She absently ruffled her fingers through her damp hair and tightened the belt around her waist before unlocking and opening the door. She was prepared to light into Dean, and was thrown off guard when she found Burke standing on the welcome mat.

For a long moment she stared wide-eyed at him, unable to fathom why he was there. He was dressed as urbanely as ever, fresh and alert for a day of business. He seemed not contrite but somewhat cool and aloof, as if this were just another matter of business. No consideration for her time or feelings.

"Good morning," he drawled.

Still Dallas stared at him and realized that it might have been weeks since she last thought about Burke.

"What are you doing here?" Dallas opened calmly.

He raised his brows and spread his hands. "That's all you have to say? I knew you'd be up. I figured I'd catch you before you left the house." He casually swept his attention over her undressed state.

"This isn't a good time," Dallas responded. Under his scrutiny she touched the front of the robe to make sure it was closed securely. She stood partially behind the door, using it somewhat as a barrier between them. "You should have called first. I . . ."

"So you could put me off? I thought I'd extend the olive branch, or whatever that saying is." He stepped toward her. "Aren't you going to let me in? I can't stay long anyway."

"I'm getting dressed . . ."

A small knowing smile lifted a corner of his mouth. "Come on . . . I've watched you get dressed before. I've seen you without a damned thing on."

His saying so seemed particularly off base to Dallas. She debated just closing the door in his face. But that was childish.

He put his hand on the door. "Come on, Dallas," he said with a touch of asperity. "I'm here and this will only take a few minutes."

She hesitated, and then stepped back to allow Burke to enter.

"Thank you," he said sarcastically, heading for the living room.

Dallas followed angrily behind. He settled himself on her sofa, crossing his legs. She remained standing to make sure that Burke understood she didn't consider this a long visit.

"Why don't you sit down? You act like we don't know each other."

"I'm not sure that we do. Maybe we never did."

"Why? Because you wanted something different from the relationship than I did? Don't say I led you on, 'cause you know that's not true."

She flushed at his admission but kept her expression neutral. "You're right."

When she didn't take the bait and become argumentative, Burke sighed and shook his head. "I thought you knew where I was coming from. We had a good thing . . ."

"*You* had a good thing. I didn't make demands. Not that it would have mattered," Dallas commented. "I only wanted you to not treat me as if I was here for your pleasure and convenience."

Burke's foot began to shake nervously. "You got something out of it, Dallas. I taught you a lot." He looked smug. "Your ex-husband didn't know a damned thing 'cept how to beat on you."

"Burke, you don't want to go there," Dallas warned softly. "You never treated me the way he did, but there is very little difference between you and Hayden."

He leaned forward and pointed his hand at her. "Hey . . . I don't have to take that . . ."

She pointed to the door. "I didn't ask you to come. What do you want?"

"Look . . . I'm sorry about the past few months. I've been under a lot of pressure. This job is coming through like I wanted, and I've been running around like crazy."

She crossed her arms over her chest. "Congratulations."

Burke stared at Dallas and finally shook his head. "Man . . . you are really going to be difficult. I came to tell you what's been going on. Things can be different now that I have this job squared away. Now we can see each other . . ."

"No."

He narrowed his gaze on her. "What? You trying to punish me or something because we haven't been together lately?"

Dallas placed her fingertips at her temples, thinking. "Look . . . let me make it easy for you. We won't see each other anymore. You were too busy to think about us for months. I'm too busy to care what or who the reason is. So why don't we just say good-bye right now?"

Burke bounded up from the sofa. His eyes sparkled with impatience. "I know what this is about. You found out about Lana. She's a new client. We signed her to an exclusive contract and were stroking her a bit."

Dallas felt her own impatience rising. She hadn't a clue who Lana was. Someone different from the woman at the lecture? Were there others? "Burke, I don't want to know. Good luck with her."

"You're jealous, aren't you?"

She glared at him. "God, you flatter yourself. I just said I don't care. You're free to go back to whatever new job or new woman you're doing this week."

He jabbed a finger at her. "I came here to see if we can work this out. You're the one . . ."

"You came here to see if you could still get me into bed. I think that's all you ever wanted."

A change came over Burke, from self-assured and sophisticated to rank and pissed.

"Goddamn bitch!" Burke said scathingly.

She'd seen Burke angry, but she'd never seen him mean or ugly. It took her by surprise. She thought she could make her feelings clear and he would just leave. No recriminations or bruised ego. But this had the potential for getting nasty.

His mouth twisted with displeasure. "Let me tell you something about yourself . . ."

"She doesn't want to hear it," came a deep voice behind them.

Dallas jumped, and Burke whirled around in stunned surprise. Alex had appeared in the living room. He looked still drowsy from sleep, but he had quickly assessed the situation.

Dallas's surprise at Alex's appearance quickly turned into relief. His presence curtailed whatever Burke was about to say. Alex was not afraid of a fight, though she hoped it wasn't going to come to that.

Burke swung from Alex to Dallas and back to Alex again. Then he cackled in amusement. "Well, I'll be *damned*!" he said wickedly.

His expression was one of vindication and righteousness. Whatever personal regard Burke might have had for her, even ten seconds ago, was irrevocably gone.

"Ain't this some shit," he said.

Dallas noted how easily Burke's demeanor slipped into the street vernacular of the urban black male. This is what he was going to use against Alex. Except that Burke didn't know that Alex was an urban street white male who could square off with him.

Alex had pulled on his jeans, but otherwise he had nothing on. Sleep was still evident around his eyes and mouth. His face was a bit flushed and his hair tousled. He looked very much at home . . . as if he'd been with her all night.

"No wonder you can't be bothered with me. You have a *white* man in your bed! Man . . . I should have known."

Alex took two steps into the room. He looked deceptively unconcerned, his hands thrust into the front pockets of his jeans. "Now that you know the deal, why don't you get out like she asked?"

Dallas moved forward, pleading with her eyes for him to stop. She touched his arm. "Alex, it's okay. We had a disagreement and he's upset . . ."

"I don't need you to make excuses for me to that white boy."

Alex smoothly ignored Dallas's entreaty and stepped around Dallas so that she was no longer between them. The muscles in his arms were taut and ready. Prepared for battle.

"Alex . . ."

"Then, let's leave Dallas out of this. You got anything to say about why I'm here, you talk to me. I'm more your size. Try getting over on me."

Burke's expression grew tight and explosive. "Who the fuck are you?"

"I'm a friend of Dallas's," Alex said patiently. "And I don't particularly like the way you're talking to her. If you can't be nice, get out."

"Oh, *man* . . ." Burke shook his head, glaring at Dallas again.

She tried not to let her hands shake. "This isn't going anywhere. We'll just end up saying horrible things to each other, Burke. Just go."

"Oh, yes, ma'am. So that's the choice, huh? You don't need my sorry black ass anymore. You've got Casper, here."

"Hey . . ." Alex began in a slightly raised voice as he stepped even closer to Burke.

Burke stood still and they faced each other. "So, you don't like how I talk. What you gonna do? Kick my ass?"

"Is that what it's going to take?"

"You and what other two *white* boys?"

"We're not going to rock and roll because you're going to leave. *Now.* That's it."

Burke sized Alex up, but Dallas could see that he wasn't about to take a chance. Besides the fact that he wasn't dressed for throwing down on her living-room floor, he was of a slighter build than Alex. It was obvious to Dallas that Alex could take him easily.

Burke had the attitude of being tough, but nothing to back it up with. He wasn't going to take the chance of making a fool of himself. And Alex was not going to back off. So Burke took the next best option. He continued to mouth off at Dallas as he backed toward the door.

"You know what? I was right about you to begin with . . ."

Alex started toward him again.

"Alex, don't. Please . . ." she said.

Burke reached the door, and pointed at her. "You're a whole lot of yelluh, wasted."

"Sorry your visit was cut short . . ." Alex said smoothly.

"Fuck you!" Burke spat out at him.

"You wish you could," Alex murmured as the door slammed.

Dallas didn't realize she'd been holding her breath until after the door shut. Alex slowly turned to face her, but she averted her eyes, feeling the heat of embarrassment spread across her face.

"Are you okay?" he asked in quiet concern.

Dallas nodded, afraid to try to talk. She merely stepped around Alex to head toward her room. But he would have followed her there . . . and that was dangerous. She went into the bathroom and closed the door instead. Dallas sat on the downed toilet seat lid and tried to stop the tremors in her body.

. . . *A whole lot of yelluh wasted* . . .

She squeezed her eyes closed but could see the look of disgust on Burke's face. She'd had no idea he really felt that way. That Burke had never taken her seriously . . . might never have considered her as black.

There was a soft knock on the bathroom door.

"Dallas?"

"Yes?" she answered wearily.

"You okay?"

"I said I was fine," she answered impatiently.

"Then open the door."

"I'll be out in a few minutes."

There was a pause.

"All right. If you're not out by then . . . I'm coming in."

She believed him. She continued to sit there for

another minute, then got up and stepped cautiously into the hall. It was very quiet. She thought that perhaps Alex had just gotten dressed and left. She passed the small office and peered in. The futon had been folded up and the bed linens neatly stacked on top. She went into the kitchen and found Alex standing at the sink, drinking a glass of juice. She stopped short when she saw him. He was still dressed in just the jeans. He put the glass into the sink and faced her.

"Come here," he murmured, reaching out for her.

Dallas didn't seem to be able to move. Alex stepped toward her to put his arms around her. That's what he'd always done. Been there. This time it was not a comforting hug, but an embrace. Dallas could feel it in the gentle tightening of Alex's arms. In the warm breath he expelled that she felt against her cheek and neck, in the overwhelming awareness of his solid masculinity.

"Stay as long as you want," he teased.

She did, closing her eyes and not moving. She let herself relax against him. Her sense of safety returned. And then the change started.

"Dallas?"

"No. No, Alex. Don't say anything." She tried to pull out of his arms.

"You feel it, too, don't you?"

"I think I . . ."

"What's happening. It's not the same anymore between us. You know it isn't." He sighed, pressing his cheek against her hair. "It's a whole lot more . . ."

She shook her head. "No . . ."

He held her, tightening his arms a little and forcing her to look into his face. "This isn't about Burke, or your ex-husband, or any other man who's given you a hard time. This isn't about you being black or me being white. This isn't about my family or yours, or the past, but right now. We have to talk."

"I . . . I don't think . . ."

"Dallas," he said urgently. "Do you realize how

long we've known each other? Do you realize we've done everything together—*everything*—except hold each other like this? Or kiss? Jesus . . . I've never kissed you . . ."

She was going to suggest that now was not the time, but Dallas looked up and already Alex's mouth was descending. His lips settled with an open eroticism on hers. The immediate effect on them both stunned her. Totally new, yet familiar. Shocking . . . yet so right. It had taken them fifteen years to get this far. And it was as if they both knew it would come to this.

Alex gently twisted his mouth over hers, forcing it open, and Dallas let his tongue slip easily in. The warm pressure and sensual manipulation disoriented her. She closed her eyes and reality dropped away. Dallas knew only the springy softness of the hair on his chest between her fingers, the massaging warmth of his hands. The supple male firmness of his skin. It was heady and wonderful, tender and knowing and amazingly familiar. It was made all the more so because she'd imagined this, and denied it. When she was sixteen. When she saw him again at Lillian and Vin's. In the kitchen at Valerie's . . .

She jumped and pulled her mouth free. She felt his lips on her neck. He thrust his hips forward against her and the hard pressure of his erection lodged a moan in her throat. "Alex, I can't. I . . . I'm so confused, I . . . we have to stop," Dallas whispered, trying to push him away.

"I don't want to," he said. "You don't want me to."

His point was proven when Alex again kissed Dallas, sabotaging her efforts to stay focused. His mouth was so knowing, making her give in to the pleasure. She did, for a long time. Finally, she broke it off again.

"We . . . can't," she forced herself to be firm. She looked into his face. She saw wonder, gentleness . . . and desire. Dallas wanted him to kiss her again. She wanted him to never stop. But she wasn't going to let it happen. "It's too soon."

"Dallas, we would have gotten to where we are now without Valerie or Burke. We both know it."

She shook her head, as his lips left kisses on her face, teased at her mouth. "You have to settle your business with Val. I can't be in the middle, Alex."

"I never made any promises to her . . ." he whispered, brushing his lips over hers when she momentarily lifted her head. "Val knows that."

She responded. It was wonderful. She stopped.

"Maybe it's not me you want, either."

She felt the reflexive tightening of Alex's arms, the restless pressure of his fingers against her spine through her clothing. "I got distracted."

"The red hair and green eyes?" she asked, bluntly.

"Trying to get what belonged to Nick, I guess. But Val and Megan need something different than what I can offer."

Dallas frowned. "I don't understand."

He hesitated, carefully thinking over his answer. Finally Alex shook his head helplessly. "Val is trying to make up for Nick. To replace him. She wants to make up for the past. Nicholas was Megan's father."

Chapter Fourteen

Alex finished getting dressed and followed the quiet sounds in Dallas's apartment until he found her in the kitchen. She too had gotten dressed, in linen slacks and a black bodysuit that defined her lithe and curvaceous build. He tried to get her to look at him, but she studiously avoided eye contact. Yet aware of his arrival, she automatically took two glasses from a cabinet and then opened the refrigerator to get a container of orange juice. She filled the glasses.

"Do you want anything to eat for breakfast? I don't have much, but . . ."

"The juice is fine, thanks."

The formality of the question and answer belied the undercurrent between them. Alex watched Dallas and tried to figure out what was going on in her head. He'd thought for sure that the truth would make it easier for Dallas to consider that something incredibly strong was happening between the two of them. But instead she had withdrawn from him.

"I really appreciate what you did for me last night," Alex said, not bothering to sit at the small kitchen table, but leaning against the door frame as he accepted the juice.

"I suppose I should thank you for trying to help with Burke."

"Would it have been better if I'd stayed out of it?"

"I don't know," Dallas said honestly. "Maybe not. He might still have . . ."

"Go on and say it. Gotten in your face the way he

did. Sorry. I wasn't going to let him go at you like that. Reminded me of Nick."

There was a ghost of a smile at the corner of her mouth. "I know."

"So then, what's really bothering you?" he pursued softly.

Dallas had her glass halfway to her mouth, changed her mind, and put it down again. Finally she looked at Alex. And immediately she felt it again. The ties that bind . . .

"You know what," she barely whispered.

"It probably would have happened sooner or later, Dallas. I do want you. I wanted you last night when I saw you standing behind the barricades on the pier. Just like that I knew. I want you right now . . ."

She closed her eyes and shook her head, as if to deny his words. Alex reached out and took her hand tightly.

"Question is, do you want me?"

Dallas winced. "I . . . I can't answer that."

"Yes, you can."

She looked at him poignantly, her eyes overly bright.

She shook her head. "No. Right now I really can't."

"All right. We'll let it go for now. I know it seems sudden, but it's not. You know it's not. And I'm going to ask you again. I promise you."

Now Alex did pull her toward him. There was a token resistance, but all he did was to settle an arm around her waist, holding Dallas at his side. "The way I look at it maybe it's been real since that day with Nick. I know you're thinking of all that crap about black and white. It wasn't on my mind when I pulled Nick off you. And I certainly didn't think about it when I made love to you for the first time . . ." He felt the slight agitation in her at the reminder.

"I have to get to work," Dallas announced quietly. She resolutely refused to go into what was happening. She couldn't deal with it.

Alex sighed in resignation. He pressed his mouth and nose to her temple, a gesture of affection and understanding. "I have things to take care of, too. When am I going to see you again?"

She extricated herself from his arm. "I can't. I don't know what I'm feeling yet. It's complicated. And you have your own thing to deal with. There's a lot to think about, Alex."

"I know," Alex admitted. But he still wouldn't let her just walk away. He held her hand again and cupped his other around the side of her neck and jaw, his thumb stroking over her cheek and the corner of her mouth. "But there's one thing you have to tell me right now." He gazed intently into her eyes, holding her attention. "Am I way off base?"

Dallas thought about all the things that would have been best to say, but she didn't know why she should. Not being honest only confused the issue. And she had nothing more to lose by doing so. She gave a slight shake of her head.

"I . . . I don't think so."

"Girl, are you listening to me?"

Dallas started and turned her attention to Maureen. But she couldn't really see her eyes behind the polarizing lenses of the large sunglasses. She pursed her lips patiently. "Yes, Maureen. I'm listening. I heard that your sister is pissing you off because she doesn't want to wear the dress you picked for the wedding party. I heard that you and Nathan changed your mind about going to Bermuda and are thinking about Bonaire instead . . ."

"And I hope you heard me when I told you to get over this business about Burke. The man isn't worth this much emotion. You added more class to his life than he knew what to do with." She waggled her head.

"I wonder what *his* friends are telling him about *me*?"

Maureen looked as if the answer were obvious. She

gestured with her hand and repeated patiently. "That you added more class to his life than he knew what . . ."

Dallas started laughing. "I appreciate your loyalty."

They sidestepped a kamikaze in-line skater who whizzed by them so fast a breeze ruffled Dallas's hair. Paralleling her and Maureen on the Park Drive South were a steady stream of joggers, roller-bladers, horse-drawn carriages with tourists, bikers, and people like her and Maureen, just walking. They'd met for brunch, Maureen's idea, after Megan had called on Friday to say she couldn't come in for her visit. She was spending the weekend with her grandmother.

Dallas had asked how Valerie was, but could read nothing into Megan's indifferent response that "she's good." Yet when Megan had asked her if she wanted to talk to Valerie, Dallas realized she had taken the safe route out by saying she knew Val was busy and would talk to her another time. She had avoided the possibility of any discussion about Alex. But she had maybe also missed an opportunity to end the standoff between them.

Maureen sighed and shook her head. "I swear some of the brothers just don't know how to do right."

"Maybe it's not the brothers. Maybe it's me."

"Uh-huh. There ain't a thing wrong with you. You just haven't found the right man yet who appreciates you."

Dallas shook her head with a frown. "Don't make it sound like I'm so different. It's not appreciation I need or want. It's respect. Love would be nice," she added dryly.

"Yeah, that's what I mean."

Dallas smiled absently. She tried not to let her thoughts drift again to Alex, but it seemed inevitable. He had not been out of her thoughts since that morning when Burke had unexpectedly appeared. It was disturbing to remember so vividly the heightened awareness that had sparked desire between them. Alex had called her just that past Wednesday. And although the conversation had been personal—about Vin and Lillian, her and her parents, Valerie—it had not been intimate . . . about them. That was precisely how she knew that Alex's intentions were real. Perversely, Dallas realized now, the safety of their conversations was disappointing.

Dallas and Maureen stopped briefly in the middle of a viaduct over one of the roads that transversed the park from east to west. They watched the cars and cabs swishing by beneath them. Maureen chuckled.

"Remember when we were kids? On Halloween we'd fill balloons with water and drop them out my bedroom window?" She turned her head and grinned at Dallas. "Remember the year we went to that party, and you came as Darla from the *Little Rascals* . . . and I came as Buckwheat?"

Dallas shook her head. "I remember everybody really got on us for doing that."

"Dummies. It was a sight gag, and they didn't get it."

They walked to a nearby bench and sat down. Maureen turned to Dallas once more. She contemplated her silently and thoughtfully shook her head.

"You know, I never even thought of how hard it was going to be for you. I thought, here's this fly girl with good hair and light skin who doesn't act like she's white . . . the guys were going to fall out over you. I never thought you'd have to go through what you did with Hayden. And now Burke. We won't *even* talk about those pimply fools when we were in school. What is it with black men?"

Dallas shrugged. "History. Hatred. Insecurity. Expectations. Maybe anger. Go ahead . . . pick one."

Maureen cackled. "Stupidity."

"Maureen, stop worrying about it."

"Well, there's a lesson here. Even if he's black, he can still be wack!"

"I'm not going to ask where you got that from," Dallas murmured in astonishment.

"My niece, Tasha. Cute little thing. She's going with a boy whose family is Portuguese! You know what she says about him? He treats her nice. He doesn't run a line on her. Now you know they've been to bed. But he uses a condom! I told her I don't care what color he is, sounds good to me."

Dallas stared at Maureen. She had never been known for her subtlety. "Maureen, what are you trying to say?"

"I think I understand why it's been so hard. But you don't deserve for it to be *that* hard. If you were anybody else, I'd be suspicious of your motives. But maybe you need to broaden your playing field a little. You need more chances in your life, more choices . . . no matter how many colors they come in."

Valerie sat so that she wasn't directly in the sun, protecting her pale skin from its unforgiving rays. To avoid the wind whipping at her hair, she had it pulled back into a ponytail and wore a beige baseball cap. The waves jostling the small boat rocked her and weren't particular conducive to looking poised and cool. But it didn't matter, Valerie decided in resignation. Alex wasn't paying any attention to her in any case.

Alex was standing behind Megan, carefully monitoring her as she steered the craft across the open channel. Valerie could hear the timbre of his voice although not his words as he instructed her daughter, and Megan laughed and responded. Of course, he had to be prepared to take over if anything went wrong, or if Megan lost control.

The boat swerved jerkily, and Megan squealed in faint terror. Alex's throaty laugher rang out. He reached around her to steady the craft and put it back on course. But Megan soon tired and gave the wheel back to Alex.

As she made her way back toward her mother, her

hair swung left and right behind her. She collapsed in a deck chair.

"That was so *cool.* Did you see Alex let me steer?"

"I guess that makes you captain," Valerie responded with a smile.

Megan giggled and nodded her head. She bounced up again, her energy barely contained in the small confines of the boat. She stood with her legs braced apart, testing her balance and swaying with the motion of the boat.

"Megan, I think you'd better either sit down or hold on to something," Valerie warned with more pettishness in her voice than she intended. She *had* been impatient with her daughter recently. That's what Dallas had said.

Megan sighed in annoyance. "I wish Aunt Dallas was here, don't you? How come she's not here?"

Valerie pushed her sunglasses up the bridge of her nose. She shrugged. "I don't know. Maybe she's busy. Her father's been sick, you know."

"Well, what about Ross?"

Valerie struggled to keep her tone even and indifferent. "Honey, I don't know." She wondered about Ross, too.

Megan grew restless and turned toward the cabin below. "I'm going to get a can of soda . . ."

"While you're down there, put on some more sunblock," Valerie shouted after her.

When Megan had disappeared below, Valerie got up and made a quick and uneven shuffle to join Alex at the wheel. They'd had no time alone since he'd picked up her and Megan that morning for the trip across the Long Island Sound to Mystic, Connecticut. She knew it wasn't deliberate. But Valerie also knew that it made a difference. She stood silently next to Alex, looking over the compass dials and the digital navigation clocks, not the least interested in what they do or how they work, but hoping for some opening to a conversation. Nothing came to mind.

Alex glanced down at her, squinting against the wind and sun. He smiled warmly at her, but clearly missing was that light of interest and intent that had flared up between them four months earlier in February. Valerie returned the smile, but she didn't flirt. There was no longer any point.

"How's Ross?" she asked, surprising even herself with the question.

Alex looked briefly at her and then back out to the sound. "I thought you didn't like Ross."

She shrugged. "That's not true. It's just that . . . he irritates me at times."

Alex slowly grinned. "Some women have called it that."

"What?" She frowned.

"Ross is okay. He just thought we needed some time together without him as the Jolly Green Giant in the background."

Valerie had to smile in spite of herself. The image was fitting. The amusement quickly faded. She moistened her lips. "Do you think Dallas is attractive?"

Alex didn't answer right away, quickly assessing how to avoid hurting her. "Yes, I do."

She pursed her lips. "You're not in love with me, are you?"

Alex's jaw flexed. He hadn't expected to discuss their relationship this way. He'd hoped for more privacy, someplace quiet where he could be tender and reassuring. "I'm sorry, Val. I've been thinking how to tell you. You're not in love with me, either."

She hadn't expected that. She hadn't even considered it. But it was true. Valerie shook her head. "No, I don't think I am."

Alex put his arm around her shoulder. It was only affectionate. "Maybe that's our problem. We've both been trying too hard. I'm sorry. It was all my fault. I shouldn't have raised your hopes."

"No. No, you're wrong. I was just trying to rewrite history and come up with a better ending."

"Nothing wrong with that. But you gotta take care of the past, Val. Tell Megan about Nick. Tell Vin and Lillian."

He stopped abruptly when they heard Megan return to the deck. But she merely sat in the canvas deck chair, snacking on popcorn and drinking her soda and ignoring them.

Valerie gave her attention back to Alex. It was over. But that wasn't what bothered her.

"Alex, I have to ask you something else. About Dallas . . . is there something going on with you two?"

Alex stiffened momentarily. But then he shook his head. "No." That was the truth.

"But . . . you like her?"

"Why do you sound so shocked? Yeah, I like her."

"Well, I just thought . . ."

He looked closely at her, trying to read into the half-finished statement. "Because she's black that it would make a difference? Why?"

Valerie thought about it for a long time. And she couldn't come up with any answer.

Yeah. Why, indeed.

Dallas was taken aback by the reception she received at the Marco house. Lillian hugged her warmly and seemed unusually happy to see her. Vin was home and said hello, and asked her if she wanted anything to drink. Iced tea? And he asked about her family. Was her father okay?

The unexpected flutter around her made Dallas suspicious.

"Vin, stop fussing," Lillian said. "The poor child hasn't even gotten through the door yet."

"Well, don't make her sit in the kitchen," Vin muttered. With a wave of his arm he indicated the front room of the house, which they never used.

"Aagh!" Lillian responded, as if he didn't know any better. "Go away. Dallas and me have been doing this for years. We like sitting in the kitchen. We're like two old biddies gossiping and drinking tea. Right, Dallas?"

Dallas only nodded with a bemused and uncertain smile, aware that both of them were agitated. But Lillian won out. The kitchen, after all, was her domain. Vin left them alone and she and Lillian settled into their familiar routine. But something was definitely different.

Lillian clasped her hands and looked at Dallas with such heart-wrenching poignancy that Dallas knew something was also wrong.

"I'm so glad to see you. Sit down, sit down!"

Dallas watched Lillian putter around the kitchen. Dallas thought of all the reasons her coming today would make such a scene and nothing she came up with made any sense. She hadn't visited in almost two months, but that wasn't strange. She'd frequently gone much longer.

Lillian was making the iced tea while Dallas hunted down the cookies. She wondered if Vin and Lillian had somehow found out about her and Alex? But there was nothing to find out . . . yet. Not for want of trying on Alex's part. He called her almost every night, now. And she kept putting him off.

"Dallas, when am I going to see you?" Alex asked. Not urgently, but repeating the question often to let her know he wasn't going to give up. He'd meant everything he'd said to her.

"I don't know. Not yet," she answered honestly. But they hung up with Dallas knowing it was inevitable. He said that he and Valerie had had a talk. They agreed mutually to break off their relationship. There was, technically, nothing to hold her back from giving in to Alex's coaxing. It's what she wanted.

Except that Dallas still had not heard directly from Val herself.

"Lillian, is everything all right?" Dallas finally asked, when everything had been served and they sat down. Lillian shook her head, her facial expression changing and re-forming into distress and weariness.

"Oh . . . I'm not sure, honey. I haven't heard from Alex in weeks, and it's got me worried. He's always so good about letting me know how he's doing. But ever since . . . well, you know how Vin gets sometimes. Anyway, the last time Alex was by . . ." Lillian shook her head again.

Dallas was stunned to see that she was perilously close to tears. She reached across the table and gently rubbed Lillian's arm. The woman welcomed the gesture almost with desperation and reached to take hold of Dallas's hand. Lillian's was ice-cold, and gripped hers tightly.

"No, no . . . don't you worry yourself. Everything is . . . well . . . I don't know. Me and Vin . . . we really need to talk to Alex."

Dallas became alert. "Did you call him?"

"Oh, yes. But I didn't want to seem . . . you know. So anxious. I didn't want to pressure him."

"Is there anything I can do?"

Lillian sighed. "Darling, you know you're like a daughter to me, but . . . it's family stuff."

More secrets, Dallas thought uneasily. Lillian, of course, had no idea how well she knew Alex or for how long. She might have been able to help. She certainly knew Alex Marco well enough to know that if she told him to, he would phone home.

Lillian never did confide her concerns, but leaving her a short time later Dallas realized she had questions of her own as she walked the three blocks to her parents' house. How to reconcile with Eleanor without feeling like she'd capitulated completely.

It helped that the front of the property was awash with color. Eleanor had a neatly manicured plot of annuals and perennials. Dallas took a deep breath before she let herself into the house. Only her father was home.

She smiled at him as she entered. She gave him a peck on the cheek.

"It's good to see you," Lyle Oliver murmured with quiet pleasure.

Dallas was gratified by his mood. She tried not to stare too closely, but after not seeing her father for two weeks she could easily see that he still seemed gaunt. His movements were still slow and careful. He seemed much more peaceful, however. They sat at the kitchen table and wryly she declined the offer of iced tea. She already felt somewhat waterlogged.

"You look good." Dallas smiled at her father.

"You lie," he scoffed, and grinned when she laughed.

"Well . . . maybe you should put some of that weight back on. Otherwise you'll slip right through my arms if I try to hug you."

"Oh, then . . . I'll definitely fatten up. Unfortunately, the doctors and Eleanor watch me like a hawk. They give me only enough to eat to keep me alive! I would kill for some fried chicken or meat loaf with brown gravy."

Dallas laughed again. "Well, I'd rather have you eat healthy."

Lyle Oliver looked at his daughter, blinking at her with incredible warmth in his eyes. Dallas could see, behind the thoughtful gaze and quiet consideration, an acknowledgment of what *she* would have killed for as a child. Perhaps his brush with a life-threatening illness had made him reflective. Whatever the reason, Dallas was grateful for the change. It wasn't often that anyone got a second chance. She and her father seemed to be discovering each other.

"So what are the doctors telling you?"

He sighed and shifted comfortably on his chair. "Oh, basically to accept that I need to watch my health. I'm not an old man yet, but I can't do what I used to do. And if I want to continue to do what I *can* do, then I have to give up the fried chicken and meat loaf with brown gravy."

Dallas chuckled. "I'll take the trade-off."

"I appreciate that," he murmured softly. "Have you heard from Dean?"

"You mean you haven't?"

Lyle Oliver scratched his ear. "Well . . . my suspicion is that he's laying low until this whole thing with that young woman blows over. He and I had a long talk about it."

Dallas tried not to show her surprise. "Did you?"

"I live with Eleanor. I know how she gets," her father commented boldly. "I thought he could use a little support. Ellie can't have her way all the time, and this time I think she's gone too far."

Dallas wondered what both of them would do if they knew about Alex. But . . . what was there to know yet.

"You know, we've seen Dean with all kinds of women. All pretty, of course, but often not much else to speak of."

"Maybe that's why he hasn't married, yet."

He nodded. "He has some growing up to do. Eleanor is a proud woman. She came a long way at a time when we had to fight every stop of the way. So she has very definite views on ethnicity."

Dallas looked at him. "Is that why you married her?"

Her father returned the look with his own knowing smile. "You mean, she reminded me I was a black man?"

Dallas blushed. Had she sounded so impertinent?

"Ellie made me feel strong again, after your mother took you back to Texas and we divorced. She helped me heal a lot of wounds. But she also made me feel needed. She has a very clear sense of herself."

"What about love?"

He raised his brows. "Of course we love each other."

Dallas began to feel uncomfortable. "Do you think Eleanor will back off?"

"Probably, if Dean feels strongly about . . . what's her name? Alikah? I think Ellie should appreciate that Alikah is so sure of herself. She's just right out there with this personal style that makes a statement. And it's true to her natural heritage. Maybe Ellie is a little threatened by that. She's made concessions to get where she is. I certainly have. You and Dean and his girlfriend are benefiting from all this multiculturalism, and ethnic pride and political correctness in ways you already take for granted. It wasn't always so."

Dallas suddenly had a clear insight into family history from her father's point of view. In many ways he had shown enormous bravery and hope, in defying tradition and marrying her mother. He had been a forerunner, a pioneer in what the world had become. She was a product of his daring. She was the future.

There was such a mood of openness and acceptance that Dallas ventured onto another sensitive topic.

"I read through all of the letters in that box." He nodded, looking carefully for her reaction. "I wish I'd seen some of those years ago."

"I'm sorry. I thought I was doing the right thing, putting it all away. You have to understand how all of that past was painful to me. It wasn't easy. And it took me a long time to get over."

"I know, Daddy." She hesitated, gauging his mood. "But . . . I want to try to find my mother's family. Some of my cousins. There's so much I want to know about her. Do you mind?"

"No. I guess I shouldn't be surprised."

"If I find them, do you want to know?"

Lyle Oliver cleared his throat and shifted in the chair again. "Let me think about it a bit."

They heard the red Camry pull into the driveway, and Dallas got up to help her stepmother with any packages she might have. There was still a great deal of reserve between the two of them and Dallas hoped that her father was not aware of the strain.

Eleanor's conversation reminded Dallas of Lillian's. Nervous behind a facade of calm and routine. The marketing was put away, and family news caught up with. Dallas didn't know if it was worth touching on the sensitive and still raw issue of the things said between herself and her stepmother when her father had fallen sick. Perhaps it was best to leave well enough alone.

"Eleanor, the front yard looks wonderful. You could see the flowers out front all the way from the corner."

"Oh, thank you. I put in some new things this year. I really need to get out there and weed," Eleanor said with a kind of breathy brightness, bustling around the kitchen putting boxes and cans away. "Would you like something from the yard? I think I have an empty clay pot somewhere in the garage. Let me put a cutting in it for you to take home with you."

Dallas didn't respond right away. She and her father exchanged surprised looks. "That's great. I'd like that," she said.

It was certainly a start.

Megan was supposed to be in bed.

When Valerie heard her daughter in the living room, she came out of the kitchen to see what she was up to. Her daughter had plopped down on the sofa and was punching in numbers on the telephone.

"Megan, who are you calling this late?"

"Aunt Dallas . . ." She had completed the numbers and put the unit to her ear.

"Put that phone down and go to bed. Right now!"

Megan looked at her, her wide eyes showing her surprise at the tone of her mother's voice. "But I'm calling Dallas. I want to go and see her this weekend."

"Megan . . ." Valerie said in a warning tone. She

started across the room at her daughter. "Did you hear what I said?"

Megan stared at her mother in disbelief as Valerie took the unit out of her hands.

"Why don't you listen to me!"

"Mom . . ." Megan whined. "What's the matter with you? I'm supposed to visit Aunt Dallas and I always call first."

"You're not calling her because you're not going into the city." Valerie detached the hand unit and put the stand on the coffee table. Then she felt foolish. What was she going to do with it? Hide it? Why was she getting angry with Megan? She saw the confusion on her daughter's face and felt terrible.

Megan bounded up from the sofa and faced off with her mother. "Why? Why can't I go? You made me go to Grandma Rosemary's that time and . . . and I didn't even want to. I haven't seen Aunt Dallas . . . for weeks."

Valerie watched as the bewilderment and frustration made her daughter whine. She tried to get hold of herself. She'd screamed at Megan like a wild woman. Her child had done nothing wrong.

"I didn't mean to yell at you, sweetie," Valerie attempted. "But you didn't ask to use the phone, and you're supposed to be in bed by now."

"That's not it," Megan said. "You won't let me 'cause you're mad at her."

"What are you talking about?" Valerie asked, although she flashed back instantly to that awful confrontation in Dallas's kitchen the month before.

"I heard the way you and she were talking that time at her place. I don't know why, but you *were* talking loud. And now you won't let me see her. That's not fair! I didn't do anything wrong."

Valerie could see that she had mishandled the situation. Maybe she shouldn't have demanded.

"Honey, of course you didn't do anything wrong.

There are reasons why you can't see Dallas. She's been *very* busy and . . ."

"You always say that. It's not true. She's *never* too busy to see me. She told me I can call or come over anytime I want to." Megan's voice began to rise to youthful hysteria.

"Calm down." Valerie put her hand out to her. "Maybe you can go and see her after school is out."

Megan looked even more astonished. "But . . . but . . . what about my graduation? She said she'd come."

"Maybe. We'll have to . . ."

"Nooooo!" Megan began to sob. "I want to talk to her. I want to see her."

Valerie tried the voice of authority. But she knew she'd already lost it. "Stop it! You're behaving like a child and I won't . . ."

"You're so unfair!" Megan wailed, out of control.

"That's it! Enough. Please go to bed like I told you. Maybe you can see Dallas sometime later, but *not* this weekend."

Megan began crying in earnest, shaking her head at her mother, her face distorted. She turned and ran back down the hall. "I wish Aunt Dallas was my mother!" she screamed. Her bedroom door slammed.

The announcement rooted Valerie to the spot. Megan might just as well have said that she hated her. She realized she was clutching the telephone receiver against her chest. She stared at it before tossing it on the sofa in disgust. Then she sat down, her hands covering her mouth, and wondered if there was a way out of this mess she'd created.

Chapter Fifteen

Dallas lay awake in the dark.

It was the third night that week that she'd been unable to get through the whole night without her sleep being interrupted by the concerns and vagaries of the day. So much had come about in just two weeks. The result of years, even decades, of events, people, places, and things that now seemed to be turning the course of everyone's lives upside down.

Dallas still didn't know what to make of Eleanor's conciliatory attitude toward her. It was no warmer than Eleanor had ever been toward her, but Dallas couldn't deny that Eleanor really seemed more aware of her feelings. Even her father, frightened by the prospects of maybe dying suddenly without having resolved his past, had been more open and affectionate, more willing to talk about her mother and their civil rights era romance that had cost them—and her—so much. Dallas had been astounded at the extent of her father's experiences.

His history quietly was becoming the basis for a book she intended to write.

Dallas shifted positions onto her back and stretched out her legs. She closed her eyes and concentrated on falling asleep. After a few seconds they shot open again and she stared at the ceiling. Her mind wouldn't stay quiet. Dallas had been thinking for the past week that maybe she should just go ahead and call Valerie and make peace. But no. There was a principle to be maintained. She had not done anything wrong to hurt

Valerie, and she resented any implication by Valerie that she had. Yet, Dallas wondered if her standoff with the person who had been her best friend forever was going to seriously affect the future relationship with her godchild. Megan hadn't called to make arrangements for her usual visit. And Dallas wondered if that was Megan's decision . . . or her mother's.

She shifted positions again.

Then there was Dean. She'd had lunch with him and Alikah just yesterday. Dallas liked her. While it was obvious that Alikah and her brother had a real relationship in progress and not one that was based purely on sex, Dallas thought that Eleanor had overreacted to her son's recent involvement. Dallas was of the opinion that there could be a few more women before Dean settled down with one.

She gave up.

Throwing off the sheet covering her, Dallas got out of bed. She glanced at the nightstand clock: 2:13 . . . A.M. In frustration she stood up and stretched, running her fingers through her curly hair. She paced in front of the bed before deciding to get a drink of water. Maybe the brief activity would cut into her restlessness.

She walked barefoot in the dark toward the kitchen. The thin cotton sleep-slip moved softly against her skin. In the kitchen Dallas poured herself a half a glass of milk. She stood there slowly drinking, still reflective. When the buzzer sounded it made her jump so badly she dropped the glass.

Dallas gasped as it shattered on the vinyl tile floor and she felt the spray of cold milk and glass shards on her feet. Her heart thundered. She didn't know what to do first. Answer the intercom or clean up the mess. Finally she pressed the talk button on her wall system.

"Who is it?" Dallas asked quietly. Pointlessly.

"Dallas . . . it's me."

She didn't hesitate an instant in pushing the release

button for the entrance into the building. Then she turned to the kitchen floor. She had to distract herself. She got paper towels and began to sop up the debris, as if it weren't the middle of the night and someone had not just rung her apartment for admission. As if she weren't nervous as a cat . . . and filled with a perverse excitement. She had most of the floor cleaned up when her doorbell rang. But again she jumped. A small piece of glass bit into her finger as she dumped the bundle of wet towels in the garbage. She still hadn't turned on the lights.

Dallas sucked on the finger when the spot of blood squeezed through the tiny puncture. She opened the door.

It seemed silly for her and Alex to just stand and stare at one another across the threshold, but that's what they did. Dallas saw no hesitation in Alex's eyes. They were alert and focused. He saw her blinking at him in the sudden bright light of the hallway, her expression nonetheless open.

She shook her head. First things first. "It's not Lillian, is it? Vin?"

Alex stepped right into the apartment, closed the door, and stood looking down on her.

"No," he murmured, reaching for her in the same breath. "It's me . . ."

She made it easy for him to put his arms around her. She reached out to him. She made it easy for him to kiss her. Her lips were already parted and waiting. And she made it easy for Alex to know that this was unimaginably satisfying. She let their tongues dance together in gentle union that clearly was the foreplay for something much grander and more stimulating.

Dallas was so ready she felt wanton.

She didn't think about what was going on with Valerie and Alex. She believed and trusted that he would not have shown up at her door in the middle of the night unless he was free to do so. She didn't question this moment at all.

She loved the way he kissed her. It was so deep and slow and thorough, as if he had no intentions of rushing, as if he wanted it to last a lifetime. But Dallas could feel his hardened penis pressed against her loins. She could sense the control of Alex's desire in the taut sinew of his arms and shoulders. The feel of him was not a surprise. She had always felt perfectly safe and at home in his arms.

Alex pulled his mouth free, but only to make one statement before reclaiming hers again.

"I don't need to think about this anymore, Dallas."

"I know," she whispered. She'd needed him to make the first move.

Alex hugged her, his hands gliding over her to find ways to bring her closer. There was an urgency that already made his breathing short and hurried. When his hands discovered that she had nothing on beneath the short gown he groaned.

"Oh, man . . ." he said hoarsely.

Dallas grinned dreamily. "Come on," she whispered, turning out of his arms and leading him by the hand down the hallway and into her room.

She still had not turned on a single light, and by mutual agreement there didn't seem to be a need to see what was happening. The feelings vibrating between them in the dark were much more enticing.

Alex began to undress. Dallas imagined she could see him smiling at her.

"Are you going to watch me this time?" he asked, referring to that time in his apartment when she'd come to him.

Dallas blushed.

Alex chuckled and caught her chin. "I was only teasing. I'm sorry. I know this is crazy. It's after two, but . . ."

"I was awake."

He stopped at her reply. He reached to put his hand to the back of her head. His fingers combed into her curls and held her still for a slow, lingering kiss. Their tongues teased, but it wasn't passionate. Just kind of sweet and gentle.

"Couldn't sleep either?" Dallas shook her head. "I thought for sure you'd tell me to go home."

"What if I had?"

"I don't know. I guess I was counting on you not doing that."

Alex dropped to the side of her bed and pulled off the cowboy boots, then his jeans. He stood up again with only gray briefs hugging his hips and restraining his erection. Slowly he bent to peel them off and then stood waiting for Dallas to make the next move.

She started by taking off the cotton nightdress and climbing onto the bed. He moved next to her. He reached to take her into his arms as he slid down on the mattress. And then all they did for a while was hug. Perhaps it was an odd way to begin to make love, but now that they were together, the urgency from that fateful morning a few weeks ago disappeared. Instead there was only a sense of relief because the anticipation was over. It had been worth the wait.

After a while Alex finally turned to Dallas and began to kiss her again. For a long time it seemed to be enough. She was grateful for the time to adjust to him. Simply because the first time they'd been together in bed she didn't know what the hell she was doing.

His stiff member surged against her and signaled the level of his arousal. She tentatively touched him to indicate her own willingness. Alex sighed and moaned.

"Alex? Do you . . . have anything with you?" she asked, staring at him.

He stroked her stomach. "Plenty."

He leaned away over the edge of the bed for his jeans and took the packets from his pocket. When he was sheathed and protected, Alex leaned over to whisper in her ear.

"I messed it up for you, didn't I? I wasn't any good the first time we were together," he whispered with regret.

"It wasn't you."

"I always wanted a chance to show you what it's really like."

"I know what it's like. I'm more experienced now."

He carefully lifted his body to rest on top of her. Dallas automatically raised her knees, and his weight spread her legs. "Yeah . . . but not with me," Alex said as he directed his penis into her body.

Alex didn't need to worry, Dallas thought as they settled into a smooth and rhythmic thrusting. She could tell from his control, his timing, that Alex was much more experienced, too. The thing that was different was that it didn't hurt and she wasn't scared, and it felt so wonderful to be together again like this. Dallas couldn't think of a thing they didn't know about each other.

It had been such a long time. But it couldn't have taken less time than it had for them to realize they wanted each other. Alex kept the pace steady and gentle. The sensual tension built slowly in their kisses and touch, where their bodies connected. It was so different because they were part of each other. Simpatico. Soul mates.

The silky friction finally culminated in a release for both of them that was not so much explosive as it was breathless and intense. They lay languishing with their bodies still joined and a sense of peace softening their limbs.

But this had only taken off the edge. They soon started again. The second climax built upon the first, and when the last tremors were wrung out of her, Dallas realized that her toes had curled.

They were together for the next two days.

Dallas thought that the most wonderful thing about it was that they didn't spend it all in bed. There had been a lot of catching up to do. Mostly they just enjoyed being together. They walked about her neighborhood, strolled Broadway and Riverside Park. They sat in noisy sidewalk bistros with flavored designer coffee and shared muffins or brownies. Doing a lot of normal couple things. They fell into an easy and smooth compatibility, so that when they returned to her apartment, there was heightened excitement and energy to get back together naked in bed.

Dallas had grown into her body and her sexuality. She had learned the things that made her feel good. Hayden had been a selfish lover. Burke had been a great improvement. Alex was totally intuitive about her needs. But it had been him, after all, who had initiated her. And set the standards. He knew instinctively how to search out each and every pleasure point, to press those buttons . . . ring them bells.

She loved that Alex liked to sleep spooned around her back, that he liked talking in the dark before they made love; before they fell to sleep. She liked that he got up and would begin breakfast—or lunch, whatever the hour called for—without being asked. And he didn't leave the toilet seat up. Dallas liked that when she really needed a few hours to finish her next article and the proposal for her book offer, Alex disappeared to entertain himself. He returned later with a bottle of wine. And a rented video.

It just seemed so easy. So natural. But Dallas was still careful. Not about Alex, but about being with him that often erupted into hope. It was too early for plans or commitments, and she didn't need any of that. But it had also been so long since she was this sure about anything.

On Saturday morning she left him sleeping to run to the post office to mail off a freelance review. Dallas took her time getting back, stopping by a florist to buy two bouquets of flowers. She bought a tub of cream cheese with lox to go with three fresh bagels. And then smiled happily to herself all the way back to the apartment.

But the telephone ringing had awakened Alex from a sound sleep. He groggily answered.

"Yeah." He cleared his throat to talk. Almost immediately he realized his mistake. He wasn't home. This wasn't a call for him.

"Hey . . . sorry. I guess I have the wrong . . ."

"You want Dallas."

There was a pause. "Yeah. This is Dean. Her brother."

Alex sighed and sat up. He was not completely awake. "I'm Alex. We met a few months ago when I drove Dallas to her parents . . ."

"Oh, yeah . . ." Dean said as the connection was made. Then he cackled wickedly. "Dilly-Dally has some explaining to do."

Alex frowned. "About me? Why should she?"

"It's a family thing. I'm not saying it's because of you, man, but . . ."

"You don't approve."

"Hey, it's none of my business. Dallas can take care of herself."

"Good. Then I guess we're cool."

"Yeah. Just don't mess with my sister if you don't mean it."

Alex grinned lopsidedly at the protective threat in Dean's tone. "I thought you said it was none of your business."

"That's right. That don't mean I don't care about what happens to her. Tell her I called." He hung up.

Alex was more amused than anything. But it did alert him to one thing. What he was doing. What he and Dallas were doing. He didn't want to hurt her. But it could happen. There was a lot they hadn't talked about, yet. Like what happens next week.

When he got out of bed Alex became suddenly anxious. Not because Dallas had left him alone, but more because she wasn't there. When Alex heard the key in the door twenty minutes later, he was waiting for her in the living room. He had pulled on his jeans. She walked into the apartment with an armful of flowers, a bright smile, and enough warmth to melt the doubt created by her brother's phone call.

"You're up. Did you miss me?" she teased.

"Yes," Alex answered without hesitation. He met her at the entrance of the kitchen and kissed her briefly as she walked past him. Alex stood and watched as Dallas deftly arranged the flowers in two separate vases, and then refrigerated the cream cheese.

"Good. Then you haven't gotten bored with me yet."

"Your brother called."

The smile faded slowly. "He did? What did he want?"

Alex thought about making a joke out of it. He thought about lying. "He warned me not to play games with you."

Dallas's mouth dropped open. "He . . . he said that to you?"

Alex nodded. He approached her and kissed her mouth again, her automatic response forcing it closed. He took Dallas by the hand and led her out of the kitchen, down the hallway, and back into the bedroom. He began to undress her.

"Alex . . . Alex, I'm sorry. Dean had no right . . ."

"You're wrong. He had every right. He cares about you. He was feeling protective toward you." He got the oversized sweater off. The leggings proved more of a problem. "The thing is . . . that's how I feel, too."

"Alex, I . . ."

He quickly discarded his jeans and, kneeling on the bed, put his arms around her and lowered her onto her back. He began to kiss her, to rub his fingertips over the peaks of her breasts slowly until she moaned and arched her back.

"Oh, my God . . . Alex . . ."

He slipped his hand between her legs and gently caressed the sensitive opening until he felt the wetness. He slowly pushed a finger inside. All the while Alex watched her face, felt her body undulate against him, heard her moan and shudder. She breathed heavily and then gasped when the pulsating release throbbed through her body. Then he carefully lay atop her. He'd already made love to her. He didn't need to be inside. He just needed to know that Dallas trusted him with her body . . . her soul.

Alex couldn't find anything he didn't like about her. And Dean's inference did not go unnoticed. It was too soon to know if he loved Dallas Oliver, but Alex did know for sure that what he felt for her was more complete, and the closest he'd ever come to it with anyone.

It was almost one in the afternoon when the phone rang again. Alex sighed and pressed a kiss onto Dallas's neck.

"I think you'd better get that," he said.

Dallas smiled and blindly reached for the receiver. "Hello?"

"Dallas, this is Valerie."

Her eyes fluttered open. She glanced at Alex, but he was sprawled on his stomach, his face now hidden by a pillow. "Hi." She didn't know what else to say.

"I'm sorry to bother you," Valerie said stiffly.

Dallas felt discouraged. It was still the same with her. "That's all right. Can I help you with something?"

"Is Megan there?" Valerie asked bluntly.

The very question made Dallas's insides curl with alarm. Why didn't Valerie know where her daughter was? Then Dallas realized that Valerie's stiff tone was not directed at her. It was controlled fear and suppressed panic.

"No, she's not. Why?"

"Don't worry about it. I'll call one of her other friends. Bye . . ."

Dallas clutched the phone. "Valerie, wait!" The imperative in her voice brought Alex instantly awake. He turned startled eyes toward her. "Don't hang up. You don't know where she is?" There was no response. "Valerie, please. Talk to me. What's going on?"

Valerie bit her lip to keep her voice from shaking. "I . . . I haven't seen her since early last night. Neither has anyone else."

"Dallas, what's happening?" Alex asked softly but in a firm voice.

Dallas shook her head at him, indicating that she didn't know yet. "Val, I don't understand. What do you mean you haven't seen her?"

"She said she was going to spend the night with a classmate. I know the girl and her family. They've stayed back and forth with each other before. So Megan left the house at about six. She told me they were going to a movie, and then back to the friend's house. I didn't think any more about it. Until the girl called me an hour ago looking for Megan. She hadn't seen her since study hall yesterday morning."

"Oh, no. Oh, Val . . ."

Alex sat up and took the phone out of Dallas's hand. "Valerie, what's wrong?"

"Alex . . . I . . . Megan is gone. I . . . I don't know where, I . . ."

"Tell me what happened."

It was another five minutes before the full story of Megan's anger at Valerie and the argument between the two of them had been fleshed out. Then Alex told her she should finish canvassing Megan's friends, and then call the police. Dallas gasped when she heard Alex's firm directive, but she knew it had to be done. Something could be horribly wrong. Alex issued more instructions and then hung up. He turned to Dallas.

"I have to go help find her."

"I'm coming, too."

"No. You have to stay here, Dallas. What if Megan is trying to reach you? What if she calls or tries to come by herself?"

Tears welled up in Dallas's eyes. She repeated all the possibilities Alex outlined and thought, *But what if Megan doesn't?* Dallas nodded her consent to remain in the apartment. They both got out of bed and dressed quickly. Alex made several other phone calls. One to Ross. One to Lillian and Vin. Dallas called her parents, just in case. Megan knew them, and they were a lot closer than trying to reach the city . . . if that was what she had set out to do. If nothing else had happened to her.

The squawk box was driving her crazy, with its scratchy loud messages in code. As were the incessant questions and the room filled with suited and strapped men. Valerie had given up control of the situation and her house, which she'd lost the moment she'd made her suspicions about where her daughter was official. But neither she nor the police had any better idea some five hours after Valerie's discovery that Megan had lied to her . . . and possibly run away.

"Miss Holland, I'm Detective Burnes. I have a few questions, please."

That's how it had gone. Answering questions. Valerie was becoming enraged by the questions. Why weren't these men and women all out looking for her child? She turned to give her attention to the newest officer. She couldn't be stubborn now. First they had to find Megan.

"Sure," Valerie whispered, her voice tired and flat as the officer sat in the chair opposite her and began.

"Now, you told Detective Tillis that you and your daughter had had an argument recently. Over what?"

Valerie felt the stress and pain press at her temples. She didn't know how to say that it was because she herself had been unreasonable and hard. That she'd been angry and disappointed and had taken it out on Megan. Because to say so would be the same as saying it was her fault that Megan was missing. That Megan might have been angry enough at her to want to run away was what tore at Valerie the most. *She* had driven her own daughter away.

And her best friend.

It was ironic that Dallas was the one person she wanted there with her.

The officers were careful not to make any promises. A twelve-year-old out alone in unfamiliar surroundings was vulnerable and easy prey to a variety of undesirables. Yet they said Megan would probably show up on her own when she got hungry and it got dark. It was going to be dark in an hour.

Valerie nodded absently as the officer assured her that all was going to be fine and walked away to join some of the other half-dozen or so detectives camped out in her dining room. She felt alone. Members of her family had already been by to offer their support, but the weeping had nearly driven Valerie to distraction. She had suggested that it was better if they went home to wait.

Valerie looked at her watch again. It had been exactly twenty-four hours since she'd seen Megan. She could feel her resolve to stay calm starting to crack around the edges. Her stomach was queasy with stress. Tension pulled at the muscles behind her eyelids, twisting into a headache.

"Ms. Holland, there's someone here who says he has to see you. Should we let him in?" the detective asked. "A Ross Manning."

Valerie stood up and nodded to the officer. "Yes, let him in." Then she waited, feeling a jolt of adrenaline that made her both apprehensive and wary. She was in no way expecting Ross, but she was not surprised that he had come. She stared in the direction of the entrance until he finally appeared, his usually mischievous and knowing gaze serious and thoughtful as it sought her out. When their eyes connected across the room, Valerie felt for the first time that she was not alone. She was glad to see him.

She noticed the slightly uneven gait in his walking as he approached, his face looking as concerned and serious as she'd ever seen it. Valerie decided she liked it the other way, when he was cheerful and bantering, flirtatious.

He stopped within a foot of her. For the first time since they'd met they were at a loss for words for their usual sparring. The dynamics were different now, and there was something else . . . someone else, at stake.

"You haven't heard anything?" he asked.

The sound of his voice was strong and solid, his presence reassuring. "No, nothing."

"Alex had some ideas to check out. Is Dallas here with you?"

Valerie shook her head. "She's at her apartment, in case Megan manages to make it there."

He looked closely at her. "How are you doing?" he asked quietly.

She wished he wouldn't be concerned and tender. She wished his voice didn't sound like it could heal anything. She wished he wouldn't look at her that way that said the horrible pain in the middle of her chest was real and it did feel that it was ripping her insides out.

"I'm okay." Valerie nodded.

Obviously Ross didn't believe her. He stepped forward and put an arm around her. Valerie felt the crack turn into splintering. Her forehead fell forward onto his chest, and she could hide the fierce pain that seemed to squeeze out through her pores. She had never been so scared in her life.

"Ross, I'm sorry. I . . ."

"Don't be."

The acceptance of her pain, the dismissal of her need for comfort and forgiveness, gave Valerie permission to cry.

Every time the phone rang, Dallas stared at it as if it contained an evil spirit. It meant that someone was calling with news. But she was afraid that the news might be something she didn't want to hear.

On the start of the third ring she picked it up. "Yes . . ."

"Dallas, anything yet?"

She sighed. "No, Ross, nothing."

"The police out here have called all of her friends, and searched the usual places where the kids hang out. No one has seen her."

"She hasn't tried to call me."

"What about Alex?"

Dallas blushed. His assumption that Alex would have been with her made her realize that Ross was aware of what was developing between them. "He left here several hours ago, but I haven't heard from him. He didn't say what he was going to check out." Dallas took a breath. "How's Val?"

"Do you want to talk to her?"

"Well, maybe I should . . ."

"Hold on . . ."

Dallas could hear the low murmur of Ross's voice and then Valerie was on the line.

"Hi, Dallas."

She sounded exhausted and Dallas wasn't surprised. But she also wondered if what had happened between them was going to prevent them from supporting each other.

"How are you holding up?"

"My nerves are raw. I want to scream at the police to do something. My mother has been hysterical."

"I'm not surprised. Is Rosemary there?"

"No. I made her go home to wait. I'm trying to stay calm, and her crying was getting to me. God knows I'm going to do enough of it myself if anything . . ."

"Don't say it, Val. I *know* Megan is okay."

"I hope to God you're right."

Dallas could hear the strain in her voice. Their mutual concern for Megan's welfare had moved them past their last difficult encounter. Dallas imagined that it was not forgotten by Valerie any more than herself, but it hardly seemed important at the moment.

"I'll call if I hear anything. You'll let me know if there's anything I can do?"

"Sure," Valerie promised, subdued and tired.

"Val . . . everything's going to be fine," Dallas whispered.

"Thanks for saying that. I . . . hope so."

"I'd better get off the phone in case Megan or Alex is trying to reach you or me."

"Yes . . ."

"Tell Ross I said thank you."

Valerie chuckled. "You noticed, too?"

"He handled this very well. Got us talking. Megan is much more important than our differences."

"She's the most important thing in my life. But I don't want to sacrifice our friendship, either."

"It's been kicked around a bit," Dallas conceded. "But I think there's some life left in it."

"Then we'll talk when this is over."

It was another two hours and dark outside before the phone rang again. It was Alex.

"Where are you?" she asked anxiously.

"I'm at Val's."

"Val's?" she repeated blankly. "Alex, what . . ."

"It's okay. I just got here. I found Megan."

"Oh, my God . . . where?"

"She was hiding out on the boat."

Chapter Sixteen

I think what people want most in their lives is love. It's surprising what we're willing to give up in order to have it and experience it. But love is not something you wish for. It's something that has to be created. And it comes not from what you can get, but what you have to give. It sounds difficult, but it really is not. Where we tend to fall short of the mark is insisting on a love we think we want and need, instead of what actually makes us feel good . . . and which lasts. Love has no boundaries, or rules, or size and, we're finding out at last, that it doesn't come in colors. When we find it in a particular person, or it is shared with us, then we are truly blessed. I have found the love I want. Not unexpected, but different than I'd planned. It is a gift. But the question I want to know about love is this . . . "If I violate the taboos defining my cultural identity, will I offend God?"

"I don't see her," Rosemary Holland whispered to her daughter.

"Mom, be quiet," Valerie whispered back. "You'll see her when she stands up."

"But she won't know where we are."

"Don't worry," Ross said. "She'll know."

Dallas, seated one row behind members of the Holland clan, grinned as Valerie turned her head to give her a look. When they had graduated from elementary school, they had tied red balloons filled with helium to the arm of the chairs assigned to their families. It was a tradition the school made sure was never repeated.

"Michael Gizzali," the principal announced, and another student stood to join the others on stage as applause broke out in the auditorium. "Janine Grant . . ."

Alex reached for Dallas's hand and threaded his fingers with hers. While she felt the need to be cautious, Alex did not. He'd made a choice, placed his affections, and didn't care a damn if anyone knew.

Dallas's gaze quickly swept around those gathered, to see if anyone else noticed the hand-holding. She was not used to this kind of open display. It made her feel peculiar. But not in the way of Hayden or Burke, both of whom had placed so much emphasis on her looks. Alex didn't take what he felt lightly. Which was a good thing. Because neither did she.

On her other side Lillian Marco fidgeted nervously with her program and craned her neck to make sure she didn't miss anything.

"Mariko Hashimoto . . . Megan Holland . . ."

Megan's contingent broke out into thunderous applause. But so did the rest of the room. Down in the front of the auditorium, where the graduating class were all seated in uniform blue, Megan stood up. Her ponytail swung left and right as she walked with jaunty confidence to the stage. A reporter and photographer from the local papers, as well as a mini cam crew from a local TV station, were positioned to photograph and tape her as she climbed onto the stage. She shook hands with the principal who gave her a folder containing her diploma.

"Oh, isn't she beautiful?" Lillian murmured rhetorically, drawing in her breath and shaking her head in wonder as she clapped.

"She sure is." Ross cranked his head around to answer. "Runs in the family."

Lillian shook her head and scoffed at the indirect compliment, but she blushed when Vin nodded in agreement.

Megan had become a celebrity.

Her twenty-four-hour adventure that had taken her from the south shore of Long Island to Brooklyn had made the newspapers. Dallas beamed as proudly as anyone else, surprised at the resourcefulness and smarts Megan had demonstrated while on her own. Disappearing the way she had had ultimately galvanized her family and brought them together again. *All* of them. She had run off just long and far enough to end the stand-off between her mother and godmother, and Dallas still speculated if the disappearance was from anger . . . or a clever plan.

Megan had known nothing of her relationship to Vin and Lillian Marco until she'd been reported missing and an item had been aired on the evening news. Lillian, notified of Megan's flight by a nearly hysterical Valerie, had received the surprise of her life when Valerie then babbled an apologetic explanation of Megan's relationship to her and Vin.

Of her part in the healing of old wounds Megan remained blissfully clueless. What she was enjoying the most was that her classmates thought what she had done was way cool.

"Aagh . . . I'm so nervous," Lillian said, leaning close to Dallas.

"No need to worry," Dallas tried to reassure her. "I think she pretty much understands about Nicholas being her father, but I'm not sure how she feels that her mother never told her. She doesn't remember you or Vin from the funeral."

"I'm so embarrassed," Lillian lamented. "I don't remember her, either."

"She's going to love you," Alex added.

Vin voiced his own uncertainty. "Maybe we shouldn't have come."

"Of course you should have," Rosemary said. "Besides, there's going to be a mob of people in my backyard for the little party Valerie planned. Some of Meggie's friends and cousins will be there."

"We can see her some other . . ."

"No, please." Valerie turned in her seat to reach out and take Lillian's hand. "You and Vin have to be there. I've handled this whole thing so badly. I should have said something years ago." She glanced briefly at Dallas, color rising in her cheeks. "I haven't been very fair or very smart."

"You know what?" Ross whispered in her ear, but loud enough for them all to hear. "I don't think Megan's going to care as long as she knows the truth. She's going to have a lot of questions."

When the ceremony was over, the auditorium emptied out onto the school grounds, where the graduating students became antsy and quickly bored with the novelty of caps and robes. Dallas stood with Alex waiting for Megan to appear and find them.

"Mommy, did you see me?" Megan interrupted, bursting into the center of the group of adults to capture everyone's attention.

"Yes, I did. Megan, honey, we're all so proud of you."

"I suppose I'll have to bow down and kiss your hand or something," Ross teased her, making her giggle.

"I'm going to be on TV again."

"I guess this makes you famous," Alex said to her as she came over to give Dallas a hug. "Can I have you autograph my program?"

"Aaaah, isn't that sweet," Rosemary crooned as Megan blushed.

Then Megan turned her attention to the older couple who stood off to the side, looking at her with great curiosity, and as if they were a little afraid of her. Valerie came forward and placed her hands on her daughter's shoulders as Megan became subdued and a little shy.

"Honey, I want you to meet Lillian and Vincent Marco. You remember me telling you about them."

Megan nodded, staring openly at them. "I know. You're my father's parents, right?"

Dallas could see that Lillian's eyes were moist with unshed tears as she nodded with a tremulous smile. "It . . . it's very nice to meet you, Megan. You look so grown-up in your cap and gown."

"Thank you," she replied quietly, taking hold of Dallas's hand and leaning against her arm.

Lillian took a step forward. "You know, you have Nicky's eyes. And the same mouth. Doesn't she, Vin?"

Behind his wife, Vin looked at Megan, equally fascinated and timid. "Yeah. But she's a lot prettier."

Everyone laughed at Vin's comment.

"I'm sorry he died," Megan said to Vin, surprising everyone with her reference to Nicholas. "I didn't get a chance to know him."

Vin cleared his throat. "I hope you'll give me and Lilly a chance to know *you*."

"Sure," Megan said with a shrug. She glanced suddenly at her mother and then back to Vin. "I don't have to call you Vin, do I?"

A slight shock went through everyone, although no one said anything. Only Lillian drew her breath in, her eyes blinking as she waited for her husband to respond.

"Not if you don't want to," Vin said softly, clearly taken aback by the question.

"Megan, why don't you want to call him Vin?" Rosemary asked her.

"Well, why can't I call him Grandfather? I never had a grandfather before," she explained.

Lillian covered her mouth to hide her quivering chin. Valerie stroked her daughter's cheek with her hand. Everyone else grinned foolishly. Vin cleared his throat.

"Sure, why not? Nobody's ever called me that before, either."

* * *

Dallas went into the kitchen balancing used paper plates, plastic forks, and crumpled napkins in both hands as she headed for the garbage. Behind her, the voices and conversation trailed from the backyard, where the adult voices were outmatched by the exuberance of Megan and several of her friends and cousins, gathered to finish the graduation celebration. She'd left Vin, Alex, and Ross engaged in a conversation about the merits of the military when Vin had served in Nam, to Alex and Ross's tour of duty in the Middle East. Valerie had approached them but Ross did not separate himself to give her his undivided attention. Instead he'd put an arm around her waist to include her. That Val consented said volumes about what was developing between them. But it was pretty much the same kind of acceptance that Dallas knew she felt with Alex. And no one seemed surprised by either couple.

Lillian was conversing with Rosemary in an attempt to learn a little of what she'd missed for the past twelve years of her granddaughter's life. She and Vin made it clear that they didn't at all consider Megan Marie any less a grandchild just because Nicholas hadn't been their birth child. In the same way, Dallas realized, that Lillian had always treated her like a daughter and Alex like a son. There had been enough love to go around. Dallas glanced out the kitchen window briefly, reflecting on the affinity she felt with Lillian. The fact that they'd both lost a first child. Was it that first failure that had sent Vin Marco to the temporary solace of another woman?

Dallas turned to the kitchen table and began clearing away things that had been opened and spread out for the party. As she worked, she imagined she understood what Lillian was feeling, meeting Megan for the first time.

She'd finally gotten up the courage to write a letter to a Brenda Coleburn of San Antonio, Texas, introducing herself as a cousin; their mothers were sisters. She explained about the letters she'd never seen until finding them recently, and that if Brenda was still interested, yes . . . she would like a chance to get to know her and her mother's side of the family.

Dallas didn't know if she would get an answer. It had been more than ten years since her cousin had attempted to reach her. But she had already decided, through the process of writing the letter, that whatever the outcome was, it was really secondary to the sense of completion she'd gained.

Dallas opened the kitchen door into the backyard and, taking a deep breath, went out into the twilight to sit alone on the top step. She was not there long before Alex slowly made his way across the yard toward her. He was interrupted in the journey as two of Megan's cousins, giggly teens two years Megan's senior, stopped Alex to innocently flirt. Dallas smiled, finding it amusing and endearing that he had a chivalrous streak that made Alex so sympathetic. So heroic.

Alex reached her and squeezed in next to her on the step. He put an arm around her waist and kissed her cheek. He could feel her relax against his side as the trust flowed through her body.

"Did you and Valerie make up?"

Dallas looked into his face, his almost-white hair making him look dark and shadowy, his eyes hidden. "Did she tell you what happened?"

He shook his head. "She didn't have to. I could tell you'd had a fight."

Dallas didn't feel the need to add to it. "Not yet," she answered thoughtfully. "She's a bit preoccupied with Megan and Ross right now. But we will."

Alex squeezed her gently. "I bet I know what you're thinking," he whispered after a moment of silence.

Dallas turned to regard him skeptically. "Oh, yeah?"

Alex nodded. "You're thinking, it feels a little strange to be part of this tonight. It's really a family thing."

She chuckled with a shake of her head. "Okay. You

win. Except I notice that Vin had an awful lot to say to Ross about you. Calling you his older son. Talking about you helping him with his business." Alex grunted. "Suddenly you're the reigning prince."

"I wouldn't put it that way," Alex murmured, encouraging her to lean against his chest. "Yeah, it was a surprise, but I'll settle for the older son title."

Alex was still adjusting to that. It was the first public acknowledgment he'd ever gotten from Vin, and it had rolled off his tongue with an ease and pride that had caught Alex up short. He didn't know if he'd expected to feel any different if Vin had ever admitted their relation, but there was this sense of closure, a final link in place.

"Aren't you happy about it?"

He thought about it. "Are you happy that your stepmother finally opened up to you and admitted that she was afraid your father favored you over Dean? Are you happy that Dean is playing protective brother all of a sudden and is ready to kick my butt if I do anything to hurt you?"

Dallas laughed lightly at the irony of it. "I'm glad to know where I stand, but it doesn't seem so important anymore. Not that I don't care, but . . ."

Alex sighed and hugged her. When she smiled at him, he kissed her briefly.

"I figured out that if you don't get love and friendship from one person, you can find it somewhere else. There are other people who love you besides your family. Lillian and Megan. Me," Alex finished, gazing at her intently.

It was the first time that word had been said between them. But Dallas wasn't really surprised. It seemed natural and a foregone conclusion. Not the end or even a beginning. It was the core of what they had always been to each other.

Dallas kept waiting for it to wear off. The joy. The near breathless wonder. She had the best of all possible worlds. They were real friends . . . and lovers. She smiled at him, rubbing her hand on his thigh.

"I have a favor to ask."

"Go ahead," Alex encouraged.

"My friend Maureen is getting married at the end of the month. I'm in the wedding party. Will you come and be my escort?"

He stared at her, and Dallas watched the thought process displayed in his features. There was consideration. Bemusement. Surprise. Love.

"Sure," he answered. "I'll be there with bells on."

She laughed. "You don't have to do all that. A tux is enough. Although . . . it's going to be a nontraditional ceremony."

"How?"

"Maureen is doing something Afro-Centric. Jump the broom."

Alex nodded. "I've been to one before. One of my buddies in the service. Best wedding I ever attended. We partied for twenty-four hours."

Alex lowered his head to kiss her. His mouth parted over hers and his tongue teased at her. There was a fearlessness that had always been a part of him and that had always made Dallas feel safe with him. It was dependable and solid.

"Alex? Do you think Vin will mind . . . about us?"

"What I think is that it doesn't matter. You know what the real acid test is going to be?"

"What?"

Alex grinned at her. "Where to spend the holidays."

Dallas shook her head, joining in the easy take on their future.

"But that's not the only question," he said.

"What else?"

"Aunt Dallas, could you come here?" Megan called out, interrupting them.

Dallas stood up, holding onto Alex's hand as she looked at him. "What were you going to say?"

Alex regarded Megan for a moment and stood up,

too, squeezing Dallas's hand. A slow enigmatic smile played on his mouth. He pecked a kiss on her lips.

"It can wait. We'll talk later," Alex assured her. "I'm not going anywhere."